Karen DeWitt

About the Editor

MICHELE SLUNG has been called "an editor and reviewer of unusual discrimination." Her works include *Crime on Her Mind*, a historical anthology of fictional women detectives; *I Shudder at Your Touch: Twenty-Two Tales of Sex and Horror* and its sequel, *Shudder Again;* two compilations of women's original erotic writing, *Slow Hand* and *Fever;* and the Book-of-the-Month Club main selection *Murder & Other Acts of Literature.* With Roland Hartman, she edited *Murder for Halloween.* She is the author of *Living with Cannibals and Other Women's Adventures.*

Her essays and criticism have appeared in the *New York Times Book Review,* the *Washington Post, USA Today,* the *Village Voice,* and *The New Republic,* and in such volumes as *The Oxford Companion to Crime and Mystery Writing, Twentieth-Century Crime and Mystery Writers, Whodunit?, The Sleuth and the Scholar,* and *The Penguin Encyclopedia of Horror and the Supernatural.*

STRANGER

DARK TALES OF EERIE ENCOUNTERS

EDITED BY MICHELE SLUNG

Perennial

An Imprint of HarperCollins*Publishers*

For Robert Wyatt, man of books

Presentiment—is that long Shadow—on the Lawn—
Indicative that Suns go down—
The Notice to the startled Grass
That Darkness—is about to pass—

EMILY DICKINSON

CONTENTS

ACKNOWLEDGMENTS

No ANTHOLOGIST IS an island. I'd like to thank, above all, Gordon Van Gelder, whose faultless generosity operates at the amazing level of his enormous knowledge. Others who've helped along the way are Jean-Daniel Brèque, Bob Eldridge of Eldritch Books, Tom Mann of the Library of Congress, the Mercantile Library's Harold Augenbraum, and Everett F. Bleiler. Additionally, John Silbersack and John Douglas deserve my gratitude for their patient overseeing of this project.

ACKNOWLEDGEMENTS

PREFACE

JUST AS ONE knows the expression "passing strangers," so have many of us also frequently heard that rather quaint descriptive phrase, "passing strange." In the stories I've chosen, more often than not, the two come together.

And usually not in the ways we might expect.

"Don't talk to strangers," of course, is the unambiguous-seeming maxim no child ever escapes hearing. But in the matter of strangers, exact definition will always be elusive. So, while life becomes an ongoing series of measured judgments (and possible bad calls), literature gets masterpieces like Shirley Jackson's "The Lottery," Ray Bradbury's *The Martian Chronicles,* or Patricia Highsmith's *The Talented Mr. Ripley.*

Perhaps more memorably than anyone else, Alfred Hitchcock

experimented with our expectations and assumptions about strangers. Not only did he shrewdly select his raw material—from writers like Buchan and Bloch, Highsmith and Christie, Du Maurier and Woolrich—but his natural instinct for the perverse consistently ensured maximum effect with *his* version of *their* strangers becoming our own.

(Besides making America head en masse for the nearest Holiday Inn, he gleefully intuited our dismayed reaction to finding out that the perky little songbird in our garden is, at heart, a conscienceless assassin.)

How to take the measure of any stranger, then, is certainly the challenge set by the tales in this volume, in which even the more apparently benign archetypes—the Good Samaritan, Prince Charming, etc.—are never exactly what they seem. When first I began planning the book, my original notion did run more narrowly along the lines of plots featuring the stereotypical (mysterious) figure and the (accidental) encounter leading to a grim conclusion.

But since Janet Leigh *didn't* choose to stop at a nationally advertised chain motel, and since Mr. Hyde may have been just as horrified by Dr. Jekyll, one winds up inevitably surprised by what begins to insinuate itself into the mix.

In the matter of "strangers," I not only found myself faced with an enormous potential population but also at every turn came across opportunities to upend the obvious. So that, while I offer here the equivalent of the good old gypsy curse, it takes the form of a savage little tale by the tirelessly inventive Christopher Fowler, who happens to be quite clear about what comprises human vulnerability.

Edith Wharton's elegiac "Afterward" had, since I first read it, always seemed to me the quintessential tale of an imperfectly understood and forever-to-be-regretted encounter with a stranger—that is, until I came across Jack Ketchum's remorseless waking nightmare, "The Box." Tabitha King's "The Women's Room," for its part, brings to hideous life that overused phrase "the wrong place at the wrong time," as does Jay Russell's sanguinary "Hides."

"The tables turned" is what we often find here. See, for instance, Thomas Tessier's spellbinding "In the Desert of Deserts" or Alex Hamilton's chill-inducing "The Baby-sitters." Yet "reversal" hardly describes, really, just how disorienting these circumstances are—and in Bradbury's "The Town Where No One Got Off," G. K. Wuori's "The General Store," John Peyton Cooke's "After You've Gone," and Tom Disch's "The Asian Shore," it's merely a single facet of the fun-house distortions taking place.

Black comedy, too, is much in evidence, probably because the power which strangers have to affect our lives is simultaneously awful and absurd. But if some selections are more obviously amusing than others—Lisa Tuttle's droll "Honey, I'm Home" or Richard Matheson's wicked "Button, Button," to name two—still the chuckles are always on the verge of being gasps.

If these stories make a difference in how you see your friends and family, or change your comfort level in any shop or elevator, if they make you that much more cautious walking out your front door on a sunny morning without a cloud in the sky, then they will have accomplished their purpose.

Certainly they have long disturbed me, returning at odd moments to scratch at the window of my consciousness, demanding to be let in again. But since I'm the one sharing them, perhaps—at this moment, anyway—I'm that very stranger you need most to avoid.

STRANGER

THE WOMEN'S ROOM

TABITHA KING

There is always a single moment that separates the mundane world, operating according to the usual, taken-for-granted rules, from unfathomable chaos. The good news is that most of us are lucky enough never to experience one; the bad, of course, is that finding one's way back to it (and to the safety it tantalizingly represents) is impossible. Simply moving forward, like a rat in a maze, is the only choice, and King's tale, brilliantly using drab detail to create an everyday labyrinth all of us can instantly recognize, is the more horrific for that familiarity.

ॐ

THE WOMAN'S EYES glittered behind bifocal lenses. Wide-bottomed with middle age, she wore her graying hair uncompromisingly short. Her khaki skirt stretched tight across her thighs and she crossed her ankles primly. In her lap she clutched a leaflet.

To one side and with empty chairs between them, Mary D. had a clear view of the woman with the leaflet. Her own folding metal chair creaked as wearily as her conscience as Mary pushed back in it. A stranger in this meeting and she was already taking the other woman's measure, indulging an instinctive dislike. The nuns, she thought. She ought to have put all that behind her. Let go and let God. Ah. The answering cliché: Easier said than done.

The woman with the leaflet was the first to speak. Introducing herself as June B., an alcoholic—*Hi, June*—she announced, with a little rattle of the leaflet, she was going to use her five minutes to read something to them.

Mary felt her face work against a sardonic smile. She stopped listening. As June B. droned on, Mary's bladder began to ache. Meeting coffee on a day of business-meeting coffee, and maybe the metal chair—the damn things were always cold when you sat down in them. June B. shot her a glare as Mary rattled her chair rising from it and made her way to the door, masking her face with the concentration of urgent need.

The air in the corridor outside the meeting room was cool on her face and she breathed deeply. Her head immediately felt much clearer. Though the meeting was nonsmoking, sticking a bunch of people in the same room for an hour inevitably thickened up the air. Though it was possible that some peculiar AA physics was at work, she supposed, the Program forcing a miasma of toxic feelings like sweat and bad breath out of those practicing it.

The doors off the corridor were all closed and locked, their frosted windows unlit by any interior illumination. Inscriptions on the windows revealed the occupants were firms of CPAs and dentists and therapists of various stripes, physical and psychological. The meeting room was apparently a lunchroom for a large partnership of family counselors by day.

Around a corner she found a women's room. Though it was locked, the combination, a simple 1–2–3, had been read off at the beginning of the meeting. She worked the combination and opened the door onto darkness. One foot over the threshold, she groped about on either side of the doorframe and found a light switch on the left.

The sudden illumination showed her a narrow room of the dreary functionality hinting at being buried alive that is the signature of the contemporary public restroom. There were no windows. The two stalls faced one side of the rectangular room, with a basin and mirror opposite, and another pair faced the other way, with a basin and mirror serving them. Everything was very clean, and the room smelled strongly of industrial antiseptic cleansers.

Giving old ex-Sister Mary June a good chunk of time to blow off, Mary dawdled, scrubbing her hands, drying them carefully, enjoying rubbing hand lotion into her skin. She tidied her hair with a brush. Chin getting a little soft, she noted, and chucked the slackening flesh ruefully with the back of her hand. There was a procedure now where you have the fat sucked out. Christ. That's what you came to.

When the lights flickered, she couldn't help a startled little cry. Then they went out.

"Shit."

She clung to the edge of the basin, the one certainty in the darkness. She didn't dare move; indeed she was rigid with the kind of anger that comes from confusion and fear. After a couple of seconds' blindness, the lights suddenly flooded the room again, seeming a little brighter than she remembered. Her anger immediately seemed silly, a familiar feeling that reminded her of how easily she angered, and all out of proportion or completely without reason.

She shoved her brush back into her handbag and hurried out of the women's room. Preoccupied with anticipating the end of the meeting, getting back to her rented Lexus out in the parking lot, and then her hotel where she planned to call home before she went to bed, she retraced her way to the meeting room on mental cruise. She tugged at the handle of the double door and was surprised by resistance. It was locked. She must have inadvertently triggered the locking mechanism when she left it to go to the women's room.

She knocked gently, then realized she heard no voices from within. Her first thought was the group was engaged in silent prayer. She stopped herself just short of knocking again. She would wait until they finished.

Her gaze wandered to the bottom of the door. Disconcertingly, there was no line of light under it. She stooped closer to be sure.

Surely the meeting had not ended that quickly; she had not been gone *that* long. Her trenchcoat was still inside, hanging over the back of the folding metal chair. Now she rapped hard on the door, but there was no response. There was a hollowness in the rattle of the door under her fist that seemed to confirm the room was empty.

There had been easily two dozen people at the meeting. Where were the inevitable few stragglers?—the Thirteenth-Steppers earnestly hitting on newcomer females, the Old-Timers grousing about the infestation of druggies, the volunteers cleaning up discarded coffee cups and emptying the coffee machine? There was not even the staling cigarette smoke in the corridor from the smokers who invariably lit up as they left a meeting. All she could think was she had radically lost track of the time while the lights had been out. But a glance at her wristwatch refuted that explanation. She had been in the women's room no more than ten minutes.

Whatever had happened, her trenchcoat was still inside. It was a beautiful matte vermeil color in a classic cut that fit her perfectly. She had bought it in Denver, on a trip with her sister Terry. They had both tried it on, and though it had fit her sister too, Terry had let her buy it. She never put it on, never, that she didn't think of Terry.

She needed to find a janitor or a security guy to unlock the room. But as she stood there, hesitating, the silence was too complete. She was sure no one else could be left in the building, unless they were very far away. It was a big funny old building, though, that had sprouted wings and ells and additions over decades. Like Topsy, it had just growed. And still was growing. She had noticed building debris in the parking lot, and a wall of bright brick seamed to one of old yellow. New window glass, still stickered, blind as a newborn kitten, in frames that did not match the ones in the yellow wall.

She guessed her best hope might be that the security guard she had passed on entering was still on duty in the lobby. Otherwise she would have to resign herself to returning tomorrow and hoping her trenchcoat would still be there. She summoned up some gratitude that she had placed her car keys and hotel room card in the outside pocket of her handbag.

She started down the corridor to the elevator but, after turning another corridor, saw there was no elevator where she remembered one. She was going the wrong way, she realized, and turned around to pass the double door of the meeting room again. Around the next corner, the corridor stretched and turned again, so much like the one she had rejected as the wrong way that again she thought herself turned around. She looked back the way she had come and then in the direction she had been headed. There were no elevator doors and no doors to stairwells either way.

In the harsh lighting, the colors had drained away, beige walls into no-color, the charcoal gray carpet into black. The carpet did not seem as worn as it had previously. The hallway seemed somewhat longer than she remembered, and indeed seemed almost to lengthen as she stared down it. Shadows cut across it like the sheets of ghostly sailboats, flat triangles dipping into impossible planes, driven by winds from another dimension.

The place had grown eerily unfamiliar. It was as if she had never been in this place before. It was the emptiness, she told herself, and being night. God, what an idiot she was to be spooked by an empty building in a strange city. Once upon a time she had been fearless, in love with strange cities and strangeness of every kind, and emptiness of every kind, too. Of course she had been drunk much of the time, too.

Meditations upon the past did not solve the problem of which direction to take. There had to be a way out, an EXIT sign around some corner. She drifted slowly the way she had been going when she stopped, hoping it wouldn't matter much which way she went. Eventually she would recognize something or stumble on an exit.

She came to an intersection with another corridor and peeked down it, but it was much the same as the others. A few yards down it, she realized there were no names on the closed office doors. Spinning around, she hurried back the way she had come. And almost immediately came to a halt again, wondering if she had somehow blundered into a new or remodeled wing of the building, as yet unoccupied. It might explain the overwhelming sense of emptiness, of abandonment, and (now it occurred to her) the lack of directional signs of any kind.

She paced the maze of corridors, no longer sure whether she was retracing her route or not. *Don't panic*, she told herself, even as her throat tightened and she drew her shoulders in and thrust her head forward. She picked up her pace a little bit at a time until she was running. The doors with their frosted-glass panes as blank as a blind man's mirrored glasses flashed by her. Stumbling, she fetched up against a wall and held on to it, gasping.

Blinking away tears, she thought, Jesus, lost in a goddamn professional building. How unbelievably stupid. She had navigated Tokyo and Rome and Beirut, for Christ's sake, while blind drunk. That's what she needed, she told herself, sardonically, a drink or two, and she'd find her way right out of the shithole. Only first she would have to break into somebody's private bar. It was not possible there was not at least one secret boozer in a building this size, with a little pick-me-up hidden in the bottom drawer.

She turned another corner. Halfway down the hallway from her, a diffuse light from the window of an office door fell in a milky rhomboid over wall and carpet. She hurried to it. With her knuckles curled against the glass, ready to knock, she cautioned herself not to count on anyone being there. Most likely someone forgot to turn the lights out. A moment of unbroken silence almost convinced her there could be no one within. Uncurling her fist, she started to let it fall to her side. Then something rustled inside the office, on the other side of the door.

Impulsively she seized the knob. It moved easily in her grasp. She let it go and stood still on the threshold as the door swung open with a faint creak. Inside was a receptionist's desk, bare except for a multi-line telephone. The receiver was off the hook, on the desk next to the base. It was dead; there was no tone.

Gingerly she stepped into the room. A door behind the desk indicated it was clearly an anteroom to another office or suite of offices. It smelled of new carpet and paint. There were no pictures on the walls, no furniture other than the desk and the chair behind it. Nor were there any windows.

Handbag tucked into her armpit, Mary slipped around the desk to pick up the telephone receiver with one hand. The line was dead.

When she picked up the wire dangling from the phone, the jack swung free and lightly stung her shin. She sank to her haunches to plug it into the wall behind the desk.

As she pushed the jack into the module in the wall, a movement at the periphery of her vision, accompanied by a single childish gurgle, distracted her. She nearly lost her balance shifting to the source of the sound and the flutter in her eye.

Within the kneehole of the desk, on the other side of the chair, was a baby. It was tightly wrapped in a blanket that effectively bound its limbs. The triangle formed by two of the chair's chrome feet made a kind of primitive pen that prevented it rolling away.

Forgetting about the phone jack, she pulled the chair away from the kneehole and reached for the child. She stayed in her crouch, staring at it in disbelief. It looked to be about six or seven months old to her, well nourished and alert. Its pate was silky with fine colorless hair and its gray eyes gazed at her as calmly and curiously as if it knew her. It smiled at her. A bubble formed in the corner of its delicate rosy lips.

She became aware that she was holding her breath. Why would anyone stick a baby under a desk? Perhaps the mother was working late—or the father, a baby-sitting arrangement falling through—the parent working late had had to go to the toilet—why not take the child with her, or him. She couldn't imagine leaving a baby alone in an otherwise empty building. What if an intruder happened on the child? It wasn't as if the world were getting any safer. There seemed to be more creeps and murderers than rocks for them to come out from under.

She rose, cradling the baby, and went back to the door to stick her head out. No little mother, no daddy, appeared in the corridor, hurrying back from the toilet.

Mary backed into the room and looked around. There was nowhere else to look for the missing parent but through the other door, as yet unbroached. The baby's weight rode in the crook of her right arm, with the fingers of her left hand spread upon its back to hold it against her bosom. She had to twist her body at the waist to grope the doorknob with her right hand. Though her turn was awkward, it moved easily and she pushed it open.

She looked into darkness. As she fumbled for the lights, she jounced the baby clumsily. Her hand found a bank of switches and the darkness was magically banished. The room was crammed with metal lockers of the kind soldiers are issued, marked with mysterious codes of numbers and letters. She edged around the lockers. With the baby on her shoulder as if she were burping it, she freed one hand to test the closure of one of the lockers. To her surprise it was unlocked. She undid the other and tipped the lid of the metal box upward. Inside was foam packing material. She poked at it, exposing brick-shapes wrapped in paper and plastic and heavy-duty tape. They looked like movie-prop kilos of dope. Probably they were plastic junk imported from Southeast Asia. Her curiosity only went so far. Getting into one of the packages would take a box cutter or a pair of scissors, and she had neither item. She dropped the lid. Turning off the lights, she gave the room up as a dead end and closed the door.

Somewhere, goddamn it, there is a parent that belongs to this baby.

The child burbled at her curiously and she cooed back. Carrying it out into the corridor again, she looked both ways, still half expecting and certainly still fully hoping that some smiling young woman would come hurrying along, blushing and full of explanations. But there was no one. She stood in the now familiar emptiness, no longer entirely alone but still lost.

She cast about, telling herself she would just go to the next corner and look around it and then double back and go the other way and if there was no parent standing there, having a smoke or kicking a vending machine for a cup of coffee, then she would just go back to the office and wait. And jack in that frigging phone and call the cops. Not only was she lost in this place, somebody needed a scare, bucking off and leaving their kid like this.

The baby seemed to like her holding it. It was making faces at her, showing a couple of teeth in its wet gums and blowing spit bubbles. She wiped its chin with the edge of the blanket a couple of times. Fortunately, it was not crying. She couldn't cope with that. She didn't really like babies. They were always so out of control.

At the corner she was surprised to see the double doors of the meeting room, halfway down the corridor. Walking slowly so as to give the baby a smooth ride—*Keep it happy, keep it in good mood*—she tried the knob compulsively. It turned. Some mechanism clicked and she knew it was open.

The baby whimpered and kicked into her thigh. Wincing and distracted, she pushed the door open. Her hand fell upon the studs of the light switches even as the terrible smell turned her stomach. *Goddamn baby*, she thought as the lights came on. For an instant, she felt as if she had her eyes tightly clenched and the light had pried her eyelids open and forced its way in. She did not want to have her eyes open. She wanted her eyes closed and to be asleep and safe.

Where the folding metal chairs had been deployed, there was a circular conference table. The terrible smell came from the several people sprawled like forgotten trenchcoats in the chairs around the table. Two had fallen forward onto the table. They were all facedown in pools of blood, their heads bloody too, bloodied and bowed. Eyes variously open and unseeing. On the floor there was a woman, her short skirt hiked nearly to her waist by her fall. Her face had been destroyed, her torso blown nearly in two. There was so much blood, she appeared to be wearing underpants somehow made of it. The other bodies were all male.

She made a sound in her throat and realized how quiet the room was. The baby dug its nails into her neck and whined softly. There was no air that did not stink. The lights were far too bright; they showed far too much she did not want to see. Her stomach lurched and cramped and her bowels ached. Her thoughts were thick and tangled, tripping over themselves like a clumsy drunk. Staggering backward out into the corridor, she clutched the baby so tightly it cried out in protest and bucked and kicked as if they were drowning together. She fell against a wall. Holding her head away from the baby, she was sick onto the carpet. The baby burst into wails, its shrieks tearing at her shattered nerves.

In a daze, she retreated around the corner to the office where she had found it. Where the phone was. Shushing the baby, she crouched behind the desk. She eased it onto the floor, between her knees. What she most wanted was to get out of the building, but she had already gotten herself lost in it. There was a killer, or maybe killers, in the vicinity, and no way was she going to wander around and walk into him, or them. At least here there was a phone, a precious phone.

She reached up and pulled the phone set off the desk and cradled it in one arm. The receiver nearly escaped her grasp and her fingertips skittered on the keypad. She missed the second 1 in 911 and started over again. As she waited for someone to answer the ringing, it occurred to her that she might have obliterated fingerprints, perhaps the murderer's fingerprints. If he had been in this office. Someone had hidden the baby in the kneehole of the desk. The dead woman. She closed her eyes briefly against a renewed onslaught of nausea.

"Police Emergency," a recorded voice said. "If this is not an emergency, please dial five-five-five-one-eight-zero-one. If this is an emergency, please wait for an operator."

Mary bit her lip, a swear word seeming stuck in her throat like a fish bone.

The tape looped and repeated itself.

"Answer, goddamn it," she muttered.

The tape repeated the message again.

She was snuffling and the tears were leaking from the corners of her eyes when an actual human being, a deep calm female voice, finally said, "Police Emergency. Please tell me where you are and who you are and then tell me the nature of your emergency."

"I'm at"—she could not remember the numbers of the address that she had jotted on a slip of paper, now on the dashboard of her rental car—"oh God, it's something like two-seven-zero-nine, two-nine-eight-seven Ohio Avenue, my name is Mary Dorr, and there's people murdered here and a baby and I don't know where I am inside this building, I came here for a meeting and got lost and found everyone dead"—her voice rose to a breathless snot-clogged squeak.

"Please give me the number of the phone you're calling from, miss," the voice asked.

She looked at the phone. "There isn't one. The little window is blank."

"Please stay on the line," the voice advised, "I'll put a trace on it. Maybe we can pinpoint your location in the building and save some time. We're dispatching officers to you right now, miss."

Mary nodded and then felt foolish, realizing the voice couldn't see her. "Okay."

"Is there anyone with you?"

"No, except for the baby—"

"You said everyone was dead—"

"I found the baby first, the baby's alive—"

"Is there anyone else in the building?"

"No," she said, "at least I haven't seen anyone." And she prayed with the frantic urgency of a child that there was no one else in the building anymore besides her and baby.

"No janitor, no night security man?"

"I don't know," she whispered, and then blurted, "I think the people were just killed. I think the murderer might still be here—"

"Why?"

"I don't know! The baby wasn't crying. It would have cried for its mother if she were gone for very long, wouldn't it?"

"Please stay on the line, miss—"

She strained to hear sirens, but there was only the sniffling of the baby and herself and their breathing. The baby's bowels gurgled and it grimaced. She shivered. Murderers didn't hang around, they killed and ran, surely, so as not to get caught. Soon the cops would be here and she would be safe.

Then she realized the voice was gone, she wasn't on hold anymore. The line was dead. Carefully, she put the receiver in its cradle and took hold of the baby. Her mouth and throat felt as if they had been packed with sand. Moving as soundlessly as she could, she wriggled out and crawled to the door and closed it, then flicked the lock over.

She sucked in a deep, shaky breath and crept back to the baby.

Pulling out the chair, she curled up into the kneehole, the baby's head against her heart, hoping the beat would reassure it and maybe make it go to sleep. She caught the chair by one of its wheels and tugged it into place so it would look as it had when she had blundered into this place.

The baby stank. The murderer would find them by following his nose. How long would it take the police to arrive? She willed them closer, willed the sound of sirens in her ears.

What she heard first were footsteps outside the door. She stopped breathing. She had not heard the sirens. It could not be the police.

A key turned in the lock, the lock tumbled over, the hinges creaked like the grate at the liquor store first thing in the morning.

She slipped her hand over the baby's mouth. It opened its lips slightly and began to gum her fingers. The intruder's breathing was audible now, hers must be too, and she had to fight not to cry out. The carpet whispered underfoot as whoever it was approached the desk, came around without hesitation, and pulled the chair gently away from the kneehole. She could see the pinstripes of his trousers, the thin silk socks, the gloss of delicately soled expensive shoes, all flecked with something darker. The trousers crinkled as his knees buckled, the instep of the shoes creasing as he supported himself on his toes. His face came into view, an ordinary face, just shy of handsome, late-thirty-something, clean-shaven tanned skin, blue eyes with thick blond lashes, an upper-class white man who might have been a high-priced lawyer or medico.

"Hi." He was smiling. His teeth were very good. His earlobes, though, were hairy, and there was a single pockmark on the edge of his upper lip.

She couldn't speak.

"Come on out," he said, holding out his hand. He wore a Rolex. "It can't be very comfortable in there."

She shrank from the outstretched hand.

He shrugged. His hand fell lightly upon one of her ankles. Her skin crawled and she could not suppress a shiver.

"Come on," he said.

Trembling, she pushed herself forward.

He grasped her wrist and then her elbow and supported her as she came to her feet. In his other hand he held a gun that seemed very large and had a very long snout on it. Something on the end of it that looked like a movie silencer. She came up to his Marlboro man chin.

He studied the baby a few seconds and then gently nudged her into motion, around the desk and out of the room, down the corridor to the meeting room where the slaughter had taken place. She balked at the door.

"Go on," he said, "there's an empty chair right there. Sit down. Put your head on the table. All you'll feel is the gun at the base of your skull."

She gasped. The baby began to cry.

"Give me the kid," he went on. "I won't hurt it."

The only thought she could form from the utter terror that possessed her was that she did not believe him. He would put the baby on the table and blow out its brains just as surely as he was going to blow out hers.

She shook her head.

He looked mildly exasperated, as if she were his wife and he had come home to be told there was no gin for his martini. Casually, he shoved her forward.

She had never been able to bear being manhandled. It sent her into a blind, red-eyed rage. She shoved back violently, putting her shoulder hard into his diaphragm. He coughed and staggered. As he took a backward step to recover his balance, she kicked upward and caught him in the testicles. A look of surprise crossed his face and then the pain turned his tan yellow and he dropped his gun. It skittered across the floor. He bellowed. She nearly lost her own balance, trying to hold on to the baby. Startled by the murderer's shout of pain, it began again to shriek. She dove out the door, carrying the baby as if it were a football. The murderer clutched at her but she slipped through his clawing fingers.

She hurtled herself down the corridor and around a corner and down the length of another corridor, with no idea where she was going. Looking wildly around, she saw the door to the women's room. A woman's room. But she had turned right from the corridor with the meeting room on it, not left. *Backward*, she thought, *it's all backward*. Behind her, she heard first hesitant, staggering footfalls, and then they began to pick up pace.

Hastily she punched 1–2–3 and jerked at the doorknob. Nothing happened. Now frantic, she punched 3–2–1 and the knob turned and she jerked open the door and thrust herself and the baby into the women's room. Once inside, she closed the door with great care, trying to make no sound. Silently she backed to the other side of the women's room. Beyond the second rank of stalls, she saw the door, the one unlocked by 1–2–3, that she must have used originally, before the lights went out. The women's room was a mirror image of itself, doors opening at either end onto different corridors in the building, those treacherous doors hidden from each other by the catercorner stalls.

She opened the 1–2–3 door and let herself out. It was all familiar here, the worn carpet, the lettered doors of the professional offices. Tiptoeing around the corner, she was not surprised to find the meeting room doors closed and locked. She had been in the other part of the building for some time. But she could smell the old cigarette smoke, that normally irritating odor reassuring her now that she knew where she was.

Behind her, around the corner, a door opened, and she broke into a run, down the hall toward the EXIT sign and the stairwell beyond the fire door. As she reached the fire door, a spurt of plaster and wood exploded from the wall behind her. When she glanced back in terror, she saw the murderer in a shooter's crouch, aiming the gun at her. The sound had been muffled. That thing on the end was not a movie prop but a real silencer, and that was not a prop gun. She stumbled down the stairs. The gun went off again behind her, the walls spitting debris at her. She threw herself sideways at the roll bars on the EXIT doors and fell with them as they opened and she tumbled out into the brightly lit night of the parking lot.

"FREEZE, POLICE," boomed an enormous amplified voice.

"He's trying to kill me," she screamed, trying to roll herself around the baby to protect it.

The baby's crying stopped abruptly as she knocked the breath out of it.

Mary stared back at the EXIT doors but the murderer did not come bursting out. Everything grew quiet again. She could hear the scuffle of hard-soled shoes on the pavement and, more distantly, the whisper of tires and the rush of vehicles on the highway nearby. She could smell the pavement she was on, and see small pebbles embedded in it. The baby wriggled against her and a small whimper escaped it.

A shadow fell on them and a uniformed policeman stooped to touch her shoulder. "You okay? Kid okay?"

Shaking her head yes, she flung an arm over his neck, and he lifted her to her feet and hustled her to the protection of an unarmed police car just beyond the lights. There were several cars there, more policemen, not very interested in her, focused on the building, guns like weapons of war in their hands.

The baby fussed. She rocked it and patted it and it quieted a little.

"You the woman that called?" the policeman asked.

"Yes."

"There's an armed man?"

She nodded.

"Just one?"

"All I saw."

The policeman opened the back door of his unit and gestured at it; she ducked inside. He addressed a walkie-talkie. Another policeman, an older man, approached, and the two men conferred. The first policeman turned to her again.

"Just one guy?" he asked absently.

"Yes." She slid into the footwell of the rear seat so her head was below the windows.

"One gun?"

"A big one. With a silencer."

He almost smiled at her. "They're all big when they're pointed at you, right?"

Exhausted and terrified, she was close to hysteria. She had to repress a giggle, promising herself she would remember that line to tell her sister. Terry would hoot.

"You know anything about guns?" the policeman asked.

She shook her head. "Just what I see in the movies."

He nodded, his opinion of the uselessness of her observations confirmed. "What's your name, ma'am?"

She told him and explained she was from out of town, staying overnight on business, and had come to a meeting at this place almost randomly.

He made notes. "Business meeting?"

"AA," she said evenly.

He looked up quickly from his notes, and the other policeman, who kept his eyes on the building, glanced back at her.

The first policeman scratched his cheek thoughtfully. "Somebody shot up an AA meeting?"

"No. I got lost going to the women's room and found this baby and a room full of bodies. The AA meeting let out before I could get back to—"

"So you don't know any of the dead people you say you saw—"

"Not a one—"

"You don't know who the kid belongs to?—"

"No—"

"Boy or girl?"

"How would I know?" she said. "I never saw this kid before in my life. What's it matter whether it's a girl or boy?"

The policeman blinked. "I'm just trying to get information to help identify it, that's all. Anyway, my wife always seems to know just looking at them—"

She rolled her eyes. "Obviously she has talents I don't—"

The policeman cleared his throat. "We, ah, could look—"

She thrust the kid's butt up at him. "Take a sniff, officer. If we open this kid's pants, we better have a clean diaper and some wet wipes handy."

He wrinkled his nose and poked at the other policeman. "We're gonna need a female officer to take custody. Get her to stop at the Seven-Eleven down the block for diapers and wet wipes, okay?"

Police cars were flocking into the parking lot. The policeman patted her shoulder. "You keep down out of sight, in case this joker's still hunting. Might be some gunfire. We're going to get you out of here real quick, take you someplace safer."

Mary snuggled into the footwell and soothed the baby. It did stink, worse all the time. It had burped up a little too, so its blanket was redolent of soured milk too. But when it smiled up at her, she felt chilled again. There was still a monster on the loose.

The older policeman who had been asked to call for diapers climbed into the car and leaned over the seat. "SWAT team's here, ma'am. They're going in now and secure the building. Anybody in there, they'll get him. Then we'll go in and take a look at the crime scene."

She heard some shouting, team leaders to one another, she guessed, and the doors being rushed, and then there was just the crackling of the radio from the front seat and the older cop in the front seat, shaking a butt out of a package.

"Would you mind opening a window?" she asked. "The cigarette smoke bothers me."

"Sorry," he muttered, cranking down his window. "I thought you wouldn't mind a little homemade air freshener to counter the load in the kid's diape—"

"So far as I know," she said, glancing up from the baby's gummy smile, "the smell of shit is not carcinogenic—"

The policeman exhaled a cloud of smoke and rolled an eye at her. "We all gotta die sometime, lady—"

A sinister rod appeared next to the policeman's left ear and there was a muffled pop. The policeman jerked and his face exploded.

Gibbering insanely, she scrambled backward toward the door as the murderer's head rose over the edge of the open window. He smiled at her. She sobbed and swore. He opened the driver's door, pushed the dead cop toward the shotgun seat, and climbed in. Casually he tossed a box of Pampers and a plastic canister of wet wipes over the back of the seat at her.

She kicked them away as if they were live snakes.

He started the car.

She couldn't take her eyes off him, certain if she turned to look at the door she was losing her nails on, groping for a door handle, he would blow out her brains with that gun.

"There are no interior handles on the backseat doors of police cruisers," he said.

Immobilized, she shrank into the footwell, against the handleless door.

Someone outside shouted and she jerked her head up to see the policeman who had put her into this vehicle, suddenly *her* policeman, in a shooter's crouch to the left of the direction they were beginning to move. The car instantly picked up speed and swerved toward him. As she was thrown against the door by her own weight and the baby's, she watched her policeman try to scramble out of the way. She screamed, the sound tearing out of her throat involuntarily, like something being ripped, and there was a thud and the policeman flew violently to one side.

She was close to fainting. Curled up in the footwell like a porcupine around the baby, she closed her eyes against dizziness and nausea, against what she could no longer comprehend. They were going very fast. She was jolted and tossed about several times. For a while there were sirens and even lights moving ahead and the thumping of helicopter rotors, but she dared not raise her head to look out.

Incredibly, she fell asleep, or at least lost so much consciousness as to amount to the same thing. She only knew, when she came to, that some time had passed and that they were traveling, without apparent pursuit, somewhere darker. Somewhere where the streetlights were scarcer. The baby woke up and began to whimper and clutch at her breasts. Poor thing must be horribly hungry by now.

From the front seat, the murderer spoke curtly. "Change the goddamn diaper."

The sound of his voice froze her again. She knew she should do as she was told but she could not.

He reached one long arm over the back of the seat and grabbed at the baby. She jerked it away from him, clawing and hitting at his hand. Slowing the car, he backhanded her casually, bouncing her head against the door. Suddenly she no longer held the baby. He had grasped it by the neck and hauled it into the front seat. It waited as he speeded up. He shook it and its blanket fell away. Its arms and legs windmilled frantically and he flung it from the open window of the moving police cruiser.

With a shriek, she hurtled herself bodily over the seat at him. He had to fight to control the vehicle with one hand, but he succeeded in punching her, giving her a glancing blow on one ear. She went for his throat.

The car swerved, throwing her backward. Her hands sought any kind of purchase and found his chin. His hands left the wheel to scrabble at hers. His eyes rolled back trying to see her and his face was transformed into a snarling inhuman mask. She felt herself falling backward again and convulsively she jerked his chin as she held on to his head as if it were a lifeline. There was a snap and all resistance seized, as if someone had let go of the other end of the line she was grabbing. The car sheered into a guardrail and bounced along it. She let go of him and a brilliant, explosive darkness rose up to meet her.

She woke to the smell of gasoline. She was in the backseat. Crawling into the front, she did not look at the body behind the wheel but just went over it, out the open window. The police cruiser had come to rest in the gully of a median strip. She could hear traffic on the divided highway above her. One of her shoes was gone. Limping, she scrabbled her way up one side and stood swaying at the edge of the highway. A little way down the road was a service station. She kicked off her remaining shoe and put one bare foot in front of the other until she reached the edge of light from the overhead arcs.

An acned adolescent attendant watched her from behind a grille.

She trudged up to him, aware she was tattered and bruised and probably bloody. She stood there and stared at him and he stared back.

"You bin in an accident, lady?"

She nodded dumbly. Then she remembered what she had been going to ask him.

"Key to the women's room?" she croaked.

"Oh sure." He shoved it through the slot at the bottom of the grille. "Round to the right."

She was putting the key in the door, without any memory of moving her feet to get there, when she heard him shout, "You know, you hadn't oughtta leave the scene of an accident, lady."

"Right," she said.

Turning the key, she leaned against the door. It was metal and cold and already she could smell the disinfectant.

She hadn't even found out what sex the baby was.

She gave the door a light push and the door creaked open. The women's room was a narrow, dark box, reeking of cleaners and cold urine, into which the light from the overhead arcs spilled through the open door in a rhomboid like a stain. A cracked mirror in a basin directly in front of her reflected purple light, and showed her the troubled image of a woman. She stared into it. The mirror rippled darkly as if she were underwater. She chucked herself under the chin. *Getting soft*, she thought.

IN THE DESERT OF DESERTS

THOMAS TESSIER

The lore of haunting long ago convinced us that an empty room can resonate with ghastliness, magnifying and mocking our deepest fears of unnatural encounters. But what about a vaster space? Thom Tessier unhesitatingly leads us to the Sahara and a sinister scenario that calls to mind a sort of alternate Robinson Crusoe. *Here, the fateful meeting with Friday might have been scripted by the ever perverse Paul Bowles—yet with a supernal assist from another master of the silenced scream, Edgar Allan Poe.*

༄

DRIVE AT NIGHT, somebody told me in Laghouat, and at first I did. But that advice was only good as long as I knew where the road was. The road was quite fair over some stretches, but then it would peter out, fading into the surrounding terrain, becoming invisible until it reappeared a mile or two farther on. That was all right too, if I didn't stray dangerously. A sensitive driver can tell where the road ought to be even when it isn't.

But I found it maddeningly difficult to follow the trail at night. My vision was restricted to the range of the headlights, and I had no useful sense of the landscape. At one point on my first night out I was driving along cautiously when the powerful beams of an oil supply truck lanced the darkness. The truck went by, nearly a mile away from me. *That* was where the road was, I realized unhappily. A trucker could make the desert run at night because he'd done it so many times he knew the way instinctively, but it was impossible for a first-timer to travel like that. I decided to travel the rest of the way by daylight.

Besides, there was more to the challenge than just making it all the way to Niamey. I wanted to experience the Sahara at its most difficult, as well as to enjoy it at its beautiful best. It would be a shame to drive through the desert mostly at night, and come away like some empty-handed thief.

I spent most of the second day in Ghardaïa, where I topped up the water and petrol tanks. I gave the Range Rover a careful examination, and was satisfied. I checked the spare parts list, but I already had everything on it. I had done these same things the day before, at Laghouat, only a hundred miles away. But this was my last chance to correct any problems or pick up something I might need. Ghardaïa has supplies, equipment, skilled mechanics and even cold soda. The oil pipeline runs nearby. It's a fairly busy town, considering the fact that it's located out on the edge of the edge.

I don't distrust people but I slept with one eye on my Rover and its load of supplies. I was up before dawn, feeling as eager as I was nervous, and I left Ghardaïa when the first infiltration of grey light began to erode the blackness. Now the crossing was truly under way.

I was travelling south through the Great Western Erg, and my next stop was In Salah, more than three hundred miles away. This would be the easy part of my journey, I reckoned. The desert was immediately fierce and formidable, but I knew there was an oasis at El Golea and some kind of a military outpost at Fort Miribel, both of which were on my route.

South of In Salah the terrain would become much rougher, the climate even more hellish, and although in theory there were more villages in that part of the country, I knew that they would prove to be fly-speck settlements that offered little. I had been told that in the Sahara what you think you see on a map is usually not what you find on the ground. I had no fear of dying of thirst or starvation, nor even of heat, but I did worry about a mechanical breakdown that could strand me indefinitely in some heat-blasted cluster of huts on the far side of nowhere.

At first I made relatively good time, but by midday the road deteriorated predictably and I had to drive more slowly. After a break for lunch I proceeded, and soon got stuck. The sand in the Sahara can be deceptive and treacherous. One moment it may be as firm and hard-packed as an old gravel road, and then it will turn into something like dry water, all but impossible to stand in or move through. My right rear tire slid into just such a hole, and it took me nearly two hours to extricate myself with the help of aluminum tracks.

Even so, I felt reasonably pleased by the time I decided to stop for the night because I had experienced no major trouble and nothing unexpected had come up. I picked a place where the road was clearly visible, then pulled off about a quarter of a mile to set up camp.

That last night of peace I fancy I absorbed something of the remorseless clarity of the Sahara. This is a world composed of a few simple elements—sand, air, the disappearing sky, then the blue, red, yellow and white stars—but each one of them is huge in its singularity. They are so vivid and immediate that after a while they begin to seem unreal to the human observer, like stage props for a drama that never happens and involves no one. In the Sahara, it is said, God talks to himself. I had not come to the desert looking for any mystical fix or tourist inspiration, but I did find something like joy in the loneliness and insignificance it constantly threw in my face.

I ate, cleaned up, drank a single neat scotch and then slept well. It was chilly, but I had of course expected that and was warmly wrapped, and if there was any night wind it didn't disturb me at all.

Before dawn, as I prepared to leave, I found the footprints. I knew at once that they were not mine.

I almost laughed. I felt a little bit like Robinson Crusoe, shocked, amused, fascinated. After the initial wave of reaction passed, I began to feel uncomfortable. Crusoe had a pretty good idea of what he was up against, but the footprints I'd discovered made no apparent sense. For one thing, they shouldn't have been there at all.

They formed a counter-clockwise trail, roughly in the shape of a circle, around my little camp. They looked like the tracks of a solitary adult male wearing ordinary shoes and walking at an ordinary pace. The footprints stopped twice, overlapping tightly before continuing, as if at those two points the unknown visitor had paused to stare and think for a moment. It was disturbing to know that he could only have been looking at me as I slept just a few yards away, inside the circle.

I calmed down after a few minutes. The headlights of an oil company truck passing by on the road must have caught part of the Rover in the darkness, and the driver stopped to investigate. It was so obvious, I felt silly. The fact that I could see no trail to or from the circle was strange, but a breeze could have hidden them or perhaps the driver had walked a particularly hard-packed stretch of ground that would show no footprints.

Once I was on the road again I thought no more about it. My progress was slow because the wind started up and the road became more difficult to follow. It was a long day, hot and demanding, but late in the afternoon the conditions changed abruptly, as so often happens in the Sahara. The wind died away and at the same time I hit a good section of the road. I covered more ground in the last four hours than I had in the previous eight.

This time I camped a little farther from the road, beyond a ridge, where no headlights could spot me. I didn't like the idea of anyone sneaking up on me in the middle of the night, out there in the depths of the desert. My vehicle and equipment were worth a small fortune, and the next person might not think twice about bashing my head in and hiding them. He could always return later with a partner to collect the goods. The chances of anybody else finding my remains would be virtually nonexistent.

I felt so secure that I was not at all prepared to come upon anything unusual the next morning, but I did. The same unmarked heels and soles, coming from nowhere, going nowhere, but circling my ground, stopping once or twice.

I was shaken. I didn't want to be there anymore, and yet I sat down. It was as if I could not bring myself to leave. I had to reason my way out of this threatening situation. Whoever had left those tracks couldn't have followed me on foot because I had come too many miles yesterday. He could have followed me by car, or truck, or even on a camel, but surely I would have seen him at some point, and if he stayed too far back he couldn't be certain of finding the point where I left the road for the night.

Besides, why would anyone bother to shadow me like this? To approach me in the darkness, but then do nothing? If he intended to attack me he could have done so twice by now. The whole thing made no sense at all. It was precisely the fact that nothing had happened that worried me most. It seemed somehow more menacing, as if I were being monitored.

Could it be a Bedouin, a nomadic Arab? It seemed unlikely. I'd been told that they travel in clans and that they seldom come through this part of North Africa. There's nothing for them here and it isn't on any of their usual routes. Besides, I doubt that the Bedouins wear ordinary Western-style shoes.

I put my hand to the ground and touched one footprint. Yes, it was real. I was not hallucinating. I traced the indentation in the sand. He had big feet, like me. I placed my right foot next to one of the footprints. Nearly a perfect match. However, my high-top camping shoes had corrugated soles, and no heels.

It was theoretically possible that I had made the footprints in the middle of the night, because I did have a pair of ordinary shoes packed away in the Rover, but I simply couldn't believe it. I had absolutely no recollection of taking them out, putting them on, walking the circles, obscuring my tracks back to the van, and then packing the shoes away again. Not the slightest glimmer of any such memory. If it was my doing, asleep or awake, I was well on the way to losing my mind.

But isn't that what the desert is supposed to do to a person who wanders through it alone? Madness creeping in, like the sand in your socks. I told myself it wasn't possible, at least not in the first three days out of Laghouat. All that desert mythology was nothing more than romantic nonsense.

Nonetheless, I decided to push on all the way until I got to In Salah. I stopped only to eat and drink, and to let the engine cool down a little. I got stuck a couple of times but never lost the road, and I made pretty good time. The changes in the Sahara were largely lost on me, however. When my eyes weren't fixed on the road ahead they were glancing up at the rearview mirror. But I never saw another vehicle or person.

When I reached In Salah I was so exhausted that I slept for eleven hours. I spent another day working on the Rover, stocking up on supplies, and enjoying the break in my journey. I even had a stroll around the town, what there was of it.

And I decided to change my plans. Instead of heading south through the moderately populated mountains of the Ahaggar, as I'd originally intended, I would now turn west to Zaouiet Reggane and then drive south through the Tanezrouft all the way to Mali, and from Bourem I would follow the course of the Niger River on into Niamey. The net effect would be to shorten my journey and make it less scenic but also perhaps more challenging. The Tanezrouft is vast, empty and closer to sea level, therefore hotter than the Ahaggar. The oil trucks don't run in that part of Algeria. Some people believe that the Tanezrouft is the worst part of the whole Sahara Desert.

So why do it? I don't know. I must have been thinking that no one would dare follow me across the Tanezrouft. Before I left In Salah I bought a gun, an ugly Czech pistol. I don't know if I was indulging my own delusions, or pursuing them.

These actions and decisions of mine had an irrelevance that I could not completely ignore. It was as if I sensed that I was merely distracting myself with them, and that they didn't really matter. If the man was real, he'd be there. And if he was other than real, well, he might be there anyway.

One hundred miles south of Zaouiet Reganne, I awoke. I went out about fifty feet, looking for the footprints. Nothing. So I went a little farther, but again found nothing, no sign, no mark, that didn't belong to that place. I broke into a trot, circling my campsite, scouring the ground as I went. Still nothing of an unusual nature.

I ran right past it, then stopped sharply, one foot skidding out from under me as I turned back. Even then I didn't see it, I smelled it. And, as the saying goes, I thought I saw a ghost. A pencil-line of blue fluttering in the air. It was smoke. In the sand were two footprints, just two, not my own. The same shoes. The heel marks were so close they almost touched each other, but the toes were apart, forming a V on the ground. It was as if the man had squatted on his haunches there, staring at me while I was sleeping. Nearby, a discarded cigarette. It was still burning, almost to the filter now, and it had an inch-long trail of intact ash. I don't smoke.

I touched the smoldering tip just to convince myself that it was real, and it was. I jumped up and looked around, but there was no one in sight for half a mile in any direction. I'd chosen a natural basin, so there was nowhere to hide and even if someone was lying flat and trying to insinuate himself into the sand he'd still be easily seen. There was no one. No tracks. Just me and those two footprints, and the cigarette.

I picked it up and examined it carefully. Any trademark had already burned away, but there was enough left for me to see that the cigarette had the slightly flattened, oval shape that is more common to the Middle East than Europe or America. But that told me nothing. I wished it had lipstick on it.

I say that, but I drove scared, and the farther I went the more frightened I became. There was nowhere on the entire planet I could feel safe, because I could drive until I passed out and I would still be in the middle of the Sahara. When I reached Bidon 5, a desperate little waterhole, I sat off by myself and let the engine cool for three hours. They thought I was another of those wandering Englishmen who go to the most awful places in the world and then write articles about it for the *Sunday Times*.

I considered driving on, but common sense finally prevailed and I stayed the night. I must have been even more tired than I thought, for I slept late into the morning and no one bothered to wake me. Early starts are like a matter of religion to me, but I felt so much better, refreshed, that I wasn't annoyed. Besides, I had plenty of time. The change of route gave me an extra three or four days.

I was also encouraged by the fact that I was approaching the southern limits of the Sahara. Another three hundred miles, and I would be rolling through the grassy plains of Mali. When I got to Bourem I might even take a side trip and visit the fabled city of Timbuktu, a center of Islamic teaching in the fifteenth century. I have heard that Timbuktu is just a dull and decayed backwater of a place nowadays, but I was tempted to take a look. How could I come to within a hundred miles or so of what was once regarded the remotest spot on earth, and pass it by?

But I still had the last of the Sahara to deal with, and the road soon disappeared. My progress was slow, I got stuck and had to dig my way out several times, and the heat was devastating. I pushed on, regarding the desert now as nothing but an obstacle to be overcome as quickly as possible. Mileage is deceptive because the road, when you haven't strayed from it, meanders this way and that in its endless pursuit of firm ground, and one hundred miles on the map is usually a hundred and twenty-five or fifty on the clock. I think I reached the border, or even crossed it, when I had to stop for the night. Another day, a day and a half, two at most, and I would leave the Sahara behind me.

This time I parked only a few yards off the road. There was no traffic at all this far south so I had nothing to fear in that respect, and the sand was too treacherous to risk venturing into any farther than necessary. I checked the air pressure in all of the tires, checked my gun, had a glass of scotch, and got into my sleeping bag.

It was still quite dark when I awoke. Just like in a film, my eyes opened but the rest of my body didn't move. I was lying on my side, and I knew immediately that I was not alone. My mind wasn't working yet, I was still in a fog, and at first I thought I saw a single red eye staring at me from some distance away. It was the glowing tip of a cigarette, I realized dimly. I couldn't make out anything of the person who held it. I was overcome by a wave of choking fear that seemed to be strangling me from within. A dozen hungry lions circling closer wouldn't have frightened me as much as that burning cigarette did.

I had the gun in my hand, my elbow dug into the sand. I was still lying there in my sleeping bag, and I forced my drowsy eyes to focus on the tiny red speck of fire. A moment later it traced a gentle arc, came to a stop, and then brightened sharply. As he inhaled, I squeezed the trigger. The explosion seemed distant, a curiously muffled noise that might have come from another part of the desert. I shut my eyes, having no idea what had taken place, and I fell back into sleep.

The brightness woke me later. I didn't believe anything had actually happened during the night because my memory was blurred, dream-like, unreal. The gun was where I had put it when I got in the sleeping bag last night, between carefully folded layers of a towel on the ground nearby. If I had fired it at some point in the night, surely I wouldn't have put it back so neatly.

But when I sat up and looked around, I saw the body. I felt calm, yet desolate. He was about twenty yards away. I got to my feet and walked slowly toward him. My shot had been true, like a sniper in one of the old European wars. The slug had smashed his face into a bowl of bloody mush.

His hair was black and curly, his skin olive-colored, and he wore a plain white short-sleeved shirt, faded khaki slacks, and a pair of ordinary shoes. A man so dressed, on foot, wouldn't last more than a few hours in the desert. His presence there was such a vast affront to sanity and nature that I felt a flash of anger. It gave way, a moment later, to cold helplessness.

I found a few loose cigarettes and a box of matches in his shirt pocket, but he carried nothing else on his person. I don't smoke, but I took them. I checked inside the shirt collar but it had no label or markings.

It seemed to me that I would never know who this man was, or how he came to be in the desert with me, what he wanted, or why I had been compelled to kill him, so I got my shovel and buried him on the spot. Dead bodies are supposed to be heavy and cumbersome but he felt as light as a bundle of sticks.

Somewhere along the way in Mali I gave up thinking about it. There was nothing to do, there were no answers to be discerned in the lingering confusion of fact and fear. Guilt? No. I've seen enough of the world to know how superfluous human life really is. I drove, losing myself once again to the rigors and pleasures of simple movement.

Bourem offered little, Timbuktu less. I looked at the dust, the mud, the crumbling and overgrown buildings that seemed to be receding into prehistory before my eyes, and I left. In Niamey I relaxed, celebrated and got laid. I made my way eventually down to the beaches at Accra. I ate with Swedish and German tourists who fretted about the unofficial fact that ninety percent of West African whores are HIV-positive.

That didn't bother me. I drank bottled French water with my scotch, but I also busied myself with the women. Day after day, night after night. There's not much else to do, except drink and lie about. Besides, there are moments in your life when you just know you're meant to live.

"Why?"

Ulf was a well-meaning, earnest and somewhat obsessive Swede who had developed a spurious concern for my reckless behavior. I shrugged absently at his question. He wanted an answer but I did not care to mislead him.

"Regardless."

Ulf had money and nothing to do, nowhere to go, like me, and so we drove to Abidjan, then Freetown, finally Banjul. I enjoyed his company, but by the time we were in the Gambia the charm wore thin and I was eager to be alone again. Still, I agreed that Ulf could tag along as far as Dakar. He was still with me days after that, as I approached Tindouf far to the north.

"I'm heading east," I told him.

"But it's just a short run to Marrakesh now." Ulf was quite disturbed. He consulted the map. "There's nothing to the east, only the Sahara. No road. Nothing."

"There's always a road."

Ulf hired someone to drive him to Marrakesh. I stayed on in Tindouf for a couple of days, working on the Rover and restocking my supplies. I was serious about driving east. True, there was no road, but I believed I could make it anyway. I had it in mind to reach Zaouiet Reggane, four hundred miles away, and then take the road south until I found my campsite near the border. It was the last arc in a big circle.

Why indeed? At times I was crazy with disbelief. I thought I had to return to the spot and dig up the dead man, just to make sure that he was real. The missing bullet in my gun was not good enough, nor were the stale cigarettes I still carried with me. I had to see the body again. In some unfathomable way, the rest of my life seemed to depend on it.

But there were moments of clarity too. I was caught up in a senseless odyssey. I could ramble around Africa until I died of old age or stupidity. I argued with myself, dawdled, hung on for days in the soporific dullness of Tindouf. I dreamed of the dead man's hands reaching up out of the sand to strangle me, like some corny turn in a horror movie. I dreamed that the grave was still there, and I found it, but it was empty. Most of all, I imagined that I would never locate the place again, that I would just burn and blister myself to a blackish lump as I dug pointless holes in the desert.

I did, after all, drive east. A few miles from the village, the ground became tricky. I pushed on, often swerving one way or another on an immediate impulse. Progress was slow. Late in the afternoon, I had a sense that I would never make it anywhere near Zaouiet Reggane. Then all four tires sank into a trough of very fine sand. I got out. The Rover was in it up to the axles, with no chance at all that I could extricate it by myself. I reckoned I was between twenty and twenty-five miles east of Tindouf, which was a long one-day walk. I prepared to spend the night there. I would set off early and reach the village by nightfall. I would return the day after, with helpers, and we would haul my vehicle onto solid ground. They would laugh, I would pay, and later I'd drive to Marrakesh, perhaps catch up with Ulf, and that would be the end of it.

I woke up in the middle of the night. Unable to get back to sleep, I pulled on my jacket and walked into the chilly darkness. I didn't go far. When the dim outline of the Rover began to fade in my vision I stopped. This is what he saw, I realized.

I was still fogged with sleepiness. I sat on my haunches, with my heels together and toes apart. It's often rather bright in the Sahara at night, when the stars form a brilliant skyscape, but some high thin clouds now cast everything in shades of black. The Rover was an inky lump against the charcoal expanse of sand. This is what he saw.

Without thinking, I took one of his crumpled cigarettes from my jacket and lit it. I didn't inhale, but puffed at it, and the glowing red tip only seemed to emphasize the blackness around me. I imagined a shape stirring out there, mysterious and unknowable, secure in the anonymity of the night. I imagined it noticing me behind my tiny pinpoint of fire, fixing on me. As if I were the only stain on all that emptiness. And then I thought that maybe I had been wrong from the beginning.

It was like looking deeply into your own eyes, and finding nothing there.

THE BABY-SITTERS

ALEX HAMILTON

The perils on tap in Alex Hamilton's wickedly nightmarish fable are the stuff of this afternoon, tonight, and tomorrow for many of us. And it's pretty hard, given the title, to distract nervous readers from that fact. But the author has surprise firmly on his side, and the breezy, brittle patter he employs manages to provide some welcome distraction from the agonies of anticipating the worst . . . for a short while, at least.

✹

A LL THE WHILE she dressed, Muriel worried.
  "If they don't come soon, we shan't be able to go."

"They'll come," said Selwyn easily; "they're not like friends, they're professionals. They won't let us down."

"Makes it a jolly expensive evening out, *hiring* people to look after your kids."

"Better than paying in kind," said Selwyn. He lay on his back on the bed, choosing the best route from a map wide enough to have been tucked in with the bedclothes on either side of him.

She turned to look at him, although she could see him perfectly well in the mirror.

"Aren't you going to finish dressing?" she asked. "I don't want them to arrive and find us both half naked."

"Stop fussing, Moo. Tie and shoes and jacket and I'm ready for all comers."

"You haven't even shaved yet!"

"That's not obscene, is it? Baby-sitters have to take you as they find you."

"Oh, you are selfish! It creates a terrible impression. You don't seem to *think* that we're leaving the children in their charge, and if they think we're sloppy they'll probably be sloppy too. I truly think you're selfish."

"Sel*wyn*, darling, not selfish."

"I suppose it'll be left to me to show them everything."

"The advertisement said they'd done it hundreds of times. I'm sure by now they have a nose for everything."

"That's just the part of them that I don't want, their nose. I'll show them all they need to put their nose into."

Selwyn slid off the bed and walked over to her. He kissed her shoulder and swivelled her to kiss her throat and the upper slopes of her breast. He rested the tip of his nose on the bridge of her bra. She stroked the back of his head.

"Darling, I *must* get ready."

He laid his head alongside hers and looked at the two faces in the mirror.

"I have powder on the tip of my nose," he said. "Do you think they'll guess where it came from?"

The bell rang. She jumped up. "There they are. Oh, Selwyn, I knew this would happen! Will you see them while I get my dress on? Then come back and zip me up. Please hurry, and put your shoes on before you answer the door. *Selwyn!* Your jacket!"

"They won't go away," said Selwyn, "they wanted to come. They don't give a damn about us and who we are. It's the kids they're coming to look after, not us."

"All the same . . ." she sighed.

She listened to Selwyn cheerily greeting the baby-sitters. He was saying *frightful* things, but he was one of those people who got away with remarks that from somebody else would be in terrible taste. He had evidently taken them into the lounge and left the door open, because she could hear his voice booming back as if he were addressing people at the back of a hall.

". . . little snifter to start the evening, eh? I'm going to draw a line on the bottle after that, but it'll be in pencil, so you can always rub it out and draw another one, eh? Gin or Scotch? That's it, touch of the old gold watch is best on a cold night. Was the house difficult to find? Can't always find it myself when I've had one too many. If you feel hungry, would you work your way through the canned stuff first? The leg of lamb in the fridge is our Sunday dinner. If you want to make love in front of the fire I should make sure the door's properly shut, because even when it is there's a draught like a gale comes in through those windows, where there's a sash cord broken . . . Here you are. Jolly good health!"

She could not hear the replies, and struggled impatiently with a dress which seemed to have got too small for her since the last party they'd been to. Ever since Mark it had been a problem to stay the same size, while David had been a greedy little chap and she'd almost wasted away. Well, they were both first-class kids, and, professionals or not, nobody could help loving them.

Selwyn came back. He gave her the thumbs-up sign.

"Very presentable," he said, "even chronically good-looking."

"Yes, dear," she said, "you'll have to zip me in, this seems to have shrunk."

She turned round and he obligingly took hold of the zip. It would not budge. He put his hand on her hip to steady her and then pulled again. It remained where it was.

"What are you doing?" she asked, trying to peer down over her shoulder.

"I think I've found the snows of yesteryear," he replied; "stop laughing, or are you trying to cause an avalanche?"

"Do be serious and get me into this damn dress. I want to go in and talk to the baby-sitters. We can't just leave them in there waiting."

"Yes, we can," he whispered, "they're the most self-possessed baby-sitters I've ever met."

"All right, all right," she said, "I get the point. I'm sure they're very efficient and reliable and I'm silly to worry. All the same, I worry."

"You've got cause," he said. "I'm going to take you out tonight and seduce you."

"If you have as much trouble getting me out of my dress as you're having getting me into it I shan't have to fight very hard for my honour."

Then the zip moved. It flashed from one end of the course to the other in a fraction of a second.

"That's what I call a zip," he said in an awed voice.

"Thank God that's done," she said. "Now take me in and give me a drink too. After that I feel there's no backing out."

He turned her, to get the effect. "I can see the escape hatch," he commented.

She tugged at the dress, trying to conceal the top of her bra. "There's too much of me," she said helplessly.

"There's never too much of you, you look grand!"

"I wish we weren't going out!"

"Everything will be all right."

"Do you really love me, Selwyn?"

"Try me! Cross that line on the carpet and you'll find out."

"Oh, you're hopeless! Come on, then, if we're going. Put the light out in the bathroom, will you?"

"That reminds me. Better show it to *them*. Don't want them peeing in the airing cupboard."

"They don't *sound* that sort." But the anxiety was back in her voice.

"In a moment you'll see for yourself. Actually I think they're our sort."

In fact a moment later she saw what he meant. There was a curious resemblance between themselves and the couple standing, each with a drink, on either side of the hearth. As the door opened they were talking quietly, seemingly into the fire, but now they turned and came forward, smiling, the man with his hand out. It was an odd, but not unpleasant sensation, taking his hand, as if she were being welcomed into her own lounge. Perhaps because he was of the same physical type as Selwyn she found the man very attractive. His hand clasp was warm and dry. As his regard rested on her she felt that she looked nice.

"Good evening, Mrs. Chievely," he said, "you're our most glamorous mother this month."

"Thank you! How long is your list of mothers this month?"

"Long enough to make it worth saying. Mothers get about these days."

"And so you do as well? Where do you actually live?"

It was the woman who answered. "On the telephone. It's our life these days, isn't it, darling?"

Her voice was thick, soupy, a fluid in which the consonants seemed merely to float. Muriel thought her overdressed for an occasion like baby-sitting, but she could see from Selwyn's face that he would think it a silly complaint to make. She felt a little embarrassed for him, staring in that fascinated way. She said briskly:

"Before we were married I felt like that. I was glad to get away from the blessed thing."

"Well, you've nothing to worry about, Mrs. Chievely, we shall be right beside the blessed thing all evening, so call us whenever you feel like it. Some parents don't trust us. We've learnt to accept that."

Muriel bridled at the satirical hint in her tone.

"We're not like that," said Selwyn, "once we're out of the house, we're out."

The thick rich voice engulfed the idea: "It's exactly what we want too."

Selwyn was standing right over the woman.

"I want you to feel absolutely at home here."

"The time will pass very quickly," said the woman, "we have lots to do."

They all found themselves looking at a suitcase standing in one corner of the room.

"We take our gear around with us wherever we go," explained the man, "hoping for the right atmosphere to work in. Your beautiful house will suit us right down to the ground."

"Right down to the basement, I hope," exclaimed Selwyn.

"What work do you do, though?" asked Muriel, and felt her drink splash on her wrist as Selwyn nudged her.

"Correlating, linking, blending, cross-indexing, all that sort of stuff," said the man. "A thorough-going pest of a job. These moments before the parents depart are almost poignant for me, I enjoy them so much for their carefree feeling, in contrast with what has to follow."

"Have a night off, on us," babbled Selwyn, still looking idiotically at the woman, "you can always come again and we'll blend a bit ourselves!"

"We can't afford to miss our opportunity," said the woman, "but isn't he nice, though?" she appealed to the man. Selwyn gave him no time to answer.

"Let me at least show you how our hi-fi stuff works. It's our great relaxation, isn't it, Moo? She's my moose, and it's her choice, all but the pops, so we call it moosic."

"Hadn't you better shave?" asked Muriel.

While he was away she showed off the children. She had meant to list their peculiarities and forewarn the baby-sitters about their little foibles, grading them in the degree of their urgency, but after Selwyn's performance she was unable to mention them. It was doubtful, in any case, whether she could have lectured this woman, with her self-assurance and style, nor did she have the inclination to play the heavy mother before this charming, reassuring man.

"As soon as they're old enough I'm going back to work," she told the man, as she quietly closed the bedroom door.

"They're beautiful children," said the man with apparently genuine enthusiasm, "an achievement in themselves. When you go back to work you must think of them, just as they are now, as something complete and perfect!"

The woman only said: "I would like children like that. One could do anything with them."

"Don't you believe it!" laughed Muriel.

Suddenly she was impatient to be away. She could think of nothing else to say, and somehow she felt in the way of this couple who wanted to get on with their work. She called to Selwyn:

"Do get a move on, darling, the invitation said seven-thirty, and it's miles!"

"Don't worry!" called back Selwyn, "it's a party, not Grand Opera. They won't close the doors on us if we don't arrive on the dot."

But to her relief he came out as soon as he had said that, and resisting the temptation to shake the hands of the baby-sitters, and thank them for putting up with them, Muriel took down her coat and let the man help her into it. She thought his hand stroked her hair as he did so, but she was not sure. Then they were ready, and Selwyn was chattering about the necessity of getting a little petrol on the way.

At the gate they looked back, and saw the baby-sitters standing in the doorway, the man with his arm around the woman's shoulders, watching them go. Muriel prayed that Selwyn would not crash the gears as they left. In the car as they pulled away (quite smoothly) she said:

"I'm sorry, Selwyn, that I carried on like that. They're certainly a perfectly reliable couple. I hadn't dreamed of anybody so mature and sophisticated when you talked about them. It was only, you see, that I anticipated some fearful teenagers trying to grub up some pocket money, and so naturally I was worried. I shan't worry any more now."

"No? Well, all the same I shall give them a tinkle now and then."

"Don't be so silly, darling, they're perfectly capable. If there were anything they could ring us. I left the number."

"Maybe. But when I think of them absorbed in their tasks, blending and all that, I wonder if they would have any time to spare for anything bourgeois like our kids."

"Oh, of course they will!" And then Muriel giggled. "I know what it is! Selwyn, you transparent thing, you're jealous!"

"Jealous! You don't mean it! What have I to be jealous of?"

"I see it all. It's sweet! It's fantastic!"

"You're raving, Muriel! For God's sake!"

"You want to ring up because you want to interrupt."

"Interrupt? Interrupt what?"

"Interrupt our baby-sitters making love."

"You have sex on the brain! Just because they look so well equipped for it doesn't mean they have any such idea themselves. And personally I don't give a damn what they do if it doesn't interfere with their keeping a sharp eye out for the kids waking."

"Funny," said Muriel, leaning over so she could get some light from passing street-lamps to examine her make-up, "because in fact that's true, isn't it? You don't think so much of their making love together, as making love with other people."

"Well, the girl certainly gave me the eye. I felt pole-axed."

"Darling, she did not! She was just there, and you were in the way of her rays. I don't blame you a bit, but I don't think you should call her a girl, she's almost as old as I am."

"Old girl, you're all girls to me, until you positively chicken out."

"I'm not going to think about them any more. I won't have my evening spoilt by being jealous of baby-sitters. It's bad enough spying on you at the party, where everybody's dolled up specifically to get at you."

"Stop harping on jealousy. If there were to be any authentic jealousy in the air it would come from me, watching you melt before that bloke."

"Melt! Oh, you liar! I did not *melt*! I thought he was a pleasing man, I admit. But *melt*, no fear!"

"Melt, get pleased, what does it matter so long as we're out for the evening together quarrelling about it?"

"We are *not* quarrelling. We are discussing the matter sensibly."

"Quarrelling, discussing, what does it matter so long as we don't go on doing it?"

"Selwyn, I love you."

"Moo, you are my queen."

They felt at the party that it was the penalty for having been so long housebound that they knew nobody. But their hosts worked hard and soon they knew almost everybody. Muriel realised, when she had circulated a little, that the party was made up mainly of married couples, and found that few of them would have been there had it not been for baby-sitters. It was a lovely party; there was something in that punch which made everybody friends; she had the nicest shoulders in the room; it was like the party where she had met Selwyn but for the fact that she had been single then and worried about who was going to take her home; she made several contacts which she was sure would be a great help to Selwyn in his career—and it annoyed her to see him standing near that telephone and finally ask their host if he minded. She prodded him as he put the receiver down. He turned guiltily.

"All quiet on the Western Front," he said.

"Who answered?"

"She did."

"Oh."

"Well, it was either him or her."

"All right, all right."

"You can make the next call if you like."

"There's no need, not for either of us, to call."

"As a father I feel it behooves me to keep in touch."

"And as a rake you feel it behooves you to chat the female up."

"Muriel, take that back."

"Selwyn, I take it back."

"Moo, you're the loveliest woman here."

"Take me home, darling!"

"We only just got here!"

"Well, leave that bloody phone alone then."

And for an hour or so he did. He made purposefully for the far corner of the room, and she was proud of him, seeing him tall against the wall, with a little semicircle of people laughing at everything he said. She could see that he was feeling like a genie let out of a bottle, and she felt guilty at having hemmed him in so long with house and kids. There was a young thing with a lot of blonde hair pouting and wriggling about in front of him, and affectionately and mentally wished them both the best of luck. Selwyn was really too indolent to be unfaithful, though he talked as if he were perpetually knocking them over. As long as she let him flirt she knew there would be no trouble. The exceptions in his behavior were easy to spot, such as that self-conscious display before the baby-sitter. Momentarily Muriel's face darkened. She *would* make the next call.

". . . so I have this need for an outside opinion," said the stout planter-like man she'd been talking to, "and it would just please me to act on a decision fallen from your fair lips."

Muriel had no idea what he was talking about.

"I should," she said quickly.

"Should? Should do what?"

"Go right ahead." She could see Selwyn disengaging himself from his group.

"Christ!" exclaimed her interlocutor, "that's a bit extreme, isn't it? This isn't China."

"Will you excuse me?" asked Muriel, working her way round his bulk, and finding another group smiling her into their company. By the time she was free of them, Selwyn was on the phone and talking. In a pleased tone he was explaining the operation of the lighting system. Seeing her at his elbow, he said:

"Trouble and strife at my side, wanting to pitch me back into the circus, so I'll sign off."

He put the receiver down and Muriel said:

"What was all that about? What have you got to go into all those details for?"

"Oh," said Selwyn casually, "something to do with small print. They wanted to fix up the Anglepoise in the lounge."

"The Anglepoise is in the study," she said, "and I locked that."

"I know," he said, "I told them where the key is."

"Who was them, this time?"

"The lady, as it happens."

"The *girl*, the *woman* we hired, as it happens," said Muriel, "and as it happens I'm going to call right back and tell her not to touch that key."

She reached out. Agitatedly Selwyn laid his hand on her arm.

"That would be very rude, Muriel."

"I don't care. I'm not having them going through my private papers."

"Don't be so silly. They're not interested in your private papers. I beg you to forget all about it."

"You'll have to go on your knees. And if you do I promise I'll pour this drink right down your collar."

"Well, I'm not going to stand here and listen to you make a fool of yourself."

"Every two's a pair, they say," commented Muriel, dialling.

She had not expected the man to answer. She instantly forgot the little speech she had formulated.

"Sorry to bother you," she got out. "I was just sort of thinking, you know how it is, wondering how everything was."

"Splendid!" she heard. "Have to congratulate you on the children. Answer to a baby-sitter's prayer. We have a little warm toddy ready in case any soothing needs to be done. Normally we're introduced to children, so we shouldn't be a shock if they wake up, but as you were in a hurry, we let it go. If they do wake up, I think we can get round them."

"Our fault. We should have thought of that. In our old place we had lots of friends all round us among the neighbors, so, of course, it wasn't necessary."

"Quite understandable. Hope you're having a good time."

"Yes, it's a very nice party, thank you."

"A woman with your style, Mrs. Chievely, has no right to stay in."

"Thank you, kind sir."

"Mustn't keep you from the gay throng. There's someone just behind you longing to make your acquaintance. Bye-bye."

Behind her in fact stood Selwyn, smiling ironically.

"Did she confess all?" asked Selwyn.

Muriel flushed. "It was him," she said.

"Do you know, I thought it might be. You positively dandled that receiver."

"You are a pig," she said. "Selwyn darling, introduce me to those people in the corner you were talking to."

"Having fun?"

"I'm going to, from now on."

The few words spoken by the baby-sitter acted on her with surprising strength. She thought that she had perhaps been seeing things out of proportion, and she realised that she was quite beautiful and clever enough to be enjoyable to talk to. She resolved not to watch Selwyn, and to make that elegant, smooth Pakistani mathematician, amongst others, remember that he had met her. She held her empty glass conspicuously before her, until, excellent-mannered man, he asked if he might fill it for her.

As they went everybody said it had been a lovely party, and meant what they said. Most of them said they would stay longer but for the necessity of getting home to relieve their baby-sitters. The Chievelys felt they could stay a little while more, each time the problem came up, because Selwyn was told, over the phone, that, if anything, the baby-sitters would welcome a late arrival, as they had not quite broken the back of their task, and a little extension of comfort and silence would help them vastly.

And of course, when the party thinned out, and there was room to talk, and to talk about the things in life that really mattered, it was even better than it had been before. And in the end it was only because Muriel could see that their hosts plainly wanted to get off to bed now that she insisted they should go. She prised Selwyn away from the daughter of the house, who obviously had the stamina to go on relating to her parents' gorgeous guest until breakfast-time, and explained for the last time that now *they* would give a party, and they had the best baby-sitters in the world to recommend.

"I'm the only baby round here," said the daughter, pertly, "and I'm not going to be left at home with any baby-sitters."

"Oh, you don't know," said Muriel, welcoming the girl into a bond of man-relishing womanhood. "If this one had been on his own you wouldn't have seen me, I don't suppose."

Selwyn looked at the daughter. "Would have suited me," he said gallantly.

"Go on with you," said the hostess, "I think you're the best-suited couple we've had here tonight. In any trouble I know you'd be a team."

"We get enough practice against each other," said Selwyn, "and now if I may I'll make one last call. Just to let them know we're coming. I'd better write you a cheque for the use of your phone. You've been most sympathetic, but I feel a little guilty over it." "Nonsense," said the host, "I know what it is. Help yourself."

But there was no reply. Selwyn tried three times, the last time through the exchange.

"Funny," he said, "number unobtainable."

"Some cross-up in the wires, probably," said their host. "Strange things happen at this time of night. I remember once I was trying to call . . ."

But his wife was offering coats, and the party was over.

In the car going home, Muriel said:

"I'm a bit sloshed, darling, we shouldn't have stayed so late, I wished it could have gone on longer, I was so enjoying myself, you were a terrific success, I was so proud of you, oh God, my head's spinning, are you sure this is the right way?"

"Damn right you're sloshed, darling. That was a hell of a sloshed sentence."

"I just want to get home."

"Soon be there."

She dozed off while the car slipped along the empty streets, so it seemed quite soon after that she was watching him take out his door keys. She leant her head against his shoulder.

"Do hurry up, darling."

"Hold up, Moo, you're leaning against the pocket. Drunken thing, you."

She shook herself awake, and watched him trying to fit the key in the lock.

"Drunken thing, yourself," she murmured; "if I were going to be seduced by you I'd have had second thoughts by now."

He straightened up, flicked his lighter on, and bent down again. She would never forget his face at that moment, as he stared back at her, still bent down, his black hair falling limp over his forehead. He

said, with unbelieving astonishment in his voice which made it
sound stupid to her:

"*The key won't go in!*"

"Nonsense, Selwyn, I'm far too tired for games. Come on, open
the door, and let's get to bed."

He fumbled with the key again.

"It's the wrong lock," he announced in a queer voice.

She drew close and clutched his arm.

"What do you mean?"

He stabbed at the aperture with the key. He shrugged. "Wrong
lock," he said again.

She snatched the key from him, and tried it herself.

"It's the wrong *key*, you idiot!" she said. Her voice was as strange
as his.

"You know bloody well it isn't," he replied. "You use it every day
of your life."

"Well, don't just stand there holding that lighter like a torch-
bearer. Ring the bell."

"Yes, I'll ring the bell. I didn't want to wake the kids."

"We'll just have to wake them. I'm not going to stand out here all
night. You'll have to get the lock seen to in the morning. Can't you
find out about these things before we go out? Honestly, Selwyn, I
have to see to everything in this house."

"That's bloody well not true!"

"I'm not going to argue about it now. Press the bell!"

"You press it. You may be tired, but you can raise your arm, I suppose. Talk about helpless femininity!"

Angrily she put her finger on the bell push. She kept it there until
he snatched her hand away.

"All right, all right, they're expecting us," he muttered.

"This is so humiliating," she said.

After a long wait the door opened a little. The man's face
appeared. There was a dim roseate light in the hallway beyond
him.

"What is it?" asked the man.

"Couldn't find the key, or something," replied Selwyn. They both moved forward, but the door did not give before them.

"I don't understand," said the man.

"Don't mess about, there's a good chap," said Selwyn. "I know we're a bit late, but you said you wanted to get on with it, so we took you at your word."

"Hope the children behaved themselves," added Muriel.

"This is a very strange time of night to call," said the man. "I think you must have the wrong house. There is nobody else in this building save my wife and myself."

The door seemed to be closing, but Selwyn suddenly leaned forward and pushed against it. It gave a little, but not enough to allow him to insert himself.

He pushed his face within six inches of the baby-sitter's, and said:

"We're bloody tired, my good friend, and in no mood for fun and games, so if you'll just move to one side we'll take over."

"Please," said Muriel pathetically.

"No bloody please about it," said Selwyn, "we're coming in."

"I should think not!" said the man. He put out a hand and seemed to lean it on Selwyn's shoulder. And suddenly Selwyn staggered back from it, as if there had been a spring in the man's forearm.

"What is it?" came the woman's voice from inside the house. "What's all the commotion?"

The door opened and revealed her in the doorway to the bedroom. She was standing with one hand clutching together the neck of her dressing gown. Muriel recognised the garment for her own. Below the hem several inches of Muriel's favorite nightie, the scarlet one that she called her "competitive nightie," fluttered in the draught flowing in from the cool outside.

"Those are mine!" shrieked Muriel.

"It's all right," said the man, in that reassuring voice, "don't worry, darling. It's only some drunken revellers."

"It's all right," repeated the woman, back into the darkness beyond her, "it's only some bad people that Daddy will soon frighten away."

"I want to see the bad people!" came the voice of a child, and as if plucked out of the darkness the woman suddenly had both the children, one on either side of her, holding on to her gown and staring at Muriel and Selwyn, with their arms around the woman's waist and their cheeks pressed against her hips. They stared accusingly, sullenly, darkly, as Muriel had never seen them stare at anything before.

She recoiled.

The door closed slowly. The man may have whispered "Satisfied?" before it clicked to, or she may have made the syllables from the sound of dead leaves blowing along the pavement.

"I'll knock the door down!" raged Selwyn.

"You said yourself it couldn't be done," said Muriel. "Why did we have to have such a perfect house?"

She began to cry.

"They can't get away with this," said Selwyn, "I'll have this looked into straight away."

"I'm scared," said Muriel. "They've thought it all out. Oh, did you see their faces?"

"To hell with their faces, we'll soon have a different look on their faces."

"But what are we going to do?"

"It's incredible. You know what they're after, don't you? They want all that equipment I've bought. They think we're going off and then they're going to ship it all out."

She backed away from him as if he had been one of them.

"Your equipment? Equipment!" she screamed. "What are they doing to my *babies*?"

The line of light under the door vanished.

AFTER YOU'VE GONE

JOHN PEYTON COOKE

Suicide is the ultimate private act, and the most intimate. But when doubts exist, many who are bent on doing away with themselves have the option of buying time by phoning a hotline; on the other end, the volunteers can only hope the delay will short-circuit the intent.

Thinking about this eerie dance of death performed with an unknown partner, John Peyton Cooke dares to acknowledge the possibility of the Bad Samaritan.

But, even more subversively, he refuses to stop there.

ⓢ

I LOVED IT SO much I was cradling it in my hands, fondling its stock, bracing its chamber between my thumbs, staring into its barrel like you'd look into a lover's eyes, in search of some kind of truth. It stared back at me deeply and gave me the ultimate truth: *Yeah, you got it right, Grant. I'm your trusty Glock. You can count on me. I'm going to kill you.*

I kissed its muzzle. My tongue tasted oil, and I could smell powder traces on my fingers. I'd cleaned it out after being down at the firing range all afternoon, blasting at all those black hanging targets, trying to get rid of all my black thoughts but only making them blacker. It was all I could do to keep from turning my Glock on myself then and there.

I didn't want to go out that way, in front of everybody. I wanted to have some privacy and leave a note—three notes, maybe, addressed to different people and taped up on my bathroom mirror. One to my landlord, saying sorry about the mess and take what you want. Another to Captain Feliciano, telling him thanks for your support when the going got tough, but face the facts, guy, I'm a screw-up. The last to Mom, saying love you lots and none of this is your fault, even if you did put Poncho to sleep.

I loved my Glock so much I was laying four of its six inches on my tongue, forming my lips around it, hooking my thumbs around its safe-action trigger. There's no such thing as a safety catch on a Glock—you have to apply direct pressure in the right spot, or the trigger acts like a safety and refuses to fire.

My thumb was in the right spot. The rest ought to be cake.

I was telling myself that if I was a real man, I'd do it.

I was sweating bullets, staring down at the trigger cross-eyed. The last thing I'd see would be the knuckly creases on my thumb parting ever so slightly.

I depressed the safe action so it wouldn't be safe anymore—and I wouldn't be depressed anymore.

I did it. I squeezed the trigger.

It should have fired. But it didn't. It jammed on me.

For the first time in my career, my Glock had let me down.

And now my hands were shaking and my heart was beating so fast I thought I was going to have a heart attack. If I tried again, I was going to screw it up. And I didn't want to fail.

I set the gun down. My stomach churned in disgust. With fumbling fingers, I tapped out a cigarette and lit it on the third match. It felt good to have that smoke in my lungs. The nicotine got my mind to thinking—maybe the ol' Glock was giving me a sign, that I needed help, that something was terribly wrong with me. And you don't argue with a Glock.

I didn't know where to begin. The brass always encouraged us to use the departmental psychiatrists—but everyone knew what that was about. I couldn't count on total confidentiality. Whatever was wrong with me might get leaked to IA. It might get subpoenaed in some future court case if my policing skills were called into question, and such a case was not outside the realm of possibility. It might simply get spread around as interprecinct gossip: *Officer Grant's a loose cannon. Yeah, you can't trust Tom Grant as your backup. The guy's nuts. Let's find him a nice desk job and pull him off the streets.*

I couldn't turn to the department. No sir, not on my life.

Facedown on the kitchen table in front of me lay the *Village Voice*. One of the classified ads on the back page caught my eye:

> **LONELY? DEPRESSED? SUIDICAL?**
> **CALL THE 24-HOUR HELP LINE!**
> **555-HELP 555-HELP 555-HELP**

It looked like what I needed. Help was only a phone call away. Even though it was two in the morning, somebody would be there on the other end of the line to talk me down.

I picked up the phone and called.

"Hello?" A man's voice, exceedingly mild, somewhat sleepy.

"Um, yes, is this the help line?" I croaked.

"Yeah, sure." He cleared his throat. "How can I help you?"

"I—I just tried to kill myself."

"Really?"

"Yes, really."

"What happened? Why didn't it work?"

"My gun jammed."

"Oh, you're using a gun? What kind?"

"What kind? Does it matter?"

"Of course it matters. What kind of gun do you own?"

"Well, it's a Glock."

"Mmm," said the guy on the help line. "What model?"

"It's a seventeen-L. Semiauto, six-inch barrel."

"What does that use? Nine-millimeters? Forty-caliber Smith & Wessons? Or forty-fives?"

"Nine-millimeters," I said.

"How many in the clip?"

"I've got seventeen in the clip and one in the chamber. The one in the chamber jammed. I'm going to have to start all over."

"How much does a gun like that cost?" the help line wanted to know.

"I don't know what it costs now. I got mine, what, four years ago, when I joined the academy. It set me back about eight hundred."

"The academy?" he said. "You mean the police academy?"

"Yes, I'm a policeman."

"How interesting."

"Listen I'm serious about this. I'm going to take my Glock apart, clean it all up, reload it, and try again. Probably one chance in a billion that it'll jam again."

"Probably," the help line said.

There was an uncomfortable silence.

"Aren't you going to try to talk me out of it?"

"Why should I?"

"I thought that's what you were there for."

"If you want to kill yourself and you thought I was going to try to talk you out of it, why would you call?" he asked.

"I don't follow," I said.

"Why don't you do it right now, while I'm on the phone?"

"What?"

"You heard me. Talk to me while you're unjamming your gun or whatever it is you have to do. I'll wait. Get it all nice and ready, and then do it. Just do it. I want to hear it."

"Listen, maybe I dialed the wrong number, buddy."

"No, you didn't. You dialed five-five-five-H-E-L-P, didn't you? That's me. I'm the help line. You got what you wanted."

"I still don't understand."

"Who cares whether you understand? You're about to kill your-

self. In a few minutes, no one's going to give a damn about you anymore. You'll be gone, and we'll still be here. It's not for you to understand. Are you beginning to see my logic?"

"Not exactly."

"How are you going to do it? Side of the head? In the mouth?
Through the chest?"

"In the mouth."

"Good," he said. "That's best. Side of the head, there's too much
chance you'll turn yourself into a vegetable. Through the chest,
you're not guaranteed to hit the heart. You might only wound yourself, pass out, and wind up in the hospital."

"I don't need your advice," I said. "I want help."

"Help? You want help? What do you think I'm giving you?"

"Not that kind of help."

"I didn't specify what kind of help in my ad, now, did I?"

"No, but—"

"Everyone always *assumes* I'm here to rescue them. I'm not. You
want to kill yourself, that's fine by me. I can't abide suicides who get
halfway there and then can't finish the job. Some of them only need
a little push to be on their way. So I put the number in the paper. I
want them to call me at that moment of crisis, when all they need is
a little encouragement."

"You're sick."

"Ho-ho!" he said. "You're the one who's already tried to kill himself once this evening, and you want to do it again. Which one of us
do you think is sick?"

"Wait a minute," I said, and began to laugh. "I see what you're
doing. I can see right through you. You're smart, you know that? You
really take the cake. You're using reverse psychology, just like my
mother used to do when I was a kid."

"Oh?" the help line said. "Just how am I doing that?"

"By pretending you want me to go ahead and do it, acting like
you get some kind of kick out of other people dying while you hang
there on the line. You think all we're doing is feeling sorry for ourselves and looking for someone to hold our hands and tell us it's

okay, tell us we're somebody special, tell us there's a brighter day dawning somewhere over the rainbow."

"Stop wasting my time. Are you going to do it or not?"

"See?" I said. "Instead of giving us soothing words, you give us abuse. You try to make us feel even more worthless, because you think we're going to react against it and tell ourselves we're really okay. We listen to you and think you're a jerk, but we say to ourselves, 'Hey, why should I listen to this guy?' and before you know it, you've cured us of our mania and sent us on our merry way. Isn't that how it goes?"

The voice on the help line gave a rude, audible yawn.

"Hello?" I said. "Are you still there?"

"I've been making a sandwich. You were saying?"

"Never mind what I was saying. I'm onto you, and it won't work. Maybe with some other schlemiel, but not with me, man."

"What won't work?"

"The reverse psychology trick. You've just proved to me what a lousy world it is that we live in. I don't want any part of it. I'm going to clean my gun up and blow my brains out."

"Do you really mean it this time?"

"Of course I mean it!" I shouted. "If you want to hear it for yourself, just stay on the line. It won't take very long."

"You promise? You're not just pulling my leg?"

"I promise. Cross my heart and hope to die."

"That's the spirit! Where do you live?"

"Oh, no," I said. "I'm not telling you. Now you believe me, and you want to send somebody over. Somebody from my precinct, maybe, or an ambulance or some goddamn social worker."

"No," he said in that calm, level voice of his. "No, I want to come over. I want to see it for myself. Maybe I can even help you do it. That is, if you really want my help—"

"I can take care of it myself, thank you very much."

"I'm not so sure. You sound chicken to me."

"Chicken?" I said. "Why don't you go fuck yourself?"

"What's your name?" he asked, unfazed by my suggestion.

"Tom," I said.

"Tom what?"

"Just Tom, okay? I don't want you reporting me."

"I'm not going to report you. You can trust me, Tom. My name's Ray. I'm your friend Ray. I'm here to help you."

"Lot of help you've given me so far, pal."

"I have," Ray said. "Only you just don't appreciate it. Now why don't you tell me where you live? I want to come over."

"As long as you promise not to interfere," I said.

"Oh, I won't," Ray said. "I wouldn't dream of it."

I gave him my address. He said he lived only fifteen blocks away and could be there in ten minutes. We hung up.

I laid out some newspaper and started cleaning my gun.

"Why a nine-millimeter?" Ray asked from across my kitchen table. He was my age, with an altogether too intense look in his eyes. "Why not a revolver? Revolvers never jam. You never would have had this problem. You never would have had to call me."

"If you must know," I said, carefully reloading seventeen live rounds into the clip, "I really believed the nine-millimeter was the way to go. Right after I joined the academy, the department had just changed regulations to allow us to carry something more powerful than a thirty-eight."

"Thirty-eight Special," Ray beamed. "Standard police issue."

"Yeah, in the old days," I said. "Most of us supported the change, but the old-timers were opposed. They kept nagging at us that semi-autos were unreliable and prone to jamming."

"See?" Ray said. "They knew whereof they spoke!"

"They were so scared of the change, they drummed up other reasons. They thought that we youngsters would lose control and empty our clips into every unlucky punk who crossed our path."

"Did they switch?"

"No. They kept their thirty-eight Specials. Switching would be like ending a love affair. Most of us under forty went for the nine-millimeters, though. We were the ones facing the front-line action. The gangstas were outgunning us, with AK-forty-sevens, sometimes. We had to be on as equal a footing as possible."

"Thus the Glock," Ray said admiringly. "It *is* nice, Tom."

"Thanks. My Glock and I have been through a lot together. I had to use it once to stop a sixteen-year-old kid who was armed with a beautiful silvery Colt Double Eagle ten-millimeter."

"Do tell!"

"The kid had just robbed a liquor store. I identified myself and asked him to drop his weapon. He refused to do so. He wanted to go out in a blaze of glory, I guess, and I had little choice but to oblige him."

"Good for you," Ray said with a gleam in his eye.

"Ever since, I wished he could have got a bead on me and let fly. Anything to make it seem less like an execution. But to do that, he would have had to have had at least a few shells in his gun. Once the kid was down, we examined his Colt, and we found his magazine just as empty as mine was after I'd shot him."

"Oh, too bad!" Ray pouted his lips. "Poor Tom!"

"It only takes a second holding that trigger down to let all those slugs come spewing out. I thought I only let him have a few, but the count we did of his chest came up seventeen."

"Wow!" Ray said. "And you didn't get in any trouble?"

"Of course not," I said. "It was all okay. I'd done what I had to do to protect my fellow officers and the citizenry. My captain, Captain Feliciano, said, 'Good work, son,' and gave me this big slap on the back. 'Don't sweat it,' he said. 'He was asking for it, and you gave it to him. Go home and take a nice long shower. You'll feel fine by tomorrow.'"

"Your captain sounds like my kind of guy," Ray said. "Was he right? Did you feel okay about it the next day?"

"Sure, I felt fine. I mean really fine. I believed what my captain said. I'd done my duty. If the kid's gun had been loaded, I might have gotten a commendation for saving the lives of all those pedestrians standing outside the store to watch all the fireworks. Officer Grant to the rescue. Handshake from the chief. Kudos from the mayor. Champagne all around."

"Tell me about the other times," Ray said huskily.

So I told him about the high-speed pursuit up the FDR Drive, when we managed to bring the driver to a stop, and I stayed by my vehicle to cover my partner while he approached the car, and the driver leapt out brandishing a Rossi 851 .38 Special in blued steel. I had no choice but to bring him down. Captain Feliciano later agreed with my course of action, and everything was okay.

Then there was the out-of-control traffic incident, when a Sikh taxi driver cut off a Jamaican bike messenger at a stoplight, and the messenger retaliated by shattering the driver's side window with his bike lock and beating the driver across the turban with it, and the bloodied driver reached under his seat and pulled out a bright stainless Colt King Cobra .357 Magnum and aimed it at the messenger's head with a shaky trigger finger. I was on the corner and calling for backup when I saw the gun. I pulled out my Glock, identified myself as a police officer, and told the Sikh to throw down his weapon. I gave him more time than I should have, really, but he kept the gun trained on the messenger. Again, I had no choice. I shot the driver dead and charged the messenger with assault as well as criminal damage to property. We later learned that the driver never understood a word of English, but Captain Feliciano insisted that I'd done the right thing. He even bought me a beer.

"I think this captain of yours has the hots for you," Ray said. "He lets you get away with murder because he wants to get into your pants."

"Feliciano? No. If you knew him, you wouldn't say that."

"Yes I would," Ray said. "Isn't that reason enough to go through with killing yourself? I mean, doesn't that just disgust you? You've killed all these people in the line of duty, and you don't even get any suspensions or reprimands because your captain thinks you're a dish. Believe me. I may never have met him, but I know human nature. You're his little buddy, his one special boy. He goes home at night and dreams of you, Tom."

"I doubt that." I laughed nervously. "Feliciano's married."

"As if that meant anything! Tom, don't be so naïve!"

"I left him a suicide note," I said.

"You did?" Ray's dark eyebrows rose. "Can I see it?"

"It's sealed, taped to the bathroom mirror."

Ray got up.

"No!" I said. "I told you, it's sealed."

"So we'll reseal it!" Ray said, heading for the bathroom.

"It's for his eyes only," I said, getting up and going after him. " I don't want you reading it!"

"I bet it's a love letter!" Ray shot ahead of me.

"It is not!"

Ray got to the mirror first and snatched the middle envelope of the three, the one clearly addressed to Captain Feliciano.

"Ha-ha!" Ray said, backing up to stand in the bathtub. "I've got it." He ripped open the envelope, started reading it, and began to laugh. "Oh, this is great! I love suicide notes!"

"Give it to me!" I said, reaching out for it.

Ray snatched it away and started reading it aloud:

"'*Dear Tony*'—Tony, eh? You two are that buddy-buddy? You don't call him captain? Oh, well, never mind—'*Dear Tony, What you see is the end result of my wasted life. I don't know what ever kept me going this long. I guess it was you. You were always there for me when the going got tough. If it weren't for you, I don't think I would have even lasted this far.*'—Oh, Tom, this is a riot!—'*But it's all catching up with me, Tony. I'm a bad cop, and you know it. I can't walk into any situation without my gun going off and leaving somebody dead. No matter what you say, this isn't the way it's supposed to be. Someone should have taken me off into a room somewhere and punished me.*'—Oh, now you're asking Captain Tony for a spanking! Tom's been a bad boy!—'*I don't deserve to wear this badge. But what else can I do? This was my last chance. If I'm a failure at this, I'll be a failure at everything else. I've failed at life. I've got no choice but to end it. Sorry for being such a screw-up. Don't bother sending flowers to the funeral. Save the money for yourself and Stella. Goodbye forever— Tom.*'"

"Give that to me," I said, finally snatching it away.

"Tom, that is so precious!" Ray said. "Can I have a copy? I could just run this down to the Kinko's around the corner—"

"No. Get away from me."

"Oh, Tom! Don't be like that!"

"I think you're the one who's got the hots for me, Ray," I said, heading back to the kitchen table.

"'I shall but love thee better after death,'" Ray said. "That's Elizabeth Barrett Browning, you know."

"I used to own a Browning," I said.

I put the letter back in the envelope, resealed it with cellophane tape, and posted it back up on the bathroom mirror.

"What do the other letters say?"

"More of the same. Don't you dare touch them."

I grabbed Ray's collar and threw him out of the bathroom.

"Hey!" he said.

"In fact, I think you'd better leave."

"Oh, no, Tom. I've got to stay and make sure you follow through with this. You might turn back for all I know. I'd hate to come back here tomorrow and find you're still alive."

"Beat it. Out. Sayonara. Asti Spumante."

I gave him a push toward the front door.

"I knew it," he said. "You're chicken. You don't want me around because you're too chicken to go through with it. You're not man enough. You don't have what it takes to put that gun in your mouth and blow the back of your head off. You're more of a pansy than I am, Thomas."

"Shut up," I said.

"Pansy, pansy, pansy,"

"I said shut up!"

"The minute I'm out that door, you're going to turn around and pout and say, 'Oh my God! What was I thinking? I can't go through with it! I love life so much! Life is so good!' And then you're going to put your gun away, lock it up in its box, get it out of your sight, and try to get it out of your mind. You'll go back into your bathroom, rip those suicide notes off the mirror, tear them into confetti, and flush them down the toilet. You'll look at yourself in the mirror and thank your lucky stars that your gun jammed and you're still alive. Only I bet it didn't jam on its own. You fixed it up that way."

"I did not," I protested.

"Did too," Ray said. "It wouldn't be so hard. You knew just what to do to make that bullet lodge there in the chamber. Maybe you did it unconsciously. Whatever, you didn't want to do it. Why not? Because you're weak! You're not a man at all. You're just a fluffy little kitten, playing a fun game with a bright, shiny toy. And when the kitten gets tired of playing, it curls up in its little basket and falls asleep. Beddy-bye. Nighty-night. Sweet dreams, little kitty."

I held Ray by the front of his shirt and gave him a left uppercut to the jaw. He swayed, but I held him up.

"Oh, Tom" he said. "You didn't have to hurt me. But the fact that you did only proves my point. What I'm saying is true. You don't have what it takes to kill yourself. You're pathetic."

I let go of Ray, went back to the kitchen table, and stared at the gun. I picked it up and put the last of the parts in place. I slammed the clip firmly into the grip and loaded one more slug directly into the chamber.

"It's all set to go, now," I said.

Rubbing his jaw, Ray came back and sat down across from me.

"You sure you're going to be able to do it?" he asked.

"Sure, I'm sure."

"If you can't quite manage it, you could let me."

"No thanks. I can do it myself."

"No one would ever know," Ray said. "I could kill you myself, and no one would ever know. Just by putting that gun in my hands and letting me do the job, why, I'd be a murderer. But you've got those notes all neatly prepared—for your landlord, your captain, your mother—and no one would ever suspect a thing. I've got no connection to you. We've never seen each other before. The only person who knows you called is me, and I won't tell anyone!"

"That won't be necessary. I can take care of myself."

"I'm not so sure," Ray said. "Let's see you do it."

"You better stand back," I said, turning the Glock around toward me, just outside my mouth. "It might get messy."

"I know where to sit to get out of the way," Ray said. "I've done this dozens of times."

"You've what?"

"You don't believe me? You think you're the only special person in the universe? That's not the first time I've run that ad, you know. You're a cop, you're probably aware of how many people commit suicide in this city every year. A lot of them call for help. Some call me. I try to talk them through it over the phone, but every once in a while I get a really special case—like you—and no matter what time of day or night it is, I drop what I'm doing and come over to see how I can help. I was asleep when you called tonight, did you know that? Yet I hopped out of bed and came on over. How's that for dedication?"

"Then it's not really a twenty-four-hour help line, is it? When you're over here helping me, you're not taking calls."

"I can only help one person at a time, you know."

I had the muzzle almost to my mouth, but I was curious:

"How many suicides have you witnessed, exactly?"

"I've lost count. Funny, isn't it? You'd think that a guy like me would keep a log or something to keep track, but I don't bother with it. Each customer deserves my undivided attention. I don't want them ending up just another statistic. I don't always just witness, you know. Sometimes I assist. It's perfectly legal, you know."

"Bull."

"Assisted suicide? Of course it is! Dr. Kevorkian paved the way. I bet he's lost count of all his assisted suicides."

"There's a difference," I said. "You're not a doctor, and you're not helping people who are terminally ill."

"Don't pick nits with me, Tom! Dr. Kevorkian helps people who are in great pain and want out. I'm no different. Everyone who calls me is in *excruciating* pain. Aren't you? I mean, Tom, the kind of sickness you have, it just eats at your heart, doesn't it? It's *painful*, and you can hardly *bear* it."

"Something like that," I said, "but—"

"But nothing, Tom! Assisted suicide is the wave of the future. The precedents are set. Soon enough, you're going to see suicide centers spring up all over the country. A whole chain of centers. Suicide superstores, next to every Barnes and Noble."

"You're insane," I said.

"If you're tired of listening to me, why don't you just pull that trigger and get it over with?"

I put the four extending inches of the barrel in my mouth, with my bottom lip resting against the trigger guard. I had it in both hands, with my thumb wrapping around the trigger. There was no chance it would jam this time. It was ready to go.

Ray looked at me with those intense eyes of his. He looked about ready to start slobbering. In fact, he looked lustful.

I shall but love thee better after death . . .

I took the gun out of my mouth.

"Wait a minute," I said, turning the gun on Ray.

Ray's lascivious grin collapsed into a thin red line.

"What's the matter, Tom? I was so proud of you. I thought you were going to make good on your promises."

"Shut up," I said. "I could kill you right now."

"You won't," Ray said confidently. "Everyone else you've killed was armed. I'm helpless, and harmless. You won't do it."

"You want to make a bet?"

"Hey, Tom, come on, buddy! Don't you see it worked?"

"What worked?"

"You were right! I was playing reverse psychology on you all along, and it worked. Another life saved. Damn, I'm good!"

"I don't believe you," I said.

"Don't, then." Ray shrugged.

"You're sick. Death turns you on. Everything about death. It gets you going. Ever since you came over here, you've had this covetous look in your eye—"

"Covetous?" Ray played the innocent. "Covetous of what?"

"Of my body, that's what!"

"Nonsense!" Ray said.

"And you know what? I don't think you're even a pansy or anything. All you care is that it's a body, and that it's dead."

"Tom, I can't believe you're saying that. It's too awful!"

"It's awful because it's true. You don't care how they do it, or why, just so long as you're alone with them afterwards."

"Tom, don't be ridiculous! I do nothing of the sort!"

"Oh yeah? I don't believe you. And I don't believe you have it in you to kill anybody yourself. In this city, you could pick up just about any stranger you saw on the street, if you were clever enough. All you'd have to do is take them home, or to a dark, secluded spot—maybe the park. If you were capable of killing anyone, that's what you'd do."

"Put the gun down, Tom. You're talking crazy! I'm—I'm worried about you. You don't really want to hurt me, do you?"

"Oh, yes, I want to hurt you, Ray. You bet I do. You're scum. You're worse than scum. You're a scavenger. I'd rather hurt you, but I'm going to take you in. Come on, get up."

I stood up and waved the gun at him. Ray got up.

"Take me in? On what charge? You can't prove anything!"

Ray had a point. I had no evidence of his crimes.

"What am I going to do with you, then?" I asked aloud.

"Why don't you just kill me?" Ray suggested.

"No good," I said. "I'd never beat the rap."

"Kill me, then kill yourself. Solves all your problems."

"You have a death wish or something? I'm sorely tempted."

"If that doesn't grab you, why not join me?"

"Join you?" I was incredulous.

"Sure, we'd make a great team! Tom and Ray, the help line boys! Two is better than one. Hey, we could use the good cop, bad cop routine on them! I bet we'd have more successes that way. It's clear to me from that suicide note that you're finished with police work. Well, now Ray's here to hand you back your future on a silver platter. You could quit your job at the police force and come work with me full time. What do you say?"

"You do this full time? How do you make a living?"

"Tom, I thought you were brighter than that! I invite myself in, I help them out, I get my kicks, and then I go rooting around for loot. They can't take it with them, and I may as well have it. That's how I collect my fee."

"Your fee," I repeated.

"You think I'd do any of this out of the goodness of my heart? It's a business, Tommy baby. So are you in or out?"

"How much do you make?"

"Some nights are better than others. I bet you don't have much dough lying around. Maybe you got some baseball cards—"

"You're not getting my baseball cards," I said. "Or me."

"And I was so close."

"Your apartment must be filled with stolen goods," I said.

"It's not easy to fence everything so fast."

"Uh-huh," I said, grinning. "That's what I figured."

I emptied my clip into Ray. He fell down all bloody.

I set my Glock down on the kitchen table. I opened my front door, looked up and down the hallway to make sure no one was watching, and went into the hall. I closed my door. I kicked it hard three times with the heel of my boot until I busted the lock and splintered the jamb and the door flew wide open. I went to the bathroom, tore down the suicide notes, and set them aflame using one match. I let them burn in my fingers until I dropped them into the toilet, and I flushed the ashes down and away.

I went to the phone and called the precinct house. Captain Feliciano happened to be the operations officer on duty tonight.

"Tony, it's Tom," I said.

"Hey, Tom!" he said. "You're off tonight, aren't you?"

"Yeah, and I had a bit of a problem here. I was just sitting here watching television in the dark, and some guy broke in through my front door. It looked like he was pointing a gun at me through the pocket of his jacket. He said if I didn't give him all my money, he was going to kill me. I didn't want to take any chances, so—"

Feliciano sighed. "How many times did you shoot him, Tom?"

"That damned trigger jammed on me again, Tony, so I blew the one in the chamber and all seventeen in the clip."

"Eighteen, huh? So I take it he's dead."

I glanced at Ray, not moving. "You take it correctly, sir."

"What kind of a gun did he have on him?"

"It wasn't a gun at all. It must have been his fingers."

"Well, that's okay," my captain said. "Just swear in court that you saw the butt of the gun poking out of his jacket. And you're sure he intended to burglarize you?"

"Oh, I'm positive," I said. "He had his moves down cold, like he's done this dozens of times before. I bet he's got tons of stolen goods at his place. Can we get a warrant?"

"Don't sweat it, Tom. You did the right thing. I'll have dispatch send a car over to take your report. Just relax. You don't have a thing to worry about. I'll see to it myself."

"Thanks, Tony, captain, sir," I said, to cover the bases.

Captain Feliciano laughed good-naturedly and hung up.

Ray lay there darkly staining my carpet.

I looked over at my Glock and smiled. In the end, it hadn't let me down at all. It had given me one last chance to prove I was worthy. I picked it up and found the barrel still warm and smoking. I cooled it off with a nice, long, sloppy kiss.

HE

H. P. LOVECRAFT

The phantasmagorical effects so integral to the Lovecraft style are peculiarly suited to the feverish panorama that is Manhattan. Yet it's provocative to contemplate how this writer, who in the 1930s recoiled from the city's arrogant modernity, would react to the New York of the new millennium.

Read carefully, however, and see not just how amazingly contemporary are some of the "tenebrous" descriptions here but also how, despite his protestations, the narrator has actually fallen prey to the dark spell of the streets.

༄

I SAW HIM ON a sleepless night when I was walking desperately to save my soul and my vision. My coming to New York had been a mistake; for whereas I had looked for poignant wonder and inspiration in the teeming labyrinths of ancient streets that twist endlessly from forgotten courts and squares and waterfronts to courts and squares and waterfronts equally forgotten, and in the Cyclopean modern towers and pinnacles that rise blackly Babylonian under waning moons, I had found instead only a sense of horror and oppression which threatened to master, paralyse, and annihilate me.

The disillusion had been gradual. Coming for the first time upon the town, I had seen it in the sunset from a bridge, majestic above its waters, its incredible peaks and pyramids rising flower-like and delicate from pools of violet mist to play with the flaming golden clouds and the first stars of evening. Then it had lighted up window by window above the shimmering tides where lanterns nodded and glided and deep horns bayed weird harmonies, and itself become a starry firmament of dream, redolent of faery music, and one with the marvels of Carcassonne and Samarcand and El Dorado and all glorious and half-fabulous cities. Shortly afterward I was taken through those antique ways so dear to my fancy—narrow, curving alleys and passages where rows of red Georgian brick blinked with small-paned dormers above pillared doorways that had looked on gilded sedans and panelled coaches—and in the first flush of realisation of these long-wished things I thought I had indeed achieved such treasures as would make me in time a poet.

But success and happiness were not to be. Garish daylight shewed only squalor and alienage and the noxious elephantiasis of climbing, spreading stone where the moon had hinted of liveliness and elder magic; and the throngs of people that seethed through the flume-like streets were squat, swarthy strangers with hardened faces and narrow eyes, shrewd strangers without dreams and without kinship to the scenes about them, who could never mean aught to a blue-eyed man of the old folk, with the love of fair green lanes and white New England village steeples in his heart.

So instead of the poems I had hoped for, there came only a shuddering blankness and ineffable loneliness; and I saw at last a fearful truth which no one had ever dared to breathe before—the unwhisperable secret of secrets—the fact that this city of stone and stridor is not a sentient perpetuation of Old New York as London is of Old London and Paris of Old Paris, but that it is in fact quite dead, its sprawling body imperfectly embalmed and infested with queer animate things which have nothing to do with it as it was in life. Upon making this discovery I ceased to sleep comfortably; though something of resigned tranquillity came back as I gradually formed the habit of keeping off the streets by day and venturing abroad only at night, when darkness calls forth what little of the past still hovers wraith-like about, and old white doorways remember the stalwart forms that once passed through them. With this mode of relief I even wrote a few poems, and still refrained from going home to my people lest I seem to crawl back ignobly in defeat.

Then, on a sleepless night's walk, I met the man. It was in a grotesque hidden courtyard of the Greenwich section, for there in my ignorance I had settled, having heard of the place as the natural home of poets and artists. The archaic lanes and houses and unexpected bits of square and court had indeed delighted me, and when I found the poets and artists to be loud-voiced pretenders whose quaintness is tinsel and whose lives are a denial of all that pure beauty which is poetry and art, I stayed on for love of these venerable things. I fancied them as they were in their prime, when Greenwich was a placid village not yet engulfed by the town; and in the hours before dawn, when all the revellers had slunk away, I used to wander alone among their cryptical windings and brood upon the curious arcana which generations must have deposited there. This kept my soul alive, and gave me a few of those dreams and visions for which the poet far within me cried out.

The man came upon me at about two one cloudy August morning, as I was threading a series of detached courtyards; now accessible only through the unlighted hallways of intervening buildings, but once forming parts of a continuous network of picturesque alleys. I had heard of them by vague rumour, and realised that they could not be upon any map of today; but the fact that they were forgotten only endeared them to me, so that I had sought them with twice my usual eagerness. Now that I had found them, my eagerness was again redoubled; for something in their arrangement dimly hinted that they might be only a few of many such, with dark, dumb counterparts wedged obscurely betwixt high blank walls and deserted rear tenements, or lurking lamplessly behind archways, unbetrayed by hordes of the foreign-speaking or guarded by furtive and uncommunicative artists whose practices do not invite publicity or the light of day.

He spoke to me without invitation, noting my mood and glances as I studied certain knockered doorways above iron-railed steps, the pallid glow of traceried transoms feebly lighting my face. His own face was in shadow and he wore a wide-brimmed hat which somehow blended perfectly with the out-of-date cloak he affected; but I was subtly disquieted even before he addressed me. His form was very slight, thin almost to cadaverousness; and his voice proved phenomenally soft and hollow, though not particularly deep. He had, he said, noticed me several times at my wanderings; and inferred that I resembled him in loving the vestiges of former years. Would I not like the guidance of one long practiced in these explorations, and possessed of local information profoundly deeper than any which an obvious newcomer could possibly have gained?

As he spoke, I caught a glimpse of his face in the yellow beam from a solitary attic window. It was a noble, even a handsome, elderly countenance; and bore the marks of a lineage and refinement unusual for the age and place. Yet some quality about it disturbed me almost as much as its features pleased me—perhaps it was too white, or too expressionless, or too much out of keeping with the locality, to make me feel easy or comfortable. Nevertheless I followed him; for in those dreary days my quest for antique beauty and mystery was all that I had to keep my soul alive, and I reckoned it a rare favor of Fate to fall in with one whose kindred seekings seemed to have penetrated so much farther than mine.

Something in the night constrained the cloaked man to silence, and for a long hour he led me forward without needless words; making only the briefest of comments concerning ancient names and dates and changes, and directing my progress very largely by gestures as we squeezed through interstices, tiptoed through corridors, clambered over brick walls, and once crawled on hands and knees through a low, arched passage of stone whose immense length and tortuous twistings effaced at last every hint of geographical location I had managed to preserve. The things we saw were very old and marvellous, or at least they seemed so in the few straggling rays of light by which I viewed them, and I shall never forget the tottering

Ionic columns and fluted pilasters and urn-headed iron fence-posts and flaring-lintelled windows and decorative fanlights that appeared to grow quainter and stranger the deeper we advanced into this inexhaustible maze of unknown antiquity.

We met no person, and as time passed the lighted windows became fewer and fewer. The street-lights we first encountered had been of oil, and of the ancient lozenge pattern. Later I noticed some with candles; and at last, after traversing a horrible unlighted court where my guide had to lead with his gloved hand through total blackness to a narrow wooden gate in a high wall, we came upon a fragment of alley lit only by lanterns in front of every seventh house—unbelievably colonial tin lanterns with conical tops and holes punched in the sides. This alley led steeply uphill—more steeply than I thought possible in this part of New York—and the upper end was blocked squarely by the ivy-clad wall of a private estate, beyond which I could see a pale cupola, and the tops of trees waving against a vague lightness in the sky. In this wall was a small, low-arched gate of nail-studded black oak, which the man proceeded to unlock with a ponderous key. Leading me within, he steered a course in utter blackness over what seemed to be a gravel path, and finally up a flight of stone steps to the door of the house, which he unlocked and opened for me.

We entered, and as we did so I grew faint from a reek of infinite mustiness which welled out to meet us, and which must have been the fruit of unwholesome centuries of decay. My host appeared not to notice this, and in courtesy I kept silent as he piloted me up a curving stairway, across a hall, and into a room whose door I heard him lock behind us. Then I saw him pull the curtains of the three small-paned windows that barely shewed themselves against the lightening sky; after which he crossed to the mantel, struck flint and steel, lighted two candles of a candelabrum of twelve sconces, and made a gesture enjoining soft-toned speech.

In this feeble radiance I saw that we were in a spacious, well-furnished, and panelled library dating from the first quarter of the eighteenth century, with splendid doorway pediments, a delightful Doric cornice, and a magnificently carved overmantel with scroll-and-urn top. Above the crowded bookshelves at intervals along the walls were well-wrought family portraits; all tarnished to an enigmatical dimness, and bearing an unmistakable likeness to the man who now motioned me to a chair beside the graceful Chippendale table. Before seating himself across the table from me, my host paused for a moment as if in embarrassment; then, tardily removing his gloves, wide-brimmed hat, and cloak, stood theatrically revealed in full mid-Georgian costume from queued hair and neck ruffles to knee-breeches, silk hose, and the buckled shoes I had not previously noticed. Now slowly sinking into a lyre-back chair, he commenced to eye me intently.

Without his hat he took on an aspect of extreme age which was scarcely visible before, and I wondered if this unperceived mark of singular longevity were not one of the sources of my original disquiet. When he spoke at length, his soft, hollow, and carefully muffled voice not infrequently quavered; and now and then I had great difficulty in following him as I listened with a thrill of amazement and half-disavowed alarm which grew each instant.

"You behold, Sir," my host began, "a man of very eccentrical habits, for whose costume no apology need be offered to one with your wit and inclinations. Reflecting upon better times, I have not scrupled to ascertain their ways and adopt their dress and manners; an indulgence which offends none if practiced without ostentation. It hath been my good-fortune to retain the rural seat of my ancestors, swallowed though it was by two towns, first Greenwich, which built up hither after 1800, then New-York, which joined on near 1830. There were many reasons for the close keeping of this place in my family, and I have not been remiss in discharging such obligations. The squire who succeeded to it in 1768 studied sartain arts and made sartain discoveries, all connected with influences residing in this particular plot of ground, and eminently desarving of the strongest guarding. Some curious effects of these arts and discoveries I now purpose to shew you, under the strictest secrecy; and I believe I may rely on my judgment of men enough to have no distrust of either your interest or your fidelity."

He paused, but I could only nod my head. I have said that I was alarmed, yet to my soul nothing was more deadly than the material daylight world of New York, and whether this man were a harmless eccentric or a wielder of dangerous arts I had no choice save to follow him and slake my sense of wonder on whatever he might have to offer. So I listened.

"To—my ancestor—" he softly continued, "there appeared to reside some very remarkable qualities in the will of mankind; qualities having a little-suspected dominance not only over the acts of one's self and of others, but over every variety of force and substance in Nature, and over many elements and dimensions deemed more univarsal than Nature herself. May I say that he flouted the sanctity of things as great as space and time, and that he put to strange uses the rites of sartain half-breed red Indians once encamped upon this hill? These Indians shewed choler when the place was built, and were plaguy pestilent in asking to visit the grounds at the full of the moon. For years they stole over the wall each month when they could, and by stealth performed sartain acts. Then, in '68, the new squire catched them at their doings, and stood still at what he saw. Thereafter he bargained with them and exchanged the free access of his grounds for the exact inwardness of what they did; larning that their grandfathers got part of their custom from red ancestors and part from an old Dutchman in the time of the States-General. And pox on him, I'm afeared the squire must have sarved them monstrous bad rum—whether or not by intent— for a week after he learnt the secret he was the only man living that knew it. You, Sir, are the first outsider to be told there is a secret, and split me if I'd have risked tampering that much with—the powers— had ye not been so hot after bygone things."

I shuddered as the man grew colloquial—and with familiar speech of another day. He went on.

"But you must know, Sir, that what—the squire—got from those mongrel salvages was but a small part of the larning he came to have. He had not been at Oxford for nothing, nor talked to no account with an ancient chymist and astrologer in Paris. He was, in fine, made sensible that all the world is but the smoke of our intellects; past the bidding of the vulgar, but by the wise to be puffed out and drawn in like any cloud of prime Virginia tobacco. What we want, we may make about us; and what we don't want, we may sweep away. I won't say that all this is wholly true in body, but 'tis sufficient true to furnish a very pretty spectacle now and then. You, I conceive, would be tickled by a better sight of sartain other years than your fancy affords you; so be pleased to hold back any fright at what I design to shew. Come to the window and be quiet."

My host now took my hand to draw me to one of the two windows on the long side of the malodorous room, and at the first touch of his ungloved fingers I turned cold. His flesh, though dry and firm, was of the quality of ice; and I almost shrank away from his pulling. But again I thought of the emptiness and horror of reality, and boldly prepared to follow whithersoever I might be led. Once at the window, the man drew apart the yellow silk curtains and directed my stare into the blackness outside. For a moment I saw nothing save a myriad of tiny dancing lights, far, far before me. Then, as if in response to an insidious motion of my host's hand, a flash of heat-lightning played over the scene, and I looked out upon a sea of luxuriant foliage—foliage unpolluted, and not the sea of roofs to be expected by any normal mind. On my right the Hudson glittered wickedly, and in the distance ahead I saw the unhealthy shimmer of a vast salt marsh constellated with nervous fireflies. The flash died, and an evil smile illumined the waxy face of the aged necromancer.

"That was before my time—before the new squire's time. Pray let us try again."

I was faint, even fainter than the hateful modernity of that accursed city had made me.

"Good God!" I whispered, "can you do that for *any time*?" And as he nodded, and bared the black stumps of what had once been yellow fangs, I clutched at the curtains to prevent myself from falling. But he steadied me with that terrible, ice-cold claw, and once more made his insidious gesture.

Again the lightning flashed—but this time upon a scene not wholly strange. It was Greenwich, the Greenwich that used to be, with here and there a roof or row of houses as we see it now, yet with lovely green lanes and fields and bits of grassy common. The marsh still glittered beyond, but in the farther distance I saw the steeples of what was then all of New York; Trinity and St. Paul's and the Brick Church dominating their sisters, and a faint haze of wood smoke hovering over the whole. I breathed hard, but not so much from the sight itself as from the possibilities my imagination terrifiedly conjured up.

"Can you—dare you—go *far?*" I spoke with awe, and I think he shared it for a second, but the evil grin returned.

"*Far?* What I have seen would blast ye to a mad statue of stone! Back, back—forward, *forward*—look, ye puling lack-wit!"

And as he snarled the phrase under his breath he gestured anew; bringing to the sky a flash more blinding than either which had come before. For full three seconds I could glimpse that pandaemoniac sight, and in those seconds I saw a vista which will ever afterward torment me in dreams. I saw the heavens verminous with strange flying things, and beneath them a hellish black city of giant stone terraces with impious pyramids flung savagely to the moon, and devil-lights burning from unnumbered windows. And swarming loathsomely on aerial galleries I saw the yellow, squint-eyed people of that city, robed horribly in orange and red, and dancing insanely to the pounding of fevered kettle-drums, the clatter of obscene crotala, and the maniacal moaning of muted horns whose ceaseless dirges rose and fell undulantly like the waves of an unhallowed ocean of bitumen.

I saw this vista, I say, and heard as with the mind's ear the blasphemous domdaniel of cacophony which companioned it. It was the shrieking fulfillment of all the horror which that corpse-city had ever stirred in my soul, and forgetting every injunction to silence I screamed and screamed and screamed as my nerves gave way and the walls quivered about me.

Then, as the flash subsided, I saw that my host was trembling too; a look of shocking fear half blotting from his face the serpent distortion of rage which my screams had excited. He tottered, clutched at the curtains as I had done before, and wriggled his head wildly, like a hunted animal. God knows he had cause, for as the echoes of my screaming died away there came another sound so hellishly suggestive that only numbed emotion kept me sane and conscious. It was the steady, stealthy creaking of the stairs beyond the locked door, as with the ascent of a barefoot or skin-shod horde; and at last the cautious, purposeful rattling of the brass latch that glowed in the feeble candlelight. The old man clawed and spat at me through the mouldy air, and barked things in his throat as he swayed with the yellow curtain he clutched.

"The full moon—damn ye—ye . . . ye yelping dog—ye called 'em, and they've come for me! Moccasined feet—dead men—Gad sink ye, ye red devils, but I poisoned no rum o' yours—han't I kept your pox-rotted magic safe?—ye swilled yourselves sick, curse ye, and ye must needs blame the squire—let go, you! Unhand that latch—I've naught for ye here—"

At this point three slow and very deliberate raps shook the panels of the door, and a white foam gathered at the mouth of the frantic magician. His fright, turning to steely despair, left room for a resurgence of his rage against me; and he staggered a step toward the table on whose edge I was steadying myself. The curtains, still clutched in his right hand as his left clawed out at me, grew taut and finally crashed down from their lofty fastenings; admitting to the room a flood of that full moonlight which the brightening of the sky had presaged. In those greenish beams the candles paled, and a new semblance of decay spread over the musk-reeking room with its wormy panelling, sagging floor, battered mantel, rickety furniture, and ragged draperies. It spread over the old man, too, whether from the same source or because of his fear and vehemence, and I saw him shrivel and blacken as he lurched near and strove to rend me with vulturine talons. Only his eyes stayed whole, and they glared with a propulsive, dilated incandescence which grew as the face around them charred and dwindled.

The rapping was now repeated with greater insistence, and this time bore a hint of metal. The black thing facing me had become only a head with eyes, impotently trying to wriggle across the sinking floor in my direction, and occasionally emitting feeble little spits of immortal malice. Now swift and splintering blows assailed the sickly panels, and I saw the gleam of a tomahawk as it cleft the rending wood. I did not move, for I could not; but watched dazedly as the door fell in pieces to admit a colossal, shapeless influx of inky substance starred with shining, malevolent eyes. It poured thickly, like a flood of oil bursting a rotten bulkhead, overturned a chair as it spread, and finally flowed under the table and across the room to where the blackened head with the eyes still glared at me. Around that heat it closed, totally swallowing it up, and in another moment it had begun to recede; bearing away its invisible burden without touching me, and flowing again out of that black doorway and down the unseen stairs, which creaked as before, though in reverse order.

Then the floor gave way at last, and I slid gaspingly down into the nighted chamber below, choking with cobwebs and half swooning with terror. The green moon, shining through broken windows, shewed me the hall door half open; and as I rose from the plaster-strown floor and twisted myself free from the sagged ceiling, I saw sweep past it an awful torrent of blackness, with scores of baleful eyes glowing in it. It was seeking the door to the cellar, and when it found it, it vanished therein. I now felt the floor of this lower room giving as that of the upper chamber had done, and once a crashing above had been followed by the fall past the west window of something which must have been the cupola. Now liberated for the instant from the wreckage, I rushed through the hall to the front door; and finding myself unable to open it, seized a chair and broke a window, climbing frenziedly out upon the unkempt lawn where moonlight danced over yard-high grass and weeds. The wall was high, and all the gates were locked; but moving a pile of boxes in a corner I managed to gain the top and cling to the great stone urn set there.

About me in my exhaustion I could see only strange walls and windows and old gambrel roofs. The steep street of my approach was nowhere visible, and the little I did see succumbed rapidly to a mist that rolled in from the river despite the glaring moonlight. Suddenly the urn to which I clung began to tremble, as if sharing my own lethal dizziness; and in another instant my body was plunging downward to I knew not what fate.

The man who found me said that I must have crawled a long way despite my broken bones, for a trail of blood stretched off as far as he dared look. The gathering rain soon effaced this link with the scene of my ordeal, and reports could state no more than that I had appeared from a place unknown, at the entrance of a little black court off Perry Street.

I never sought to return to those tenebrous labyrinths, nor would I direct any sane man thither if I could. Of who or what that ancient creature was, I have no idea; but I repeat that the city is dead and full of unsuspected horrors. Whither *he* has gone, I do not know; but I have gone home to the pure New England lanes up which fragrant sea-winds sweep at evening.

THE NATURE OF THE THING

PATRICIA HIGHSMITH

Superbly in control of her effects, Patricia Highsmith never for an instant hid the fact that she was obsessed with outsiders, those figures living willfully or vulnerably or perhaps just matter-of-factly beyond the expected regularities. But since her characters invariably find themselves perched on or near the edge, it always takes only the slightest of pushes for that slow tumble into disaster to begin.

Nonetheless, nothing about the dignified and rather plucky Eleanor Heathcote seems automatically to qualify her as one of this author's typical heroines—nothing, that is, except for the sudden presence in her life of an antagonist who in his perfect amorality is quintessentially Highsmithian.

ᔐ

ELEANOR HAD BEEN sewing nearly all day, sewing after dinner, too, and it was getting on for eleven o'clock. She looked away from her machine, sideways towards the hall door, and saw something about two feet high, something greyish black, which after a second or two moved and was lost from view in the hall. Eleanor rubbed her eyes. Her eyes smarted, and it was delicious to rub them. But since she was sure she had not really seen something, she did not get up from her chair to go and investigate. She forgot about it.

She stood up after five minutes or so, after tidying her sewing table, putting away her scissors, and folding the yellow dress whose side seams she had just let out. The dress was ready for Mrs. Burns tomorrow. Always letting out, Eleanor thought, never taking in. People seemed to grow sideways, not upward any more, and she smiled at this fuzzy little thought. She was tired, but she had had a good day. She gave her cat Bessie a saucer of milk—rather creamy milk, because Bessie liked the best of everything—heated some milk for herself and took it in a mug up to bed.

The second time she saw it, however, she was not tired, and the sun was shining brightly. This time, she was sitting in the armchair, putting a zipper in a skirt, and as she knotted her thread, she happened to glance at the door that went into what she called the side room, a room off the living room at the front of the house. She saw a squarish figure about two feet high, an ugly little thing that at first suggested an upended sandbag. It took a moment before she recognized a large square head, thick feet in heavy shoes, incredibly short arms with big hands that dangled.

Eleanor was half out of her chair, her slender body rigid.

The thing didn't move. But it was looking at her.

Get it out of the house, she thought at once. Shoo it out the door. What *was* it? The face was vaguely human. Eyes looked at her from under hair that was combed forward over the forehead. Had the children put some horrid toy in the house to frighten her? The Reynoldses next door had four children, the oldest eight. Children's toys these days—You never knew what to expect!

Then the thing moved, advanced slowly into the living room, and Eleanor stepped quickly behind the armchair.

"Get out! Get away!" she said in a voice shrill with panic.

"Um-m," came the reply, soft and deep.

Had she really heard anything? Now it looked from the floor—where it had stared while entering the room—to her face. The look at her seemed direct, yet was somehow vague and unfocused. The creature went on, towards the electric bar heater, where it stopped and held out its hands casually to the warmth. It was masculine,

Eleanor thought, its legs—if those stumpy things could be called legs—were in trousers. Again the creature took a sidelong look at her, a little shyly, yet as if defying her to get it out of the room.

The cat, curled on a pillow in a chair, lifted her head and yawned, and the movement caught Eleanor's eye. She waited for Bessie to see the thing, straight before her and only four feet away, but Bessie put her head down again in a position for sleeping. That was curious!

Eleanor retreated quickly to the kitchen, opened the back door and went out, leaving the door open. She went round to the front door and opened that wide, too. Give the thing a chance to get out! Eleanor stayed on her front path, ready to run to the road if the creature emerged.

The thing came to the front door and said in a deep voice, the words more a rumble than articulated, "I'm not going to harm you, so why don't you come back in? It's your house." And there was the hint of a shrug in the chunky shoulders.

"I'd like you to get out, please!" Eleanor said.

"Um-m." He turned away, back into the living room.

Eleanor thought of going for Mr. Reynolds next door, a practical man who probably had a gun in the house, as he was a captain in the Air Force. Then she remembered the Reynoldses had gone off before lunch and that their house was empty. Eleanor gathered her courage and advanced towards the front door.

Now she didn't see him in the living room. She even looked behind the armchair. She went cautiously towards the side room. He was not in there, either. She looked quite thoroughly.

She stood in the hall and called up the stairs, really called to all the house, "If you're still in this house, I wish you would leave!"

Behind her a voice said, "I'm still here."

Eleanor turned and saw him standing in the living room.

"I won't do you any harm. But I can disappear if you prefer. Like this."

She thought she saw a set of bared teeth, as if he were making an effort. As she stared, the creature became paler grey, more fuzzy at the edges. And after ten seconds, there was nothing. *Nothing!* Was she losing her mind? She must tell Dr. Campbell, she thought. First thing tomorrow morning, go to his office at 9 A.M. and tell him honestly.

The rest of the day, and the evening, passed without incident. Mrs. Burns came for her dress, and brought a coat to be shortened. Eleanor watched a television programme, and went to bed at half past ten. She had thought she would be frightened, going to bed and turning all the lights out, but she wasn't. And before she had time to worry about whether she could get to sleep or not, she had fallen asleep.

But when she woke up, he was the second thing she saw, the first thing being her cat, who had slept on the foot of the bed for warmth. Bessie stretched, yawned and miaowed simultaneously, demanding breakfast. And hardly two yards away, he stood, staring at her. Eleanor's promise of immediate breakfast to Bessie was cut short by her seeing him.

"I could use some breakfast myself." Was there a faint smile on that square face? "Nothing much. A piece of bread."

Now Eleanor found her teeth tight together, found herself wordless. She got out of bed on the other side from him, quickly pulled on her old flannel robe, and went down the stairs. In the kitchen, she comforted herself with the usual routine: put the kettle on, fed Bessie while the kettle was heating, cut some bread. But she was waiting for the thing to appear in the kitchen doorway, and as she was slicing the bread, he did. Trembling, Eleanor held the piece of bread towards him.

"If I give you this, would you go away?" she asked.

The monstrous hand reached out and up, and took the bread. "Not necessarily," rumbled the bass voice. "I don't need to eat, you know. I thought I'd keep you company, that's all."

Eleanor was not sure, really not sure now if she had heard it. She was imagining telling Dr. Campbell all this, imagining the point at which Dr. Campbell would cut her short (politely, of course, because he was a nice man) and prescribe some kind of sedative.

Bessie, her breakfast finished, walked so close by the creature,

her fur must have brushed his leg, but the cat showed no sign of seeing anything. That was proof enough that he didn't exist, Eleanor
thought.

A strange rumbling. "Um-hm-hm," came from him. He was
laughing! "Not everyone—or everything—can see me," he said to
Eleanor. "Very few people can see me, in fact." He had eaten the
bread, apparently.

Eleanor steeled herself to carry on with her breakfast. She cut
another piece of bread, got out the butter and jam, scalded the
teapot. It was ten to eight. By nine she'd be at Dr. Campbell's.

"Maybe there's something I can do for you today," he said. He had
not moved from where he stood. "Odd jobs. I'm strong." The last
word was like a nasal burr, like the horn of a large and distant ship.

At once, Eleanor thought of the rusty old lawn roller in her barn.
She'd rung up Field's, the second-hand dealers, to come and take it
away, but they were late as usual, two weeks late. "I have a roller out
in the barn. After breakfast, you can take it to the edge of the road, if
you will." That would be further proof, Eleanor thought, proof he
wasn't real. The roller must weigh two or three hundred pounds.

He walked, in a slow, rolling gait, out of the kitchen and into the
sitting room. He made no sound.

Eleanor ate her breakfast at the scrubbed wooden table in the
kitchen, where she often preferred to eat instead of in the dining
room. She propped a booklet on sewing tips before her, and after a
few moments, she was able to concentrate on it.

At 8:30, dressed now, Eleanor went out to the barn behind her
house. She had not looked for him in the house, didn't know where
he was now, in fact, but somehow it did not surprise her to find him
beside her when she reached the barn door.

"It's in the back corner. I'll show you." She removed the padlock
which had not been fully closed.

He understood at once, rubbed his big yellowish hands together,
and took a grip on the wooden stick of the roller. He pulled the
thing towards him with apparently the greatest ease, then began to
push it from behind, rolling it. But the stick was easier, so he took

the stick again, and in less than five minutes, the roller was at the edge of the road, where Eleanor pointed.

Jane, the girl who delivered morning papers, was cycling along the road just then.

Eleanor tensed, thinking Jane would cry out at the sight of him, but Jane only said shyly (she was a very shy girl), "'Morning, Mrs. Heathcote," and pedalled on.

"Good morning to you, Jane," Eleanor answered.

"Anything else?" he asked.

"I can't think of anything, thank you," Eleanor replied rather breathlessly.

"It won't do you any good to speak to your doctor about me," he said.

They were both walking back towards the house, up the carelessly flagged path that divided Eleanor's front garden.

"He won't be able to see me, and he'll just give you useless pills," he continued.

What made you think I was going to a doctor? Eleanor wanted to ask. But she knew. He could read her mind. *Is he some part of myself?* she asked herself, with a flash of intuition which went no further than the question. If no one *else* can see him—

"I am myself," he said, smiling at her over one shoulder. He was leading the way into the house. "Just me." And he laughed.

Eleanor did not go to Dr. Campbell. She decided to try to ignore him, and to go about her usual affairs. Her affairs that morning consisted of walking a quarter of mile to the butcher's for some liver for Bessie and a half-chicken for herself, and of buying several things at Mr. White's, the grocer. But Eleanor was thinking of telling all this to Vance—Mrs. Florence Vansittart—who was her best friend in the town. Vance and she had tea together, at one or the other's house, at least once a week, usually once every five days, in fact, and Eleanor rang up Vance as soon as she got home.

The creature was not in sight at that time.

Vance agreed to come over at four o'clock. "How *are* you, dear?" Vance asked as she always did.

"All right, thanks!" Eleanor replied, more heartily than usual. "And you? . . . I'll make some blueberry muffins if I get my work done in time . . ."

That afternoon, though he had kept out of sight since the morning, he lumbered silently into the room just as Eleanor and Vance were starting on their second cups of tea, and just as Eleanor was drawing breath for the first statement, the first introductory statement, of her strange story. She had been thinking, the roller at the edge of the road (she must ring Field's again first thing in the morning) would be proof that what she said was not a dream.

"What's the matter, Eleanor?" asked Vance, sitting up a little. She was a woman of Eleanor's age, about fifty-five, one of the many widows in the town, though unlike Eleanor, Vance had never worked at anything, and had been left a little more money. And Vance looked to her right, at the side room's door, where Eleanor had been looking. Now Eleanor took her eyes away from the creature who stood four feet within the room.

"Nothing," Eleanor said. Vance didn't see him, she thought. Vance can't see him.

"She can't see me," the creature rumbled to Eleanor.

"Swallow something the wrong way?" Vance asked, chuckling, helping herself to another blueberry muffin.

The creature was staring at the muffins, but came no closer.

"You know, Eleanor—" Vance chewed, "—if you're still charging only a dollar for putting a hem up, I think you need your head examined. People around here, all of them could afford to give you two dollars. It's criminal the way you cheat yourself."

Vance meant, Eleanor thought, that it was high time she had her house painted, or re-covered the armchair, which she could do herself if she had the time. "It's not easy to mention raising prices, and the people who come to me are used to mine by now."

"Other people manage to mention price-raising pretty easily," Vance said as Eleanor had known she would. "I hear of a new one every day!"

The creature took a muffin. For a few seconds, the muffin must have been visible in mid-air to Vance, even if she didn't see him. But suddenly the muffin was gone, being chewed by the massive, wooden-looking jaw.

"You look a bit absent today, my dear," Vance said. "Something worrying you?" Vance looked at her attentively, waiting for a confidence—such as another tooth extraction that Eleanor felt doomed to, or news that her brother George in Canada, who had never made a go of anything, was once more failing in business. Eleanor braced herself and said, "I've had a visitor for the last two days. He's standing right here by the table." She nodded her head in his direction.

The creature was looking at Eleanor.

Vance looked where Eleanor had nodded. "What do you mean?"

"You can't see him?—He's quite friendly," Eleanor added. "It's a creature two feet high. He's right there. He just took a muffin! I know you don't believe me," she rushed on, "but he moved the roller this morning from the barn to the edge of the road. You saw it at the edge of the road, didn't you? You *said* something about it."

Vance tipped her head to one side, and looked in a puzzled way at Eleanor. "You mean a handyman. Old Gufford?"

"No, he's—" But at this moment, he was walking out of the room, so Vance couldn't possibly have seen him, and before he disappeared into the side room, he gave Eleanor a look and pushed his great hands flat downward in the air, as if to say, "Give it up," or "Don't talk." "I mean what I said," Eleanor pursued, determined to share her experience, determined also to get some sympathy, even protection. "I am not joking, Vance. It's a little—creature two feet high, and he talks to me." Her voice had sunk to a whisper. She glanced at the side room doorway, which was empty. "You think I'm seeing things, but I'm not, I swear it."

Vance still looked puzzled, but quite in control of herself, and she even assumed a superior attitude. "How long have you—been seeing him, my dear?" she asked, and chuckled again.

"I saw him first two nights ago," Eleanor said, still in a whisper. "Then yesterday quite plainly, in broad daylight. He has a deep voice."

"If he just took a muffin, where is he now?" Vance asked, getting up. "Why can't I see him?"

"He went into the side room. All right, come along." Eleanor was suddenly aware that she didn't know his name, didn't know how to address him. She and Vance looked into an apparently empty room, empty of anything alive except some plants on the windowsill. Eleanor looked behind the sofa end. "Well—he has the faculty of disappearing."

Vance smiled, again superiorly. "Eleanor, your eyes are getting worse. Are you using your glasses? That sewing—"

"I don't need them for sewing. Only for distances. Matter of fact I did put them on when I looked at him yesterday across the room." She was wearing her glasses now. She was near-sighted.

Vance frowned slightly. "My dear, are you afraid of him?—It looks like it. Stay with me tonight. Come home with me now, if you like. I can come back with Hester and look the house over thoroughly." Hester was her cleaning woman.

"Oh, I'm sure you wouldn't see him. And I'm not afraid. He's rather friendly. But I *did* want you to believe me."

"How can I believe you, if I don't see him?"

"I don't know." Eleanor thought of describing him more accurately. But would this convince Vance, or anybody? "I think I could take a photograph of him. I don't think he'd mind," Eleanor said.

"A good idea! You've got a camera?"

"No. Well, I have, an old one of John's, but—"

"I'll bring mine. This afternoon.—I'm going to finish my tea."

Vance brought the camera just before six. "Good luck, Eleanor. This should be interesting!" Vance said as she departed.

Eleanor could tell that Vance had not believed a word of what she had told her. The camera said "4" on its indicator. There were eight more pictures on the roll, Vance had said. Eleanor thought two would be enough.

"I don't photograph, I'm sure," his deep voice said on her left, and Eleanor saw him standing in the doorway of the side room. "But I'll pose for you. Um-hm-hm." It was the deep laugh.

Eleanor felt only a mild start of surprise, or of fear. The sun was still shining. "Would you sit in a chair in the garden?"

"Certainly," the creature said, and he was clearly amused.

Eleanor picked up the straight chair which she usually sat on when she worked, but he took it from her and went out the front door with it. He set the chair in the garden, careful not to tread on flowers. Then with a little boost, he got himself on to the seat and folded his short arms.

The sunlight fell full on his face. Vance had showed Eleanor how to work the camera. It was a simple one compared to John's. She took the picture at the prescribed six-foot distance. Then she saw old Gufford, the town handyman, going by in his little truck, staring at her. They did not usually greet each other, and they did not now, but Eleanor could imagine how odd he must think she was to be taking a picture of an ordinary chair in the garden. But she had seen him clearly in the finder. There was no doubt at all about that.

"Could I take one more of you standing by the chair?" she asked.

"Um-m." That was not a laugh, but a sound of assent. He slid off the chair and stood beside it, one hand resting on the chair's back.

This was splendid, Eleanor thought, because it showed his height in proportion to the chair.

Click!

"Thank you."

"They won't turn out, as they say," he replied, and took the chair back into the house.

"If you'd like another muffin," Eleanor said, wanting to be polite and thinking also he might have resented her asking him to be photographed, "they're in the kitchen."

"I know. I don't need to eat. I just took one to see if your friend would notice. She didn't. She's not very observant."

Eleanor thought again of the muffin in mid-air for a few seconds— it must have been—but she said nothing. "I—I don't know what to call you. Have you got a name?"

A fuzzy, rather general expression of amusement came over his square face. "Lots of names. No one particular name. No one speaks to me, so there's no need of a name."

"I speak to you," Eleanor said.

He was standing by the stove now, not as high, not nearly as high

as the gas burners. His skin looked dry, yellowish, and his face somehow sad. She felt sorry for him.

"Where have you been living?"

He laughed. "Um-hm-hm. I live anywhere, everywhere. It doesn't matter."

She wanted to ask some questions, such as, "Do you feel the
cold?" but she did not want to be personal, or prying. "It occurred to
me you might like a bed," she said more brightly. "You could sleep
on the sofa in the side room. I mean, with a blanket."

Again a laugh. "I don't need to sleep. But it's a kind thought.
You're very kind." His eyes moved to the door, as Bessie walked in,
making for her tablecloth of newspaper, on which stood her bowl of
water and her unfinished bowl of creamy milk. His eyes followed
the cat.

Eleanor felt a sudden apprehension. It was probably because
Bessie had not seen him.

That was certainly disturbing, when she could see him so well
that even the wrinkles in his face were quite visible. He was clothed
in strange material, grey-black, neither shiny nor dull.

"You must be lonely since your husband died," he said. "But I
admit you do well. Considering he didn't leave you much."

Eleanor blushed. She could feel it. John hadn't been a big earner,
certainly. But a decent man, a good husband, yes, he had been that.
And their only child, a daughter, had been killed in a snow avalanche
in Austria when she was twenty. Eleanor never thought of Penny. She
had set herself never to think of Penny. She was disturbed, and felt
awkward, because she thought of her now. And she hoped the creature would not mention Penny. Her death was one of life's tragedies.
But other families had similar tragedies, only sons killed in useless
wars.

"Now you have your cat," he said, as if he read her thoughts.

"Yes," Eleanor said, glad to change the subject. "Bessie is ten.
She's had fifty-seven kittens. But three—no four years ago, I finally
had her doctored. She's a dear companion."

Eleanor slipped away and got a big grey blanket, an army surplus
blanket, from a closet and folded it in half on the sofa in the side

room. He stood watching her. She put a pillow under the top part of the blanket. "That's a little cosier," she said.

"Thank you," came the deep voice.

In the next days, he cut the high grass around the barn with a scythe, and moved a huge rock that had always annoyed Eleanor, embedded as it was in the middle of a grassy square in front of the barn. It was August, but quite cool. They cleared out the attic, and he carried the heaviest things downstairs and to the edge of the road to be picked up by Field's. Some of these things were sold a few days later at auction, and fetched about thirty dollars. Eleanor still felt a slight tenseness when he was present, a fear that she might annoy him in some way, and yet in another way she was growing used to him. He certainly liked to be helpful. At night, he obligingly got on to his sofa bed, and she wanted to tuck him in, to bring him a cup of milk, but in fact he ate next to nothing, and then, as he said, only to keep her company. Eleanor could not understand where all his strength came from.

Vance rang up one day and said she had the pictures. Before Eleanor could ask about them, Vance had hung up. Vance was coming over at once.

"You took a picture of a chair, dear! Does he look like a chair?" Vance asked, laughing. She handed Eleanor the photographs.

There were twelve photographs in the batch, but Eleanor looked only at the top two, which showed him seated in the straight chair and standing by it. "Why, there he *is!*" she said triumphantly.

Vance hastily, but with a frown, looked at the pictures again, then smiled broadly. "Are you implying there's something wrong with *my* eyes? It's a chair, darling!"

Eleanor knew Vance was right, speaking for herself. Vance couldn't see him. For a moment, Eleanor couldn't say anything.

"I told you what would happen. Um-hm-hm."

He was behind her, in the doorway of the side room, Eleanor knew, though she did not turn to look at him.

"All right. Perhaps it's my eyes," Eleanor said. "But I *see* him there!" She couldn't give up. Should she tell Vance about his Herculean feats in the attic? Could she have got a big chest of drawers down the stairs by herself?

Vance stayed for a cup of tea. They talked of other things—everything to Eleanor was now "other" and a bit uninteresting and unimportant compared to *him*—and then Vance left, saying, "Promise me you'll go to Dr. Nimms next week. I'll drive you, if you don't want to drive. Maybe you shouldn't drive if your eyes are acting funny."

Eleanor had a car, but she seldom used it. She didn't care for driving. "Thanks, Vance, I'll go on my own." She meant it at that moment, but when Vance had gone, Eleanor knew she would not go to the eye doctor.

He sat with her while she ate her dinner. She now felt defensive and protective about him. She didn't want to share him with anyone.

"You shouldn't have bothered with those photographs," he said. "You see, what I told you is true. Whatever I say is true."

And yet he didn't look brilliant or even especially intelligent, Eleanor reflected.

He tore a piece of bread rather savagely in half, and stuffed a half into his mouth. "You're one of the very few people who can see me. Maybe only a dozen people in the world can see me. Maybe less than that.—Why should the others see me?" he continued, and shrugged his chunky shoulders. "They're just like me."

"What do you mean?" she asked.

He sighed. "Ugly." Then he laughed softly and deeply. "I am not nice. Not nice at all."

She was too confused to answer for a moment. A polite answer seemed absurd. She was trying to think what he really meant.

"You enjoyed taking care of your mother, didn't you? You didn't mind it," he said, as if being polite himself and filling in an awkward silence.

"No, of course not. I loved her," Eleanor said readily. How could he know? Her father had died when she was eighteen, and she hadn't been able to finish college because of a shortage of money. Then her mother had become ill with leukaemia, but she had lived on for ten years. Her treatment had taken all the money Eleanor had been able to earn as a secretary, and a little more besides, so that everything of value they had possessed had finally been sold. Eleanor had married at twenty-nine, and gone with John to live in Boston. Oh, the gone and lovely days! John had been so kind, so understanding of the fact that she had been exhausted, in need of human company—or rather, the company of people her own age. Penny had been born when she was thirty.

"Yes, John was a good man, but not so good as you," he said, and sighed. "Hm-mm."

Now Eleanor laughed spontaneously. It was a relief from the thoughts she had been thinking. "How can one be good—or bad? Aren't we all a mixture? You're certainly not all bad."

This seemed to annoy him. "Don't tell me what I am."

Rebuffed, Eleanor said nothing more. She cleared the table.

She put him to bed, thanked him for his work in the garden that day—gouging up dandelions, no easy task. She was glad of his company in the house, even glad that no one else could see him. He was a funny doll that belonged to her. He made her feel odd, different, yet somehow special and privileged. She tried to put these thoughts from her mind, lest he disapprove of them, because he was looking, vaguely as usual, at her, with a resentment or a reproach, she felt. "Can I get you anything?" she asked.

"No," he answered shortly.

The next morning, she found Bessie in the middle of the kitchen floor with her neck wrung. Her head sat in the strangest way on her neck, facing backwards. Eleanor seized up the corpse impulsively and pressed the cat to her breast. The head lolled. She knew he had done it. But why?

"Yes, I did it," his deep voice said.

She looked at the doorway, but did not see him. "How could you? Why did you do it?" Eleanor began to weep. The cat was not warm any longer, but she was not stiff.

"It's my nature." He did not laugh, but there was a smile in his voice. "You hate me now. You wonder if I'll be going. Yes, I'll be going." His voice was fading as he walked through the living room, but still she could not see him. "To prove it, I'll slam the door, but I don't need to use the door to get out." The door slammed.

She was looking at the front door. The door had not moved.

Eleanor buried Bessie in the back lawn by the barn, and the pitch-fork was heavy in her hands, the earth heavier on her spade. She had waited until late afternoon, as if hoping that by some miracle the cat might come alive again. But Bessie's body had grown rigid. Eleanor wept again.

She declined Vance's next invitation to tea, and finally Vance came to see her, unexpectedly. Eleanor was sewing. She had quite a bit of work to do, but she was depressed and lonely, not knowing what she wanted, there being no person she especially wanted to see. She realized that she missed him, the strange creature. And she knew he would never come back.

Vance was disappointed because she had not been to see Dr. Nimms. She told Eleanor that she was neglecting herself. Eleanor did not enjoy seeing her old friend Vance. Vance also remarked that she had lost weight.

"That—little monster isn't annoying you still, is he? Or is he?" Vance asked.

"He's gone," Eleanor said, and managed a smile, thought what the smile meant, she didn't know.

"How's Bessie?"

"Bessie—was hit by a car a couple of weeks ago."

"Oh, Eleanor! I'm sorry.—Why didn't you—You should've *told* me! What bad luck! You'd better get another kitty. That's always the best thing to do. You're so fond of cats."

Eleanor shook her head a little.

"I'm going to find out where there's some nice kittens. The Carters' Siamese might've had another illegitimate batch." Vance smiled. "They're always nice, half-Siamese. Really!"

That evening, Eleanor ate no supper. She wandered through the empty-feeling rooms of her house, thinking not only of him, but of her lonely years here, and of the happier first three years here when John had been alive. He had tried to work in Millersville, ten miles away, but the job hadn't lasted. Or rather, the company hadn't lasted. That had been poor John's luck. No use thinking about it now, about what might have been if John had had a business of his own. Yes, once or twice, certainly, he had failed at that, too. But she thought more clearly of when *he* had been here, the funny little fellow who had turned against her. She wished he were back. She felt he would not do such a horrid thing again, if she spoke to him the right way. He had grown annoyed when she had said he was not entirely bad. But she knew he would not come back, not ever. She worked until ten o'clock. More letting out. More hems taken up. People were becoming square, she thought, but the thought did not make her smile that night. She tried to add three times eighty cents plus one dollar and twenty-five cents, and gave it up, perhaps because she was not interested. She looked at his photographs again, half expecting not to see him—like Vance—but he was still there, just as clear as ever, looking at her. That was some comfort to her, but pictures were so flat and lifeless.

The house had never seemed so silent. Her plants were doing beautifully. She had not long ago repotted most of them. Yet Eleanor sensed a negativity when she looked at them. It was very curious, a happy sight like blossoming plants causing sadness. She longed for something, and did not know what it was. That was strange also, the unidentifiable hunger, this loneliness that was worse and more profound than after John had died.

Tom Reynolds rang up one evening at 9 P.M. His wife was ill and he had to go at once to an "alert" at the Air Base. Could she come over and sit with his wife? He hoped to be home before midnight. Eleanor went over with a bowl of fresh strawberries sprinkled with powdered sugar. Mary Reynolds was not seriously ill, it was a day-long virus attack of some kind, but she was grateful for the strawberries. The bowl was put on the bed-table. It was a pretty color to look at, though Mary could not eat anything just then. Eleanor felt herself, heard herself smiling and chatting as she always did, though in an odd way she felt she was not really present with Mary, not really even in the Reynoldses' house. It wasn't a "miles away" feeling, but a feeling that it was all not taking place. It was not even as real as a dream.

Eleanor went home at midnight, after Tom returned. Somehow she knew she was going to die that night. It was a calm and destined sensation. She might have died, she thought, if she had merely gone to bed and fallen asleep. But she wished to make sure of it, so she took a single-edged razor blade from her shelf of paints in the kitchen closet—the blade was rusty and dull, but no matter—and cut her two wrists at the bathroom basin. The blood ran and ran, and she washed it down with running cold water, still mindful, she thought with slight amusement, of conserving the hot water in the tank. Finally, she could see that the streams were lessening. She took her bath towel and wrapped it around both her wrists, winding her hands as if she were coiling wool. She was feeling weak, and she wanted to lie down and not soil the mattress, if possible. The blood did not come through the towel before she lay down on her bed. Then she closed her eyes and did not know if it came through or not. It really did not matter, she supposed. Nor did the finished and unfinished skirts and dresses downstairs. People would come and claim them.

Eleanor thought of him, small and strong, strange and yet so plain and simple. He had never told her his name. She realized that she loved him.

THE GENERAL STORE

G. K. WUORI

Are we still shockable? Thresholds differ, but I know that the matter-of-fact unfolding of this brilliantly unpleasant tale certainly helped it work its shriek-making magic on me. Writing in a vein one can think of as "noir-ror," G. K. Wuori ruthlessly ambushes our attention with the first words we read—"Johnny had fingernails"—and then stomps on from there, dragging our sensibilities behind him.

◈

JOHNNY HAD FINGERNAILS—truly, not nubby, chewed things but products of pride in his appearance—yet they were not good enough. The two men had taped his one hand to the cooler door handle with damned tough tape, taped it round and round and round, and he couldn't even make a nick or slice in it with the nails on his free hand. He'd even walked the door around until it was almost closed so he could reach in and grab a thing of yogurt and rip the lid off—the stuff spilling down his leg as it plopped to the floor—and slice at the tape with the plastic lid but it did no good.

Time was going on and they had his wife.

Without that, he would have been calmer. He would not have wasted time hefting the door to see if he could get it off its stainless steel hinges.

He wouldn't have taken those few moments to assess the bottles of oil behind him on the shelf to see if he could grab one and smash the glass of the door. That, too, wouldn't have done any good since the bottles were plastic. It was just the idea that some kind of trashing might indicate progress toward getting out of this.

They were still out there. One of them was doing something to his, Johnny's, car, while the other was gassing up their own. Janice was out there, too, and looking in at him, her wrists taped together, one end of a short piece of rope tied around her arm just above the elbow, while the other end was looped and tied into the rear door handle.

In the beginning, he had looked closely at the two men. No masks. No panty hose pulled down to the neck. Two men as visible as anybody coming in for chips and soda or a sub and a six-pack of beer. Clean-shaven, both of them easily in their forties, maybe fifties, one of them over six foot with red hair—that bothered Johnny because Janice had red hair—and the other up in the high fives and fat, wearing khaki pants and a wide, black belt that cradled his pot, a stiff-legged walker with 'roids and workman's hands, liver spots, too, and mostly gray hair.

Then Janice had come out of the bathroom and had seen the gun and the two men. She had seen them and been calm, acting poised but irritated the way women sometimes do in a crisis while men stand around with their thumbs up their butts plotting later revenge. Johnny had been standing there, his hands out but not quite elevated—no one had said, "Hands up, Buster!"—palms out, willing to go through all of this and give the men everything they wanted if only they didn't go crazy with the gun. He wondered why they had to bring the gun into it along with the loose bowels and the adrenaline burp when it all could have been so easy without it. After all, Quilli had only one night-shift cop and no dispatcher. Didn't they know? Everyone knew that.

Janice, though, went right to the register and opened it. She put all the bills and change into a bag, even the stash of bills and checks under the register tray. Unchoreographed, they had all moved then. Johnny raised his arms way up in the air and stepped toward the cooler. The man with the gun looked right at him and smiled, even though Johnny didn't want to see him at all, didn't want that face locked so tight in his brain that only a bullet would get it out.

The other man, the one with the pot and poached hands, walked over to Janice and shoved his hand right into the top of her dress, squeezing, Johnny thought, hard enough to bring an awful look to Janice's face.

All right, Johnny decided, so a free feel is part of this. You lose your livelihood and you lose—other things. We know this.

She dropped the bag when he did it, and when she went to pick it up the man rammed her hard in the hip with his knee and sent her sprawling behind the counter. Janice's dress flew up around her waist and Johnny could see she was embarrassed.

In those few moments Johnny felt successive waves of just about everything passing over him, including amazement as the man reached down and pulled off Jan's stockings and her shoes. Johnny continued to stand by the cooler. He wanted to shout "Just cooperate, Jan!" except that she was, or was trying to. Johnny felt as though he were being held in place by other forces—good sense, he hoped—the gun merely molded metal, his thoughts much more than that.

Finally, the gunman said, "Let's get this guy secured," and Jan stood up as her attacker moved away to get a roll of duct tape for Johnny's hands.

Let's get this guy secured? These were no leak-nosed dopers out for cash and wine. In fact, Johnny had already noticed that the gunman was wearing a class ring and had his neck shaved the way a hairstylist or good barber will do. Again, that thought bothered him since he thought he now had far too good a description of both of them than was healthy. On health, his feelings almost gave out: they still had Jan tied to the side of the car.

As the gunman, outside, tossed something from Johnny's car out back he looked in through the window of the store, and Johnny tried to look passive or cooperative or just generally not causing any trouble.

The gunman pulled a pint bottle of liquor from his own car and came back inside. He walked to the paper goods shelf and ripped open a bag of plastic cups. He poured some into a cup and drank it, then poured some more that he started sipping as he walked back outside.

Janice looked right at Johnny and Johnny stood as straight as he could. He wanted to look strong and ready for her should something come up. He worked hard on the tape and he hoped she could see that, although if he worked too hard the freezer door would pop open, so he had to watch it. There might be some glare from the drive lights that could attract attention but he wanted to gauge that. Jan's eyes looked glazed, an odd look, something wicked in her fear. He continued working on the tape. There was movement there, progress, but not freedom. Not yet.

Jan hadn't had to come down from upstairs. She'd said she couldn't sleep, but that happened often and mostly she would read for a time, using the tiny reading flashlight so as not to disturb Johnny, even if it was a Saturday night when they stayed open until two or three and he wasn't even in bed yet.

But she'd come down, had gotten dressed and put on some makeup and hose and brought him a piece of pie from their kitchen and a glass of milk. She'd also put a piece of cheddar on the plate and they'd talked, a gentle and nowhere talk, a small laugh, a breathy sigh, not anything to add up to anything and all the more worthwhile for that.

Now Jan was out there. She had already put up with things you don't put up with in a normal day, had been handled and forced around in a way that, as Johnny saw it, meant that those two guys had given up their right to live.

They had given it up.

Johnny was startled by the thought, a heavy, bold thought, though it was not a hard thought in a place like Quilli, where the fine points of anything get smoothed out so quickly they often disappear.

Fine minds in courtrooms could decide what they wanted but,

whatever this was, as Johnny lived it, it was just a people thing, the four of them, and something would be worked out. Even executioners can think things through.

Both of the men got in the car and Johnny looked down to his hand to see if the tape had really loosened up or if it felt that way because he'd managed to rip all the hairs out around his wrist. You cooperate and it does no good. You don't cooperate and suddenly you're someone's problem and they don't have much time. He heard the engine of the car start and he looked out to see Jan bending toward the driver's window. She was trying to talk, Johnny saw, trying very hard.

As the car began to move Johnny bent his head down to his wrist and began chewing on the tape, funny thoughts coming to mind like the way Jan had been suggesting they blacktop the drive and now she was out there on that gravel with no shoes on.

He was chewing furiously, certain that he'd heard Jan yell but not wanting to take even a moment to look up. The thing was, he thought, if you could get through the first thirty seconds of this you could make it, those first instants being the time when you had to plan something, try something, with nothing in your head functioning very well. That was your disadvantage because no matter how impulsive the event was, the intruder still knew what he wanted to do. His end was clear and all you had was time.

They were driving around the parking lot in a circle, going slowly with Jan tied to the car, speeding up for an instant, slowing, stopping hard—repeating that. Jan kept up. She held herself just inches from the car, strength, Johnny saw, still there, an abundant poise.

She lost her balance once. Her hip hit hard against the car as they came around the gas pumps. She went down on one knee and ended up sitting on the drive as he speeded up again, dragging her with her arms overhead but still working the situation, her legs pumping furiously until she finally managed to lurch to her feet.

Her dress was ripped and her mouth bleeding from where she'd bitten her tongue. She leaned forward to the window and shouted something at the driver. In a blind, backward punch, though, his fist came out and caught her on the nose, not enough to knock her out, but enough to bloody it and stagger her backward and off her feet again.

All Johnny saw was Jan losing her balance, her body going per-pendicular to the car as they made the turn around the pumps. Her legs swung out over the island and knocked over the windshield wash and a rack of oil containers.

Jan, on her feet, limped badly as Johnny came through the door. His hands were red with blood from several bad cuts he'd chewed into the one wrist. He knew he didn't have much thought left inside at all, but his life seemed tool enough—a thing to use. No thoughts of bravery came to mind, nothing of courage or heroism. It was just a matter of tools, of craft.

For several years they'd kept a gun near the register until he'd finally decided he couldn't do business that way. Too many locals felt free enough to ring up their own sales if Johnny was busy.

The gun was packed away. Although he tried to think if there was anything else around that he could use as a weapon he knew there was not. He had some garden tools toward the back but the executive out there had his own gun and all Johnny could do was test his will, which seemed considerable now and cruel as well.

The car was parallel to the porch as Johnny stepped outside. It was barely moving and both men had their heads turned sharply toward Jan, the executive with his arm in the passenger window, gun in hand and pointed forward. Fat boy, Johnny thought, the driver, looked like he was trying to pop Jan again.

Johnny did two things then where he might have surprised him-self by being able to do even one. He walked up to the car, his eyes on the gun and nothing else. The man's hand was on the butt of the gun, and Johnny found his mind thinking, *That's good*, no finger on the trigger. Johnny put both hands on the gun and pulled so hard on it he spun himself around in a complete circle. He ended up still facing the car with only a second's worth of disorientation to get through.

He knew the next step was panic—theirs—and that if the driver floored the gas pedal he'd have one good shot from the gun (which

had damn well better be loaded, he hoped—after all this) and if that
didn't work, well, he just couldn't think of how bad, how awful it
would be for Jan.

By the time he completed his disorienting spin the gun was in
Johnny's right hand and his left was already wrapped into the executive's hair. Johnny forced the man's head back onto the headrest so
that he could rest the barrel of the gun on the bridge of the executive's nose—the effect was noticeable—while still pointing it directly
at the driver's head.

"I don't want you to step on the gas," Johnny said quietly. "None
of us knows what'll happen if you do. Maybe nothing. Maybe everything. Uncertainty's a bitch, we all know that."

"What do you want us to do?" the executive said. His words
sounded packed in clay as they came out of his tightened throat.

"I don't know," Johnny said. "Shit, I'm pretty scared."

"Okay," the driver said. "My foot's off the gas. It's off the goddamn gas."

Hostaging doesn't work unless someone cares, Johnny thought.
He didn't know if either of these guys cared about the other. He also
didn't know if there might not be more weapons lying about. For a
moment, he felt more vulnerable than when he'd been tied to the
freezer with the smiling corporate type holding the gun on him. It
was all in Johnny's hands now and it was quiet, yet he felt unprepared for leadership.

"It's off the gas, guy," the driver said again. He had his foot up on
the hump, wiggled it almost cutely so that Johnny would see. Johnny
looked at the foot and noticed he was wearing the kind of sneakers
you can pump air into for a tight fit. Ruined, he thought, as he fired
the gun into that foot.

The noise was horrible, yet through it he could hear a scream from
Jan.

Under Johnny's other hand, the executive's head was shaking, his
body nearing a spasm. Johnny couldn't tell what kind of state the

driver was in (awkwardly, the thought popped in, Footloose?, strange as could be). With his knee jammed onto the hump and with the steering wheel there the driver couldn't reach his foot, but he kept trying. He was noisy, too. He moaned a lot, cursed and cried, finally threw up all over the wheel and his lap and the dashboard.

Time to act, Johnny thought. If they had any more weapons or any presence of mind at all to try something they'd all just have to duke it out because he had to tend to Jan now. He released the executive to his tremors and walked around the rear of the car, grabbing a utility knife near the fallen oil rack as he did so.

Jan's dress was in shreds and she was standing mostly on one leg, the other bent slightly at the knee. Both legs were bloody. She looked up at him and Johnny thought, *You're such a peach* as she tried to bring a smile to that dirty and puffy face. Johnny noticed the contact lens sitting there on her cheek, looked like an edge of it had dried into a bit of blood, a fascinating bit of something, but he didn't think there was anybody he could ever tell it to. He picked it off with his fingernail and dropped it into his shirt pocket. He hoped it hadn't been scratched.

"I kept thinking of it, Johnny," she said.

"It's all right," he told her. He had the knife down to her wrists now, the tape all twisted up and tight and tough. A breast had come out of her bra and he brushed it with his ear as he bent close to try to find a spot to stick the knife in.

"Like when I'm raking or mowing," Jan went on, "or painting or doing anything long and repetitive and a song goes through my mind, just one or two lines which might be all I know of it, going over and over again except that now I can't even remember what it was."

The men had been looking at Jan's dishevelment and the breast and laughing when Johnny'd grabbed the gun and he thought, Sonofabitch, just making fun of someone like that. She had to stand there showing them her blood, more intimate than a striptease. It pissed Johnny off.

He understood how a cop might haul off and whack somebody he'd been chasing even though the person was finally subdued. A lot had gone out of him—Johnny—with that bullet into the guy's foot. Jesus, it's a mess in there. Blood and vomit and sneaker bits, a gun smell mixing with the moans and squirming going on in the car, all of it awful, and Jan still standing there humming and talking. "Can you believe that, Johnny? In my head I was joking all the time. I had my own death on my mind but I was going to laugh all the way and I don't suppose I took it serious enough, but, anyway, how'd all this happen, Johnny? What's going on here?"

Johnny's action had not been cathartic. A scruffy fizz still boiled within and the quiet evening of before refused to return. Worse, things seemed to be building up again. He even thought he was smiling—calmly and approvingly—when Jan, her hands finally free, reached in to the driver and patted his cheek, almost tenderly, then dug her nails in and dragged them from just under his ear to his mouth.

"I guess it's a shitty glory, though," she said, looking down at her hand and going "ugh" as she wiped it again and again on her torn dress.

Together they walked around to the other side of the car. Both of them concluded that the driver would be fine for a time, somewhat removed, change coming over him like a quality anesthetic.

"Why don't you get out of the car now," Johnny said to the executive. The man made no sound but his arm, not an aggressive arm, Johnny thought, flopped out of the door with his wallet in his hand. The wallet was open and Johnny could see the edges of some cash and some credit cards tucked in there. "I understand," Johnny said. "I really do. It just doesn't apply here, though. Not really, fella."

"We don't take American Express," Jan said from behind Johnny. An acceptable attempt at a laugh came out as she said it and Johnny smiled at her.

Johnny didn't think it fair that the driver should have to take the brunt of their trying to even all of this out. He brought Jan around and, after taking the wallet from the outstretched arm, brought that hand up onto Jan's breast.

"Johnny?"

"What it's all about, isn't it buddy?" Johnny said. "Something like that. Goddamn mean thing to do though, isn't it?" He pushed the arm away then and bent down to look at the man. "You do anything with that besides chew gum? Do you talk?"

"Whatever you want. This is all yours now."

Johnny stood up. "Well shit—sure. It's all me now. You make the mess, I clean it up."

"Take the wallet," the executive said. "I got cash, credit cards. I got ID in there and it's really me. Do whatever you want."

"Really you?" Johnny asked, quite loud. "Why in the hell would it be really you? Why would you do that?"

Johnny shot him in the wrist then. He heard a hard gasp from inside, a strange breathing. Obviously, things had evened out now, the lines redrawn for a relationship.

The arm was still straight out. The door opened slowly as the man tried to keep the arm centered in the window opening. His hand was a mess, not bleeding all that much, but distorted from where the bones were broken.

"You would have killed her," Johnny said. Jan was holding the door open while the man sat sideways on the seat, his feet on the gravel. He had taken his arm by the wrist and was trying to press it into his stomach: painful, but protective.

Johnny thought: I have hurt them worse than they'd hurt Jan, but still the tension isn't draining. They probably didn't know she'd never bring him pie and cheese again and you had to think about that. That was a change and it was no damn good.

"We wouldn't have killed her," the man said. "My God—listen, we need some help here."

Don't sneak that goddamn tone of authority in here, thought Johnny.

"Are you listening to me?"

There was no reason why Johnny couldn't lose his mind in all of this—he hadn't been in a courtroom in at least twenty years yet already possible defenses were popping up—though at the time he was feeling much more complex than someone who just happened to have this simple thing to lose—there it goes—to be found again after some calm searching. I run a little shop here, is all, he thought, Route 161, Quillifarkeag, Maine, occasionally omitted on cheap maps. It's in my interest to be cheerful, to smile until my ears feel heavy. No one comes here to buy despondency or the rage of a merchant. I am tone deaf, yet the tone is upbeat. Gently do you lead the grumpy to the door and wish them a good day. Of course, it is not always what you want. These two here—a case of a case in point. Mean people and ransackers, brutalizers high on the Lord. Oh, hell.

"What's the other guy doing, Jan?" Johnny asked.

"He's not dancing," she said.

"Honey."

"I don't want it to end, Johnny."

"I know."

The old garage with its two bays was empty and had been that way ever since Don's Grocery had built its Auto Centre. Johnny had thrown some plastic on the floor to protect the cases of hard goods he occasionally stored there, but other than that it was unused and it was rare that Johnny even went out there.

He took Jan over to the old spring-loaded door and together they lifted it, both of them keeping an eye on the car, both of them hoping, in a way, to see it start to drive slowly off, to let this thing, through default or neglect, simply be over.

"Any idea how pissed off those two are right now?" Johnny said.

"Like me," Jan said quietly, the fact simply there and not necessarily being driven into any point.

Johnny reached over and touched her face where there was redness and some swelling. "I know," he said. "I wasn't forgetting you." He put his arm around her and held her for a moment, then stepped back and tried to smooth and fold the ripped pieces of dress over her breast.

"I guess I thought all I had to do was grab the gun, call the police, and make a pot of potato salad for tomorrow," Johnny said. "Little moments like this still get by me. What do you need?"

"Nothing. I feel stiff and getting stiffer. My hands hurt but I don't think anything's broken. I'm all right."

"I shot them, shot them both. Just like that. I wonder if I could do it again?"

"You did it once. That was fine. They're not going to go, are they?"

"No. I don't see how."

"They're pissed. You said so. They'd come back someday."

"Think so? I don't know. The one guy seems pretty smart, seems a guy who knows his beginnings and his endings."

"Careful, Johnny. Right now they could say the couple up at the store just went crazy and shot them. I don't know if anyone would believe that but if you can start out off the hook it's harder for them to put you back on it."

"Any ideas? Find the night-shift cop?"

"Sure, but Johnny—"

If there was an old self to Jan, something of constancy and prediction that had vacated itself for a time, Johnny thought he saw it again. Maybe a furrow to the brow, pursing of lips—answers to practical problems. For a moment she seemed uninjured, unbludgeoned, the night not so bad after all.

"—I don't want to. Not yet."

Neither of them protested as Johnny led them toward the grease pit. Johnny assumed they were thinking he was taking them inside to tend their wounds before the police came. "John, John, John," he sighed aloud, the executive saying, "Excuse me?" as Johnny brought him to the edge of the pit, surprising himself—this guy really has no idea what's coming, he thought—at how light a touch to the shoulders it took to push him in. He did notice a flash of residual instinct as the man wrenched himself around enough to avoid falling on the injured hand. Johnny thought he heard an ominous crack, though. Bones, he thought, bones, bones.

The other man was even easier, limping and trusting, weeping. Johnny was holding one of his arms with his hand and had his other arm across the man's shoulders. A strong smell of shit and sweat was coming off the man, a lot of iron in the blood, Johnny decided. They approached the pit and before the man even noticed anything amiss Johnny took a sharp turn and just let go.

There were cries as Johnny slid a plywood sheet over the hole. He thought of weighing it down with some cinder blocks in the garage but didn't. Those two boys weren't climbing anywhere.

Strange feelings were going at Johnny. Hard feelings, conciliation and lots of regret over things he thought were stupid, a sense that, pain for pain, things were about at a match, except for the living part. He couldn't get rid of the feeling that they'd given up any right to continue the process. No downward sloping of the high spirits of combat seemed able to change that, yet he couldn't pin down where he might be at in the agent business.

Certainly, he could not stand above them at the edge of the pit and fire shots down into them. He couldn't do that. Nor could he give chase if they somehow managed to climb out, one of them standing on the other's back, maybe, pretty tough considering the injuries he knew about, the ones before the fall. But if they did, if they really did, he wouldn't care. Let them go wherever they might, tell whatever stories they wanted. Location, he thought, is all the truth you ever need, and he and Jan were here.

"Jan?"

She was standing behind the counter inside, one foot on a chair, putting an elastic bandage on an ankle.

"Did we kill them, Johnny?"

"Come here, Jan."

"What?"

"I want to look at you. Are you all right?"

"I'm all right."

In the morning he went out back first thing to check on where he'd put the car. It was in an ∟ where the garage attached to the house and store, parked and locked and looking normal, as though anyone who would need to would know whose car it was.

Johnny was pleased about the morning, one of those perfect fall sunrises that brought back the memory of other perfections, the sharpness of chill with the promise of warmth later on, the sky a bottle blue and no clouds anywhere.

He went into the garage expecting to find the plywood sheet thrown and the pit empty. The sheet was in place, causing him to look around quickly—someone waiting, two-by-four in hand. There wasn't even a sound.

He took an old furring strip and pushed it against the corner of the plywood. I anticipate a smell, he thought, and it's bad enough that I have to go out and clean your car. Foot blood, smelly foot blood and a lot of puke from your favorite foods.

"Morning, boys," he said. There was no response.

"Hello?" He leaned over and looked into the pit.

The executive was lying in a corner, one pant leg pulled up over his knee. Even in the dimness Johnny could see the swollen shin, the bone—no sliver here, looked like the whole lower bone—sticking out. He'd taken his shoe off and the foot was swollen, too, the tiny red dots of his painted toes gleaming a happiness certainly inappropriate for the moment. You should be careful of your toes if you think you might be in an accident. Sounds like something a mother would say.

He looked at the other man in the other corner who was looking up at him with tears running down his cheeks—or cheek. The
nose was clearly broken, mashed really—he must have landed on
his face, Johnny decided—the one cheekbone caved in, the skin raw.
These two dogs been out in the sun too long. Still, he bet they both
had children, probably grown children by now, some sort of assort-
ment between the two who would have been stunned—stunned?
decimated? traumatized?—or just upset to see their dads like this.
It's just your tragic gore, you know, the thin air, the fetid smell, a
touch of slime, of offal. Bones break under stress. "That's my
thought, gentlemen," he said. "Maybe later we can all go down to
Bud's and have a drink."

The only movement was in the workman's eyes as Jan and
Johnny stood over the pit some days later. Johnny had brought a case
of baking soda out and together they were emptying the boxes onto
the men. "Hold your hand over your face," Johnny said softly to him.
His eyes blinked but there was no other motion.

"I understand," Johnny said.

Earlier, he had opened the door to the other bay to let some fresh
air in and Jan had suggested the baking soda for the smell. Even with
the chill nights and cooling days the smell had been sour and growing. Both of the men were covered with the powder now, looking
ghostly and the workman a trifle bizarre as that red-rimmed stare
locked on to them through his dusted face. Johnny wondered if he
was trying to see up under Jan's shorts.

He closed the door then and Jan waited while he took the case of
empty boxes out to the Dumpster in back.

It was nearly noon and the morning had been busy with both of
them working the register and Jan running out to pump gas. Technically, their two pumps were self-serve, but they offered the service
whenever they could because a lot of the women felt comfortable
with Jan and knew her anyway. The men just seemed to enjoy the
service.

Jan was wearing sandals and shorts and a heavy sweater, her
short, reddish hair shining in the high sun. Only a small red mark

under her eye and the slightest limp remained of her encounter with the two men. The incident was done, however, for her. It had been an unfortunate thing, but you either let it scar and cripple or you didn't and much of that was just a function of what you thought about.

Johnny, though, had this idea that the two men in the pit had corporate origins, that the one with the silver-reddish hair and the tanning salon look was too distinguished to be some sort of ordinary stick-up guy, whatever that was, and Jan disagreed with that. Neither thought it was an important disagreement.

As they'd driven her around the parking lot she'd heard them talking in the midst of their laughter and great fun and she'd noticed that the corporate one had a lisp, nothing prissy but a hard garbling of certain sounds, enough, she thought, to keep you from going very far up anyone's ladder, let alone any corporate ladder. That was her point and Johnny just said, "Okay."

They were both disappointed that the two hadn't tried to escape, had felt fear change to a sense of burden by the way they just lay there, the pit, Johnny thought, not all *that* deep. After Sunday he'd even left the plywood sheet askew so they could see the opening and have some light to think and talk about things. Sunday, too, he and Jan had even talked about feeding them, but the conversation had been brief.

"Are you going to give them something to eat?" she asked.

"Are you serious?"

"Very—I mean in an abstract way."

"Oh. Well, no, I'm not going to feed them. Are you?"

"I couldn't do that. I don't even want to go in there, Johnny. Scares me just to think about it."

"Of course."

"I know."

So they hadn't, relying on escape instead, and now growing frustrated, even angered, because that didn't seem to be happening. Jesus, he thought, they don't even yell.

"Do you suppose we're letting them die?" she asked when

Johnny finally came around from the Dumpster. Johnny hadn't been thinking at all at the time so her question caught him off guard.

"Who?"

"Johnny!"

"No—I mean, you just caught my mind out of gear. Uh—"

"I think we are," she said.

"They're free to go."

"Yes and no. They can but they can't."

"I know. So are we. We could take a trip. Just go and go for a few days."

"Why?"

"I'm bothered by being bothered," Johnny said. "Even annoyed."

"It's almost noon, Johnny. It'll be busy soon."

"Let's have lunch. I made some shrimp salad this morning."

"Johnny—I threw an apple down there earlier. I didn't mean to, but it hit the one guy on his head, near that bad cheek."

"And?"

"He looked at me. It landed in his lap but he didn't move. I'm still wondering if he ate it."

"Do you want to go see?"

"No."

"Good."

"But what if he did? What if he wanted the food, the strength? I felt bad when I gave it to him, like I was betraying us or something. Then I was pissed because he just sat there, like he doesn't care or—"

"Hush, Jan. It's all right."

"I don't know."

Johnny's arm was across her shoulder, his fingers on her neck and gently rubbing it. Jan told Johnny she was hungry and that they ought to eat before things got busy the way they usually did from noon until two. Then she said she had to go to the bathroom but stopped on the way in to pick up an old comb that was lying on the ground.

"Look Johnny," she said. "I bet it's theirs, or one of theirs. Older guys like that—they still carry combs, you know? What do we do with the damn comb?"

Johnny thought for a moment it was all hysteria, parts of an old Jan from a lot of years of marriage mixing with something new here. She was not—he could see this—sad, not even confused. Once, she even said, "It's, really, just a trash problem. I think so." There was a harder look to her eyes now and Johnny felt proud of her.

"Jan?"

"What, Johnny?"

"Everything's all right. It really is."

"Oh, I know that—damned all right, too. I have to kick me once in a while for my lack of faith in us, how we keep making it, you and I day after day, problems booted in the butt that I couldn't even have imagined before, let alone resolved, but we do it, the two of us, and when it's all done I wonder what in the hell's going to happen next when I should be looking in a mirror and smiling like a crazy person. Sonofagun. Holy cow. Jan and Johnny—what a pair. Am I making any sense?"

"Dignity?"

"Is that what I'm talking about?"

"I am."

"Okay. Sure. You might say it has a certain ring to it. A little old-fashioned, maybe, but—here." She handed Johnny the comb and walked inside. He threw it in the trash can on the pump island.

By Saturday the treat and spectacle of early fall had passed and it was warm and rainy. Neither of them had been in the bay area since early in the week, although Johnny had closed the one overhead door on Thursday morning, concerned finally about what might start to creep in there rather than whether or not it was possible to get out. Before doing so he had stepped inside holding his nose, and pushed the plywood sheet back squarely over the pit. He saw it then and lamented that sometimes things just happen too late. Whatever you try there is a timing, often a split second between a deed and indifference, things done that might be noticed, or the hole in one by the solo golfer where there was so much more involved than a ball and a cup and a word of honor. My word, my honor, he thought, but only at the right time. Otherwise, it was nothing at all. He kicked the half-eaten apple core outside before closing the door, then picked it up and threw it hard toward the woods on the other side of the road.

HONEY, I'M HOME

LISA TUTTLE

One knows already that there are a great many different ways in which the familiar can suddenly turn strange: trust the ever inventive Lisa Tuttle, though, to come up with a completely unexpected one. So sly is her take on the small-screen illusions we unquestioningly welcome into our lives every day that this story almost seems a true cautionary tale and not at all the nasty little fantasy that it is.

҉

A S SOON AS she got home Gina turned on the television for company. She'd started doing it while living alone in New York, and although she wasn't as paranoid about living alone in London—that was the idea of the move—the habit persisted. She watched it hardly at all; it was wallpaper. Last week she'd succumbed to a salesman's spiel and had a satellite receiving dish fixed to the side of her building. The new channels she paid for offered more to choose from, but little of it choice. Much of the "entertainment" was imported from America or Australia and distinctly past its "Best By" date.

Standing in the kitchenette slicing chicken, mushrooms and zucchini for her dinner, feeling her usual faint regret that there would be no one to share it with her, no lover or husband soon to walk through the door, Gina was aware of the television playing in the sitting room behind her, and heard it call, in a voice from her childhood:

"Honey, I'm home!"

Memory tagged it instantly: Hugh Beaumont as Ward Cleaver in *Leave It to Beaver*. She marvelled at time's magic which turned any boring old sitcom into a cultural classic.

Then somebody grabbed her by the waist, and she screamed. At the same time she twisted in his grasp, half turned and drove her fist straight into his midriff. It was a response drilled into her by years of self-defense classes, but this time, the first time she'd done it for real, in her fist was a long, very sharp kitchen knife, and it went straight into the living body of Ward Cleaver.

He let go of her, looking surprised and sorry. Her eyes went from the kindly face, as familiar as a member of her own family, to the black knife handle protruding from his belly, and she couldn't have said whether guilt or disbelief was the stronger emotion.

"Gosh, honey, what's wrong? Did I forget our anniversary again?" With a visible wince, he grasped the handle and pulled the knife out. He laid it down on the counter and patted himself gingerly where she had stabbed him. Except she couldn't have stabbed him really. There was no blood on his white shirt, no rent in the cloth. She looked at the knife and could see no blood on the blade. Maybe her usual sharp chopper had been replaced by a stage prop. When she tried to pick it up to check he grabbed her hand.

"Easy," he said, half laughing. "Truce? I'm sorry, whatever I've done, I'm sorry."

His hand holding hers was solid and warm and very real. She stared at him, grasped at a mental straw. "Is Allen Funt about?"

"Huh?"

"Candid Camera?"

He shook his head. "It *is* our anniversary, isn't it? Why don't I take you out to dinner. Wherever you want, price no object. Okay, honey? Whaddaya say."

She said yes. She was so befuddled she forgot to turn off the television set when they left, and would have forgotten to lock the door if he hadn't reminded her.

"This is London, you know. Have to be careful. Not like back home."

"It's worse back home," she said sharply. "London isn't full of people carrying guns, or psychos who'd rather kill the people they rob than let them live."

"Whatever you say, dear." Ward Cleaver's face, like his voice, was good-humored, handsome, warm, yet somehow blank. She didn't think there was anybody home behind the eyes. She hoped he wasn't a psycho. Was he a robot? Were those Disneyland kind of things that good now? But how did it get into her apartment? And why?

Her choice for dinner was the Café Pelican in St. Martin's Lane. It was a place she often went for drinks, particularly in the summer, and there was a good chance she would see someone she knew. London might be a big city, but the world of publishing was more like a small town. Think about changing jobs, or get too interested in a married colleague, and suddenly everybody was talking about it. Although she still traded on the aura of Manhattan sharpness with which she had won her first London job, Gina suspected it was wearing as thin as her accent by now. She didn't care. This was home. She had never found the husband she had hoped for, and dating wasn't any easier in London, but she had her own flat, a job she liked, and lots of interesting friends.

"If I'm so happy, why am I hallucinating?"

"What's that, dear?"

He hadn't gone away. He was still beside her in a carriage on the Northern line. She broke into a cold sweat. What if she wasn't single, didn't have a career, didn't live in London. What if this refugee from an imaginary 1950s America was really her husband, and they had two sons, Wallace and Theodore. And she did the housework in high heels and pearls. She moaned softly. It wasn't possible. Please, let it not be possible.

They got off at Charing Cross and walked up past the opera house, towards the café. Her heart lifted. There, sitting at one of the tables on the pavement, was someone she knew, an editor at Gollancz in conversation with a rumpled, seedy-looking individual, undoubtedly an author. His name flew away without alighting; Gina's concentration was fixed on her friend when she introduced Ward.

"Hello, Ward, nice to meet you."

No reaction at all. Gina could not contain herself. With the barest sketch of an apology, she dragged the other woman off to the ladies' room.

"What's up?"

"Doesn't he remind you of someone? Doesn't he look a lot like . . . Ward Cleaver?"

"I thought you said that was his name."

"But don't you remember *Leave It to Beaver*? No?" Gina groaned. She'd grown up on the series, but that was in another country, and besides . . . "Just answer this: was there a man in my life the last time I saw you?"

"I don't think so. No, definitely not. You were talking about putting an ad in *Time Out*. Is that where he came from?"

"No. I don't know. He just turned up and . . . there's something strange about him. I can't explain."

"Mmmm. Well, be careful. I'd ask you to join us, but I'm afraid I'm on my last drink. I really have to get home to the boy."

"Oh, I'll be all right. I'm not afraid of him—he's just . . . boring."

"They're the ones you have to look out for. Whatever you do, don't let him take you home."

"Oh, no!"

After dinner (which was, thanks to Ward's conversation about the life he presumed they shared, the most surrealistically boring meal of her life) Gina tried to lose him in the crowds at Leicester Square, but he stuck like a limpet. She realized that even if she lost him now he'd turn up at the flat later since he believed it was his home. Anything she said which disagreed with his version of reality he treated either as a joke or as an understandable expression of womanly pique.

"I know you're mad because I forgot our anniversary, honey, but I'm trying to make up for it."

"It's not our anniversary!"

"Is it your birthday? Come on, honey, give me a break, you know I can't remember dates."

"It's nothing! You're nothing to me. I never met you before today when you turned up in my apartment! Can't you hear what I'm saying?"

"Aw, honey, just tell me what you're so mad about."

"Stop calling me honey!"

When they got home Gina leaped up the stairs like a gazelle and managed to get the door shut and locked with him on the outside. But Ward had his own key and he used it, chuckling indulgently at her cute, wifely tricks.

"I give up," said Gina wearily, sinking down on the sofa. "What do I have to do to get rid of you, put on the ruby slippers and click my heels together and say there's no place like home?"

Ward stood smiling fondly down at her. "You're right, honey, there's no place like home. I'll sure be glad when we can get out of London and back to the boys and our own house."

Gina shuddered. "I don't suppose a bucket of water would wash you away?"

"Would you like a drink, honey?"

"That's not a bad idea. There's some Scotch up over the sink. A little water, no ice." She watched him as he went to fetch it. He had a nice build on him, she had to admit. Maybe he had his uses.

When he returned with her drink, she scrutinized his face, remembering that, as a child, she had thought him handsome. There had even been a time—she'd forgotten until this moment—when she'd imagined she would grow up to marry someone just like the Beaver's father. As the old memories came back she began to thaw, and as she took the first warming swallow of Scotch she turned a genuine smile on the man in front of her. Maybe he really had come in response to an unarticulated wish, to fill her subconscious desire.

"Sit down, why don't you. Make yourself comfortable."

He fidgeted and tossed back his drink. "Mmm, strong stuff!" He turned away to set down his glass and then yawned exaggeratedly, balling his fists and stretching his arms out at his sides. "Man, oh, man, am I tired! That city really takes it out of you. Think I might just get ready . . ." His voice trailed off as he went into the bedroom.

Gina smiled after him, feeling a definite spark of interest. "Yes, dear, why don't you get ready for bed, and I'll join you."

There was a shout and Ward reappeared, glaring. "What did you do with the beds, for Pete's sake?"

"What?"

"The beds! There's only one bed in there!"

"One that's big enough for two." She smirked.

"But we always—you know I can't—*you* always say you can't sleep with anybody else in the same bed."

"I don't always say that. Do I always say that? Well, maybe I don't feel like sleeping tonight." She was enjoying herself.

Ward was definitely sweating. She'd seen that look on his face before, when his high-heeled, aproned, screen wife ran mental circles around him.

"I've got to get some sleep tonight because . . . because I've got a meeting, yes that's right, a meeting, very important, in the office, first thing tomorrow morning."

Gina shrugged. "Well, I'm sorry. But there's nothing I can do. I only have one bed, as you can see . . . *honey*. Unless you want to check into a hotel."

"Oh, no, no, no need for tha . . . I'll sleep on the couch!"

"You can't sleep on the couch. It's not even big enough for me to sleep on. You're way too tall. You'd put your back out even trying."

"Um . . . the floor! That would be good for my back, yeah. Perfect. I need something hard—that mattress is much too soft. Right. I'll sleep on the floor."

"You can sleep in hell for all I care," Gina said. She was tired of this game. If he was that nervous about sex, where had the two boys come from? She could just imagine June, who had probably never lost her figure, turning up one day with two little bundles. *There was a special on at the hospital, two for the price of one!* Back when Gina had watched *Leave It to Beaver* for the first time she had believed babies came from hospitals like bread or ice cream, untouched by human hands. She looked at her "husband," terrified at the prospect of a night in the same bed with his wife, and remembered another childhood fantasy caused by the ambiguity of adult language. In overheard, barely comprehended gossip, as well as in the *Confessions* magazines read by the baby-sitter, unmarried women got in trouble—which meant pregnant—by "sleeping with" men. Maybe Ward, too, thought sex was something that happened while you slept. Maybe for him it did. She had to sympathise. The prospect of fathering another Beaver was worth going to any lengths to avoid.

She got up and walked away from him to turn off the television. She had just realized it had been left on all evening. "I'm going to bed," she said, and turned back to face him.

"You—"

He was gone.

"Ward?" She already knew from the way her voice sounded when she called that she was alone in the flat, but she checked out the bedroom and bathroom, just in case. Then she looked at the silenced television set. That simple? She laughed with relief.

But old habits die hard, and the very next evening, as soon as she came in, Gina turned the television on before hurrying back to the bathroom for a shower. Ward Cleaver was an imaginary character, better forgotten, and although she was feeling vaguely sexy she certainly wasn't expecting company when she emerged from the bathroom wearing only a light cotton wrap, her hair turbanned in a fluffy white towel.

"Hi, honey," said the man on the bed.

She let out a blood-curdling scream. A few seconds after fear, recognition kicked in. "Ricky?" she said weakly, clutching the robe to her breast.

"Sure," said the man she recognized as Desi Arnaz, a.k.a. Ricky Ricardo, from *I Love Lucy.* His face took on a scowl of distrust. "Who else you esspecting besides your husband? You esspecting maybe somebody else? Somebody I don' know about?"

She didn't think about it, her voice fell into Lucy's high-pitched, husband-placating cadences. "No, of course not, no, how can you say that, Ricky? You just startled me, that's all. I didn't hear you come in. I thought I was all alone."

"Yeah? Well, you're not all alone now. You happy to see me? Come and show me you're happy to see me, *querida*."

Ricky, it became clear, was not made nervous by double beds, nor did he think they were only for use by the terminally tired at bedtime. Sex with him was pretty sensational. Gina was very late for work the next day. First she overslept, then Ricky wouldn't let her up.

"Look, I'd love to stay in bed all day, but I can't," she said, laughing, gently disentangling herself from him. "I have to work."

"Why? Do it later, do it when I'm at work, tonight. I don' mind a little dust."

"I'm not talking about housework—I mean my job."

His face darkened. "Job? Don' I make good money, my wife goes out to work?"

"It's nothing to do with you—I mean, it's my choice, I *like* my job—I had it before I met you—why shouldn't I have a job?" To her own amazement she heard herself babbling as if it mattered what he thought, as if she must, at all costs, placate him.

"Ricky Ricardo's wife does not have to work," he said sternly. Then, more gently, sweetening it with kisses: "I don' want you out there working for strangers, wearing yourself out. I want you here, making a nice home for me."

"But—but I'd get bored here alone all day."

"You don' have to stay in all the time. I'm here in the mornings. In the afternoons you can come to the club and watch me rehearse, or go out shopping. I know how you love to shop! Don' waste your time on some silly job."

"But, Ricky—"

"No buts!" He landed a playful slap on her bottom, and she jumped. "Go cook my breakfast, *mujer*, I am starving!"

She went out as if obediently to the kitchen, but really to turn off the television. She felt guilty doing it, and knew she would miss him, but it meant she was able to get dressed and go out to work without having to cook his breakfast.

It wasn't so easy to cancel out the memory of him. She hadn't had sex that hot for a very long time, and although her uncharacteristically meek response to his typical *machismo* worried her, she reminded herself how simple it had been to get rid of him.

After work she went out for drinks and dinner with a friend, and she deliberately did not turn on the television when she got home. She thought about it, though; she thought a lot about Ricky. The memories were especially poignant when she was alone in bed. It wasn't fair, dammit. Why shouldn't she have a little fun? When it was as easy as turning a television on or off—could it really be that easy? She got up and went to find out.

There was no sign of *I Love Lucy* or any American sitcoms from that era on any of the channels. She wondered if that meant she would have to wait until the right program was playing or make a choice from what was available. One channel had a group of real people sitting in a studio having a serious discussion about the euro. Another was showing a French movie with English subtitles. There was something with sinister music that looked like an American made-for-TV movie, something that was either a soft-core film or an ad for chocolates, the shopping channels, boxing, talking cats, dancing cows, a very old Western and championship darts. She wondered if what was on the screen was related to the men who turned up in her flat. She hoped not. The French movie seemed her best bet for sex (the chocolate ad didn't feature any men), but without the use of subtitles communication would probably break down long before they got to bed.

Restless, horny and bored, she prowled her flat, looking in the refrigerator, picking up books and setting them down, deliberately ignoring the TV.

"Come on, Ricky," she muttered, praying that it would be enough to want him to get him. She wondered why he had turned up in the first place. If desire—her desire—was involved it didn't make sense. She was ready to believe that Ward Cleaver had been summoned by some deeply buried but still potent wish for the loving husband, two kids and house in the suburbs which had signified happiness in her childhood, but—Ricky Ricardo? Come on! She had never found him sexy—she would not believe she found him sexy now except for the memories of her body. But subconsciously, if Ward represented the safe, nonsexual side of marriage, then Ricky, a musician and a foreigner with a mercurial temper, might stand for the more exotic and sexual possibilities in a marriage. Wasn't it, after all, the lure of the artistic and exotic which had drawn her to publishing, and to London? Maybe the start of her whole career could be located in those childhood hours spent watching, through a haze of boredom, *I Love Lucy*.

What else would she learn about her own desires? Who would be the next character to appear—Fred Flintstone? The thought made her shudder, and she cast about desperately for some other televisual memories. She had been an ardent fan of the old *Dick Van Dyke Show*; Rob Petrie might have been a bit of a bumbler at times, but she'd had a crush on him, and measured herself sadly against his wife, the cute, pert Laura. She tried to revive her old enthusiasm for Rob, but then she realized the Petries were, like the Cleavers, definitely a twin-bedded couple, and gave up. It was no good. Perverse her desire might be, but she wanted Ricky.

She went to bed, leaving the TV on. She was barely asleep when Ricky woke her with a kiss and the welcome warmth of his body.

She had meant to avoid a replay of their last argument by getting rid of him first thing in the morning, but he woke before she did. Then he insisted on taking her out to breakfast at the Ritz. At least there she was able to pay a visit to the ladies' room and secretly call the office. She claimed a touch of flu and said she hoped to be in on Monday, or Tuesday at the latest. After a long weekend of playing Lucy she thought she'd be eager to return to real life, but she hadn't realized how much, when she was with Ricky, his reality became hers.

She couldn't bring herself to turn off the television. On Tuesday, she lied about a doctor's appointment and managed to get to work on time. On Wednesday another lie got her out the door only an hour late, Thursday the same, and by Friday, at work right on time, she was congratulating herself on how easy it was to keep Ricky in the dark. She'd been in her office less than an hour when she got a phone call from Jill in reception saying, mysteriously, that there was someone waiting downstairs to see her.

"Well," she said, puzzled. "Send him up. Who is it?"

"He *says* he's your *husband*."

Jill knew perfectly well Gina wasn't married.

"Oh. It's all right. I know who—I'll come down and see him, Jill. Thanks."

She knew it was going to be trouble; she didn't realize quite what kind. "I can explain," she said, and then Ricky grabbed her and—to her complete and helpless disbelief—turned her over his knee and *spanked* her. With a slipper. Shouting triumphantly in Spanish the while.

She wept. Not in pain—although it was surprising how much it did hurt—but rage. He hugged and kissed her then, her tears his proof of victory, and took her home in a cab. She let him, she had to let him, because she couldn't stop crying and, anyway, she needed time to figure out how the hell she was going to explain this one to Jill. And not just Jill. It would be all over the building in five minutes. How could she go back? How could she ever face anyone at work again?

He had planned it that way, of course. The public humiliation was meant to ensure that she would stay home where he wanted her. He seemed to think it was what she wanted, too. Maybe, if she had been Lucy, he would have been right. But she wasn't Lucy and didn't want to be. He was taking his clothes off, as if the spanking had been their customary foreplay, when she turned him off.

Gina extinguished Ricky in the white heat of anger, but no regret or calmer reflection would make her summon him back. It was time to be sensible about this. For some reason, or none at all, she'd been given a powerful gift, and it was up to her to use it wisely. She supposed it must have something to do with the satellite receiver dish. In the old days (she reflected) there would have been a fairy or a dusty old shopkeeper to mutter a cryptic warning if not tell you the rules, but these days it was all so impersonal, *caveat emptor* and no one but yourself to blame when the magic did you in.

This time she would wish for a man she wanted now, not just in her childish subconscious. It made perfect sense that the man of her dreams should be found on television. It was television more than anything else, more than movies or rock 'n' roll, that had shaped her sexuality, had given her the images and vocabulary of desire. Other people her age talked about movies, but she'd never seen anything but the occasional Walt Disney film until she was old enough to date, and by then the pattern would have been well established. Popular music had stirred strange longings in her soul, of course, but those longings were directed not at the unimaginably distant musicians, but at actors, the men whose faces she gazed at, intimately close, night after night in the half-dark of the family room. (The Beatles were an exception; but she'd only fallen in love with the Beatles after seeing them on *The Ed Sullivan Show*.)

Gina stretched out on the carpeted floor. The silence was eerie. Silent, it didn't even feel like her apartment. On a weekday morning even the usual noises from her upstairs neighbors were missing. Uneasy, she got up and switched on Radio Two. Even real life should have a soundtrack. Returning to the floor, she closed her eyes and let her mind drift back to the time when she had been madly in love with Napoleon Solo and Illya Kuryakin, unable to decide (just as she had always been unable to choose just one favorite Beatle) which of the men from U.N.C.L.E. she preferred, Napoleon with his suave charm or Illya with his icy cool. Yet now that she thought of them, neither alternative was very appealing. It was all new and thrilling when she was twelve, but in the years since she'd been out with enough bed-hoppers to have the measure of Solo, and she'd broken her heart against icebergs like Kuryakin enough to resent all that unreciprocated effort.

She was no longer a girl, and the world had moved on. Napoleon Solo would seem as ridiculously out of date and sexist now as Ricky Ricardo.

★ ★ ★

The problem with finding a contemporary TV lover was that she never watched TV anymore except for movies and the news—well, and the occasional American sitcom when she was too tired to do anything else.

She thought of *Friends* and wrinkled her nose. She couldn't seriously imagine dating any of those boys. *Seinfeld* was out because he was a real person, and she wasn't crazy enough to think she had the power to transport real, live men from their homes into hers at the press of a button—even presuming she was interested in such a whiny, self-absorbed New Yorker.

She recalled photographs of gorgeous George Clooney, but she'd never tuned in to *ER* and didn't even know the name of the character he played. She'd given up on cop shows when they turned to dirty realism, and when she'd grown tired of *Eastenders* no other soap had taken her fancy.

Besides, the sexiest men in the soaps were generally villains any sane woman would stay away from. She wondered if that was a contemporary equation—safe and boring or attractive but dangerous—or if it had been ever thus. It seemed an awfully immature attitude towards sex, but maybe the television idea of romance was inescapably adolescent. She tried to remember the last time she'd found any character from a television series sexually interesting, let alone compelling, and then remembered Frank Furillo from *Hill Street Blues*. There was a man to make her heart beat a little faster. Not only sexy but *nice*. She considered his eyes, his laugh, the way he moved, and then she remembered something about his character which made her sigh in a different way. He was a recovering alcoholic. She had played partner to one of those before—also a "pizza-man." That had been one of the several last straws before she left New York, and she had sworn never again.

Familiar music impinged upon her consciousness, jarring, percussive, a popular track from several years back, carrying a freight of memory.

She sat up and stared at the blank screen while the radio played the theme music from *Miami Vice*.

It came back in a rush: the curious, guilty pleasure of it, like eating a whole batch of brownies, delicious and comforting and yet sickening. Something she could never talk about. For those few months, one night a week, she had a secret, a pleasure waiting for her, like having someone to go home to. She'd get in from somewhere, maybe a union meeting, maybe a disappointing tryst in a pub. Sometimes she'd be a little drunk, sometimes she would pour herself a glass of white wine, sometimes she'd have a packet of fish and chips, sometimes she would have been crying. She'd turn on the television and curl up in the comfy chair with her wine or her chips and gaze at the screen entranced by the brilliantly colored, designer vision of Florida. She knew Miami wasn't like that—and she knew cops didn't dress like that, but watching *Miami Vice*, she was as uncritical as any dreamer in her own dream.

What was the name of the character played by Don Johnson? Sonny. Sonny something. King of the wild frontier.

Gina smiled, sank back on the carpet and closed her eyes, remembering. Sonny Crockett. How many years ago was it? Three? Four? It was the time she was hung up on Lane, and it must be nearly three years now since she'd seen him at all. They used to go out for drinks and talk for hours on the phone. Mostly they acted like pals, but sometimes they were like lovers, edgy and flirtatious. He was married, so of course he couldn't be interested in her, she thought, and so her crush on him grew, unspoken, until he started telling her things about his marriage that she didn't want to know. As he seemed more interested in her she began to question her own interest in him; getting to know him better, she liked him less while becoming more involved—it was all very emotionally confusing and exhausting.

What a relief it had been to go home and forget all that, to feel straightforward, uncomplicated lust for someone she didn't know and would never meet. Someone who would never burden her with the secrets of his soul, complaints about his wife, the problems of his childhood, his health worries. Someone who was fit and strong and unattached, with a smashing wardrobe and his own boat.

For nearly an hour every week she was able to forget Lane, forget work, forget money worries, forget being lonely or being in love and simply be warmed by the sunlight, the jewel colors, and Sonny Crockett's sexy smile.

That was what she wanted. A smart, funny, tough, slightly scruffy fashion plate. A man of the eighties, he would expect his girlfriend to have her own demanding career rather than wait at home for him all day. He probably wouldn't be around all that much himself, since he was usually working undercover to bust evil drug dealers and mob kingpins. As far as women were concerned he was neither a Don Juan nor emotionally retarded. He lived by himself but sometimes fell in love.

Heart pounding hard, Gina got up, turned off the radio and turned on the TV, then went into the kitchenette, thinking of that bottle of chardonnay in the fridge. Would it be jumping the gun to open it now? He might not turn up for hours. Or, of course, he might not turn up at all, in which case at least she'd have the wine for comfort.

Why not, it was nearly lunchtime. There were eggs and cheese for an omelette, lettuce and tomato for a salad, and the wine to make it special. She got eggs, cheese and butter from the refrigerator and put them to one side on the counter. She took out two glasses and uncorked the bottle. She had just put down the corkscrew when she felt a presence behind her. She smiled and leaned back as his arms slipped around her waist, inhaling the scent she already seemed to know.

"Perfect timing," she said as his cheek scraped hers. She'd forgotten the designer stubble. She felt his grin against her mouth as she turned. "You're perfection," he said, and then gave her the best kiss she'd ever had.

"Can lunch wait?" he asked.

"Mmm-hmmm."

"Good, 'cause I can't."

Having said that, though, he made a detour on the way to the bedroom and spent what seemed an unnecessarily long time going through her CDs in search of the perfect mood music.

"Don't you have any Whitney Houston?"

"Afraid not."

"Gloria Estefan? Sheena Easton?"

"Suzanne Vega?" she suggested.

"You gotta be kiddin'."

"Carly Simon? Look, does it matter? We don't need music."

"I think you been sleepin' alone too long," he said, very gently, shaking his head at her unsatisfactory recordings. Gina knew a moment of disbelieving despair: this was worse than high school, it was worse than *junior* high school, to be judged and found lacking for her taste in pop stars. She shot a glance at the television set, deciding she would pre-empt him rather than suffer rejection. Then, with a tiny grunt of satisfaction, he found something he liked, slipped it in, and they continued to the bedroom. As his hands, his mouth, his body moved against hers it was to the rhythms of Tina Turner steaming up the windows.

And Gina was in heaven. He was better than her dreams. It was all very much the way she used to imagine sex would be, before she'd learned otherwise.

After they'd made love he cooked a perfect omelette which they ate from the same plate, sitting cosily together on the floor, not far from the television which flashed unregarded pictures, the sound turned down.

"Thanks for takin' the time off work," Sonny said. "I wish all my lunchtimes could be like this."

"Why can't they?"

"Only in heaven. Listen, if you don't hear from me for a while, don't think it has anything to do with you and me, know what I mean? This case I'm workin' on is heatin' up. So you might not see too much of me for the next couple of weeks."

"Well, the door's always open . . ."

"What did I tell you about that? Keep it closed and locked." He put his arms around her and grinned. "Anyway, I got my own key. The problem is time. This case . . ." He shook his head, his face briefly grim. "Never mind. When it's all over maybe you and me could take the boat somewhere, get away from it all. Could even call it a honeymoon—maybe even for real. Think you could go for that?"

"I think I could," she said, managing to keep her tone as casual as his.

"Good deal. I gotta move." He looked at her tenderly, touched her mouth with a finger. "*Hasta la vista.*"

Gina was in a daze of physical happiness, loose and relaxed as she began to clean up the kitchen. She wondered if it would really be a couple of weeks before she saw Sonny again, or if time would be compressed the way it was in an hour-long drama.

"The door's always open," she murmured, thinking of the television in the room behind her. "I'll never turn it off again."

She heard the slightest sound, a footfall, from the other room, and looked up in surprise.

"Honey, I'm home."

The voice was a stranger's, yet somehow familiar, falsely falsetto. The adrenaline of fear was shooting through her veins as she turned and saw them.

One was short, white, with thinning hair and a lived-in, almost ravaged face. She had seen him somewhere before—maybe she had known him when he was younger?—but she couldn't quite place him. He was wearing a nasty-looking suit and a skinny tie. The other, in an understated track suit of the most pristine white was young, black, and quite startlingly beautiful. She had seen that face before, on posters, on album covers. Everybody had.

"What are *you* doing here?" she asked. Her fear vanished in astonishment.

The beautiful one smiled like an angel. It was the other one who spoke. "I think you know that, my lovely."

The London vowels teased at her memory. He must be an actor, she thought. Confused, she shook her head. "But—I didn't want *you.* There must have been a mistake."

The man in the nasty suit nodded. "And you're the one who made it."

The beautiful one laughed. It was an utterly mad laugh.

A little over the top, thought Gina, as objectively as if she was watching this on television. Real villains aren't like this, and it's impossible to take rock stars seriously when they try to act.

Then she felt herself freeze as she understood. These weren't actors, these weren't people, they were characters who had come from the same place as Sonny. And she knew very well why they had come.

"Your boyfriend hurt a friend of ours, rather badly," said the white guy. A part of her mind was still scrabbling to come up with his name. He'd played drums once, hadn't he? "And I'm afraid that, in return, we'll have to hurt a friend of *his*. Tit for tat, you know."

"Tit for tat," said the beauty, and shrieked.

If this was a movie Sonny could return unexpectedly, in the nick of time, to save her. But this wasn't a movie, this was series television, and everybody knew the fate of the hero's girlfriend in a TV series. The hero had to be available, free to begin again with each new episode. She should have been smart and stuck with a sitcom husband. They might be dumb, but they were safe. The price of loving a hero was death.

Unless she could get to the television and turn this episode off.

The white guy took a step towards her. "Nothing personal, lovey," he said in a world-weary voice.

Instinctively, she moved away. Two steps backed her into a corner. It was, however, the corner where she kept the knives. She remembered the knife's lack of effect on Ward Cleaver, but he was a character from an old-fashioned sitcom for whom death by stabbing was unimaginable. These men obeyed an altogether different set of rules.

So she snatched up a carving knife. But they had been waiting for it, and now acted in concert, far swifter and more brutal than she could ever be, and had the knife away from her before she could even scream.

"Little girls shouldn't play with knives," whispered the mad one into her face. "They could hurt themselves. They could even kill themselves."

Desperately, staring at those too-familiar faces as if hypnotized, she told herself that this was not happening. They were not real. If they weren't real, they couldn't hurt her, not really. But even if she had been right—and if right, what about Ricky's spanking?—the knife that one of them now held was as real as her own agonized body. She might try to deny it, but she knew what was going to happen before it did.

LETTERS FROM THE *SAMANTHA*

MARK HELPRIN

The vastness of the sea, like the trackless wastes of the desert, adds the weight of long odds to any unlooked-for encounter. And the unknown—something as unrevealed as it is indisputably present— will always be more threatening in the eerie isolation of such settings. Here, the mostly silent creature whom Mark Helprin floats into our consciousness, thrown up out of nowhere and returning there soon after, must have his own vision of his circumstances.

But we are given little help in imagining it.

⟳

THESE LETTERS WERE recovered in good condition from the vault of the sunken *Samantha*, an iron-hulled sailing ship of one thousand tons, built in Scotland in 1879 and wrecked during the First World War in the Persian Gulf off Basra.

20 August, 1909, 20° 14' 18" S,
43" 51' 57" E
Off Madagascar

Dear Sir:

Many years have passed since I joined the Green Star Line. You may note in your records and logs, if not, indeed, by memory, the complete absence of disciplinary action against me. During my command, the Samantha has been a trim ship on time. Though my subordinates sometimes complain, they are grateful, no doubt, for my firm rule and tidiness. It saves the ship in storms, keeps them healthy, and provides good training—even though they will be masters of steamships.

No other vessel of this line has been as punctual or well run. Even today we are a week ahead and our Madagascar wood will reach Alexandria early. Bound for London, the crew are happy, and though we sail the Mozambique Channel, they act as if we had just caught sight of Margate. There are no problems on this ship. But I must in conscience report an irregular incident for which I am ready to take full blame.

Half a day out of Androka, we came upon a sea so blue and casual that its waters seemed fit to drink. Though the wind was slight and we made poor time, we were elated by perfect climate and painter's colors, for off the starboard side Madagascar rose as green and tranquil as a well-watered palm, its mountains engraved by thrashing fresh-water streams which beat down to the coast. A sweet upwelling breeze blew steadily from shore and confounded our square sails. Twenty minutes after noon, the lookout sighted a tornado on land. In the ship's glass I saw it, horrifying and enormous. Though at a great distance, its column appeared as thick as a massive tree on an islet in an atoll, and stretched at least seventy degrees upward from the horizon.

I have seen these pipes of windy fleece before. If there is sea nearby, they rush to it. So did this. When it became not red and black from soil and debris but silver and green from the water it drew, I began to tighten ship. Were the typhoon to have struck us directly, no preparation would have saved us. But what a shame to be swamped by high waves, or to be dismasted by beaten sea and wind. Hatches were battened as if for storm, minor sails furled, and the mainsail driven down half.

It moved back and forth over the sea in illegible patterning, as if tacking to changing winds. To our dismay, the distance narrowed.

We were afraid, though every man on deck wanted to see it, to feel it, perhaps to ride its thick swirling waters a hundred times higher than our mast—higher than the peaks inland. I confess that I have wished to be completely taken up by such a thing, to be lifted into the clouds, arms and legs pinned in the stream. The attraction is much like that of phosphorescent seas, when glowing light and smooth swell are dangerously magnetic even for hardened masters of good ships. I have wanted to surrender to plum-colored seas, to know what one might find there naked and alone. But I have not, and will not.

Finally, we began to run rough water. The column was so high that we bent our heads to see its height, and the sound was greater than any engine, causing masts and spars to resonate like cords. Waves broke over the prow. Wind pushed us on, and the curl of the sea rushed to fill the depression of the waters. No more than half a mile off the starboard bow, the column veered to the west, crossing our path to head for Africa as rapidly as an express. Within minutes, we could not even see it.

As it crossed our bows, I veered in the direction from which it had come. It seemed to communicate a decisiveness of course, and here I took opportunity to evade. In doing so we came close to land. This was dangerous not only for the presence of reefs and shoals but because of the scattered debris. Trees as tall as masts and much thicker, roots sucked clean, lay in puzzlement upon the surface. Brush and vines were everywhere. The water was reddish brown from earth which had fallen from the cone. We were meticulously careful in piloting through this fresh salad, as a good ram against a solid limb would have been the end. Our cargo is hardwoods, and would have sunk us like granite. I myself straddled the sprit stays, pushing aside small logs with a boat hook and calling out trim to the wheel.

Nearly clear, we came upon a clump of tangled vegetation. I could not believe my eyes, for floating upon it was a large monkey, bolt upright and dignified. I sighted him first, though the lookout called soon after. On impulse, I set trim for the wavy mat and, as we smashed into it, offered the monkey an end of the boat hook.

When he seized it I was almost pulled in, for his weight is nearly equal to mine. I observed that he had large teeth, which appeared both white and sharp. He came close, and then took to the lines until he sat high on the topgallant. As he passed, his foot cuffed my shoulder and I could smell him.

My ship is a clean ship. I regretted immediately my gesture with the hook. We do not need the mysterious defecations of such a creature, or the threat of him in the rigging at night. But we could not capture him to throw him back into the sea and, even had we collared him, might not have been able to get him overboard without danger to ourselves. We are now many miles off the coast. It is dark, and he sits high off the deck. The night watch is afraid and requests that I fell him with my rifle. They have seen his sharp teeth, which he displays with much screaming and gesticulating when they near him in the rigging. I think he is merely afraid, and I cannot bring myself to shoot him. I realize that no animals are allowed on board and have often had to enforce this rule when coming upon a parrot or cat hidden belowdecks where some captains do not go. But this creature we have today removed from the sea is like a man, and he has ridden the typhoon. Perhaps we will pass a headland and throw him overboard on a log. He must eventually descend for want of food. Then we will have our way. I will report further when the matter is resolved, and assure you that I regret this breach of regulations.

Yours & etc.,
Samson Low
Master, S/V Samantha

23 August, 1909, 10° 43' 3" S,
49° 5' 27" E
South of the Seychelles

Dear Sir:

We have passed the Channel and are heading north-northeast, hoping to ride the summer monsoon. It is shamefully hot, though the breeze is less humid than usual. Today two men dropped from the heat but they resumed work by evening. Because we are on a homeward tack, morale is at its best, or rather would be were it not for that damned ape in the rigging. He has not come down, and we have left behind his island and its last headland. He will have to have descended by the time we breach passage between Ras Asir and Jazirat Abd al-Kuri. The mate has suggested that there we throw him into the sea on a raft, which the carpenter has already set about building. He has embarked upon this with my permission, since there is little else for him to do. It has been almost an overly serene voyage and the typhoon caused no damage.

The raft he designed is very clever and has become a popular subject of discussion. It is about six feet by three feet, constructed of spare pine dunnage we were about to cast away when the typhoon was sighted. On each side is an outrigger for stability in the swell. In the center is a box, in which is a seat. Flanking this box are several smaller ones for fruit, biscuit, and a bucket of fresh water, in case the creature should drift a long time on the sea. This probably will not be so; the currents off Ras Asir drive for the beach, and we have noted that dunnage is quickly thrown upon the strand. Nevertheless, the crew have added their own touch—a standard distress flag flying from a ten-foot switch. They do not know, but I will order it replaced by a banner of another color, so that a hapless ship will not endanger itself to rescue a speechless monkey.

The crew have divided into two factions—those who wish to have the monkey shot, and those who would wait for him to descend and then put him in his boat. I am with the latter, since I would be the huntsman, and have already mentioned my lack of enthusiasm for this. A delegation of the first faction protested. They claimed that the second faction comprised those who stayed on deck, that the creature endangered balance in the rigging, and that he produced an uncanny effect in his screeching and bellicose silhouettes, which from below are humorous but which at close range, they said, are disconcerting and terrifying.

Since I had not seen him for longer than a moment and wanted to verify their complaint, I went up. Though sixty years of age, I did not use the bosun's chair, and detest those masters who do. It is pharaonic, and smacks of days in my father's youth when he saw with his own eyes gentlemen in sedan chairs carried about the city. The sight of twenty men laboring to hoist a ship's rotund captain is simply Egyptian, and I will not have it. Seventy feet off the deck, a giddy height to which I have not ascended in years, I came even with the ape. The ship was passing a boisterous sea and had at least a twenty-degree roll, which flung the two of us from side to side like pendula.

I am not a naturalist, nor have we on board a book of zoology, so the most I can do is to describe him. He is almost my height (nearly five feet ten inches) and appears to be sturdily built. Feet and hands are human in appearance except that they have a bulbous, skew, arthritic look common to monkeys. He is muscular and covered with fine reddish-brown hair. One can see the whiteness of his tendons when he stretches an arm or leg. I have mentioned the sharp, dazzling white teeth, set in rows like a trap, canine and pointed. His face is curiously delicate, and covered with orange hair leading to a snow-white crown of fur. My breath nearly failed when I looked into his eyes, for they are a bright, penetrating blue.

At first, he began to scream and swing as if he would come at me. If he had, I would have fared badly. The sailors fear him, for there is no man on board with half his strength, no man on the sea with a tenth his agility in the ropes, and if there is a man with the glacierlike pinnacled teeth, then he must be in a Scandinavian or Eastern European circus, for there they are fond of such things. To my surprise, he stopped his pantomime and, with a gentle and quizzical tilt of the head, looked me straight in the eyes. I had been sure that as a man I could answer his gaze as if from infallibility, and I calmly looked back. But he had me. His eyes unset me, so that I nearly shook. From that moment, he has not threatened or bared his teeth, but merely rests near the top of the foremast. The crew have attributed his conversion to my special power. This is flattering, though not entirely, as it assumes my ability to commune with an ape. Little do they suspect that it is I and not the monkey who have been converted, although to what I do not know. I am still thoroughly ashamed of my indiscretion and the trouble arising from it. We will get him and put him adrift off Ras Asir.

This evening, the cook grilled up some beef. I had him thoroughly vent the galley and use a great many herbs. The aroma was maddening. I sat in near-hypnotic ease in a canvas chair on the quarterdeck, a glass of wine in hand, as the heat fell to a cool breeze. We are all sunburnt and have been working hard, as the ape silently watches, to trim regularly and catch the best winds. We are almost in the full swift of the monsoon, and shortly will ride it in all its speed. It was wonderful to sit on deck and smell the herb-laden meat. The sea itself must have been jealous. I had several men ready with cargo net and pikes, certain that he would come down. We stared up at him as if he were the horizon, waiting. He smelled the food and agitated back and forth. Though he fretted, he did not descend. Even when we ate we saw him shunting to and fro on a yardarm. We left a dish for him away from us but he did not venture to seize it. If he had, we would have seized him.

From his impatience, I predict that tomorrow he will surrender to his stomach. Then we will catch him and this problem will be solved. I truly regret such an irregularity, though it would be worthwhile if he could only tell us how far he was lifted inside the silvered cone. And what it was like.

Yours & etc.,
Samson Low

25 August, 1909, 2° 13' 10" N,
51° 15' 17" E
Off Mogadishu

Dear Sir:

Today he came down. After the last correspondence, it occurred to me that he might be vegetarian, and that though he was hungry,

the meat had put him off. Therefore, I searched my memory for the
most aromatic vegetable dish I know. In your service as a fourth
officer, I called at Jaffa port, in Palestine, in January of 1873. We
went up to Sfat, a holy town high in the hills, full of Jews and
Arabs, quiet and mystical. There were so many come into that
freezing velvet dome of stars that all hostelries were full. I and
several others paid a small sum for private lodging and board. At
two in the morning, after we had returned from Mt. Jermak, the
Arabs made a hot lively fire from bundles of dry cyprus twigs, and
in a great square iron pan heated local oil and herbs, in which they
fried thick sections of potato. I have never eaten so well. Perhaps it
was our hunger, the cold, the silence, being high in the mountains
at Sfat, where air is like ether and all souls change. Today I made
the cook follow that old receipt.

We had been in the monsoon for several hours, and the air was
littered with silver sparks—apparitions of heat from a glittering
afternoon. Though the sun was low, iron decks could not be tread.
In the rigging, he appeared nearly finished, limp and slouching, an
arm hanging without energy, his back bent. We put potatoes in a
dish on the forecastle. He descended slowly, finally touching deck
lightly and ambling to the bows like a spider, all limbs brushing the
planks. He ate his fill, and we threw the net over him. We had
expected a ferocious struggle, but his posture and expression were so
peaceful that I ordered the net removed. Sailors stood ready with
pikes, but he stayed in place. Then I approached him and extended
my hand as if to a child.

In imitation, he put out his arm, looking much less fearsome.
Without a show of teeth, in his tired state, crouched on all fours
to half our heights, he was no more frightening than a hound. I
led him to the stern and back again while the crew cheered and
laughed. Then the mate took him, and then the entire hierarchy
of the ship, down to the cabin boys, who are smaller than he
and seemed to interest him the most. By dark, he had strolled
with every member of the crew and was miraculously tame. But
I remembered his teeth, and had him chained to his little boat.

He was comfortable there, surrounded by fruit and water
(which he ate and drank methodically) and sitting on a throne of
sorts, with half a dozen courtiers eager to look in his eyes and hold
his obliging wrist. Mine is not the only London post in which he
will be mentioned. Those who can write are describing him with
great zeal. I have seen some of these letters. He has been portrayed
as a "mad baboon," a "man-eating gorilla of horrible colors,
muscled but as bright as a bird," a "pygmy man set down on the sea
by miracle and typhoon," and as all manner of Latin names, each
different from the others and incorrectly spelled.

Depending on the bend of the monsoon and whether it
continues to run strongly, we will pass Ras Asir in three days. I
thought of casting him off early but was implored to wait for the
Cape. I relented, and in doing so was made to understand why
those in command must stay by rules. I am sure, however, that my
authority is not truly diminished, and when the ape is gone I will
again tighten discipline.

I have already had the distress flag replaced by a green banner.
It flies over the creature on his throne. Though in splendor, he is in
chains and in three days' time will be on the sea once more.

Yours & etc.,
Samson Low

28 August, 1909, 12" 4' 39" N,
50° 1' 2" E
North of Ras Asir

Dear Sir:

A most alarming incident has occurred. I must report, though it
is among the worst episodes of my command. This morning, I
arose, expecting to put the ape over the side as we rounded Ras Asir
at about eleven. (The winds have been consistently excellent and a
northward breeze veering off the monsoon has propelled us as
steadily as an engine.) Going out on deck, I discovered that his boat

was nowhere to be seen. At first, I thought that the mate had already disposed of him, and was disappointed that we were far from the coast. Then, to my shock, I saw him sitting unmanacled atop the main cargo hatch.

I screamed at the mate, demanding to know what had happened to the throne (as it had come to be called). He replied that it had gone overboard during the twelve-to-four watch. I stormed below and got that watch out in a hurry. Though sleepy-eyed, they were terrified. I told them that if the guilty one did not come forth I would put them all in irons. My temper was short and I could have struck them down. Two young sailors, as frightened as if they were surrendering themselves to die, admitted that they had thrown it over. They said they did not want to see the ape put to drift.

They are in irons until we make Suez. Their names are Mulcahy and Esper, and their pay is docked until they are freed. As we rounded the Cape, cutting close in (for the waters there are deep), we could see that though the creature would have been immediately cast up on shore, the shore itself was barren and inhospitable, and surely he would have died there. My Admiralty chart does not detail the inland topography of this area and shows only a yellow tongue marked "Africa" thrusting into the Gulf of Aden.

I can throw him overboard now or later. I do not want to do it. I brought him on board in the first place. There is nothing with which to fashion another raft. We have many tons of wood below, but not a cubic foot of it is lighter than water. The wind is good and we are making for the Bab al-Mandab, where we will pass late tomorrow afternoon—after that, the frustrating run up the Red Sea to the Canal.

The mate suggests that we sell him to the Egyptians. But I am reluctant to make port with this in mind, as it would be a victory for the two in chains and in the eyes of many others. And we are not animal traders. If he leaves us at sea the effects of his presence will be invalidated, we will touch land with discipline restored, and I will have the option of destroying these letters, though everything

here has been entered in short form in the log. I have ordered him
not to be fed, but they cast him scraps. I must get back my proper
hold on the ship.

> Yours & etc.,
> Samson Low

30 August, 1909, 15° 49' 30" N,
41° 5' 32" E
Red Sea off Massawa

Dear Sir:

I have been felled by an attack of headaches. Never before has
this happened. There is pressure in my skull enough to burst it. I
cannot keep my balance; my eyes roam and I am drunk with pain.
For the weary tack up the Red Sea I have entrusted the mate with
temporary command, retiring to my cabin with the excuse of heat
prostration. I have been in the Red Sea time and again but have
never felt apprehension that death would follow its heat. We have
always managed. To the east, the mountains of the Hijaz are so dry
and forbidding that I have seen sailors look away in fright.

The ape has begun to suffer from the heat. He is listless and
ignored. His novelty has worn off (with the heat as it is) and no
one pays him any attention. He will not go belowdecks, but spends
most of the day under the canvas sun shield, chewing slowly,
though there is nothing in his mouth. It is hot there—the light so
white and uncompromising it sears the eyes. I have freed his
champions from irons and restored their pay. By this act I have won
over the crew and caused the factions to disappear. No one thinks
about the ape. But I dare not risk a recurrence of bad feeling and
have decided to cast him into the sea. Where we found him, a
strong seaward current would have carried him to the open ocean.
Here, at least, he can make the shore, although it is the most barren
coast on earth. But who would have thought he might survive the
typhoon? He has been living beyond his time. To be picked up and

whirled at incomprehensible speed, carried for miles above the earth where no man has ever been, and thrown into the sea is a death sentence. If he survived that, perhaps he can survive Arabian desert.

His expression is neither sad nor fierce. He looks like an old man, neutral to the world. In the last two days he has become the target of provocation and physical blows. I have ordered this stopped, but a sailor will sometimes throw a nail or a piece of wood at him. We shall soon be rid of him.

Yesterday we came alongside another British ship, the Stonepool, of the Dutch Express Line. On seeing the ape, they were envious. What is it, their captain asked, amazed at its coloring. I replied that he was a Madagascar ape we had fished from the sea, and I offered him to them, saying he was as tame as a dog. At first, they wanted him. The crew cried out for his acceptance, but the captain demurred, shaking his head and looking into my eyes as if he were laughing at me. "Damn!" I said, and went below without even a salute at parting.

My head aches. I must stop. At first light tomorrow, I will toss him back.

> Yours & etc.,
> Samson Low

3 September, 1909
Suez

Dear Sir:

The morning before last I went on deck at dawn. The ape was sitting on the main hatch, his eyes upon me from the moment I saw him. I walked over to him and extended my arm, which he would not take in his customary manner. I seized his wrist, which he withdrew. However, as he did this I laid hold of the other wrist, and pulled him off the hatch. He did not bare his teeth. He began to scream. Awakened by this, most of the crew stood in the companionways or on deck, silently observing.

He was hard to drag, but I towed him to the rail. When I took his other arm to hoist him over, he bared his teeth with a frightening shriek. Everyone was again terrified. The teeth must be six inches long.

He came at me with those teeth, and I could do nothing but throttle him. With my hands on his throat, his arms were free. He grasped my side. I felt the pads of his hands against my ribs. I had to tolerate that awful sensation to keep hold of his throat. No man aboard came close. He shrieked and moaned. His eyes reddened. My response was to tighten my hold, to end the horror. I gripped so hard that my own teeth were bared and I made sounds similar to his. He put his hands around my neck as if to strangle me back, but I had already taken the inside position and, despite his great strength, lessened the power of his grip merely by lifting my arms against his. Nevertheless he choked me. But I had a great head start. We held this position for long minutes, sweating, until his arms dropped and his body convulsed. In rage, I threw him by the neck into the sea, where he quickly sank.

Some of the crew have begun to talk about him as if he were about to be canonized. Others see him as evil. I assembled them as the coasts began to close on Suez and the top of the sea was white and still. I made my views clear, for in years of command and in a life on the sea I have learned much. I felt confident of what I told them.

He is not a symbol. He stands neither for innocence nor for evil. There is no parable and no lesson in his coming and going. I was neither right nor wrong in bringing him aboard (though it was indeed incorrect) or in what I later did. We must get on with the ship's business. He does not stand for a man or men. He stands for nothing. He was an ape, simian and lean, half sensible. He came on board, and now he is gone.

Yours & etc.,
Samson Low

THE BOX

JACK KETCHUM

Children, naturally curious, are perpetually at odds with adults, schooled in the life lessons of keeping a safe distance. And the eventual indulgence of a kid's stubborn desire to see, to know, to experience something new, is equally natural. How else do they learn? one reasons, giving in. Shrugging: it's harmless.

But what if it's not?

And never, never will be.

Jack Ketchum paints a trompe l'oeil picture of a split second of deadly menace that to any onlooker will resemble a moment much like any other. Arising vaporously out of the hectic cheer of a Christmas shopping expedition, it's a now-you-see-it-now-you-don't situation, but with an added twist to make sure our unease is chronic, not acute.

⟳

W HAT'S IN THE box?" my son said.
"Danny," I said. "Leave the man alone."
It was two Sundays before Christmas and the Stamford local was packed—shoppers lined aisles and we were lucky to have found seats. The man sat facing my daughters Clarissa and Jenny and me,

the three of us squeezed together across from him and Danny in the seat beside him.

I could understand my son's curiosity. The man was holding the red square gift box in his lap as though afraid that the Harrison stop, coming up next, might jolt it from his grasp. He'd been clutching it that way for three stops now—since he got on.

He was tall, perhaps six feet or more and maybe twenty pounds overweight and he was perspiring heavily despite the cold dry air rushing over us each time the train's double doors opened behind our backs. He had a black walrus mustache and sparse thinning hair and wore a tan Burberry raincoat that had not been new for many years now over a rumpled grey business suit. I judged the pant-legs to be an inch too short for him. The socks were grey nylon, a much lighter shade than the suit, and the elastic in the left one was shot so that it bunched up over his ankle like the skin of one of those ugly pug-nosed pedigree dogs that are so trendy nowadays. The man smiled at Danny and looked down at the box, shiny red paper over cardboard about two feet square.

"Present," he said. Looking not at Danny but at me.

His voice had the wet phlegmy sound of a heavy smoker. Or maybe he had a cold.

"Can I see?" Danny said.

I knew exactly where all of this was coming from. It's not easy spending a day in New York with two nine-year-old girls and a seven-year-old boy around Christmas time when they know there is such a thing as FAO Schwarz only a few blocks away. Even if you *have* taken them to the matinee at Radio City and then skating at Rockefeller Center. Even if all their presents had been bought weeks ago and were sitting under our bed waiting to be put beneath the tree. There was always something they hadn't thought of yet that Schwartz *had* thought of and they knew that perfectly well. I'd had to fight with them—with Danny in particular—to get them aboard the 3:55 back to Rye in time for dinner.

But presents were still on his mind.

"Danny . . ."

"It's okay," said the man. "No problem." He glanced out the window. We were just pulling in to the Harrison Station.

He opened the lid of the box on Danny's side, not all the way open but only about three inches—enough for him to see but not the rest of us, excluding us three—and I watched my son's face brighten at that, smiling, as he looked first at Clarissa and Jenny as if to say *nyah nyah* and then looked down into the box.

The smile was slow to vanish. But it did vanish, fading into a kind of puzzlement. I had the feeling that there was something in there that my son did not understand—not at all. The man let him look a while but his bewildered expression did not change and then he closed the box.

"Gotta go," the man said. "My stop."

He walked past us and his seat was taken immediately by a middle-aged woman carrying a pair of heavy shopping bags which she placed on the floor between her feet—and then I felt the cold December wind at my back as the double-doors slid open and closed again. Presumably the man was gone. Danny looked at the woman's bags and said shyly, "Presents?"

The woman looked at him and nodded, smiling.

He elected to question her no further.

The train rumbled on.

Our own stop was next. We walked out into the wind on the Rye platform and headed clanging down the metal steps.

"What did he have?" asked Clarissa.

"Who?" said Danny.

"The man, dummy," said Jenny. "The man with the box! What was in the *box*?"

"Oh. Nothing."

"Nothing? What? It was *empty*?"

And then they were running along ahead of me toward our car off to the left in the second row of the parking lot.

I couldn't hear his answer. If he answered her at all.

And by the time I unlocked the car I'd forgotten all about the guy.

★ ★ ★

That night Danny wouldn't eat.

It happened sometimes. It happened with each of the kids. Other things to do or too much snacking during the day. Both my wife Susan and I had been raised in homes where a depression-era mentality still prevailed. If you didn't like or didn't want to finish your dinner that was just too bad. You sat there at the table, your food getting colder and colder, until you pretty much cleaned the plate. We'd agreed that we weren't going to lay that on *our* kids. And most of the experts these days seemed to agree with us that skipping the occasional meal didn't matter. And certainly wasn't worth fighting over.

So we excused him from the table.

The next night—Monday night—same thing.

"What'd you do," my wife asked him, "have six desserts for lunch?" She was probably half serious. Desserts and pizza were pretty much all our kids could stomach on the menu at the school cafeteria.

"Nope. Just not hungry, that's all."

We let it go at that.

I kept an eye on him during the night, though—figuring he'd be up in the middle of a commercial break in one of our Monday-night sitcoms, headed for the kitchen and a bag of pretzels or a jar of honey-roasted peanuts or some dry fruit loops out of the box. But it never happened. He went to bed without so much as a glass of water. Not that he looked sick or anything. His color was good and he laughed at the jokes right along with the rest of us.

I figured he was coming down with something. So did Susan. He almost had to be. Our son normally had the appetite of a sumo wrestler.

I fully expected him to beg off school in the morning, pleading headache or upset stomach.

He didn't.

And he didn't want his breakfast, either.

And the next night, same thing.

Now this was particularly strange because Susan had cooked spaghetti and meat sauce that night and there was nothing in her considerable repertoire that the kids liked better. Even though—maybe because of the fact—that it was one of the simplest dishes she ever threw together. But Danny just sat there and said he wasn't hungry, contented to watch while everybody else heaped it on. I'd come home late after a particularly grueling day—I work for a brokerage firm in the City—and personally I was famished. And not a little unnerved by my son's repeated refusals to eat.

"Listen," I said. "You've got to have something. We're talking *three days* now."

"Did you eat lunch?" Susan asked.

Danny doesn't lie. "I didn't feel like it," he said.

Even Clarissa and Jenny were looking at him like he had two heads by now.

"But you *love* spaghetti," Susan said.

"Try some garlic bread," said Clarissa.

"No thanks."

"Do you *feel* okay, guy?" I asked him.

"I feel fine. I'm just not hungry's all."

So he sat there.

Wednesday night Susan went all out, making him his personal favorite—roast leg of lemon-spiced lamb with mint sauce, baked potato and red wine gravy, and green snap-peas on the side.

He sat there. Though he seemed to enjoy watching *us* eat.

Thursday night we tried takeout—Chinese food from his favorite Szechuan restaurant. Ginger beef, shrimp fried rice, fried wonton and sweet-and-sour ribs.

He said it smelled good. And sat there.

By Friday night whatever remnants of depression-era mentality lingered in my own personal psyche kicked in with a vengeance and I found myself standing there yelling at him, telling him he wasn't getting up from his chair, *young man,* until he finished at least *one slice* of his favorite pepperoni, meatball and sausage pizza from his favorite Italian restaurant.

The fact is I was worried. I'd have handed him a twenty, gladly, just to see some of that stringy mozzarella hanging off his chin. But I didn't tell him that. Instead I stood there pointing a finger at him and yelling until he started to cry—and then, second-generation Depression-brat that I am, I ordered him to bed. Which is exactly what my parents would have done.

Scratch a son, you always get his dad.

But by Sunday you could see his ribs through his tee shirt. We kept him out of school Monday and I stayed home from work so we could both be there for our appointment with Dr. Weller. Weller was one of the last of those wonderful old-fashioned GP's, the kind you just about never see anymore. Over seventy years old, he would still stop by your house after office hours if the need arose. In Rye that was as unheard-of as an honest mechanic. Weller believed in home-care, not hospitals. He'd fallen asleep on my sofa one night after checking in on Jenny's bronchitis and slept for two hours straight over an untouched cup of coffee while we tiptoed around him and listened to him snore.

We sat in his office Monday morning answering questions while he checked Danny's eyes, ears, nose and throat, tapped his knees, his back and chest, checked his breathing, took a vial of blood and sent him into the bathroom for a urine sample.

"He looks perfectly fine to me. He's lost five pounds since the last time he was in for a checkup but beyond that I can't see anything wrong with him. Of course we'll have to wait for the blood work. You say he's eaten *nothing?*"

"Absolutely nothing," Susan said.

He sighed. "Wait outside," he said. "Let me talk with him."

In the waiting room Susan picked up a magazine, looked at the cover and returned it to the pile. "*Why?*" she whispered.

An old man with a walker glanced over at us and then looked away. A mother across from us watched her daughter coloring in a Garfield book.

"I don't know," I said. "I wish I did."

I was aware sitting there of an odd detachment, as though this were happening to the rest of them—to them, not me—not *us*.

I have always felt a fundamental core of loneliness in me. Perhaps it comes from being an only child. Perhaps it's my grandfather's sullen thick German blood. I have been alone with my wife and alone with my children, untouchable, unreachable, and I suspect that most of the time they haven't known. It runs deep, this aloneness. I have accommodated it. It informs all my relationships and all my expectations. It makes me almost impossible to surprise by life's grimmer turns of fate.

I was very aware of it now.

Dr. Weller was smiling when he led Danny through the waiting room and asked him to have a seat for a moment while he motioned us inside. But the smile was for Danny. There was nothing real inside it.

We sat down.

"The most extraordinary thing." The doctor shook his head. "I told him he had to eat. He asked me why. I said, 'Danny, people die every day of starvation. All over the world. If you don't eat, you'll die—it's that simple.' Your son looked me straight in the eye and said, '*So?*'"

"Jesus," Susan said.

"He wasn't being flip, believe me—he was asking me a serious question. I said, 'Well, you want to live, don't you?' He said, '*Should* I?' Believe me, you could have knocked me right off this chair. '*Should* I!' I said, 'Of course you should! *Everybody* wants to live.'

"'*Why?*' he said.

"My God. I told him that life was beautiful, that life was sacred, that life was *fun*! Wasn't Christmas just around the corner? What about holidays and birthdays and summer vacations? I told him that it was everybody's duty to try to live life to the absolute fullest, to do everything you could in order to be as strong and healthy and happy as humanly possible. And he listened to me. He listened to me and I knew he understood me. He didn't seem the slightest bit worried about any of what I was saying or the slightest bit concerned or unhappy. And when I was done, all he said was, 'Yes—yes, but *I'm not hungry.*'"

The doctor looked amazed, confounded.

"I really don't know what to tell you." He picked up a pad. "I'm writing down the name and phone number of a psychotherapist. Not a psychiatrist, mind—this fellow isn't going to push any pills at Danny. A therapist. The only thing I can come up with pending some—to my way of thinking, practically unimaginable—problem with his blood work is that Danny has some very serious emotional problems that need exploring and need exploring immediately. This man Field is the best I know. And he's very good with children. Tell him I said to fit you in right away, today if at all possible. We go back a long time, he and I—he'll do as I ask. And I think he'll be able to help Danny."

"Help him do what, doctor?" Susan said. I could sense her losing it. "Help him do what?" she said. *"Find a reason for living?"*

Her voice broke on the last word and suddenly she was sobbing into her hands and I reached over and tried to contact that part of me which might be able to contact her and found it not entirely mute inside me, and held her.

In the night I heard them talking. Danny and the two girls.

It was late and we were getting ready for bed and Susan was in the bathroom brushing her teeth. I stepped out into the hall to go downstairs for one last cigarette from my pack in the kitchen and that was when I heard them whispering. The twins had their room and Danny had his. The whispering was coming from their room.

It was against the rules but the rules were rapidly going to hell these days anyway. Homework was being ignored. Breakfast was coffee and packaged donuts. For Danny, of course, not even that much. Bedtime arrived when we felt exhausted.

Dr. Field had told us that that was all right for a while. That we should avoid all areas of tension or confrontation within the family for at least the next week or so.

I was *not* to yell at Danny for not eating.

Field had spoken first to him for half an hour in his office and then, for another twenty minutes, to Susan and me. I found him personable and soft-spoken. As yet he had no idea what Danny's problem could be. The gist of what he was able to tell us was that he would need to see Danny every day until he started eating again and probably once or twice a week thereafter.

If he did start eating.

Anyhow, I'd decided to ignore the whispering. I figured if I'd stuck to my guns about quitting the goddamn cigarettes I'd never have heard it in the first place. But then something Jenny said sailed through the half-open door loud and clear and stopped me.

"I still don't get it," she said. "What's it got to do with that *box*?"

I didn't catch his answer. I walked to the door. A floorboard squeaked. The whispering stopped.

I opened it. They were huddled together on the bed.

"What's what got to do with *what* box?" I said.

They looked at me. My children, I thought, had grown up amazingly free of guilty conscience. Rules or no rules. In that they were not like me. There were times I wondered if they were actually my children at all.

"Nothing," Danny said.

"Nothing," said Clarissa and Jenny.

"Come on," I said. "Give. What were you guys just talking about?"

"Just stuff," said Danny.

"*Secret* stuff?" I was kidding, making it sound like it was no big deal.

He shrugged. "Just, you know, stuff."

"Stuff that maybe has to do with why you're not eating? That kind of stuff?"

"Daaaad."

I knew my son. He was easily as stubborn as I was. It didn't take a genius to know when you were not going to get anything further out of him and this was one of those times. "Okay," I said, "back to bed."

He walked past me. I glanced into the bedroom and saw the two girls sitting motionless, staring at me.

"What," I said.

"Nothing," said Clarissa.

"G'night, Daddy," said Jenny.

I said good night and went downstairs for my cigarettes. I smoked three of them. I wondered what this whole box business was.

The following morning my girls were not eating.

Things occurred rapidly then. By evening it became apparent that they were taking the same route Danny had taken. They were happy. They were content. And they could not be budged. To me, *we're not hungry* had suddenly become the scariest three words in the English language.

A variation became just as scary when, two nights later, sitting over a steaming baked lasagna she'd worked on all day long, Susan asked me how in the world I expected her to eat while all her children were starving.

And then ate nothing further.

I started getting takeout for one.

McDonald's. Slices of pizza. Buffalo wings from the deli.

By Christmas Day, Danny could not get out of bed unassisted.

The twins were looking gaunt—so was my wife.

There was no Christmas dinner. There wasn't any point to it.

I ate cold fried rice and threw a couple of ribs into the microwave and that was that.

Meantime Field was frankly baffled by the entire thing and told me he was thinking of writing a paper—did I mind? I didn't mind. I didn't care one way or another. Dr. Weller, who normally considered hospitals strictly a last resort, wanted to get Danny on an IV as soon as possible. He was ordering more blood tests. We asked if it could wait till after Christmas. He said it could but not a moment longer. We agreed.

Despite the cold fried rice and the insane circumstances Christmas was actually by far the very best day we'd had in a very long time. Seeing us all together, sitting by the fire, opening packages under the tree—it brought back memories. The cozy warmth of earlier days. It was almost, though certainly not quite, normal. For this day alone I could almost begin to forget my worries about them, forget that Danny would be going into the hospital the next morning—with the twins, no doubt, following pretty close behind. For her part Susan seemed to *have* no worries. It was as though in joining them in their fast she had also somehow partaken of their lack of concern for it. As though the fast were itself a drug.

I remember laughter from that day, plenty of laughter. Nobody's new clothes fit but my own but we tried them on anyway—there were jokes about the Amazing Colossal Woman and the Incredible Shrinking Man. And the toys and games all fit, and the brand-new hand-carved American-primitive angel I'd bought for the tree.

Believe it or not, we were happy.

But that night I lay in bed and thought about Danny in the hospital the next day and then for some reason about the whispered conversation I'd overheard that seemed so long ago and then about the man with the box and the day it had all begun. I felt like a fool, like somebody who was awakened from a long confused and confusing dream.

I suddenly had to know what *Danny* knew.

I got up and went to his room and shook him gently from his sleep.

I asked him if he remembered that day on the train and the man with the box and then looking into the box and he said that yes he did and then I asked him what was in it.

"Nothing," he said.

"Really *nothing*? You mean it was actually empty?"

He nodded.

"But didn't he . . . I remember him telling us it was a *present*."

He nodded again. I still didn't get it. It made no sense to me.

"So you mean it was some kind of joke or something? He was playing some kind of joke on somebody?"

"I don't know. It was just . . . the box was empty."

He looked at me as though it was impossible for him to understand why *I* didn't understand. Empty was empty. That was that.

I let him sleep. For his last night, in his own room.

I told you that things happened rapidly after that and they did, although it hardly seemed so at the time. Three weeks later my son smiled at me sweetly and slipped into a coma and died in just under thirty-two hours. It was unusual, I was told, for the IV not to have sustained a boy his age but sometimes it happened. By then the twins had beds two doors down the hall. Clarissa went on February 3rd and Jenny on February 5th.

My wife, Susan, lingered until the 27th.

And through all of this, through all these weeks now, going back and forth to the hospital each day, working when I was and *am* able and graciously being granted time off whenever I can't, riding into the City from Rye and from the City back to Rye again alone on the train, I look for him. I look through every car. I walk back and forth in case he should get on one stop sooner or one stop later. I don't want to miss him. I'm losing weight.

Oh, I'm eating. Not as well as I should be, I suppose, but I'm eating.

But I need to find him. To know what my son knew and then passed on to the others. I'm sure that the girls knew, that he passed it on to them that night in the bedroom—some terrible knowledge, some awful peace. And I think somehow, perhaps by being so very much closer to all of my children than I was ever capable of being, that Susan knew too. I'm convinced it's so.

I'm convinced that it was my essential loneliness that set me apart and saved me, and now of course which haunts me, makes me wander through dark corridors of commuter trains waiting for a glimpse of him—him and his damnable present, his gift, his box.

I want to know. It's the only way I can get close to them.

I want to see. I *have* to see.

I'm *hungry*.

AFTERWARD

EDITH WHARTON

If there is a story that inspired this collection, it is this one. Long ago, when I first read it, its parting revelation lodged in my mind as a truth that made sense of many situations.

Acceptance, however, is not remedy, and far too often we are all, as Edith Wharton realizes, unthinking attendants at the altar of our own tragedies.

ℭ

I

OH, THERE *IS* ONE, of course, but you'll never know it."

The assertion, laughingly flung out six months earlier in a bright June garden, came back to Mary Boyne with a new perception of its significance as she stood, in the December dusk, waiting for the lamps to be brought into the library.

The words had been spoken by their friend Alida Stair, as they sat at tea on her lawn at Pangbourne, in reference to the very house of which the library in question was the central, the pivotal "feature." Mary Boyne and her husband, in quest of a country place in one of the southern or southwestern counties, had, on their arrival in England, carried their problem straight to Alida Stair, who had successfully solved it in her own case, but it was not until they had rejected, almost capriciously, several practical and judicious suggestions that she threw out: "Well, there's Lyng, in Dorsetshire. It belongs to Hugo's cousins, and you can get it for a song."

The reason she gave for its being obtainable on these terms—its remoteness from a station, its lack of electric light, hot water pipes, and other vulgar necessities—were exactly those pleading in its favor with two romantic Americans perversely in search of the economic drawbacks which were associated, in their tradition, with unusual architectural felicities.

"I should never believe I was living in an old house unless I was thoroughly uncomfortable," Ned Boyne, the more extravagant of the two, had jocosely insisted; "the least hint of convenience would make me think it had been bought out of an exhibition, with the pieces numbered. And set up again." And they had proceeded to enumerate, with humorous precision, their various doubts and demands, refusing to believe that the house their cousin recommended was *really* Tudor till they learned it had no heating system, or that the village church was literally in the grounds till she assured them of the deplorable uncertainty of the water supply.

"It's too uncomfortable to be true!" Edward Boyne had continued to exult as the avowal of each disadvantage was successively wrung from her; but he had cut short his rhapsody to ask, with a relapse to distrust: "And the ghost? You've been concealing from us the fact that there is no ghost!"

Mary, at the moment, had laughed with him, yet almost with her laugh, being possessed of several sets of independent perceptions, had been struck by a note of flatness in Alida's answering hilarity.

"Oh, Dorsetshire's full of ghosts, you know."

"Yes, yes; but that won't do. I don't want to have to drive ten miles to see somebody else's ghost. I want one of my own on the premises. *Is* there a ghost at Lyng?"

His rejoinder had made Alida laugh again, and it was then that she had flung back tantalizingly: "Oh, there *is* one, of course, but you'll never know it."

"Never know it?" Boyne pulled her up. "But what in the world constitutes a ghost except the fact of its being known for one?"

"I can't say. But that's the story."

"That there's a ghost, but that nobody knows it's a ghost?"

"Well—not till afterward, at any rate."

"Till afterward?"

"Not till long long afterward."

"But if it's once been identified as an unearthly visitant, why hasn't it *signalement* been handed down in the family? How has it managed to preserve its incognito?"

Alida could only shake her head. "Don't ask me. But it has."

"And then suddenly"—Mary spoke up as if from cavernous depths of divination—"suddenly, long afterward, one says to one's self *'That was it?'*"

She was startled at the sepulchral sound with which her question fell on the banter of the other two, and she saw the shadow of the same surprise flit across Alida's pupils. "I suppose so. One just has to wait."

"Oh, hang waiting!" Ned broke in. "Life's too short for a ghost who can only be enjoyed in retrospect. Can't we do better than that, Mary?"

But it turned out that in the event they were not destined to, for within three months of their conversation with Mrs. Stair they were settled at Lyng, and the life they had yearned for, to the point of planning it in advance in all its daily details, had actually begun for them.

It was to sit, in the thick December dusk, by just such a wide-hooded fireplace, under just such black oak rafters, with the sense that beyond the mullioned panes the downs were darkened to a deeper solitude: it was for the ultimate indulgence of such sensations that Mary Boyne, abruptly exiled from New York by her husband's business, had endured for nearly fourteen years the soul-deadening ugliness of a Middle Western town, and that Boyne had ground on doggedly at his engineering till, with a suddenness that still made her blink, the prodigious windfall of the Blue Star Mine had put them at a stroke in possession of life and the leisure to taste it. They had never for a moment meant their new state to be one of idleness; but they meant to give themselves only to harmonious activities. She had her vision of painting and gardening (against a background of grey walls), he dreamed of the production of his long-planned book on the "Economic Basis of Culture"; and with such absorbing work ahead no existence could be too sequestered: they could not get far enough from the world, or plunge deep enough into the past.

Dorsetshire had attracted them from the first by an air of remoteness out of all proportion to its geographical position. But to the Boynes it was one of the ever-recurring wonders of the whole incredibly compressed island—a nest of counties, as they put it— that for the production of its effects so little of a given quality went so far: that so few miles made a distance, and so short a distance a difference.

"It's that," Ned had once enthusiastically explained, "that gives such depth to their effects, such relief to their contrasts. They've been able to lay the butter so thick on every delicious mouthful."

The butter had certainly been laid on thick at Lyng: the old house hidden under a shoulder of the downs had almost all the finer marks of commerce with a protracted past. The mere fact that it was neither large nor exceptional made it, to the Boynes, abound the more completely in its special charm—the charm of having been for centuries a deep dim reservoir of life. The life had probably not been of the most vivid order: for long periods, no doubt, it had fallen as noiselessly into the past as the quiet drizzle of autumn fell, hour after hour, into the fish pond between the yews; but these backwaters of existence sometimes breed, in their sluggish depths, strange acuities of emotion, and Mary Boyne had felt from the first the mysterious stir of intenser memories.

The feeling had never been stronger than on this particular afternoon when, waiting in the library for the lamps to come, she rose from her seat and stood among the shadows of the hearth. Her husband had gone off, after luncheon, for one of his long tramps on the downs. She had noticed of late that he preferred to go alone; and, in the tried security of their personal relations, had been driven to conclude that his book was bothering him, and that he needed the afternoons to turn over in solitude the problems left from the morning's work. Certainly the book was not going as smoothly as she had thought it would, and there were lines of perplexity between his eyes such as had never been there in his engineering days. He had often, then, looked fagged to the verge of illness, but the native demon of worry had never branded his brow. Yet the few pages he had so far read to her—the introduction, and a summary of the opening chapter—showed a firm hold on his subject, and an increasing confidence in his powers.

The fact threw her into deeper perplexity, since, now that he had done with business and its disturbing contingencies, the one other possible source of anxiety was eliminated. Unless it were his health, then? But physically he had gained since they had come to Dorsetshire, grown robuster, ruddier and fresher eyed. It was only within the last week that she had felt in him the undefinable change which made her restless in his absence, and as tongue-tied in his presence as though it were *she* who had a secret to keep from him!

The thought that there *was* a secret somewhere between them struck her with a sudden rap of wonder, and she looked about her down the long room.

"Can it be the house?" she mused.

The room itself might have been full of secrets. They seemed to be piling themselves up, as evening fell, like the layers and layers of velvet shadow dropping from the low ceiling, the rows of books, the smoke-blurred sculpture of the hearth.

"Why, of course—the house is haunted!" she reflected.

The ghost—Alida's imperceptible ghost—after figuring largely in the banter of their first month or two at Lyng, had been gradually left aside as too ineffectual for imaginative use. Mary had, indeed, as became the tenant of a haunted house, made the customary inquiries among her rural neighbors, but, beyond a vague "They do say so, Ma'am," the villagers had nothing to impart. The elusive specter had apparently never had sufficient identity for a legend to crystallize about it, and after a time the Boynes had set the matter down to their profit-and-loss account, agreeing that Lyng was one of the few houses good enough in itself to dispense with supernatural enhancements.

"And I suppose, poor ineffectual demon, that's why it beats its beautiful wings in vain in the void," Mary had laughingly concluded.

"Or, rather," Ned answered in the same strain, "why, amid so much that's ghostly, it can never affirm its separate existence as *the* ghost." And thereupon their invisible housemate had finally dropped out of their references, which were numerous enough to make them soon unaware of the loss.

Now, as she stood on the hearth, the subject of their earlier curiosity revived in her with a new sense of its meaning—a sense gradually acquired through daily contact with the scene of the lurking mystery. It was the house itself, of course, that possessed the ghost-seeing faculty, that communed visually but secretly with its own past; if one could only get into close enough communion with the house, one might surprise its secret, and acquire the ghost sight on one's own account. Perhaps, in his long hours in this very room, where she never trespassed till the afternoon, her husband *had* acquired it already, and was silently carrying about the weight of whatever it had revealed to him. Mary was too well versed in the code of the spectral world not to know that one could not talk about the ghosts one saw: to do so was almost as great a breach of taste as to name a lady in a club. But this explanation did not really satisfy her. "What, after all, except for the fun of the shudder," she reflected, "would he really care for any of their old ghosts?" And thence she was thrown back once more on the fundamental dilemma: the fact that one's greater or less susceptibility to spectral influences had no particular bearing on the case, since, when one *did* see a ghost at Lyng, one did not know it.

"Not till long afterward," Alida Stair had said. Well, supposing Ned had seen one when they first came, and had known only within the last week what had happened to him? More and more under the spell of the hour, she threw back her thoughts to the early days of their tenancy, but at first only to recall a lively confusion of unpacking, settling, arranging of books, and calling to each other from remote corners of the house as, treasure after treasure, it revealed itself to them. It was in this particular connection that she presently recalled a certain soft afternoon of the previous October, when, passing from the rapturous flurry of exploration to a detailed inspection of the old house, she had pressed (like a novel heroine) a panel that opened on a flight of corkscrew stairs leading to a flat ledge of the roof—the roof which, from below, seemed to slope away on all sides too abruptly for any but practiced feet to scale.

The view from this hidden coign was enchanting, and she had flown down to snatch Ned from his papers and give him the freedom of her discovery. She remembered still how, standing at her side, he had passed his arm about her while their gaze flew to the long tossed horizon line of the downs, and then dropped contentedly back to trace the arabesque of yew hedges about the fish pond, and the shadow of the cedar on the lawn.

"And now the other way," he had said, turning her about within his arm, and closely pressed to him, she had absorbed, like some long satisfying draught, the picture of the grey-walled court, the squat lions on the gates, and the lime avenue reaching up to the highroad under the downs.

It was just then, while they gazed and held each other, that she had felt his arm relax, and heard a sharp "Hullo!" that made her turn to glance at him.

Distinctly, yes, she now recalled that she had seen, as she glanced, a shadow of anxiety, of perplexity, rather, fall across his face; and, following his eyes, had beheld the figure of a man—a man in loose greyish clothes, as it appeared to her—who was sauntering down the lime avenue to the court with the doubtful gait of a stranger who seeks his way. Her shortsighted eyes had given her but a blurred impression of slightness and greyishness, with something foreign, or at least unlocal, in the cut of the figure or its dress; but her husband had apparently seen more—seen enough to make him push past her with a hasty "Wait!" and dash down the stairs without pausing to give her a hand.

A slight tendency to dizziness obliged her, after a provisional clutch at the chimney against which they had been leaning, to follow him first more cautiously; and when she had reached the landing she paused again, for a less definite reason, leaning over the banister to strain her eyes through the silence of the brown sun-flecked depths. She lingered there till, somewhere in those depths, she heard the closing of a door; then, mechanically impelled, she went down the shallow flights of steps till she reached the lower hall.

The front door stood open on the sunlight of the court, and hall and court were empty. The library door was open, too, and after listening in vain for any sound of voices within, she crossed the threshold, and found her husband alone, vaguely fingering the papers on his desk.

He looked up, as if surprised at her entrance, but the shadow of anxiety had passed from his face, leaving it even, as she fancied, a little brighter and clearer than usual.

"What was it? Who was it?" she asked.

"Who?" he repeated, with the surprise still all on his side.

"The man we saw coming toward the house."

He seemed to reflect. "The man? Why, I thought I saw Peters; I dashed after him to say a word about the stable drains, but he had disappeared before I could get down."

"Disappeared? But he seemed to be walking so slowly when we saw him."

Boyne shrugged his shoulders. "So I thought; but he must have got up steam in the interval. What do you say to our trying a scramble up Meldon Steep before sunset?"

That was all. At the time the occurrence had been less than nothing, had, indeed, been immediately obliterated by the magic of their first vision from Meldon Steep, a height which they had dreamed of climbing ever since they had first seen its bare spine rising above the roof of Lyng. Doubtless it was the mere fact of the other incident's having occurred on the very day of their ascent to Meldon that had kept it stored away in the fold of memory from which it now emerged; for in itself it had no mark of the portentous. At the moment there could have been nothing more natural than that Ned should dash himself from the roof in the pursuit of dilatory tradesmen. It was the period when they were always on the watch for one or the other of the specialists employed about the place; always lying in wait for them, and rushing out at them with questions, reproaches or reminders. And certainly in the distance the grey figure had looked like Peters.

Yet now, as she reviewed the scene, she felt her husband's explanation of it to have been invalidated by the look of anxiety on his face. Why had the familiar appearance of Peters made him anxious? Why, above all, if it was of such prime necessity to confer with him on the subject of the stable drains, had the failure to find him produced such a look of relief? Mary could not say that any one of these questions had occurred to her at the time, yet, from the promptness with which they now marshalled themselves at her summons, she had a sense that they must all along have been there, waiting their hour.

II

Weary with her thoughts, she moved to the window. The library was now quite dark, and she was surprised to see how much faint light the outer world still held.

As she peered out into it across the court, a figure shaped itself far down the perspective of bare limes: it looked a mere blot of deeper grey in the greyness, and for an instant, as it moved toward her, her heart thumped to the thought "It's the ghost!"

She had time, in that long instant, to feel suddenly that the man of whom, two months earlier, she had had a distant vision from the roof, was now, at his predestined hour, about to reveal himself as *not* having been Peters; and her spirit sank under the impending fear of the disclosure. But almost with the next tick of the clock the figure, gaining substance and character, showed itself even to her weak sight as her husband's; and she turned to meet him, as he entered, with the confession of her folly.

"It's really too absurd," she laughed out, "but I never *can* remember!"

"Remember what?" Boyne questioned as they drew together.

"That when one sees the Lyng ghost one never knows it."

Her hand was on his sleeve, and he kept it there, but with no response in his gesture or in the lines of his preoccupied face.

"Did you think you'd seen it?" he asked, after an appreciable interval.

"Why, I actually took *you* for it, my dear, in my mad determination to spot it!"

"Me—just now?" His arm dropped away, and he turned from her with a faint echo of her laugh. "Really, dearest, you'd better give it up, if that's the best you can do."

"Oh, yes, I give it up. Have *you*?" she asked, turning round on him abruptly.

The parlormaid had entered with letters and a lamp, and the light struck up into Boyne's face as he bent above the tray she presented.

"Have *you*?" Mary perversely insisted, when the servant had disappeared on her errand of illumination.

"Have I what?" he rejoined absently, the light bringing out the sharp stamp of worry between his brows as he turned over the letters.

"Given up trying to see the ghost." Her heart beat a little at the experiment she was making.

Her husband, laying his letters aside, moved away into the shadow of the hearth.

"I never tried," he said, tearing open the wrapper of a newspaper.

"Well, of course," Mary persisted, "the exasperating thing is that there's no use trying, since one can't be sure till so long afterward."

He was unfolding the paper as if he had hardly heard her; but after a pause, during which the sheets rustled spasmodically between his hands, he looked up to ask, "Have you any idea *how long*?"

Mary had sunk into a low chair beside the fireplace. From her seat she glanced over, startled, at her husband's profile, which was projected against the circle of lamplight.

"No; none. Have *you?*" she retorted, repeating her former phrase with an added stress of intention.

Boyne crumpled the paper into a bunch, and then, inconsequently, turned back with it toward the lamp.

"Lord, no! I only meant," he exclaimed, with a faint tinge of impatience, "is there any legend, any tradition, as to that?"

"Not that I know of," she answered; but the impulse to add "What makes you ask?" was checked by the reappearance of the parlormaid, with tea and a second lamp.

With the dispersal of shadows, and the repetition of the daily domestic office, Mary Boyne felt herself less oppressed by that sense of something mutely imminent which had darkened her afternoon. For a few moments she gave herself to the details of her task, and when she looked up from it she was struck to the point of bewilderment by the change in her husband's face. He had seated himself near the farther lamp, and was absorbed in the perusal of his letters; but was it something he had found in them, or merely the shifting of her own point of view, that had restored his features to their normal aspect? The longer she looked the more definitely the change affirmed itself. The lines of tension had vanished, and such traces of fatigue as lingered were of the kind easily attributable to steady mental effort. He glanced up, as if drawn by her gaze, and met her eyes with a smile.

"I'm dying for my tea, you know; and here's a letter for you," he said.

She took the letter he held out in exchange for the cup she proffered him, and, returning to her seat, broke the seal with the languid gesture of the reader whose interests are all enclosed in the circle of one cherished presence.

Her next conscious motion was that of starting to her feet, the letter falling to them as she rose, while she held out to her husband a newspaper clipping.

"Ned! What's this? What does it mean?"

He had risen at the same instant, almost as if hearing her cry before she uttered it; and for a perceptible space of time he and she studied each other, like adversaries watching for an advantage, across the space between her chair and his desk.

"What's what? You fairly made me jump!" Boyne said at length, moving toward her with a sudden half-exasperated laugh. The shadow of apprehension was on his face again, not now a look of fixed foreboding, but a shifting vigilance of lips and eyes that gave her the sense of his feeling himself invisibly surrounded.

Her hand shook so that she could hardly give him the clipping.

"This article—from the *Waukesha Sentinel*—that a man named Elwell has brought suit against you—that there was something wrong about the Blue Star Mine. I can't understand more than half."

They continued to face each other as she spoke, and to her astonishment she saw that her words had the almost immediate effect of dissipating the strained watchfulness of his look.

"Oh, *that!*" He glanced down the printed slip, and then folded it with the gesture of one who handles something harmless and familiar. "What's the matter with you this afternoon, Mary? I thought you'd got bad news."

She stood before him with her undefinable terror subsiding slowly under the reassurance of his tone.

"You knew about this, then—it's all right?"

"Certainly I knew about it; and it's all right."

"But what *is* it? I don't understand. What does this man accuse you of?"

"Pretty nearly every crime in the calendar." Boyne had tossed the clipping down, and thrown himself into an armchair near the fire. "Do you want to hear the story? It's not particularly interesting—just a squabble over interests in the Blue Star."

"But who is this Elwell? I don't know the name."

"Oh, he's a fellow I put into it—gave him a hand up. I told you all about him at the time."

"I dare say. I must have forgotten." Vainly she strained back among her memories. "But if you helped him, why does he make this return?"

"Probably some shyster lawyer got hold of him and talked him over. It's all rather technical and complicated. I thought that kind of thing bored you."

His wife felt a sting of compunction. Theoretically, she deprecated the American wife's detachment from her husband's professional interests, but in practice she had always found it difficult to fix her attention on Boyne's report of the transactions in which his varied interests involved him. Besides, she had felt during their year of exile, that, in a community where the amenities of living could be obtained only at the cost of efforts as arduous as her husband's professional labors, such brief leisure as he and she could command should be used as an escape from immediate preoccupations, a flight to the life they always dreamed of living. Once or twice, now that this new life had actually drawn its magic circle about them, she had asked herself if she had done right; but hitherto such conjectures had been no more than the retrospective excursions of an active fancy. Now, for the first time, it startled her a little to find how little she knew of the material foundation on which her happiness was built.

She glanced at her husband, and was again reassured by the composure of his face; yet she felt the need of more definite grounds for her reassurance.

"But doesn't this suit worry you? Why have you never spoken to me about it?"

He answered both questions at once. "I didn't speak of it at first because it *did* worry me—annoyed me, rather. But it's all ancient history now. Your correspondent must have got hold of a back number of the *Sentinel*."

She felt a quick thrill of relief. "You mean it's over? He's lost his case?"

There was a just perceptible delay in Boyne's reply. "The suit's been withdrawn—that's all."

But she persisted, as if to exonerate herself from the inward charge of being too easily put off. "Withdrawn it because he saw he had no chance?"

"Oh, he had no chance," Boyne answered.

She was still struggling with the dimly felt perplexity at the back of her thoughts.

"How long ago was it withdrawn?"

He paused, as if with a slight return to his former uncertainty. "I've just had the news now; but I've been expecting it."

"Just now—in one of your letters?"

"Yes; in one of my letters."

She made no answer, and was aware only, after a short interval of waiting, that he had risen, and, strolling across the room, had placed himself on the sofa at her side. She felt him, as he did so, pass an arm about her, she felt his hand seek hers and clasp it, and turning slowly, drawn by the warmth of his cheek, she met his smiling eyes.

"It's all right—it's all right?" she questioned, through the flood of her dissolving doubts; and "I give you my word it was never righter!" he laughed back at her, holding her close.

III

One of the strangest things she was afterward to recall out of all the next day's strangeness was the sudden and complete recovery of her sense of security.

It was in the air when she woke in her low-ceiled, dusky room; it went with her downstairs to the breakfast table, flashed out at her from the fire, and reduplicated itself from the flanks of the urn and the sturdy flutings of the Georgian teapot. It was as if in some roundabout way, all her diffused fears of the previous day, with their moment of sharp concentration about the newspaper article—as if this dim questioning of the future, and startled return upon the past, had between them liquidated the arrears of some haunting moral obligation. If she had indeed been careless of her husband's affairs, it was, her new state seemed to prove, because her faith in him instinctively justified such carelessness; and his right to her faith had now affirmed itself in the very face of menace and suspicion. She had never seen him more untroubled, more naturally and unconsciously himself, than after the cross-examination to which she had subjected him: it was almost as if he had been aware of her doubts, and had wanted the air cleared as much as she did.

It was as clear, thank heaven, as the bright outer light that surprised her almost with a touch of summer when she issued from the house for her daily round of the gardens. She had left Boyne at his desk, indulging herself, as she passed the library door, by a last peep at his quiet face, where he bent, pipe in mouth, above his papers; and now she had her own morning's task to perform. The task involved, on such charmed winter days, almost as much happy loitering about the different quarters of her domain as if spring were already at work there. There were such endless possibilities still before her, such opportunities to bring out the latent graces of the old place, without a single irreverent touch of alteration, that the winter was all too short to plan what spring and autumn executed. And her recovered sense of safety gave, on this particular morning, a peculiar zest to her progress through the sweet still place. She went first to the kitchen garden, where the espaliered pear trees drew complicated patterns on the walls, and pigeons were fluttering and preening about the silvery-slated roof of their cot. There was something wrong about the piping of the hothouse, and she was expecting an authority from Dorchester, who was to drive out between trains and make a diagnosis of the boiler. But when she dipped into the damp heat of the greenhouses, among the spiced scents and waxy pinks and reds of old-fashioned exotics—even the flora of Lyng was in the note!—she learned that the great man had not arrived, and, the day being too rare to waste in an artificial atmosphere, she came out again and paced along the springy turf of the bowling green to the gardens behind the house. At their farther end rose a grass terrace, looking across the fish pond and yew hedges to the long house front with its twisted chimney stacks and blue roof angles all drenched in the pale gold moisture of the air.

Seen thus, across the level tracery of the gardens, it sent her, from open windows and hospitably smoking chimneys, the look of some warm human presence, of a mind slowly ripened on a sunny wall of experience. She had never before had such a sense of her intimacy with it, such a conviction that its secrets were all beneficent, kept, as they said to children, "for one's good," such a trust in its power to gather up her life and Ned's into the harmonious pattern of the long long story it sat there weaving in the sun.

She heard steps behind her, and turned, expecting to see the gardener accompanied by the engineer from Dorchester. But only one figure was in sight, that of a youngish slightly built man, who, for reasons she could not on the spot have given, did not remotely resemble her notion of an authority on hothouse boilers. The newcomer, on seeing her, lifted his hat, and paused with the air of a gentleman—perhaps a traveler—who wishes to make it known that his intrusion is involuntary. Lyng occasionally attracted the more cultivated traveler, and Mary half expected to see the stranger dissemble a camera, or justify his presence by producing it. But he made no gesture of any sort, and after a moment she asked, in a tone responding to the courteous hesitation of his attitude: "Is there anyone you wish to see?"

"I came to see Mr. Boyne," he answered. His intonation, rather than his accent, was faintly American, and Mary, at the note, looked at him more closely. The brim of his soft felt hat cast a shade on his face, which, thus obscured, wore to her shortsighted gaze a look of seriousness, as of a person arriving on business, and civilly but firmly aware of his rights.

Past experience had made her equally sensible to such claims; but she was jealous of her husband's morning hours, and doubtful of his having given anyone the right to intrude on them.

"Have you an appointment with my husband?" she asked.

The visitor hesitated, as if unprepared for the question.

"I think he expects me," he replied.

It was Mary's turn to hesitate. "You see this is his time for work: he never sees anyone in the morning."

He looked at her a moment without answering; then, as if

accepting her decision, he began to move away. As he turned, Mary saw him pause and glance up at the peaceful house front. Something in his air suggested weariness and disappointment, the dejection of the traveler who has come from far off and whose hours are limited by the timetable. It occurred to her that if this were the case her refusal might have made his errand vain, and a sense of compunction caused her to hasten after him.

"May I ask if you have come a long way?"

He gave her the same grave look. "Yes—I have come a long way."

"Then, if you'll go to the house, no doubt my husband will see you now. You'll find him in the library."

She did not know why she had added the last phrase, except from a vague impulse to atone for her previous inhospitality. The visitor seemed about to express his thanks, but her attention was distracted by the approach of the gardener with a companion who bore all the marks of being the expert from Dorchester.

"This way," she said, waving the stranger to the house; and an instant later she had forgotten him in the absorption of her meeting with the boiler maker.

The encounter led to such far-reaching results that the engineer ended by finding it expedient to ignore his train, and Mary was beguiled into spending the remainder of the morning in absorbed confabulation among the flower pots. When the colloquy ended, she was surprised to find that it was nearly luncheon time, and she half expected, as she hurried back to the house, to see her husband coming out to meet her. But she found no one in the court but an under-gardener raking the gravel, and the hall, when she entered it, was so silent that she guessed Boyne to be still at work.

Not wishing to disturb him, she turned into the drawing room, and there, at her writing table, lost herself in renewed calculations of the outlay to which the morning's conference had pledged her. The fact that she could permit herself such follies had not yet lost its novelty; and somehow, in contrast to the vague fears of the previous days, it now seemed an element of her recovered security, of the sense that, as Ned had said, things in general had never been "righter."

She was still luxuriating in a lavish play of figures when the par-lormaid, from the threshold, roused her with an inquiry as to the expediency of serving luncheon. It was one of their jokes that Trimmle announced luncheon as if she were divulging a state secret, and Mary, intent upon her papers, merely murmured an absent-minded assent.

She felt Trimmle wavering doubtfully on the threshold, as if in rebuke of such unconsidered assent; then her retreating steps sounded down the passage, and Mary, pushing away her papers, crossed the hall and went to the library door. It was still closed, and she wavered in her turn, disliking to disturb her husband, yet anxious that he should not exceed his usual measure of work. As she stood there, balancing her impulses, Trimmle returned with the announcement of luncheon, and Mary, thus impelled, opened the library door.

Boyne was not at his desk, and she peered about her, expecting to discover him before the bookshelves, somewhere down the length of the room; but her call brought no response, and gradually it became clear to her that he was not there.

She turned back to the parlormaid.

"Mr. Boyne must be upstairs. Please tell him that luncheon is ready."

Trimmle appeared to hesitate between the obvious duty of obedience and an equally obvious conviction of the foolishness of the injunction laid on her. The struggle resulted in her saying: "If you please, Madam, Mr. Boyne's not upstairs."

"Not in his room? Are you sure?"

"I'm sure, Madam."

Mary consulted the clock. "Where is he, then?"

"He's gone out," Trimmle announced, with the superior air of one who has respectfully waited for the question that a well-ordered mind would have put first.

Mary's conjecture had been right, then. Boyne must have gone to the gardens to meet her, and since she had missed him, it was clear that he had taken the shorter way by the south door, instead of going round to the court. She crossed the hall to the French window opening directly on the yew garden, but the parlormaid, after another moment of inner conflict, decided to bring out: "Please, Madam, Mr. Boyne didn't go that way."

Mary turned back. "Where *did* he go? And when?"

"He went out of the front door, up the drive, Madam." It was a matter of principle with Trimmle never to answer more than one question at a time.

"Up the drive? At this hour?" Mary went to the door herself, and glanced across the court through the tunnel of bare limes. But its perspective was as empty as when she had scanned it on entering.

"Did Mr. Boyne leave no message?"

Trimmle seemed to surrender herself to a last struggle with the forces of chaos.

"No, Madam. He just went out with the gentleman."

"The gentleman? What gentleman?" Mary wheeled about, as if to front this new factor.

"The gentleman who called, Madam," said Trimmle resignedly.

"When did a gentleman call? Do explain yourself, Trimmle!"

Only the fact that Mary was very hungry, and that she wanted to consult her husband about the greenhouses, would have caused her to lay so unusual an injunction on her attendant; and even now she was detached enough to note in Trimmle's eye the dawning defiance of the respectful subordinate who has been pressed too hard.

"I couldn't exactly say the hour, Madam, because I didn't let the gentleman in," she replied, with an air of discreetly ignoring the irregularity of her mistress's course.

"You didn't let him in?"

"No, Madam. When the bell rang I was dressing, and Agnes—"

"Go and ask Agnes, then," said Mary.

Trimmle still wore her look of patient magnanimity. "Agnes would not know, Madam, for she had unfortunately burnt her hand in trimming the wick of the new lamp from town"—Trimmle, as Mary was aware, had always been opposed to the new lamp—"and so Mrs. Dockett sent the kitchenmaid instead."

Mary looked again at the clock. "It's after two! Go and ask the kitchenmaid if Mr. Boyne left any word."

She went into luncheon without waiting, and Trimmle presently brought her there the kitchenmaid's statement that the gentleman had called about eleven o'clock, and that Mr. Boyne had gone out with him without leaving any message. The kitchenmaid did not even know the caller's name, for he had written it on a slip of paper, which he had folded and handed to her, with the injunction to deliver it at once to Mr. Boyne.

Mary finished her luncheon, still wondering, and when it was over, and Trimmle had brought the coffee to the drawing room, her wonder had deepened to a first faint tinge of disquietude. It was unlike Boyne to absent himself without explanation at so unwonted an hour, and the difficulty of identifying the visitor whose summons he had apparently obeyed made his disappearance the more unaccountable. Mary Boyne's experience as the wife of a busy engineer, subject to sudden calls and compelled to keep irregular hours, had trained her to the philosophic acceptance of surprises; but since Boyne's withdrawal from business he had adopted a Benedictine regularity of life. As if to make up for the dispersed and agitated years, with their "stand-up" lunches, and dinners rattled down to the joltings of the dining cars, he cultivated the last refinements of punctuality and monotony, discouraging his wife's fancy for the unexpected, and declaring that to a delicate taste there were infinite gradations of pleasure in the recurrences of habit.

Still, since no life can completely defend itself from the unforeseen, it was evident that all Boyne's precautions would sooner or later prove unavailable, and Mary concluded that he had cut short a tiresome visit by walking with his caller to the station, or at least accompanying him for part of the way.

This conclusion relieved her from further preoccupation, and she went out herself to take up her conference with the gardener. Thence she walked to the village post office, a mile or so away; and when she turned toward home the early twilight was setting in.

She had taken a footpath across the downs, and as Boyne, meanwhile, had probably returned from the station by the highroad, there was little likelihood of their meeting. She felt sure, however, of his having reached the house before her; so sure that, when she entered it herself, without even pausing to inquire of Trimmle, she made directly for the library. But the library was still empty, and with an unwonted exactness of visual memory she observed that the papers on her husband's desk lay precisely as they had lain when she had gone in to call him to luncheon.

Then of a sudden she was seized by a vague dread of the unknown. She had closed the door behind her on entering, and as she stood alone in the long silent room, her dread seemed to take shape and sound, to be there breathing and lurking among the shadows. Her shortsighted eyes strained through them, half discerning an actual presence, something aloof, that watched and knew; and in the recoil from that intangible presence she threw herself on the bell rope and gave it a sharp pull.

The sharp summons brought Trimmle in precipitately with a lamp, and Mary breathed again at this sobering reappearance of the usual.

"You may bring tea if Mr. Boyne is in," she said, to justify her ring.

"Very well, Madam. But Mr. Boyne is not in," said Trimmle, putting down the lamp.

"Not in? You mean he's come back and gone out again?"

"No, Madam. He's never been back."

The dread stirred again, and Mary knew that now it had her fast.

"Not since he went out with—the gentleman?"

"Not since he went out with the gentleman."

"But who *was* the gentleman?" Mary insisted, with the shrill note of someone trying to be heard through a confusion of noises.

"That I couldn't say, Madam." Trimmle, standing there by the lamp, seemed suddenly to grow less round and rosy, as though eclipsed by the same creeping shade of apprehension.

"But the kitchenmaid knows—wasn't it the kitchenmaid who let him in?"

"She doesn't know either, Madam, for he wrote his name on a folded paper."

Mary, through her agitation, was aware that they were both designating the unknown visitor by a vague pronoun, instead of the conventional formula which, till then, had kept their allusions within the bounds of conformity. And at the same moment her mind caught at the suggestion of the folded paper.

"But he must have a name! Where's the paper?"

She moved to the desk, and began to turn over the documents that littered it. The first that caught her eye was an unfinished letter in her husband's hand, with his pen lying across it, as though dropped there at a sudden summons.

"My dear Parvis"—who was Parvis?—"I have just received your letter announcing Elwell's death, and while I suppose there is now no further risk of trouble, it might be safer—"

She tossed the sheet aside, and continued her search; but no folded paper was discoverable among the letters and pages of manuscript which had been swept together in a heap, as if by a hurried or a startled gesture.

"But the kitchenmaid *saw* him. Send her here," she commanded, wondering at her dullness in not thinking sooner of so simple a solution.

Trimmle vanished in a flash, as if thankful to be out of the room, and when she reappeared, conducting the agitated underling, Mary had regained her self-possession, and had her questions ready.

The gentleman was a stranger, yes—that she understood. But what had he said? And, above all, what had he looked like? The first question was easily enough answered, for the disconcerting reason that he had said so little—had merely asked for Mr. Boyne, and, scribbling something on a bit of paper, had requested that it should at once be carried in to him.

"Then you don't know what he wrote? You're not sure it *was* his name?"

The kitchenmaid was not sure, but supposed it was, since he had written it in answer to her inquiry as to whom she should announce.

"And when you carried the paper in to Mr. Boyne, what did he say?"

The kitchenmaid did not think that Mr. Boyne had said anything, but she could not be sure, for just as she had handed him the paper and he was opening it, she had become aware that the visitor had followed her into the library, and she had slipped out, leaving the two gentlemen together.

"But then, if you left them in the library, how do you know that they went out of the house?"

This question plunged the witness into a momentary inarticulateness, from which she was rescued by Trimmle, who, by means of ingenious circumlocutions, elicited the statement that before she could cross the hall to the back passage she had heard the two gentlemen behind her, and had seen them go out of the front door together.

"Then, if you saw the strange gentleman twice, you must be able to tell me what he looked like."

But with this final challenge to her powers of expression it became clear that the limit of the kitchenmaid's endurance had been reached. The obligation of going to the front door to "show in" a visitor was in itself so subversive of the fundamental order of things that it had thrown her faculties into hopeless disarray, and she could only stammer out, after various panting efforts: "His hat, mum, was different-like, as you might say—"

"Different? How different?" Mary flashed out, her own mind, in the same instant, leaping back to an image left on it that morning, and then lost under layers of subsequent impressions.

"His hat had a wide brim, you mean, and his face was pale—a youngish face?" Mary pressed her, with a white-lipped intensity of interrogation. But if the kitchenmaid found any adequate answer to this challenge, it was swept away for her listener down the rushing current of her own convictions. The stranger—the stranger in the garden! Why had Mary not thought of him before? She needed no one now to tell her that it was he who had called for her husband and gone away with him. But who was he, and why had Boyne obeyed him?

IV

It leaped out at her suddenly, like a grin out of the dark, that they had often called England so little—"such a confoundedly hard place to get lost in."

A confoundedly hard place to get lost in! That had been her husband's phrase. And now, with the whole machinery of official investigation sweeping its flashlights from shore to shore, and across the dividing straits; now, with Boyne's name blazing from the walls of every town and village, his portrait (how that wrung her!) hawked up and down the country like the image of a hunted criminal; now the little compact populous island, so policed, surveyed and administered, revealed itself as a Sphinxlike guardian of abysmal mysteries, staring back into his wife's anguished eyes as if with the wicked joy of knowing something they would never know!

In the fortnight since Boyne's disappearance there had been no word of him, no trace of his movements. Even the usual misleading reports that raise expectancy in tortured bosoms had been few and fleeting. No one but the kitchenmaid had seen Boyne leave the house, and no one else had seen "the gentleman" who accompanied him. All inquiries in the neighborhood failed to elicit the memory of a stranger's presence that day in the neighborhood of Lyng. And no one had met Edward Boyne, either alone or in company, in any of the neighboring villages, or on the road across the downs, or at either of the local railway stations. The sunny English noon had swallowed him as completely as if he had gone out into Cimmerian night.

Mary, while every official means of investigating was working at its highest pressure, had ransacked her husband's papers for any trace of antecedent complications, of entanglements or obligations unknown to her, that might throw a ray into the darkness. But if any such had existed in the background of Boyne's life, they had vanished like the slip of paper on which the visitor had written his name. There remained no possible thread of guidance except—if it were indeed an exception—the letter which Boyne had apparently

been in the act of writing when he received his mysterious summons. That letter, read and reread by his wife, and submitted by her
to the police, yielded little enough to feed conjecture.

"I have just heard of Elwell's death, and while I suppose there is
now no further risk of trouble, it might be safer—" That was all. The
"risk of trouble" was easily explained by the newspaper clipping
which had apprised Mary of the suit brought against her husband by
one of his associates in the Blue Star enterprise. The only new information conveyed by the letter was the fact of its showing Boyne,
when he wrote it, to be still apprehensive of the results of the suit,
though he had told his wife that it had been withdrawn, and though
the letter itself proved that the plaintiff was dead. It took several
days of cabling to fix the identity of the "Parvis" to whom the fragment was addressed, but even after these inquiries had shown him to
be a Waukesha lawyer, no new facts concerning the Elwell suit were
elicited. He appeared to have had no direct concern in it, but to have
been conversant with the facts merely as an acquaintance, and possible intermediary; and he declared himself unable to guess with what
object Boyne intended to seek his assistance.

This negative information, sole fruit of the first fortnight's
search, was not increased by a jot during the slow weeks that followed. Mary knew that the investigations were still being carried on,
but she had a vague sense of their gradually slackening, as the actual
march of time seemed to slacken. It was as though the days, flying
horror-struck from the shrouded image of the one inscrutable day,
gained assurance as the distance lengthened, till at last they fell back
into their normal gait. And so with the human imaginations at work
on the dark event. No doubt it occupied them still, but week by
week and hour by hour it grew less absorbing, took up less space,
was slowly but inevitably crowded out of the foreground of consciousness by the new problems perpetually bubbling up from the
cloudy caldron of human experience.

Even Mary Boyne's consciousness gradually felt the same lowering of velocity. It still swayed with the incessant oscillations of conjecture; but they were slower, more rhythmical in their beat. There

were even moments of weariness when, like the victim of some poi-
son which leaves the brain clear, but holds the body motionless, she
saw herself domesticated with the Horror, accepting its perpetual
presence as one of the fixed conditions of life.

These moments lengthened into hours and days, till she passed
into a phase of stolid acquiescence. She watched the routine of daily
life with the incurious eye of a savage on whom the meaningless
processes of civilization make but the faintest impression. She had
come to regard herself as part of the routine, a spoke of the wheel,
revolving with its motion; she felt almost like the furniture of the
room in which she sat, an insensate object to be dusted and pushed
about with the chairs and tables. And this deepening apathy held her
fast at Lyng, in spite of the entreaties of friends and the usual med-
ical recommendation of "change." Her friends supposed that her
refusal to move was inspired by the belief that her husband would
one day return to the spot from which he had vanished, and a beautiful legend grew up about this imaginary state of waiting. But in
reality she had no such belief: the depths of anguish enclosing her
were no longer lighted by flashes of hope. She was sure that Boyne
would never come back, that he had gone out of her sight as completely as if Death itself had waited that day on the threshold. She
had even renounced, one by one, the various theories as to his disappearance which had been advanced by the press, the police, and her
own agonized imagination. In sheer lassitude her mind turned from
these alternatives of horror, and sank back into the blank fact that he
was gone.

No, she would never know what had become of him—no one
would ever know. But the house *knew*; the library in which she spent
her long lonely evenings knew. For it was here that the last scene had
been enacted, here that the stranger had come, and spoken the word
which had caused Boyne to rise and follow him. The floor she trod
had felt his tread; the books on the shelves had seen his face; and
there were moments when the intense consciousness of the old
dusky walls seemed about to break out into some audible revelation
of their secret. But the revelation never came, and she knew it would

never come. Lyng was not one of the garrulous old houses that betray the secrets entrusted to them. Its very legend proved that it had always been the mute accomplice, the incorruptible custodian, of the mysteries it had surprised. And Mary Boyne, sitting face to face with its silence, felt the futility of seeking to break it by any human means.

V

"I don't say it *wasn't* straight, and yet I don't say it *was* straight. It was business."

Mary, at the words, lifted her head with a start, and looked intently at the speaker.

When, half an hour before, a card with "Mr. Parvis" on it had been brought up to her, she had been immediately aware that the name had been a part of her consciousness ever since she had read it at the head of Boyne's unfinished letter. In the library she had found awaiting her a small sallow man with a bald head and gold eye-glasses, and it sent a tremor through her to know that this was the person to whom her husband's last known thought had been directed.

Parvis, civilly, but without vain preamble—in the manner of a man who has his watch in his hand—had set forth the object of his visit. He had "run over" to England on business, and finding himself in the neighborhood of Dorchester, had not wished to leave it without paying his respects to Mrs. Boyne; and without asking her, if the occasion offered, what she meant to do about Bob Elwell's family.

The words touched the spring of some obscure dread in Mary's bosom. Did her visitor, after all, know what Boyne had meant by his unfinished phrase? She asked for an elucidation of his question, and noticed at once that he seemed surprised at her continued ignorance of the subject. Was it possible that she really knew as little as she said?

"I know nothing—you must tell me," she faltered out; and her visitor thereupon proceeded to unfold his story. It threw, even to her confused perceptions, and imperfectly initiated vision, a lurid glare on the whole hazy episode of the Blue Star Mine. Her husband had made his money in that brilliant speculation at the cost of "getting ahead" of someone less alert to seize the chance; and the victim of his ingenuity was young Robert Elwell, who had "put him on" to the Blue Star scheme.

Parvis, at Mary's first cry, had thrown her a sobering glance through his impartial glasses.

"Bob Elwell wasn't smart enough, that's all; if he had been, he might have turned round and served Boyne the same way. It's the kind of thing that happens every day in business. I guess it's what the scientists call the survival of the fittest—see?" said Mr. Parvis, evidently pleased with the aptness of his analogy.

Mary felt a physical shrinking from the next question she tried to frame: it was as though the words on her lips had a taste that nauseated her.

"But then—you accuse my husband of doing something dishonorable?"

Mr. Parvis surveyed the question dispassionately. "Oh, no, I don't. I don't even say it wasn't straight." He glanced up and down the long lines of books, as if one of them might have supplied him with the definition he sought. "I don't say it *wasn't* straight, and yet I don't say it *was* straight. It was business." After all, no definition in his category could be more comprehensive than that.

Mary sat staring at him with a look of terror. He seemed to her like the indifferent emissary of some evil power.

"But Mr. Elwell's lawyers apparently did not take your view, since I suppose the suit was withdrawn by their advice."

"Oh, yes; they knew he hadn't a leg to stand on, technically. It was when they advised him to withdraw the suit that he got desperate. You see, he'd borrowed most of the money he lost in the Blue Star, and he was up a tree. That's why he shot himself when they told him he had no show."

The horror was sweeping over Mary in great deafening waves.

"He shot himself? He killed himself because of *that*?"

"Well, he didn't kill himself, exactly. He dragged on two months before he died." Parvis emitted the statement as unemotionally as a gramophone grinding out its record.

"You mean that he tried to kill himself, and failed? And tried again?"

"Oh, he didn't have to *try* again," said Parvis grimly.

They sat opposite each other in silence, he swinging his eye-glasses thoughtfully about his finger, she, motionless, her arms stretched along her knees in an attitude of rigid tension.

"But if you knew all this," she began at length, hardly able to force her voice above a whisper, "how is it that when I wrote you at the time of my husband's disappearance you said you didn't understand his letter?"

Parvis received this without perceptible embarrassment: "Why, I didn't understand it—strictly speaking. And it wasn't the time to talk about it, if I had. The Elwell business was settled when the suit was withdrawn. Nothing I could have told you would have helped you to find your husband."

Mary continued to scrutinize him. "Then why are you telling me now?"

Still Parvis did not hesitate. "Well, to begin with, I supposed you knew more than you appear to—I mean about the circumstances of Elwell's death. And then people are talking of it now; the whole matter's been raked up again. And I thought if you didn't know you ought to."

She remained silent, and he continued: "You see, it's only come out lately what a bad state Elwell's affairs were in. His wife's a proud woman, and she fought on as long as she could, going out to work, and taking sewing at home when she got too sick—something with the heart, I believe. But she had his mother to look after, and the children, and she broke down under it, and finally had to ask for help. That called attention to the case, and the papers took it up, and a subscription was started. Everybody out there liked Bob Elwell, and most of the prominent names in the place are down on the list, and people began to wonder why—"

Parvis broke off to fumble in an inner pocket. "Here," he continued, "here's an account of the whole thing from the *Sentinel*—a little
sensational, of course. But I guess you'd better look it over."

He held out a newspaper to Mary, who unfolded it slowly,
remembering as she did so, the evening when, in that same room the
perusal of a clipping from the *Sentinel* had first shaken the depths of
her security.

As she opened the paper, her eyes, shrinking from the glaring
headlines, "Widow of Boyne's Victim Forced to Appeal for Aid,"
ran down the column of text to two portraits inserted in it. The first
was her husband's, taken from a photograph the year they had
come to England. It was the picture of him that she liked best, the
one that stood on the writing table upstairs in her bedroom. As the
eyes in the photograph met hers, she felt it would be impossible to
read what was said of him, and closed her lids with the sharpness of
the pain.

"I thought if you felt disposed to put your name down—" she
heard Parvis continue.

She opened her eyes with an effort, and they fell on the other
portrait. It was that of a youngish man, slightly built, with features
somewhat blurred by the shadow of a projecting hat brim. Where
had she seen that outline before? She stared at it confusedly, her
heart hammering in her ears. Then she gave a cry.

"This is the man—the man who came for my husband!"

She heard Parvis start to his feet, and was dimly aware that she
had slipped backward into the corner of the sofa, and that he was
bending above her in alarm. She straightened herself, and reached
out for the paper, which she had dropped.

"It's the man! I should know him anywhere!" she persisted in a
voice that sounded to her own ears like a scream.

Parvis's answer seemed to come to her from far off, down endless fog-muffled windings.

"Mrs. Boyne, you're not very well. Shall I call somebody? Shall I
get a glass of water?"

"No, no, no!" She threw herself toward him, her hand frantically clutching the newspaper. "I tell you, it's the man! I *know* him! He spoke to me in the garden!"

Parvis took the journal from her, directing his glasses to the portrait. "It can't be, Mrs. Boyne. It's Robert Elwell."

"Robert Elwell?" Her white stare seemed to travel into space. "Then it was Robert Elwell who came for him."

"Came for Boyne? The day he went away from here?" Parvis's voice dropped as hers rose. He bent over, laying a fraternal hand on her, as if to coax her gently back into her seat. "Why, Elwell was dead! Don't you remember?"

Mary sat with her eyes fixed on the picture, unconscious of what he was saying. "Don't you remember Boyne's unfinished letter to me—the one you found on his desk that day? It was written just after he'd heard of Elwell's death." She noticed an odd shake in Parvis's unemotional voice. "Surely you remember!" he urged her.

Yes, she remembered: that was the profoundest horror of it. Elwell had died the day before her husband's disappearance; and this was Elwell's portrait; and it was the portrait of the man who had spoken to her in the garden. She lifted her head and looked slowly about the library. The library could have borne witness that it was also the portrait of the man who had come in that day to call Boyne from his unfinished letter. Through the misty surgings of her brain she heard the faint boom of half-forgotten words—words spoken by Alida Stair on the lawn at Pangbourne before Boyne and his wife had ever seen the house at Lyng, or had imagined that they might one day live there.

"This was the man who spoke to me," she repeated.

She looked again at Parvis. He was trying to conceal his disturbance under what he probably imagined to be an expression of indulgent commiseration; but the edges of his lips were blue. "He thinks me mad; but I'm not mad," she reflected; and suddenly there flashed upon her a way of justifying her strange affirmation.

She sat quiet, controlling the quiver of her lips, and waiting till she could trust her voice; then she said, looking straight at Parvis:

"Will you answer me one question, please? When was it that Robert Elwell tried to kill himself?"

"When—when?" Parvis stammered.

"Yes; the date. Please try to remember."

She saw that he was growing still more afraid of her. "I have a reason," she insisted.

"Yes, yes. Only I can't remember. About two months before, I should say."

"I want the date," she repeated.

Parvis picked up the newspaper. "We might see here," he said, still humoring her. He ran his eyes down the page. "Here it is. Last October—the—"

She caught the words from him. "The 20th, wasn't it?" With a sharp look at her, he verified. "Yes, the 20th. Then you *did* know?"

"I know now." Her gaze continued to travel past him. "Sunday, the 20th—that was the day he came first."

Parvis's voice was almost inaudible. "Came *here* first?"

"Yes."

"You saw him twice, then?"

"Yes, twice." She just breathed it at him. "He came first on the 20th of October. I remember the date because it was the day we went up Meldon Steep for the first time." She felt a faint gasp of inward laughter at the thought that but for that she might have forgotten.

Parvis continued to scrutinize her, as if trying to intercept her gaze.

"We saw him from the roof," she went on. "He came down the lime avenue toward the house. He was dressed just as he is in that picture. My husband saw him first. He was frightened, and ran down ahead of me; but there was no one there. He had vanished."

"Elwell had vanished?" Parvis faltered.

"Yes." Their two whispers seemed to grope for each other. "I couldn't think what had happened. I see now. He *tried* to come then; but he wasn't dead enough—he couldn't reach us. He had to wait for two months to die; and then he came back again—and Ned went with him."

She nodded at Parvis with the look of triumph of a child who has worked out a difficult puzzle. But suddenly she lifted her hands with a desperate gesture, pressing them to her temples.

"Oh, my God! I sent him to Ned—I told him where to go! I sent him to this room!" she screamed.

She felt the walls of books rush toward her, like inward falling ruins; and she heard Parvis, a long way off, through the ruins, crying to her, and struggling to get at her. But she was numb to his touch, she did not know what he was saying. Through the tumult she heard but one clear note, the voice of Alida Stair, speaking on the lawn at Pangbourne.

"You won't know till afterward," it said. "You won't know till long, long afterward."

THE TOWN WHERE NO ONE GOT OFF

RAY BRADBURY

Travel by air has long been commonplace. But even in the twenty-first century, it is trains, snaking across the landscape and whistling through our nerve endings, that time and again give rise to the sort of unsettling encounters that might make one prefer to stay at home.

Ray Bradbury has, like many of us, looked out those dusty windows into the not-quite void and felt that deep, near-anguished yearning for places never to be known.

Yet except in (and because of) such cautionary fables as this one, journeys are rarely broken on impulse. Protected by our itineraries, sheltered by habit, content to watch impossible destinations recede into the distance, we step out of safety onto strange platforms only in our dreams—praying, of course, as we glance around, that dream it is, and not anything more diabolical.

ᔕ

CROSSING THE CONTINENTAL United States by night, by day, on the train, you flash past town after wilderness town where nobody ever gets off. Or rather, no person who doesn't *belong*, no person who hasn't roots in these country graveyards, ever bothers to visit their lonely stations or attend their lonely views.

I spoke of this to a fellow passenger, another salesman like myself, on the Chicago–Los Angeles train as we crossed Iowa.

"True," he said. "People get off in Chicago; everyone gets off there. People get off in New York, get off in Boston, get off in L.A. People who don't live there go there to see and come back to tell. But what tourist ever just got off at Fox Hill, Nebraska, to *look* at it? You? Me? No! I don't know anyone, got no business there, it's no health resort, so why bother?"

"Wouldn't it be a fascinating change," I said, "some year to plan a really different vacation? Pick some village lost on the plains where you don't know a soul and go there for the hell of it?"

"You'd be bored stiff."

"I'm not bored thinking of it!" I peered out the window. "What's the next town coming up on this line?"

"Rampart Junction."

I smiled. "Sounds good. I might get off there."

"You're a liar and a fool. What you want? Adventure? Romance? Go ahead, jump off the train. Ten seconds later you'll call yourself an idiot, grab a taxi, and race us to the next town."

"Maybe."

I watched telephone poles flick by, flick by, flick by. Far ahead I could see the first faint outlines of a town.

"But I don't think so," I heard myself say.

The salesman across from me looked faintly surprised.

For slowly, very slowly, I was rising to stand. I reached for my hat. I saw my hand fumble for my one suitcase. I was surprised myself.

"Hold on!" said the salesman. "What're you doing?"

The train rounded a curve suddenly. I swayed. Far ahead I saw one church spire, a deep forest, a field of summer wheat.

"It looks like I'm getting off the train," I said.

"Sit down," he said.

"No," I said. "There's something about that town up ahead. I've got to go see. I've got the time. I don't have to be in L.A., really, until next Monday. If I don't get off the train now, I'll always wonder what I missed, what I let slip by when I had the chance to see it."

"We were just talking. There's nothing there."

"You're wrong," I said. "There is."

I put my hat on my head and lifted the suitcase in my hand.

"By God," said the salesman, "I think you're really going to do it."

My heart beat quickly. My face was flushed.

The train whistled. The train rushed down the track. The town was near!

"Wish me luck," I said.

"Luck!" he cried.

I ran for the porter, yelling.

There was an ancient flake-painted chair tilted back against the station-platform wall. In this chair, completely relaxed so he sank into his clothes, was a man of some seventy years whose timbers looked as if he'd been nailed there since the station was built. The sun had burned his face dark and tracked his cheek with lizard folds and stitches that held his eyes in a perpetual squint. His hair smoked ash-white in the summer wind. His blue shirt, open at the neck to show white clock springs, was bleached like the staring late afternoon sky. His shoes were blistered as if he had held them, uncaring, in the mouth of a stove, motionless, forever. His shadow under him was stenciled a permanent black.

As I stepped down the old man's eyes flicked every door on the train and stopped, surprised, at me.

I thought he might wave.

But there was only a sudden coloring of his secret eyes; a chemical change that was recognition. Yet he had not twitched so much as his mouth, an eyelid, a finger. An invisible bulk had shifted inside him.

The moving train gave me an excuse to follow it with my eyes. There was no one else on the platform. No autos waited by the cobwebbed, nailed-shut office. I alone had departed the iron thunder to set foot on the choppy waves of platform lumber.

The train whistled over the hill.

Fool! I thought. My fellow passenger had been right. I would panic at the boredom I already sensed in this place. All right, I thought, fool, yes, but run, no!

I walked my suitcase down the platform, not looking at the old man. As I passed, I heard his thin bulk shift again, this time so I could hear it. His feet were coming down to touch and tap the mushy boards.

I kept walking.

"Afternoon," a voice said faintly.

I knew he did not look at me but only at that great cloudless spread of shimmering sky.

"Afternoon," I said.

I started up the dirt road toward the town. One hundred yards away, I glanced back.

The old man, still seated there, stared at the sun, as if posing a question.

I hurried on.

I moved through the dreaming late afternoon town, utterly anonymous and alone, a trout going upstream, not touching the banks of a clear-running river of life that drifted all about me.

My suspicions were confirmed: it was a town where nothing happened, where occurred only the following events:

At four o'clock sharp, the Honneger Hardware door slammed as a dog came out to dust himself in the road. Four-thirty, a straw sucked emptily at the bottom of a soda glass, making a sound like a great cataract in the drugstore silence. Five o'clock, boys and pebbles plunged in the town river. Five-fifteen, ants paraded in the slanting light under some elm trees.

And yet—I turned in a slow circle—somewhere in this town there must be something worth seeing. I knew it was there. I knew I had to keep walking and looking. I knew I would find it.

I walked. I looked.

All through the afternoon there was only one constant and unchanging factor: the old man in the bleached blue pants and shirt was never far away. When I sat in the drugstore he was out front spitting tobacco that rolled itself into tumblebugs in the dust. When I stood by the river he was crouched downstream making a great thing of washing his hands.

Along about seven-thirty in the evening, I was walking for the seventh or eighth time through the quiet streets when I heard footsteps beside me.

I looked over, and the old man was pacing me, looking straight ahead, a piece of dried grass in his stained teeth.

"It's been a long time," he said quietly.

We walked along in the twilight.

"A long time," he said, "waitin' on that station platform."

"You?" I said.

"Me." He nodded in the tree shadows.

"Were you waiting for someone at the station?"

"Yes," he said. "You."

"Me?" The surprise must have shown in my voice. "But why . . . ? You never saw me before in your life."

"Did I say I did? I just said I was waitin'."

We were on the edge of town now. He had turned and I had turned with him along the darkening riverbank toward the trestle where the night trains ran over going east, going west, but stopping rare few times.

"You want to know anything about me?" I asked, suddenly. "You the sheriff?"

"No, not the sheriff. And no, I don't want to know nothing about you." He put his hands in his pockets. The sun was set now. The air was suddenly cool. "I'm just surprised you're here at last, is all."

"Surprised?"

"Surprised," he said, "and . . . pleased."

I stopped abruptly and looked straight at him.

"How long have you been sitting on that station platform?"

"Twenty years, give or take a few."

I knew he was telling the truth; his voice was as easy and quiet as the river.

"Waiting for me?" I said.

"Or someone like you," he said.

We walked on in the growing dark.

"How you like our town?"

"Nice, quiet," I said.

"Nice, quiet." He nodded. "Like the people?"

"People look nice and quiet."

"They are," he said. "Nice, quiet."

I was ready to turn back but the old man kept talking and in order to listen and be polite I had to walk with him in the vaster darkness, the tides of field and meadow beyond town.

"Yes," said the old man, "the day I retired, twenty years ago, I sat down on that station platform and there I been, sittin', doin' nothin', waitin' for something to happen, I didn't know what, I didn't know, I couldn't say. But when it finally happened, I'd know it, I'd look at it and say, yes sir, that's what I was waitin' for. Train wreck? No. Old woman friend come back to town after fifty years? No. No. It's hard to say. Someone. Something. And it seems to have something to do with you. I wish I could say—"

"Why don't you try?" I said.

The stars were coming out. We walked on.

"Well," he said slowly, "you know much about your own insides?"

"You mean my stomach or you mean psychologically?"

"That's the word. I mean your head, your brain, you know much about *that*?"

The grass whispered under my feet. "A little."

"You hate many people in your time?"

"Some."

"We all do. It's normal enough to hate, ain't it, and not only hate but, while we don't talk about it, don't we sometimes want to hit people who hurt us, even *kill* them?"

"Hardly a week passes we don't get that feeling," I said, "and put it away."

"We put away all our lives," he said. "The town says thus and so, Mom and Dad say this and that, the law says such and such. So you put away one killing and another and two more after that. By the time you're my age, you got lots of that kind of stuff between your ears. And unless you went to war, nothin' ever happened to get rid of it."

"Some men trapshoot or hunt ducks," I said. "Some men box or wrestle."

"And some don't. I'm talkin' about them that don't. Me. All my life I've been saltin' down those bodies, puttin' 'em away on ice in my head. Sometimes you get mad at a town and the people in it for makin' you put things aside like that. You like the old cave men who just gave a hell of a yell and whanged someone on the head with a club."

"Which all leads up to . . . ?"

"Which all leads up to: everybody'd like to do one killin' in his life, to sort of work off that big load of stuff, all those killin's in his mind he never did have the guts to do. And once in a while a man has a chance. Someone runs in front of his car and he forgets the brakes and keeps goin'. Nobody can prove nothin' with that sort of thing. The man don't even tell himself he did it. He just didn't get his foot on the brake in time. But you know and I know what really happened, don't we?"

"Yes," I said.

The town was far away now. We moved over a small stream on a wooden bridge, just near the railway embankment.

"Now," said the old man, looking at the water, "the only kind of killin' worth doin' is the one where nobody can guess who did it or why they did it or who they did it to, right? Well, I got this idea maybe twenty years ago. I don't think about it every day or every week. Sometimes months go by, but the idea's this: only one train stops here each day, sometimes not even that. Now, if you wanted to kill someone you'd have to wait, wouldn't you, for years and years, until a complete and actual stranger came to your town, a stranger who got off the train for no reason, a man nobody knows and who don't know nobody in the town. Then, and only then, I thought, sittin' there on the station chair, you could just go up and when nobody's around, kill him and throw him in the river. He'd be found miles downstream. Maybe he'd never be found. Nobody would ever think to come to Rampart Junction to find him. He wasn't goin' there. He was on his way someplace else. There, that's my whole idea. And I'd know that man the minute he got off the train. Know him, just as clear . . ."

I had stopped walking. It was dark. The moon would not be up for an hour.

"Would you?" I said.

"Yes," he said. I saw the motion of his head looking at the stars. "Well, I've talked enough." He sidled close and touched my elbow. His hand was feverish, as if he had held it to a stove before touching me. His other hand, his right hand, was hidden, tight and bunched, in his pocket. "I've talked enough."

Something screamed.

I jerked my head.

Above, a fast-flying night express razored along the unseen tracks, flourished light on hill, forest, farm, town dwellings, field, ditch, meadow, plowed earth and water, then, raving high, cut off away, shrieking, gone. The rails trembled for a little while after that. Then, silence.

The old man and I stood looking at each other in the dark. His left hand was still holding my elbow. His other hand was still hidden.

"May I say something?" I said at last.

The old man nodded.

"About myself," I said. I had to stop. I could hardly breathe. I forced myself to go on. "It's funny. I've often thought the same way as you. Sure, just today, going cross-country, I thought, How perfect, how perfect, how really perfect it could be. Business has been bad for me, lately. Wife sick. Good friend died last week. War in the world. Full of boils, myself. It would do me a world of good—"

"What?" the old man said, his hand on my arm.

"To get off this train in a small town," I said, "where nobody knows me, with this gun under my arm, and find someone and kill them and bury them and go back down to the station and get on and go home and nobody the wiser and nobody ever to know who did it, ever. Perfect, I thought, a perfect crime. And I got off the train."

We stood there in the dark for another minute, staring at each other. Perhaps we were listening to each other's hearts beating very fast, very fast indeed.

The world turned under me. I clenched my fists. I wanted to fall. I wanted to scream like the train.

For suddenly I saw that all the things I had just said were not lies put forth to save my life.

All the things I had just said to this man were true.

And now I knew why I had stepped from the train and walked up through this town. I knew what I had been looking for.

I heard the old man breathing hard and fast. His hand was tight on my arm as if he might fall. His teeth were clenched. He leaned toward me as I leaned toward him. There was a terrible silent moment of immense strain as before an explosion.

He forced himself to speak at last. It was the voice of a man crushed by a monstrous burden.

"How do I know you got a gun under your arm?"

"You don't know." My voice was blurred. "You can't be sure."

He waited. I thought he was going to faint.

"That's how it is?" he said.

"That's how it is," I said.

He shut his eyes tight. He shut his mouth tight.

After another five seconds, very slowly, heavily, he managed to take his hand away from my own immensely heavy arm. He looked down at his right hand then, and took it, empty, out of his pocket.

Slowly, with great weight, we turned away from each other and started walking blind, completely blind, in the dark.

The midnight Passenger-to-be-picked-up flare sputtered on the tracks. Only when the train was pulling out of the station did I lean from the open Pullman door and look back.

The old man was seated there with his chair tilted against the station wall, with his faded blue pants and shirt and his sun-baked face and his sun-bleached eyes. He did not glance at me as the train slid past. He was gazing east along the empty rails where tomorrow or the next day or the day after the day after that, a train, some train, any train, might fly by here, might slow, might stop. His face was fixed, his eyes were blindly frozen, toward the east. He looked a hundred years old.

The train wailed.

Suddenly old myself, I leaned out, squinting.

Now the darkness that had brought us together stood between. The old man, the station, the town, the forest, were lost in the night.

For an hour I stood in the roaring blast staring back at all that darkness.

HATED

CHRISTOPHER FOWLER

*"You have to be in a pretty bad mood to write a story like this one,"
says Christopher Fowler. Even the stripped-down title—five letters
baring their teeth at us—drips venom in its wake.*

*Happily for the author, he may himself have cheered up after get-
ting such a misanthropic little tale out of his system.*

The question is, where does that leave the reader?

⑨

THE FIRST INKLING Michael Everett Townsend had that something was wrong was when his wife slapped him hard around
the face.

She had never slapped his face before. Michael hadn't been
expecting the blow. He was carrying a glass of milk, and it shot out
of his hand, spattering them both. The glass was cheap and just
bounced on the rug, but he jumped back in shock and stepped on it,
cracking the thing into shards, one of which pierced his bare foot.
Gasping in pain, he dropped down on the edge of the bed just as the
blood began to pour freely from his wounded sole. Instead of the
sympathy he expected to receive, however, his wife gave a scream of
rage and a mighty shove, and tipped him onto the floor. Then she
began looking for a knife.

Michael's wife really loved him.

But then, everyone did. Michael was the most popular man in the entire apartment building. The superintendent gave him preferential treatment because unlike the other tenants he never complained about the heating, which was always too hot or nonexistent. Betty, Michael's next-door neighbor, adored him because he had once scared a drugged-up burglar from the hallway at two in the morning, because he professed an admiration for the people of North Yorkshire where she had grown up, and because he had shown her how to replace the washers in her bathroom taps. Mitzi and Karen, the two blonde Australian flight attendants on the floor below, liked him because he was cute and a gentleman, because he paid them the respect they were denied in the air and because they were attuned to potential romantic material, married or otherwise.

But it wasn't just the apartment building. The staff at work loved Michael and showed it, which was unusual, because in London-based companies very few people are willing to reveal their personal loyalties in any direction. The Asian couple who ran the deli at the corner doted on him, because he always asked after their handicapped son, and managed to pronounce the boy's name correctly. And dozens of other people whose lives crossed Michael's felt a little bit richer for knowing him. He was a popular guy. And if he was honest with himself, he knew it.

Michael had been aware of his popularity since the age of five, winning over creepy aunts and tobacco-stained uncles with an easy smile. An only child in a quiet middle-class family, he had grown up in sun-dappled suburbia, lavished with love. His parents still worshipped him, calling once a week to catch up with his latest exploits. He had been a golden child who remained golden in adulthood.

Golden. That was the perfect word.

Blond-haired, blue-eyed, broad-shouldered, thirty-two, and married to an intelligent, talented, attractive woman. When Michael spoke others listened, nodding sagely as they considered his point. They wanted to call him by a nickname that would imply intimate friendship, Micky or Mike. What they liked about him was hard for them to define; perhaps they enjoyed basking in the reflection of his success. Perhaps he made them feel more confident in their own abilities.

The truth was simpler than that. Michael was at ease in his world. Even his most casual conversations made sound sense. In a life that was filled with uncertainties he was a totally reliable factor, a bedrock, a touchstone. And others sensed it. Everyone knew that they were in the presence of a winner.

Until the night of the accident, that is.

It really wasn't Michael's fault. The rain was beating so heavily that the windscreen wipers couldn't clear it on the fastest setting. It was a little after 11 P.M., and he was driving slowly and carefully back from the office, where he had been working late. He was thinking about Marla curled up in bed, waiting to hear his key in the lock. He had just coasted the Mercedes through the water chute that a few hours ago had been the road leading to Muswell Hill Broadway when a bicycle materialised from the downpour. On it sat a heavy-set figure in a yellow slicker—but not for long. The figure slammed into the bonnet of the car, then rolled off heavily and fell to the ground. Michael stamped his boot down on the brake, caused the car to fish-tail up against the curb in a spray of dirty water.

He jumped out of the vehicle and ran to the prostrate figure.

"Jeesus *focking* Christ!" The cyclist was in his late forties, possibly South American, very pissed off. Michael tried to help him to his feet but was shoved away. "Don' touch me, man, just don't *focking* touch me!" He turned back to his bicycle and pulled it upright. The thing had no lights, no brakes, nothing. And the guy sounded drunk or stoned. Michael was feeling less guilty by the second.

"Look, I'm really sorry I hit you, but you just appeared in front of me. It's lucky I wasn't going any faster."

"Yeah, right—lucky me." The handlebars of the bike were twisted, and it didn't look like they could be straightened out without a spanner. He hurled the bicycle onto the verge in disgust.

"I can give you a ride," offered Michael. The driver door of the Mercedes was still open. The leather upholstery was getting wet.

"I don' want no *focking* ride in a rich man's car, asshole!" shouted the cyclist, pushing him away.

"Look, I'm trying to be civilised about this," said Michael, who was always civilised. "You had no lights on, you came straight through a stop sign without even slowing down, what on earth was I supposed to do?"

"I could sue your ass off is what *I* could do." The cyclist stared angrily as he gingerly felt his neck and shoulder. "I don' know that nothin' is broken here."

"You've probably pulled a muscle," said Michael, trying to be helpful.

"What, are you a doctor?" The reply was aggressive, the glare relentless.

It was a no-win situation. Time to get away from this crazy person and go back to the car, dry off the seats and head for home. Michael started to back away.

"I've offered you a lift, but if you're going to be—"

"Don' put yoursel' out. I live right over there." The cyclist pointed across the block. "Just give me your address. Write it down so I can contact you."

Michael hesitated. He didn't like the idea of giving his address to a stranger. "Why would you need to call me?" he asked.

"Jee*sus*, why do you think? It turns out I got a dislocated shoulder or something, I gonna get a claim in on you, make you pay to get it fixed. You just better pray they don' find nothin' wrong with me, man."

Reluctantly, Michael pulled a business card from his wallet and passed it across. Moments later he was heading back to the car and checking his watch. The whole business had lasted less than a couple of minutes. Behind the wheel once more, he watched the yellow slicker drift away into the rain mist and thought about the accident.

It was unusual for him to be placed in any kind of confrontational situation and not come out a winner. His likeability could defuse the most volatile of personalities. As he turned the key in the ignition, he wondered if there would be any repercussions. Suppose this chap had actually broken something and didn't know it yet? How did he stand, insurance-wise? He was thinking of himself, but hell, it had been the other party's fault. Michael was nice but no saint. His comfortable life made few allowances for upsets, and breaks in the smooth running of his routine irritated the hell out of him.

"Darling, you're all wet. What have you been doing?" Marla reached up and hugged him, her bed-warm breasts goose-pimpling against his damp jacket.

"There was a bit of an accident. I hit a cyclist. Had to get out of the car." He gently disentangled himself and began removing his clothes.

She pulled the sheet around her. "How awful. What happened?"

"He wasn't looking where he was going. I could have killed him. Luckily, he didn't seem hurt, but—"

The telephone rang. Marla shared his look of surprise. Their friends all knew that they had a seven-year-old son in the next room and never called the house late. Michael pulled the instrument toward him by the cord and raised the receiver. A wail of bizarre music squealed from the earpiece. "Hello, who is this?"

"This the guy you *hit* tonight, brother."

"How did you get my ho—"

"My shoulder's dislocated. Bad news for you. Real bad karma."

The guy couldn't have seen a doctor already, even if he'd gone straight to casualty.

"Are you sure? I mean, how—"

"Sure I'm sure, you think you're dealing with a fockin' idiot? Patty, she says it's all bust up. Which means I can't work. An' you have to pay me compensation. S'gon be a *lot* of money, man."

"Now wait a minute . . ." Maybe this was some kind of scam, a professional con trick.

Marla was tapping his arm, mouthing "Who is it?"

He slipped his hand over the mouthpiece. "The chap I hit tonight."

"You still there? You gonna pay me to get fixed up or what?"

"Look, if you think you have a case for extracting money from me, I think you're wrong." Michael's famous niceness was starting to slip. Who the hell did this guy think he was, finding his home number and calling so late at night? "But if you really have damaged yourself, it's your own fault for riding without lights and not watching the traffic."

"You don' know who you're dealing with," came the reply. "You just made the biggest mistake of your life."

"Are you threatening me?"

"I'm just saying that people like you need to be taught a fockin' lesson, treating guys like me as if we don' exist."

Michael stared at the receiver. This was bullshit. He was in the right, the other party was in the wrong. The law was on his side. And he cared, he had a social conscience. But the thought struck him, what if the accident had somehow been his fault after all?

"You still there? Tell me, Mr. Townsend, what's your biggest fear? That your child get sick? That your wife get up and leave you?"

A chill prickled at Michael's neck. He didn't like this crazy man using his name, talking about his family. And how did he know he was even married? Was it that obvious, just by looking at the car?

"No, you scared o' something else even more, but you don't even know it. I see through people like you. Don't take much to break a man like you." There was contempt in the voice, as if the caller was reading his mind.

"Now listen," Michael snapped, "you have no right to threaten me, not when you endangered my life as well as your own. I could get the police—"

The voice on the line cut in. "When you come to find me—an' you will—it won' be with no damn police."

Suddenly the line went dead. Michael shrugged and replaced the handset.

"Well, what did he say?"

"Oh, he was just—abusive," he replied distractedly, watching the rain spangle over the streetlights.

"Do you have his number?"

"Hmm?"

"His number, do you have it in case there's a problem?"

Michael realised that he didn't even know the name of the man he'd hit.

He rose early, leaving his wife curled beneath the duvet. Surprisingly, even little Sean had slept on in the adjoining bedroom. Michael showered and donned a shirt, grabbed a piece of toast and poured himself a glass of milk. Then he climbed the stairs and gently woke his wife.

And she slapped his face.

The glass broke. The milk splashed. He stepped back and cut his foot, but the pain had already given way to hurt. Puzzled, he ran his fingers across his reddening cheek.

"What the hell—what are you looking for?"

She was frantically searching beneath the mattress, then pulled up short in confusion.

"You—shouldn't creep up on me like that." Marla slunk back beneath the covers, sleep-pressed hair folding over her eyes. She turned her back to him, embarrassed by the vivid dream that had leaked over into reality. Picking the glass from his foot, he watched a drop of crimson blood disperse in an alabaster puddle of milk like a spreading virus.

An Elastoplast took care of the wound. He rattled the glass fragments into a box which he sealed and placed in the pedal bin beneath the sink, then listened as his son thumped downstairs.

"Sean? You want Crunchy-Crunch?" He cocked his head. No answer. Odd. The boy could always be drawn by mention of his favorite breakfast cereal. "Seanie?"

He looked around to find the boy glaring distrustfully at him through the bannisters. "Sean, what's the matter? Come down and pour your milk on."

The child shook his head slowly and solemnly, mumbling something to himself. He pulled his stripy sweatshirt over his chin and locked his arms around his knees. He stared through the bars, but he wouldn't descend any further.

"Come and have your breakfast, Sean. We can take some up to Mummy." Another muffled reply.

Michael set the dustpan aside and took a step toward his son. "I can't hear what you're saying."

"*You're not my daddy*," the boy screamed suddenly, scrambling back up the stairs to the safety of his bedroom.

Michael checked himself in the rear-view mirror. The same pleasant, confident face looked back, although the smile was a little less certain than usual. He drove through the avenue of sodden embankment trees heading into the city and wondered about the behavior of his family. He didn't wonder for long; the three of them had managed to maintain a problem-free existence until now, cushioned perhaps by Marla's inherited wealth and his own easy-going attitude. If they got under each other's feet in town there was always the cottage in Norfolk, a convenient ivy-covered bolt hole that provided healing seclusion. But the memory of the slap lingered as clearly as if the hand print had remained on his face.

Michael parked the car in the underground garage and took the lift to the seventh floor where he worked for Aberfitch McKiernny, a law firm dealing primarily with property disputes. The receptionist glanced up as he passed but failed to grant him her usual morning smile. The switchboard operators glared sullenly in his wake. Even the postboy seemed to be ignoring him. Why was everyone in such a bad mood today?

Michelle was already waiting by his door. She was the most efficient secretary he had ever employed. Power-dressed in tight black raw cotton, her pale hair knotted carefully at her neck, she impatiently tapped a pair of IBM disks against the palm of her hand while she waited for him to remove his coat.

"You were supposed to take these home with you last night," she explained, passing them over.

"I didn't get around to them. The Trowerbridge case took up all my time. I'll try to run them later this morning."

She reached over and took the disks back. "I don't think that will do any good. Your 'opinion' was needed yesterday. No one will want it today."

She stressed the words strangely, as if she no longer held much respect for him. Michael seated himself behind his desk and studied her. What was going on here? Michelle had always been his biggest fan, his greatest supporter. It was obvious to everyone that she was more than a little in love with him, and he played on the knowledge mercilessly. But today her tone had changed. There was a testiness in her voice, as if she had seen inside him and no longer desired what she saw.

"Michelle, are you okay?"

She folded her arms across her chest, pure frost. "Fine. Why?"

"I don't know, you sound so—"

"You'd better get into Leo's office. He's been calling for you. He sounds pretty angry about something."

Leo Tarrant, fifty-seven, the calm center of the firm, was at peace because he knew he was retiring in a year, and no longer let anything in the world worry him. But this morning he wasn't like that. His usually slick grey mane was ruffled about his head. His face was sclerotic and mottled with suppressed rage. He tipped back his chair and flicked rhythmically at the sides of a gold cigarette case, reminder of his past habit, now a talisman of his strengthened heart.

"You've let me down badly with this Trowerbridge business," he admitted. "I thought I'd get an early result by placing it in your hands. Instead it now looks as if they'll have to go to court after all."

Michael shifted uncomfortably in his seat. He simply couldn't comprehend Leo's attitude. Trowerbridge Developments had been sued by one of its tenants for failing to maintain a property. The company, aware that it had little chance of winning the case, had requested the negotiation of an out-of-court settlement by its long-standing legal representatives. Michael had done everything within his power to ensure that this would happen. After all, the clients were friends of his. They saw each other socially. Their kids even played together.

"I don't know what you're talking about, Leo," Michael confessed. "I completed my end of the deal in plenty of time to prevent the planned court action from going ahead."

"That's exactly the opposite of what I've heard," said his boss, clicking away at the clasp of the cigarette box. "According to the client's own progress report you've been holding back the negotiations and leaning so far in favor of the tenants that there's precious little time left for Trowerbridge to cut himself a deal. Neither he nor his son can see any way of making a satisfactory settlement. And there's something else."

Michael was dumbfounded. He couldn't have worked any harder for these people. If this was their way of showing gratitude . . .

"Have you ever received any financial inducements from the Trowerbridge family? Negative-equity absorbers, anything like that?"

The old man was accusing him of taking a bribe? He could scarcely believe his ears.

"No, of course not," he spluttered furiously. "I'm amazed that you could even consider—"

"Calm down, I'm not saying you did. It's something that the corporation suggested I look into. Think back over your relationship with Trowerbridge during the past few months, would you? You'd better make damned sure that there's nothing in your recent dealings with them that could damage your standing with this firm. Now let's go over these complaints in detail." He produced a slim red file and carefully unfolded it.

For the next hour and a half Michael was interrogated about his handling of the impending lawsuit. Although he left Leo's office more or less vindicated, he knew from the look on the old man's face that something irretrievable had been lost; a level of trust had been removed. The layer of good faith that had always existed between himself and his superiors had been torn away like the stripes from a dishonored soldier's tunic. It wasn't just a matter of rebuilding Leo's confidence in him. He wanted to know why his abilities had been so quickly doubted. Clearly the Trowerbridge family, father and son, had lied, and Leo had believed them. But why should they do that? What had they to gain beyond an undesired delay to the lawsuit? It made no sense.

He considered the problem for the rest of the morning, during which time his secretary proved barely capable of common civility. She appeared briefly throughout the day to dump dockets on his desk, and at one point when he glanced up at her looked as if she was about to file a harassment suit against him. Michael felt the ground shifting fast beneath him. As he was leaving the building that evening, the doorman grumpily revealed that his parking space had been switched to a smaller, more awkward stall further away from the main doors.

Marla already sounded bored with the topic of conversation. They had washed up the dinner things together. Now she had turned back to the sink and was wiping down surfaces unnecessarily; the cleaning lady was due first thing tomorrow. Eventually aware that he had asked her a question, she sighed and faced him. "I just don't know, Michael. These things happen. There's no point in getting paranoid. Nobody's out to get you."

"Well, it certainly feels like they are," he complained, digging a bottle of Scotch from the cupboard and pouring himself a generous measure.

His wife made a face; disbelief, dissatisfaction, he couldn't read which. "You know," she said slowly, "maybe you're just experiencing the real world for a change."

"What the hell is that supposed to mean?"

She gestured vaguely about her. "You know what you're like. You've always had this kind of—aura of perfection surrounding you. People go out of their way to make things easy for you. Perhaps they're not doing it this once, and you've simply noticed for the first time."

He drained the glass and set it down on the kitchen table. "Marla, that's ridiculous and you know it."

"Is it? You glide through life in a golden haze expecting people to move out of your way just because you're you." She fell silent for a moment, then turned back to the sink. "It was something I noticed about you the day we met. A quality very few men ever possess. It's something you normally only find in very pretty girls, and then just for a couple of years. Doors automatically open. No one has ever found me special like that, only you. The rest of us trail in your wake. Well, maybe it's our turn in the sun for a while."

It seemed to Michael that he was being presented with a day of revelations, that he was somehow seeing himself clearly for the first time, from above, perhaps, or from a distance.

He rose and moved to his wife's side, gently placing his hands upon her hips. "I can't understand why you've never talked to me about this before," he said softly, "why you couldn't have been more honest with me."

"What's the point when you're not prepared to be honest about yourself?" she asked, coolly removing his hands. "If you want complete candor, then I'll tell you. I really don't think I can bear you touching me any more."

The room fell silent and remained so. Sean would not come down to kiss him goodnight and hid behind his mother's skirt until she took him up to bed.

He didn't think the situation could get any worse, but it did.

Marla would not talk about her refusal to allow his touch. At night she kept to the far side of the bed and took to sleeping in a T-shirt and pants. In the mornings she was up and dressed before him. She had usually washed and fed her son by the time he arose, so that the pair of them presented his sleepy form with a smart united front. Although she refused to be drawn on the subject of their halted sex life, she conceded that no one else was stealing her affection from him. It was simply something that had finally, and perhaps inevitably, occurred.

Frozen out of his own home, he increased his hours in the office.

But there the situation was just as bad. The Trowerbridge case had been lost and everyone now regarded him with suspicion, as if he'd been caught stealing office supplies and let off with a warning. Sometimes members of staff insulted him just out of earshot. At the very least they ignored him. Michael became aware that parties and dinners were being arranged behind his back and that he had become the butt of cheap, stupid jokes. Much of the time no one seemed to notice him at all. If he joined a group at the coffee machine and struck up a conversation, they would glance over his shoulder, noting something or someone that interested them more. If he tried to make a social arrangement they cried off with transparently feeble excuses, not even bothering to convince him of their unavailability.

Petty grievances, of a kind that had never occurred before, began to accumulate. He was given the dullest briefs to work on. Someone left a bottle of Listerine on his desk in response to an office perception that he suffered from halitosis. Even the parking attendant had the temerity to suggest that he attend more carefully to his personal hygiene.

At last, at the end of his tether, he asked his secretary to enter his office and to close the door behind her.

"I want you to be honest with me, Michelle," he said carefully, seating himself and bidding her do the same. "I find everyone's attitude towards me has changed drastically in the last two weeks, and I'm at a loss to understand why."

"You want the honest truth?" asked Michelle, pointedly examining her cuticles.

"Please," pleaded Michael, ready to absorb her reply and analyse it at length.

"Well, it's the way you treat people, like they're satellites around your planet. I used to find it exciting, very masculine. I rather fancied you, all that rugged decisiveness. Others did too. Now I wonder how I could have been so blind." She shifted uncomfortably. "Can I go now?"

"Certainly not!" He snorted, wondered, shook his head in bewilderment. "Explain what you mean. What do the others say about me?"

Michelle stared up at the ceiling and blew the air from her cheeks. "Oh, you know, the usual . . . that you're self-centered, boring, pushy, less clever than you think you are. You're just not a very likeable man any more."

"And you can sit there and say this to my face?" he asked.

"I've already applied for a transfer," she answered, rising.

Michael realised then that if he went out and bought a dog it would probably run off, just to be away from him. Seated on a wet bench in the bedraggled little park beneath the office, watching as the pigeons strutted toward his shoes and then veered away, he became seized with the idea that someone had placed a curse on him. Not your usual get-boils-and-die curse, but something subtler. There was only one wild card to consider, one suspect, and that was Mr. Whatever-his-name-was on the bike, the Latin chap he'd knocked over. The more Michael considered it, the clearer it became that his troubles had truly begun after that angry night-time phone call. He remembered the voice on the line: "What's your biggest fear? . . . Don't take much to break a man like you . . . When you come to find me—an' you will . . ." It all began to make sense. Could there be a rational explanation for what was happening to him? Was the guy some kind of shaman in touch with the supernatural, a malevolent hypnotist, or just someone with the power of suggestion? Wasn't that how voodoo worked? He was determined to take positive action.

It was dark by the time he finally got out of the office. Nosing the car back toward the intersection where the accident had occurred, he remembered the cyclist's response to his offer of a lift. "I just live over there."

"*Over there*" proved to be a prefabricated two-story block of council flats. With no other way of locating his tormentor, he began ringing doorbells and facing irate residents, most of whom were in the middle of eating dinner. One of them even swore and spat at him, but by now he was used to that kind of behavior. Trudging along the cracked, flooded balconies like a demented rent collector, he suddenly recalled a name mentioned in the phone call—Patty. Hadn't she checked out the cyclist's damaged shoulder? At least it was something specific, a person he could ask to see.

After being abused in four more doorways, he was nearing the end of the first floor with only a few apartments remaining when a young Asian man with dragons tattooed on his arms pointed to the flat at the end of the corridor.

"She's married to a Mexican guy who plays weird music all night," he complained.

Leaning against the garbage chute was the bicycle that he had hit, now repaired.

"That's the one," said Michael, thanking him and setting off. He stood before the door and read the printed card wedged next to the broken bell.

"You're back sooner than I expected," said Ramon del Tierro, faith healer, opening the door at his knock and ushering him in. "I didn't think you'd come to me for at least another week."

The hallway was in darkness. Mariachi music was playing in one of the bedrooms. The flat was slightly perfumed, as though someone had been burning incense earlier. Ramon was slighter and smaller than he remembered, pallid and unhealthy looking. His left eye was milky, blinded. He led the way to a small, smartly decorated lounge and waved him to a seat. Michael didn't want to sit. He no longer considered the situation absurd. He just wanted an answer, and an end to the hatred.

"You did this to me, didn't you?" The tightness in his voice made him realise how much anger he was holding back.

"Did what? Tell me what I did." Ramon shrugged, faking puzzlement.

"You made me—made everyone detest me."

"Hey, how could I do that? You soun' like a crazy man. You want to know how my shoulder is? Thank you for askin', it's gonna be okay." He turned away. "I'm gonna make some coffee. You wan' some?"

"I want you to tell me *what you did*, damn it!" Michael shouted, grabbing a scrawny arm.

Ramon glared fiercely and remained silent until he released his grip. Then he softly spoke.

"I have a gift, Mr. Townsend. A crazy, pointless gift. If it had been second sight or somethin' I might have made some money from it, but no. When I come into contact with strangers I can see what makes them happy or sad. Sometimes I can sense what they fear or who they love. It depends on who I touch. Sometimes I don't feel nothin' at all. But I felt it with you. An' I made you see how life can be when you don't have the one thing you value most. In your case, it's your popularity. I took away your charm. You're no longer a like-able guy. I just didn't think it would screw you up as bad as this. I guess you must love yourself a whole lot more than you love anyone else."

Michael ran a hand across his face, suddenly tired. "Why did you pick on me for this particular—experiment?"

"Because I can, and because you deserved it. Now, what you gonna do about that? Go cryin' to the police, tell them nobody likes you?"

Fury was rising within Michael, bubbling to the surface in a malignant mist. "What—do you want—from me?"

"I don' want nothing from you, Mr. Townsend. You got nothin' I want."

"You sabotaged my job."

Ramon shook his head. "No sir, I did not. Anythin' that's happening to you is happening 'cause people just don't like you no more."

"Then you can make it end."

The healer considered this for a moment, scratching at his chin with a thumbnail. "I guess I could, but I don't want to. See, it's better for you to relearn yourself from scratch. Won't be easy the way you are now, but just makin' the effort would turn you into a better person."

Michael knew that if he moved too close he would lash out at Ramon. His temper was slow to rise but formidable to witness. Now he clenched his fists and advanced on the little Mexican. "You get this fucking thing off me straight away, you filthy little spic, or I will beat you unconscious and burn this shit hole down with you in it, do you understand?"

"Now you're showin' your true colors, Mr. Townsend." Ramon took a step back, wary but not nervous. "A soul like yours takes an awful lot of fixin'. Tell me what it is you want."

"I want you to make everyone love me again," he said, suddenly embarrassed by the realisation of his needs.

"That I can do."

"How soon?"

"In a few seconds, with just a touch. But you won't like it. Consider the other way, I beg you. Relearn. Begin again with the personality you have now. It will be more difficult, but the rewards will be much greater."

"I can't do that. I need this to happen tonight."

"Then it will have to be the hard way. Come closer to me."

Michael walked into Ramon's outstretched arms. Before he had time to realise what was happening, he felt the thin-bladed knife that Ramon had pulled from his pocket bite between the ribs traversing his heart. The fiery razor edge sliced through the beating muscle, piercing a ventricle and ending his life in a single crimson moment.

So many people turned up at St. Peter's Church that they ran out of parking spaces and had to leave their cars on the grass verges lining the road. The funeral service boasted eulogies from the senior partners of Aberfitch McKiernny, from friends and relatives, from his colleagues and from his adoring wife. Everyone who went to the burial of Michael Everett Townsend volubly agreed; the man being laid to rest here was truly loved by everyone.

BEING KIND

VICTORIA ROTHSCHILD

Somewhere between déjà vu and prescience exists another state of knowing, an almost-recognition that won't quite let us call it by name. Throughout Victoria Rothschild's story of an English gentility overmatched by greedy shadows, the author maintains both a discreet distance and a subtly shifting point of view.

✿

So, SAID DAISY FERN, birdy and bright, pecking a little bit closer to her neighbor, "so when is your day?"

Edith took her stand on the other side, on her side of the vestigial hedge—lavender, the two women had managed to agree on that. It was a moment before she gave her answer; this was not out of forgetfulness but because she wanted to give weight to her reply. At last:

"Friday," she told her friend portentously, "Anthony will come on Friday. This Friday."

"Oh." Daisy jerked her head excitedly. "What happened? Has anything happened? She hasn't gone back to him, has she? Oh, *Edith*—" But Edith reassured her: Anthony, Edith's only son, only offspring, was still bereft, still abandoned, he remained attractively and interestingly heartbroken. The dreaded Belinda had not gone back to him, had not summonsed or even visited their children, she had indeed bolted into the blue and everyone in this enclave of retired gentlewomen still reeled from the excitement. It was by now six o'clock and a soft warm evening. The Downs stretched fat and lazy towards light woodland and the coast. You could see right across the valley to the spires of Chichester and the pale ribbon of the sea beyond. There was not a hint of cold. All the same it was time for the two women to go indoors.

The friends complemented each other: where Daisy had changed everything she'd brought with her from her family home and went on changing, banging up new pictures and knocking through old walls, Edith had let her half of the twin houses be as it always had been. Whether from laziness, languor or a peculiar kind of stubbornness, her side did not change; Edith and her past, Daisy said, Edith and her dead, for Pleasance resembled an unchanged but miniature version of the home where Edith and Peter had lived. With Anthony. The front door gave immediately onto a small sitting room. The dividing wall had been knocked out some time before to give a view straight through to the back and up towards the gentle inland hills, with their sprinkling of woodland and ponies grazing in the scrub in between. The back door was never used.

To divide up the room and create a sense of passage Edith had brought the old pine kitchen dresser from home to bisect it. It would also form a sort of windbreak for the winters. She had hoarded everything else for Pleasance herself during the long years of anticipation of her retirement. That's what Peter had called it cynically, the time they had both imagined for her after he'd gone. She had crammed the shelves full of the little figurines, Delft and Dresden and Staffordshire, which she had collected—shepherds and shepherdesses, dogs, miniature platters, china books, two cats, a cricketer that must have come from Peter, and of course the actor and actress, Garrick and Bellamy, which the company had given her when she left them for marriage. There were also the leather-bound two-volume life of Garrick and the tiny stiff six-volume memoirs of George Anne herself. But the photos which had always been kept under glass at home she'd put up newly framed on the shelves: herself as Gertrude, herself as

Desdemona, being decorously strangled by the man she didn't marry—what had his name been? She'd been so sad when she heard of his death those years ago—how terrible it was, she thought, that she could not for the moment remember his name.

Edith reached down to the cupboard underneath, brought out tumblers and poured a couple of hefty vodka martinis. She passed the drink over to Daisy—already installed at the chess set—and wondered why it was that she minded this bolting so much less than her friend. Daisy hadn't even met Anthony yet—not since he was a child. He could mean nothing to her. Edith had moved into Pleasance nearly two months ago now but her arrival had coincided almost exactly with Belinda's departure. As a consequence Anthony had been too upset to visit his mother in her new home. And then there were the arrangements to be made, details over the children's schooling, and holidays, and diseases over which Edith fancied she had clucked and fussed in an acceptably grandparental telephonic manner. But now—without guilt but with genuine curiosity—she thought of how she had been able to listen to her son's broken voice during those weeks, and register the cost to him of stifling unmanly tears, and that she had managed to brood over all those endless practical problems—the measles, the school play, the this, the that—without any real pang of unhappiness at all. What she really felt was a pang which she suspected was unseemly for the frightful Belinda, who she knew was appalling, who had certainly behaved appallingly, but whom she almost irresistibly wanted to help in some way, to have over, and cosset, and nurture. She wanted to enfold her in loving, accepting arms; to bake bread just for her, the errant daughter-in-law. By contrast with her excitable friend, Edith heard all her son's misery, his quite broken, his surprisingly broken spirit, his abandonment, with considerable interest but quite without feeling.

She joined Daisy at the chess set and made her move. In the second she swiped one of her friend's pawns.

"Ouch," said Daisy, "that was unusually ferocious of you," and swung out her bishop. "I never liked the sound of her, you know, *Belinda*." She helped herself to a refill. "She always sounded *to me* like one of those women who are too *big* and blonde and, well, I'm thinking of that photo which you have of her, the *clothes*—attention-seeking, I thought. *Loud.*" Suddenly Edith found Daisy Fern loud and Daisy's excited concern attention-seeking, because suddenly she found that after all she did want to mourn, for Anthony she supposed it must be, for his lost happiness, some idea of a family. But here was Daisy energetically chatterboxing on and being so distracting. Edith made a stab at the bishop. She got him too.

"*Edith*, this is unprecedented," chortled her friend. "*Nice* Edith on the war path?"

That was Wednesday.

The Thursday was Daisy Fern's day for visiting. She rather liked to make this distinction—for distinction was certainly what she considered it to be—because in contrast to the other ladies in this enclave and particularly in contrast to nice, *still* Edith, Daisy was the visitor, not the visited. None of this waiting like an old person. Her day came every couple of weeks when she travelled by train down to Brighton to visit her brother in the home there. Bernard was five years older, somewhat brighter and much iller. A stroke had partially paralysed him on the left side but he still enjoyed sea air and company. He and Daisy played their own game of chess every two weeks. They were also good friends. He was very tall and thin and stooped a little and hobbled because of this stiff gammy leg. His face was still handsome and long. He had never married. They had tried sharing a house at one point but found that they preferred each other's company at greater remove. They enjoyed confiding details of their separate lives. This week's news from the home was that Colonel Patterson, who always sat under a rug in the bay window and was visited regularly by his dutiful son, had suddenly run amok. He had thrown the young man out with menaces from his walking stick and then gone out onto the sea front and held up the rock shop next door, demanding money and sweets and to be left alone for God's sake for once. He had not yet been let out of protective custody. The place in the bay which overlooked the sea had been only briefly vacant before Bernard shuffled his chair into it. He was extremely pleased with himself for this maneuver. They basked in his glory, brother and sister, by the window which overlooked the beach. And settled to their game. Bernard won because he always did. Just as surely as Daisy won over Edith. These things did not change.

It was a late summer English seaside day and the light was soft and balmy over the pebbles on the shore. The place had all but emptied. A couple of people on the beach walked dogs, which ambled, carolled ahead.

Daisy told Bernard about Edith's son. She had formed a very vivid picture of him. Out of boredom more than malice she had a secret desire for it all to get just a little bit worse. But oh then, she checked herself, poor sweet-natured Edith would *mind*. And bake more bread and do all the things that she did, things that she should have left behind at the Old House with Peter. Daisy was going on with this, which was her news, how Anthony would finally come this Friday and then perhaps things would settle down at last, but in the middle of the story she found herself wondering what it was precisely she was telling her brother. What was this story? The tale of someone else's abandonment, someone she didn't even know, or remembered only as a dumpy toddler. She was amused at herself, at the lively and voracious way in which she had pounced on all this, while Edith—the more placid soul—had seemed strangely unperturbed. Anyway. It was a pleasant summer. A pleasant day. Thanks to the new diet and the warmth, her rheumatism had gone. And now that Edith had at last moved into Pleasance instead of just filling it up with all her things and going away again, the world seemed altogether a more benign place. Even their friendly bickering was an entertainment. The lavender would grow and all would be well.

So. Daisy, then, was in an uncharacteristically dreamy mood—noticed with competitive pleasure by her brother as he easily scored another gain—and gazed out over the sea gently washing over the pebbled shore. Idly, her eyes took in the figure of a solitary youth walking on the beach. What caught her eye was that he walked with speed and a sense of purpose which struck her as out of place for someone in a lazy seaside resort. It also made her want to go after him. He was tall and upright and went swiftly. His clothes were dark, slightly austere and something about them and his posture said to her old-fashioned. He wasn't in jeans, he seemed to have none of the scruffiness of youth. She didn't know quite why he so caught her imagination except that he also looked familiar to her, and when he turned his head slightly she tried to identify where she'd seen him before. Perhaps he was only the dreary son of the delinquent colonel, perhaps that was it—and she started to point him out to Bernard. But by then the young man was out of sight.

"Oh, nothing," said Daisy, "It was nothing." And she returned her bright attention to their game.

On the way back later that afternoon Daisy thought contentedly about homecoming and looked out at the sweet Englishness of the landscape as it chugged by. Painton hove into view looking as charming as one of those watercolors, like something out of a different era in the way it nestled into the deep cleft of the Downs themselves. The countryside held the small town on all sides, the demarcations were clear, not blurred by modern outskirts. As she approached on foot from the little station the row which concluded in their twin habitations Daisy Fern was suffused with a sense of contentedness.

That morning, the Thursday, in her half of the house Edith had woken to another lovely Sussex late summer day. There was no need to draw the curtains round here as the house looked straight out across the Downs to the coast with no opposing buildings at all, so a fresh stillness of the place and the sun all streamed into her new bedroom. She thought no further than to the impending visit; just took a good deal of pleasure in the comfortable knowledge that Peter was not one to begrudge her such moments. She still considered herself to be newly widowed—probably always would—although now three years had passed. To Edith it could have been this morning. Well, yesterday. Or last week. But the Peter, her Peter, with whom she checked in on an almost hourly basis would never begrudge her current pleasures. Her darling Peter on the other side was a much more generous man with her time than he had been in life. Still, it had been a marriage and she missed him. Edith stretched her arms and saw the skin of her hands ravel like gloves. Well, she told herself, make the coffee, make the place bright and nice for their poor son. Do this work until evening and the drink and the game when Daisy gets back. Almost like an evening at home, she thought. It would be all right, thought Edith. She would start with the sitting room.

But what would she do to welcome their wretched boy? She knew that Anthony always minded the slightest change in familiar surroundings. Edith felt a tiredness she could not explain. She had turned every room here into a mausoleum to family niceness in obedience to this one overgrown son. To be fair to Peter, he had always encouraged her, however caustically, in planning for her Retirement, but after his death Edith found that, instead of flourishing, her visits to junk shops and bookshops had grown furtive. It was as if she feared that their son would be shocked and unforgiving. That she would irredeemably let him down. As mother. Still, she had sold up and eventually moved here, and of course it was then, when she was finally installed, that his Belinda, large, blonde and certainly attention-seeking in her after-effects and shocks, had done her bunk. Bunked off from poor Anthony and the children with a man younger and even poorer than Edith's poor son.

So. At last it was time for Edith to get things ready for her son's visit. To be maternal even in retirement. And make him feel always at home. She'd do a bit of baking to fill the place with warm and summery smells of fresh mint and peas, the first apples, bread and then she'd start with the sitting room. Lovingly, Edith began to touch the figurines she had accumulated over the years.

When Daisy Fern checked in later with her friend she noticed that something was different about Pleasance. It smelt lovely—sort of homely, of fresh tomatoes, and herbs, and the sun. Edith had always had this womanly way about her. But there was something new. A different quality of light in the room, a kind of clarity, an edge. Then she saw what it was: that Edith must have spent the entire day rearranging her furniture. Somehow she had managed to move the dresser so that it was sideways on from the front door and you had a clear view through the whole house to the wooded hills behind. The figurines had come down from the dresser and crowded round the fireplace where Edith always sat. Also from the window sill at the back. The window there now stood open and a soft breeze lifted the blue curtains and riffled through the room. Edith's photos stood proud on all the low surfaces—herself as Gertrude, herself as Desdemona, herself with the company nearest the door.

"Oh," Daisy exclaimed, "but you've *worked*. It looks, it looks lovely." But she felt unsure of herself, because this wasn't the place she had left and wasn't the place she was used to. Edith smiled a secret smile.

"But why did you move the things from the window sill?"

"Just letting the light and the air in. The wind off the Downs comes right through the house—blows my cobwebs away. Peter was pleased," Edith added with a smile, the friends sharing the joke now. Nevertheless, in this nice, good life there was an edge and an edginess tonight. The Thursday. The two women would have dinner shortly, prepared by Edith, pecked at and commented on by Daisy. After the meal they would play cards and then watch News at ten last thing. There would be wine.

That night Daisy Fern's sleep was disturbed by a dream. In it she saw the man from the beach standing out on the Downs in front of their houses. He stood quite stiff, upright, and motionless but Daisy knew in that certain way one does in sleep that he was poised, coiled with desire to be inside. She also understood that she knew him, and in her sleep turned to Bernard to inform him that now she could remember. Bernard wasn't there. Quickly Daisy got up and ran into the night and next door and began to shore up the place against all the gaps and gapings which Edith had made, to pile back the china figurines and framed photos in a great immovable mountain against the back window, piling them so high that you couldn't even see out, so that the window was completely blocked. Up and up they went, her hands scrabbling frantically until Garrick and Bellamy were back on top and wedged around by portraits and sheep. In relief and exhaustion she set her back to the pile. And just as she did so a tumultuous noise started up which seemed to thunder all around the house. With that she felt a scratching and the slight movement begin. Daisy sat upright in bed and woke with a gasp. She looked out over the deep blue moonlit English landscape where not a soul stirred. She did not go down.

The morning of the Friday was as bright and fearless as ever and Daisy's dream had almost receded. As soon as she was up she went next door.

"I'll be a moment," called Edith from above. "Put on the volcano." Now this was the one gadget which Daisy had never mastered, so, to play for time really until Edith came to put in the correct proportions of coffee, she let in some light. She went round the room drawing back the curtains. She wasn't really looking when she pulled back the curtains at the back of the house. So it was a scream from Edith coming downstairs which told her to look. Bulging through the entire frame of the window was the massive head of one of the Downs ponies. Brown and protuberant and indifferent.

"Oh shoo," cried Edith, "shoo away." The horse stared blankly in, its black eyes gleaming.

"I *did* think I heard something, did *you*, in the night?" flapped Daisy.

But Edith, nice and calm again, had heard nothing, had slept better than for years, was only just up in fact. She made the coffee and they took it upstairs and when they came down eventually the horse had gone. Then they began to clear. Daisy as always rushed to get the washing up done, while Edith was still rather idling behind. Suddenly Daisy was irritated and snapped at her friend and she didn't know where it had come from but she snapped out:

"Oh, Edith, you're sitting there." It was angrier than she meant. And even as it came out of her she clamped a hand over her mouth as they both instantly realised it was what *he* used to say, it was the

Peter voice, his bullying voice, the real one, come out of nowhere, out of the blue out of her. Daisy didn't know, neither of them knew, what had got into them that morning. Fairly soon Daisy went back to her side. They'd meet later of course. And of course Anthony would be there.

When Daisy went she noticed that the turves of their garden and the lavender were all heaved up, the poor roots were out and drying, and the ground was all churned. That horse, horses in the night. Later, she walked up over the ridge of the hill, partly to see where the horses had gone. She could see them like little dots, like small dark maggots on the distant hill, doing nothing, like a picture, like nothing which should bother them. From there she could also see down and see the row of cottages and see how the land was lying before going on. As she came over the top of the ridge she noticed something different about Edith's cottage but couldn't see what it was until she was almost upon it. Then she saw that the back window had been shut up tight again and the curtains on the hill side of the house redrawn. It was all tucked up and Daisy felt that it was shut against her. She didn't know why and that made her cross, she was a person who liked to know the ins and outs of things and now here were these odd sudden feelings, and she didn't know them.

Restlessly Daisy walked back to town and to the shops, to keep herself busy and also she half kept watch for Anthony. She'd know him at once, she was sure of that. So when the faintly—faint as a photo that hasn't quite come through—the faintly familiar figure of a young man in dark and slightly old-fashioned clothes strode down the middle of the High Street as if he knew exactly where he was going, she confidently identified him. The familiarity was with Edith, of course, he had a look of her. Edith when young, Edith in her day. Daisy hustled down the street and after him. She felt the same need she'd had in Brighton, when she'd noticed his purposiveness and wanted to rush after him. He was going without hesitation towards their cottages, as if he must have been there before, and he walked so fast that Daisy lost him. By the time she rounded the last bend he was nowhere to be seen.

When she got within sight of their houses she saw that Pleasance was all still determinedly shut up. Exceptionally Edith had closed the front door and drawn down the blinds over the Downs view as well. Well, thought Daisy, well. She stood outside and looked at the house for a while. Well, she would be let in soon enough, soon enough. Mother and son, plenty of catching up to do—though Anthony had hardly struck her as depleted or sad. He looked pale, to be sure, but—striding along the pebbled beach, striding down the High Street—the impression in his wake was not of grief but of directed and powerful energy. Daisy shivered. Then she started to dig in the lavender between the houses and lay turves until the time when she would be invited inside.

Six o'clock came and so did seven. Forced inside by the failing light, Daisy could hear nothing from next door. By seven-thirty she could bear it no longer. She got up, and darted round the remains of their hedge and scratched at the front door.

Edith arrived at once:

"Oh," she cried. "Come in, come in, where have you been all day? I've had the most marvellous, you must come in, it's really been the most, come in and meet—"

He was rising up behind Edith:

"But we've met, haven't we?" His voice was low and courteous, with a sort of curl of mischief.

"Have you?" Edith asked. "Where ever did you meet?"

"Well, certainly, I—" Daisy began to correct the impression he had given.

"Brighton," he said with confidence, "and of course just now."

Edith looked from one to the other. "All the same, I haven't introduced you, so Baxter, this is Daisy Fern, and Daisy—"

"*Baxter?*" Daisy blurted. "*Baxter.*"

"Who did you—?"

"Aren't you Anthony? I thought you were Anthony. It is Friday." She added by way of explanation.

The others laughed and Daisy felt like a child. Edith fixed her a drink:

"*He's* not here. There'll be one of his excuses, the letter, the telephone call. Something has kept him. Taken him off. Can't face the journey. Or it's the children. Or *something*. But Baxter's here in his place. Baxter's an old friend, aren't you? Such a special old friend. But why haven't I heard anything in all this time—after all this time? And now here you are, with your news—I can't wait—" It was quite clear which of the two visitors Edith would have preferred.

"But he looks, he looks—"

"Oh, those photos aren't very good. I don't think the resemblance is there. No, not really at all."

"Not like *Anthony*"—Daisy tried to remember what Anthony looked like—"like *you*. As if he's out of you." The man standing there behind Edith all this time.

Edith gave a girlish kind of laugh and points of blood appeared high on her cheeks:

"Baxter's from the theatre, aren't you? Of course, Anthony didn't stay long there—but Baxter's *in* the business. Has always been. He was a great Othello, weren't you? We've had such fun. We were talking about the old days. I mean the real old days. Before—weren't we?"

Baxter nodded, eyebrows ironically raised.

"You mean the theatre. Your day," cried Daisy, knowing that she sounded too sharp. She couldn't help herself, she could not. She cried out the word theatre as a kind of brake, a warning, as well as a cry at being left out. But Edith and her Baxter were talking on, and Daisy had a choking sensation in her throat. The room was too close for her. She must leave them. Forgo the evening, their meal—leave her friend—

"Oh, you won't go, will you? Oh, well. See you in the morning then," and it was Edith who was gone, gone to Baxter. The door shut on them.

So. Daisy spent her evening out in the garden again fiercely putting back, tramping down even in the dark every one back and front of the turves lifted by the horse's hooves the night before, and scrabbling into the dry summer earth the rest of the bedraggled lavender hedge which separated and joined the two houses. She worked until the veins stood out on her forehead, her mouth grim and her work frantic and taut, until at last she had exhausted herself and went indoors and shut her own door and slept a deep, unchallenged sleep until morning.

She woke with a sense of exhaustion; everything ached on her and inside her, more than the rheumatism ever did. Drawing back her curtains there was a day pouring into her bedroom with long shadows and clouds which swiftly perused the sun. She had a premonitory whiff of autumn. A single chestnut leaf curled upon the grass in front. The lavender looked strong enough, as if it had already taken. The turves all lay flat. And Pleasance, Edith's house, was shut up still. The door closed, the curtains drawn, not a glimmer of light in or out, dead quiet.

There were things Daisy had to do. There were the beginnings of the autumn plantings, seeds to buy from the village shop, the new blanket to be finished for Bernard, she would be busy. Really she was waiting for Edith to emerge so that she would find out how it had all gone, this, this visit. So she stayed close to home for the morning and when midday came went up to the village by the road from which she could see Pleasance. Coming back, she could tell at once that something had changed again: the back door had been opened, the window gaped and the curtains fluttered out in the breeze from the hills. The front door was open as well.

"Edith," her friend called out, "are you in? Are you alone?"

Edith was in her chair by the fire. The figurines were all in different places away from the windows and the photos, familiar photos, were all on the floor by the fire. Husband, grandchildren, Gertrude, Desdemona, Othello and Edith. They must have been going through them, she imagined jealously.

As Daisy stepped in she was aware that a figure was leaving by the back door with a peculiar speed.

"Ho," she called, "Baxter?" and though he did turn once she found she was unsure, there was a doubt in her mind. He had this high-fevered color quite unlike the pale and stately Baxter of the night before, or the old-fashioned creature from the beach. He was in the cast of Baxter, but he moved with a kind of ferocious speed, like a thief; he had a look of florid and furious bewilderment which belonged to Peter, and he held the unmistakable stamp of Edith which could only have marked their son: this person leaving was both intimate and unidentifiable, the person now running triumphantly away.

"Edith," she called out in alarm at she didn't know what, "*Edith.*" So he's gone, has he, your, your—I don't know, Edith—*friend*, and how nice, what a *nice* thing really, Daisy's thoughts bolted uneasily ahead, to have spent time with an old trout like one of us, drawing out the past, flirting, warming memories, what an *act*, what an act of *kindness.* For so it *must* have been. Must have. As if to think it made it so.

"Were you very late?" Daisy tried to coax, and not to pry. Then, "Was there news?" she said, and "I'll do the tea," and walked past Edith into the kitchen. At last Edith lifted her head and Daisy saw into her face. For the face was quite drained, transparent and the eyes stared with a hollow dullness. Daisy felt for a moment that she could see right through the pallor into Edith's life, that there was no barrier there, just a membrane to be broken.

"How nice," Daisy's chatter ran on, "how *nice* of the young man, I mean we must be awfully boring for the young really, but how nice to spend an evening and a night—and what did *he* say, what did Peter have to say?" For she and Peter, she realised, were on the same side in this, so what *did* he have to say, the dead husband, on all this? She was almost chiding now. Edith lifted those terrible empty eyes. And Daisy then knew for certain that Peter on the other side, the Peter who watched over her, had not been consulted.

"That's right, dear," Daisy went on, and began the tea routine with an energy she tried to summons. "Perhaps I'll have some of your nice bread too." But the teacup chattered too in its saucer. When the telephone started to ring she heard herself say in the bullying voice, "Oh, *Edith*, you're sitting there." But it was of course Daisy Fern who had to take the call, to take the news of Anthony's death. Edith said nothing.

★   ★   ★

"Bernard," Daisy began later when she tried to explain to her brother what had happened on that day, the Saturday. And then she tried again to tell him of the events which seemed to have led to it. But what had happened? she asked herself, as she would do for the rest of her life. *Do they come?* she wondered. Are there those out there who come and take you, well, as a shark might take you from a beach? But she couldn't say anything to him, she was not as she had been, she was quiet and dull and apologetic. Bernard won easily. And told her that the delinquent colonel was now in the permanent custodial protection of his dull son.

"You think things come back?" he chuckled unperturbably. "D'you think? I mean there he was the old fellow, quite the warrior in his youth too apparently, and here it is all flooding back. And the poor boy had to cope. Not an ounce of fight in him, just duty. I feel sorry for him, the boy, I mean really." And he laughed and checkmated and sort of smiled to himself because he was all right there in the window watching the empty sea.

"Blast," said Daisy. "Blast it," staring out at the horizon and the pebbled beach as if, if she stared hard enough, searched fast enough, and could find some speck in the distance, she could herself reverse the time, reverse *him* before he burst into sight and send him back. As if you could. Because yes, she thought that things come back, for there was her Edith pulled back to before it all started, before *Anthony* started, that is, wishing now that she could end it. Because of the intrusion, that disturbance of nature.

Bloody Anthony.

METEOR

JOHN WYNDHAM

Off in a corner, away from the main arena, epic events continue to have their own reality, despite the audience's attention being elsewhere. And, in fact, who is to say whether the main players are the ones we're watching?

Perhaps the truth is, they're the ones watching us.

John Wyndham, writing in postwar Britain, here proposes a confusion of strangers—and in doing so manages quite poignantly to prick our complacency. An old-fashioned story, it's one that to my way of thinking will never go out of style.

⟲

THE HOUSE SHOOK, the windows rattled, a framed photograph slipped off the mantel-shelf and fell into the hearth. The sound of a crash somewhere outside arrived just in time to drown the noise of the breaking glass. Graham Toffts put his drink down carefully, and wiped the spilt sherry from his fingers.

"That sort of thing takes you back a bit," he observed. "First installment of the new one, would you think?"

Sally shook her head, spinning the fair hair out a little so that it glistened in the shaded light.

"I shouldn't think so. Not like the old kind, anyway—they

used to come with a sort of double-bang as a rule," she said.

She crossed to the window and pulled back the curtain. Outside there was complete darkness and a sprinkle of rain on the panes.

"Could have been an experimental one gone astray?" she suggested.

Footsteps sounded in the hall. The door opened, and her father's head looked in.

"Did you hear that?" he asked, unnecessarily. "A small meteor, I fancy. I thought I saw a dim flash in the field beyond the orchard." He withdrew. Sally made after him. Graham, following more leisurely, found her firmly grasping her father's arm.

"No!" she was saying, decisively. "I'm not going to have my dinner kept waiting and spoiled. Whatever it is, it will keep."

Mr. Fontain looked at her, and then at Graham.

"Bossy; much too bossy. Always was. Can't think what you want to marry her for," he said.

After dinner they went out to search with electric lamps. There was not much trouble in locating the scene of the impact. A small crater, some eight feet across, had appeared almost in the middle of the field. They regarded it without learning much, while Sally's terrier, Mitty, sniffed over the newly turned earth. Whatever had caused it had presumably buried itself in the middle.

"A small meteorite, without a doubt," said Mr. Fontain. "We'll set a gang on digging it out tomorrow."

Extract from Onns's journal

As an introduction to the notes which I intend to keep, I can scarcely do better than give the gist of the address given to us on the day preceding our departure from Forta* by his Excellency Cottafts. In contrast to our public farewell, this meeting was

---

*Onns gives no clues to Forta's position, nor as to whether it is a planet, a moon, or an asteroid.

deliberately made as informal as a gathering of several thousands can be.

His Excellency emphasized almost in his opening words that though we had leaders for the purposes of administration, there was, otherwise, no least amongst us.

"There is not one of you men and women* who is not a volunteer," looking slowly round his huge audience. "Since you are individuals, the proportions of the emotions which led you to volunteer may differ quite widely, but, however personal, or however altruistic your impulses may have been, there is a common denominator for all—and that is the determination that our race shall survive.

"Tomorrow the Globes will go out.

"Tomorrow, God willing, the skill and science of Forta will break through the threats of Nature.

"Civilization is, from its beginning, the ability to co-ordinate and direct natural forces—and once that direction has been started, it must be constantly maintained. There have been other dominant species on Forta before ours: they were not civilized, they did not direct nature: they dwindled and died as conditions changed. But we, so far, have been able to meet conditions as they have changed, and we flourish.

"We flourish, moreover, in such numbers as undirected Nature could never have sustained. In the past we have surmounted problem after problem to make this possible, but now we find ourselved faced with the gravest problem yet. Forta, our world, is becoming senile, but we are not. We are like spirits that are still young, trapped in a failing body . . .

"For centuries we have kept going, adapted, substituted, patched, but now the trap is closing faster, and there is little left to prop it open with. So it is now, while we are still healthy and strong, that we must escape and find ourselves a new home.

"I do not doubt that great-grandchildren of the present generation's great-grandchildren will be born on Forta, but life will

---

*The terms "men" and "women" are not used biologically, but in the sense of the dominant species referring to its own members.

be harder for them: they will have to spend much more labor simply to keep alive. That is why the Globes must go now, while we have strength and wealth to spare.

"And for you who go in them—what? Even guesses are vain. The Globes will set out for the four corners of the heavens, and where they land they may find anything—or nothing. All our arts and skills will set you on your courses. But, once you have left, we can do no more than pray that you, our seed, will find fruitful soil."

He paused, lengthily. Then he went on:

"Your charge you know, or you would not have offered yourselves. Nevertheless, it is one which you will not be able to learn too well, nor teach too often. In the hands of each and every one of you lies a civilization. Every man and woman of you is at once the receptacle and the potential fountain of all that Forta signifies. You have the history, the culture, the civilization of a planet. Use it. Use it well. Give it to others where it will help. Be willing to learn from others, and improve it if you can. Do not try to preserve it intact; a culture must grow to live. For those who cling too fondly to the past there is likely to be no future. Remember that it is possible that there is no intelligence elsewhere in the universe, which means that some of you will hold a trust not only for our race, but for all conscious life that may evolve.

"Go forth, then. Go in wisdom, kindliness, peace, and truth.

"And our prayers will go out with you into the mysteries of space . . ."

. . . I have looked again through the telescope at our new home. Our group is, I think, lucky. It is a planet which is neither too young nor too old. Conditions were better than before, with less cloud over its surface. It shines like a blue pearl. Much of the part I saw was covered with water—more than two-thirds of it, they tell me, is under water. It will be good to be in a place where irrigation and water supply are not one of the main problems of life. Nevertheless, one hopes that we shall be fortunate enough to make our landing on dry ground or there may be very great difficulties . . .

I looked, too, at some of the places to which other Globes are bound, some small, some large, some new, with clouded surfaces that are a mystery. One at least is old, and in not much better case than our own poor Forta—though the astronomers say that it has the ability to support life for several millions of years. But I am glad that our group is going to the blue, shining world: it seems to beckon us, and I am filled with a hope which helps to quieten my fears of the journey.

Not that fears trouble me so much now; I have learnt some fatalism in the past year. I shall go into the Globe, and the anaesthetic gas will lull me to sleep without my being aware of it. When I wake again it will be on our shimmering new world . . . If I do not wake, something will have gone wrong, but I shall never know that . . .

Very simple, really—if one has faith . . .

This evening I went down to look at the Globes; to see them objectively for the last time. Tomorrow, in all the bustle and preparation there will be no time for reflection—and it will be better so.

What a staggering, amazing—one had almost said impossible—work they are! The building of them has entailed labor beyond computation. They look more likely to crush the ground and sink into Forta herself than to fly off into space. The most massive things ever built! I find it almost impossible to believe that we can have built thirty of these metal mountains, yet there they stand, ready for tomorrow . . .

And some of them will be lost . . .

Oh, God, if ours may survive, let us never forget. Let us show ourselves worthy of this supreme effort . . .

It can well be that these are the last words I shall ever write. If not, it will be in a new world and under a strange sky that I continue . . .

"You shouldn't have touched it," said the Police Inspector, shaking his head. "It ought to have been left where it was until the proper authorities had inspected it."

"And who," inquired Mr. Fontain coldly, "are the proper authorities for the inspection of meteors?"

"That's beside the point. You couldn't be sure it was a meteor, and these days a lot of other things besides meteors can fall out of the sky. Even now you've got it up you can't be sure."

"It doesn't look like anything else."

"All the same, it should have been left to us. It might be some device still on the Secret List."

"The Police, of course, knowing all about things on the Secret List?" Sally considered it time to break in.

"Well, we shall know what to do next time we have a meteor, shan't we? Suppose we all go and have a look at it? It's in the out-house now, looking quite unsecret."

She led the way round to the yard, still talking to stave off a row between the Inspector and her father.

"It only went a surprisingly short way down, so the men were soon able to get it out. And it turned out to be not nearly as hot as we'd expected, either, so they could handle it quite easily."

"You'd not say 'quite easily' if you'd heard the language they used about the weight of it," observed her father.

"It's in here," Sally said, leading the party of four into a musty, single-story shed.

The meteor was not an impressive sight. It lay in the middle of the bare board floor; just a rugged, pitted, metallic-looking sphere something over two feet in diameter.

"The only kind of weapon that it suggests to me is a cannon-ball," said Mr. Fontain.

"It's the principle," retorted the Inspector. "We have standing orders that any mysterious falling object is to remain untouched until it has been examined by a War Office expert. We have already informed them, and it must not be moved again until their man has had a look at it."

Graham, who had hitherto taken no part, stepped forward and put his hand on it.

"Almost cold now," he reported. "What's it made of?" he added curiously.

Mr. Fontain shrugged.

"I imagine it's just an ordinary chunk of meteoric iron. The only odd thing about it to me is that it didn't come down with more of a bump. If it were any kind of secret weapon, it would certainly be an exceedingly dull one."

"All the same, I shall have to give orders that it is not to be moved until the W.O. man has seen it," said the Inspector.

They started to move back into the yard, but on the threshold he paused.

"What's that sizzling sound?" he inquired.

"Sizzling?" repeated Sally.

"Kind of hissing noise. Listen!"

They stood still, the Inspector with his head a little on one side. Undeniably there was a faint, persistent sound on a note just within the range of audibility. It was difficult to place. By common impulse they turned back to regard the ball uneasily. Graham hesitated, and then stepped inside again. He leaned over the ball, his right ear turned down to it.

"Yes," he said. "It is."

Then his eyes closed, and he swayed. Sally ran forward and caught him as he sagged. The others helped her to drag him out. In the fresh air he revived almost immediately.

"That's funny. What happened?" he asked.

"You're sure the sound is coming from that thing?" asked the Inspector.

"Oh, yes. Not a doubt about it."

"You didn't smell anything queer?"

Graham raised his eyebrows: "Oh, gas, you mean. No, I don't think so."

"H'm," said the Inspector. He turned a mildly triumphant eye on the older man. "Is it usual for meteors to sizzle?" he inquired.

"Er—I really don't know. I shouldn't think so," Mr. Fontain admitted.

"I see. Well, in the circumstances I suggest that we all withdraw—preferably to a well-shielded spot on the other side of the house, just in case—while we wait for the expert," announced the Inspector.

Extract from Onns's journal

I am bewildered. I have just woken. But has it happened or have we failed to start? I cannot tell. Was it an hour, a day, a year, or a century ago that we entered the Globe? No, it cannot have been an hour ago; I am sure of that by the tiredness of my limbs, and the way my body aches. We were warned about that:

"You will know nothing," they said, "nothing until it is all over. Then you will feel physically weary because your bodies will have been subjected to great strains. That should pass quite soon, but we shall give you some capsules of concentrated food and stimulants to help you overcome the effects more quickly."

I have taken one capsule, and I begin to feel the benefit of it already, but it is still hard to believe that it is over.

It seems such a short time ago that we climbed the long passage into the interior of the Globe and dispersed as we had been instructed. Each of us found his or her elastic compartment, and crawled into it. I released the valve to inflate the space between the inner and outer walls of my compartment. As the lining distended I felt myself lifted on a mattress of air. The top bulged down, the sides closed in, and so, insulated from shock in all directions, I waited.

Waited for what? I still cannot say. One moment, it seems, I lay there fresh and strong: the next, I was tired and aching.

Only that, to indicate that one life has ended and a new one is about to begin. My compartment has deflated. The pumps have been exchanging the gas for fresh air. That must mean that we are now on that beautiful, shining blue planet, with Forta only a speck in our new heavens.

I feel different for knowing that. All my life hitherto has been spent on a dying planet where our greatest enemy was lethal discouragement. But now I feel rejuvenated. There will be work, hope, and life here: a world to build, and a future to build it for . . .

I can hear the drills at work, cutting a way out for us. What, I wonder, shall we find? We must watch ourselves closely. It may be easier for us to keep faith if we face hardships than if we find ourselves among plenty. But, whatever this world is like, faith must be kept. We hold a million years of history, a million years of knowledge, that must be preserved.

Yet we must also, as His Excellency said, be ready to adapt ourselves. Who can tell what forms of life may already exist here? One could scarcely expect to find real consciousness on a planet so young, but there may be the first stirrings of intelligence here. We must watch for them, seek them out, cultivate them. They may be quite different from us, but we must remember that it is their world, and help them where we can. We must keep in mind that it would be a wicked thing to frustrate even an alien form of life, on its own planet. If we find any such beings, our task must be to teach, to learn, to co-operate with them, and perhaps one day we may achieve a civilization even greater than Forta's own . . .

"And just what," inquired the Inspector, "do you think you're doing with that, Sergeant Brown?"

The police-sergeant held the limp, furry body dangling by its tail.

"It's a cat, sir."

"That's what I meant."

"Well, I thought the W.O. gentleman might want to examine it, sir."

"What makes you think the War Office is interested in dead cats, Sergeant?"

The sergeant explained. He had decided to risk a trip into the outhouse to note developments, if any. Bearing in mind the Inspector's suggestion of gas, he had tied a rope round his waist so that he could be dragged back if he were overcome, and crawled in, keeping as low as possible. The precautions had proved unnecessary, however. The hissing or sizzling had ceased, and the gas had evidently dispersed. He had been able to approach the ball without feeling any effects whatever. Nevertheless, when he had come so close to it that his ear was almost against it he had noticed a faint buzzing.

"Buzzing?" repeated the Inspector. "You mean sizzling!"

"No, sir, buzzing." He paused, searching for a simile. "The nearest thing, to my mind, would be a circular saw, but as you might hear it from a very long way off."

Deducing from this that the thing, whatever it was, was still active, the sergeant had ordered his constables away to cover on the far side of an earth bank. He himself had looked into the shed from time to time during the next hour and a half, but observed no change.

He had noticed the cat prowl into the yard just as they were settling down to a snack of sandwiches. It had gone nosing round the shed door, but he had not bothered about it. Half an hour later, when he had finished his meal and cigarette, he had gone across to take another look. He had discovered the cat lying close to the "meteor." When he brought it out, he had found it was dead.

"Gassed?" asked the Inspector.

The sergeant shook his head. "No, sir. That's what's funny about it."

He laid the cat's body on top of a convenient wall, and turned the head to expose the underside of the jaw. A small circle of the black fur had been burnt away, and in the center of the burn was a minute hole.

"H'm," said the Inspector. He touched the wound, and then sniffed at his forefinger. "Fur's burnt, all right, but no smell of explosive fumes," he said.

"That's not all, sir."

The sergeant turned the head over to reveal an exactly similar blemish on the crown. He took a thin, straight wire from his pocket, and probed into the hole beneath the jaw. It emerged from the other hole at the top of the head.

"Can you make anything of that, sir?" he asked.

The Inspector frowned. A weapon of minute bore, at point-blank range, might have made one of the wounds. But the two appeared to be entrance and exit holes of the same missile. But a bullet did not come out leaving a neat hole like that, nor did it singe the hair about its exit. To all appearances, two of these microscopic bullets must have been fired in exactly the same line from above and below the head—which made no kind of sense.

"Have you any theories?" he asked the sergeant.

"Beats me, sir," the other told him.

"What's happened to the thing now? Is it still buzzing?" the Inspector inquired.

"No, sir. There wasn't a sound from it when I went in and found the cat."

"H'm," said the Inspector. "Isn't it about time that W.O. man showed up?"

Extract from Onns's journal

This is a terrible place! As though we were condemned to some fantastic hell. Can this be our beautiful blue planet that beckoned us so bravely? We cannot understand, we are utterly bewildered, our minds reel with the horror of this place. We, the flower of civilization, now cower before the hideous monstrosities that face us. How can we ever hope to bring order into such a world as this?

We are hiding now in a dark cavern while Iss, our leader, consults to decide our best course. None of us envies him his responsibility. What provisions can a man make against not only the unknown, but the incredible? Nine hundred and sixty-four of us depend on him. There were a thousand: this is the way it happened.

I heard the drill stop, then there was a clanking as it was dismantled and drawn from the long shaft it had bored. Soon after that came the call for assembly. We crawled out of our compartments, collected our personal belongings, and met in the center hall. Sunss, our leader then, himself called the roll. Everyone answered except four poor fellows who had not stood the strain of the journey. Then Sunss made a brief speech.

He reminded us that what had been done was irrevocable. No one yet knew what awaited us outside the Globe. If it should somehow happen that our party was divided, each group must elect its leader and act independently until contact with the rest was re-established.

"We need long courage, not brief bravery," he said. "Not heroics. We have to think of ourselves always as the seed of the future; and every grain of that seed is precious."

He hammered home the responsibility to all of us.

"We do not know, and we shall never know, how the other Globes may have fared. So, not knowing, we must act as though we alone had survived, and as if all that Forta has ever stood for is in our hands alone."

It was he who led the way down the newly bored passage, and he who first set foot in the new land. I followed with the rest, filled with such a conflict of feelings as I have never known before.

And this world into which we have emerged: how can I describe it in all its alien qualities?

To begin with; it was gloomy and shadowed—and yet it was not night-time. Such light as there was came from a vast, grey panel hanging in the dusky sky. From where we stood it appeared trapezoid, but I suspect that was a trick of perspective, and that it was in fact a square, bisected twice, by two dark bars, into four smaller squares. In the murk over our heads it was possible to make out dimly faint darker lines intersecting at strange angles. I could not guess at their significance.

The ground we stood on was like nothing I had known. It was a vast level plain, but ridged, and covered with small, loose boulders. The ridges were somewhat like strata that had been laid side by side instead of one on another. They lay all one way, disappearing into gloomy distance before and behind. Close beside us was a crevasse, as wide as my own height, also running either way, in a perfectly straight line. Some considerable distance beyond it was another, similar crevasse running exactly parallel to it, and beyond that a third, and an indication of a fourth.

The man beside me was nervous. He muttered something about a geometrical world lit by a square sun.

"Rubbish!" I told him shortly.

"Then how do you explain it?" he asked.

"I do not rush into swift, facile explanations," I told him. "I observe, and then, when I have gathered enough data, I deduce."

"What do you deduce from a square sun?" he asked, but I ignored him.

Soon we were all assembled outside the Globe, and waiting for Sunss to give directions. He was just about to speak when we were interrupted by a strange sound—a kind of regular soft padding, sometimes with a rasping scratch accompanying it. There was something ominous about it, and for a moment we were all frozen with apprehension—then, before we could move, the most fearsome monster emerged from behind our Globe.

Every historic traveller's tale pales beside the reality of the thing we faced. Never would I have believed that such a creature could exist had I not seen it for myself. The first we saw of it was all enormous face, thrusting round the side of the Globe, hanging in the air far above us. It was a sight to make the bravest shudder.

It was black, too, so that in the darkness it was difficult to be certain of its outline; but it widened across the top and above the head itself one seemed to catch a glimpse of two towering pointed ears. It looked down on us out of two vast, glowing eyes set somewhat aslant.

It paused for a moment, the great eyes blinked, and then it came closer. The legs which then came into view were like massive pillars, yet they moved with a dexterity and control that was amazing in anything so vast. Both legs and feet were covered with close-set fibers that looked like strands of shining black metal. It bent its legs, lowering its head to look at us, and the fearful stench of its breath blew over us. The face was still more alarming at close quarters. It opened a cavern of a mouth; an enormous pink tongue flicked out and back. Above the mouth huge, pointed spines stood out sideways, trembling. The eyes which were fixed on us were cold, cruel, nonintelligent.

Until then we had been transfixed, but now panic took some of us. Those nearest to it fell back hurriedly, and at that one of the monstrous feet moved like lightning. A huge black paw with suddenly out-thrust claws smacked down. When it drew back, twenty of our men and women were no more than smears on the ground.

We were paralysed, all of us except Sunss. He, forgetting his instructions about personal safety, ran towards the creature. The great paw rose, hovered, and struck again. Eleven more fell at that second murderous blow.

Then I noticed Sunss again. He was standing right between the paws. His fire-rod was in his hands, and he was looking up at the monstrous head above him. As I watched, he lifted the weapon, and aimed. It seemed such folly against that huge thing, heroic folly. But Sunss was wiser than I. Suddenly the head jerked, a tremor shook the limbs, and without a sound the monster dropped where it stood.

And Sunss was under it. A very brave man . . .

Then Iss took charge.

He decided that we must find a place of safety as soon as possible in case there were other such monsters lurking near. Once we had found that, we could start to remove our instruments and equipment from the Globe, and consider our next step. He decided to lead us forward down the broad way between two of the crevasses.

After travelling a considerable distance we reached the foot of a towering and completely perpendicular cliff with curiously regular rectangular formations on its face. At the base of it we found this cavern which seems to run a great distance both inwards and to both sides, and with a height that is oddly regular. Perhaps the man who spoke about a geometrical world was not so stupid as he seemed . . .

Anyway, here we have a refuge from monsters such as that which Sunss killed. It is too narrow for those huge paws to reach, and even the fearful claws could only rake a little way inside.

Later. A terrible thing has happened! Iss and a party of twenty went exploring the cavern to see if they could find another way out other than on to the plain where our Globe lay.

Yes—lay! Past tense. That is our calamity.

After he had gone off, the rest of us waited, keeping watch. For some time nothing happened. Evidently and mercifully the monster had been alone. It lay in a great black mound where it had fallen, close to the Globe. Then a curious thing took place.

More light suddenly poured over the plain. An enormous hooked object descended upon the slain monster, and dragged it away out of sight. Then there was a thunderous noise which shook everything about us, and the light dimmed again.

I do not pretend to explain these things: none of us can understand them. I simply do my best to keep a faithful record.

Another, much longer, period passed without any event. We were beginning to worry about what might have happened to Iss and his party for they had been a long time away, when almost the worst thing that could happen to us occurred without warning.

Again the plain became lighter. The ground beneath us set up a reverberating rumble and shook so violently to a series of shocks that we were hard put to keep on our feet. Peering out of the cavern I saw a sight that even now I can scarcely credit. Forms beside which our previous monster was insignificant: living, moving creatures reared up to three or four times the height of our vast Globe. I know this will not be believed but it is the truth. Little wonder that the whole plain groaned and rumbled under the burden of four such. They bent over our Globe, they put their forelegs to it, and lifted it—yes, actually lifted that stupendous mass of metal from the ground. Then the shaking all about us became worse as they took its weight and tramped away on colossal feet.

The sight of that was too much for some of us. A hundred men ran out from our cavern, cursing, weeping, and brandishing their fire-rods. But it was too late, and the range was too great for them to do anything effective, besides, how could we hope to affect colossi such as these?

Now our Globe, with all its precious contents, is lost. Our inheritance is gone. We have nothing now; nothing, but our own few trifling possessions, with which to start building our new world . . .

It is bitter, bitter to have worked so hard and come so far, for this . . .

Nor was that the only calamity. Only a little later two of Iss's companions came back with a dreadful tale.

Behind our cavern they had discovered a warren of broad

tunnels, foul with the smell of unknown creatures and their
droppings. They had made their way down them with difficulty.
Several times they had been beset by different varieties of six-
legged creatures, and sometimes eight-legged ones, all of horrible appearance. Many of these were a great deal larger than
themselves, armed with fearful jaws and claws, and filled with a
vicious ferocity which made them attack on sight. Terrifying
though they looked, it soon became clear, however, that they
were only really dangerous when they made unexpected attacks
for they were non-sentient and the fire-rods made short work of
them once they had been seen.

After a number of such encounters Iss had succeeded in
reaching open country beyond the tunnels without the loss of a
man. It had been when they were on the way back to fetch us
that catastrophe had overtaken them. They had been attacked by
fierce grey creatures about half the size of our first monster,
which they guessed to be the builders of the tunnels. It was a terrible fight in which almost all the party perished before the monsters were overcome. Iss himself had fallen, and of all his men
only these two had been left in a fit condition to make the journey back to the rest of us.

This new, ghastly tragedy is starting to sap our spirits, and
our courage . . .

We have chosen Muin as our new leader. He has decided that
we must go forward, through the tunnels. The plain behind us is
quite barren, our Globe is gone, if we stay here we shall starve;
so we must try to get through to the open country beyond, trusting that Iss's sacrifice has not been in vain, and that there are no
more grey monsters to attack us . . .

God grant that beyond the tunnels this nightmare world
gives place to sanity . . .

Is it so much that we ask—simply to live, to work, to build, in
peace . . . ?

Graham looked in to see Sally and her father a couple of days later.

"Thought you might like an interim report on your 'meteor,'" he
said to Mr. Fontain.

"What was it, actually?" asked the older man.

"Oh, I don't say they've got that far. They've established that it was no meteor; but just what it really was still has them absolutely guessing. I'd got pretty curious by the time they decided to take it away, and after I'd talked big and waved my wartime status at them a bit, they consented to stretch a point and take me along, too. So you'd better grade this as confidential.

"When we went over the thing carefully at the research place it appeared to be simply a solid ball of some metal on which there's been no report issued as yet. But in one place there was a hole, quite smooth, about half an inch in diameter, which went straight in, roughly to the middle. Well, they scratched their heads about the best way to tackle it, and decided in the end to cut it in half and see what. So they rigged up an automatic sawing device in a pit and set it going, and we all retreated to a reasonable distance, just in case. Now they're all a bit more puzzled than they were before."

"Why, what happened?" Sally asked.

"Well, nothing actually *happened*. When the saw ran free we switched off and went back, and there was the ball lying in neat halves. But they weren't solid halves as we had expected. There *was* a solid metal rind about six inches thick, but then there was an inch or so of soft, fine dust, which has insulating qualities that seem to be interesting them quite a bit. Then inside a thinner metal wall was an odd formation of cells; more like a section of honeycomb than anything, only made of some flexible, rubbery material, and every one empty. Next a belt about two inches wide, divided into metal compartments this time, all considerably larger than the cells in the outer part, and crammed with all sorts of things—packs of minute tubes, things that look like tiny seeds, different sorts of powders that have spilled about when the thing came apart, and which nobody's got around to examining properly yet, and finally a four-inch space in the middle separated into layers by dozens of paper-thin fins, and absolutely empty otherwise.

"So there is the secret weapon—and if you can make anything of that lot, I'm sure they'll be pleased to hear about it. Even the dust layer disappointed them by not being explosive. Now they're asking one another what the hell such a thing could be remotely expected to do."

"That's disappointing. It seemed so like a meteor—until it started sizzling," said Mr. Fontain.

"One of them has suggested that in a way it may be. A sort of artificial meteor," Graham said. "That's a bit too fancy for the rest, though. They feel that if something could be sent across space at all, surely it would be something more intelligible."

"It would be exciting if it were," Sally said. "I mean, it would be such a much more hopeful thing than just another secret weapon—a sort of sign that perhaps one day we shall be able to do it ourselves . . ."

"Just think how wonderful it might be if we really could do that! Think of all the people who are sick to death of secret weapons, and wars and cruelties, setting out one day in a huge ship for a clean, new planet where we could start again. We'd be able to leave behind all the things that make this poor old world get boggier and boggier. All we'd want is a place where people could live, and work, and build, and be happy. If we could only start again somewhere else, what a lovely, lovely world we might—" She stopped suddenly at the sound of a frenzied yapping outside. She jumped up as it changed to a long-drawn howl.

"That's Mitty!" she said. "What on earth—?"

The two men followed her out of the house.

"Mitty! Mitty!" she called, but there was no sign of the dog, nor sound from it now.

They made round to the left, where the sound had seemed to come from. Sally was the first to see the white patch lying in the grass beside the outhouse wall. She ran towards it, calling; but the patch did not move.

"Oh, poor Mitty!" she said. "I believe she's dead!"

She went down on her knees beside the dog's limp body.

"She *is*!" she said. "I wonder what—" She broke off abruptly, and stood up. "Oh, something stung me! Oh, it *hurts*!" She clutched at her leg, tears of anguish suddenly coming into her eyes.

"What on earth—?" began her father, looking down at the dog. "What are all those things—ants?"

Graham bent down to look.

"No, they're not ants. I don't know what they are."

He picked one of the little creatures up and put it on the palm of his hand to look at it more closely.

"Never seen anything like that before," he said.

Mr. Fontain, beside him, peered at it, too.

It was a queer-looking little thing, under a quarter of an inch long. Its body seemed to be an almost perfect hemisphere with the flat side below and the round top surface coloured pink, and as shiny as a ladybird's wing-cases. It was insect-like, except that it stood on only four short legs. There was no clearly defined head; just two eyes set in the edge of the shiny dome. As they watched, it reared up on two of its legs, showing a pale, flat underside, with a mouth set just below the eyes. In its forelegs it seemed to be holding a bit of grass or thin wire.

Graham felt a sudden, searing pain in his hand.

"Hell's bells!" he said, shaking it off. "The little brute certainly can sting. I don't know what they are, but they're nasty things to have around. Got a spray handy?"

"There's one in the scullery," Mr. Fontain told him. He turned his attention to his daughter. "Better?" he inquired.

"Hurts like hell," Sally said, between her teeth.

"Just hang on a minute till we've dealt with this, then we'll have a look at it," he told her.

Graham hurried back with the spray in his hand. He cast around and discovered several hundreds of the little pink objects crawling towards the wall of the outhouse. He pumped a cloud of insecticide over them and watched while they slowed, waved feeble legs, and then lay still. He sprayed the locality a little more, to make sure.

"That ought to fix 'em," he said. "Nasty, vicious little brutes. Never seen anything quite like them—I wonder what on earth they were?"

SHITE-HAWKS

MURIEL GRAY

Obscene rites have long been a staple of eerie literature, so it's not surprising that Muriel Gray, with her classical bent, should wish to ring changes on the theme. But that she should get so down and dirty—filthy, really—while going about it is fairly startling, and squeamish readers are under advisement to approach carefully.

This is the kind of story that not only packs a wallop, it leaves a large, spreading bruise.

ৡ

I HATE THE WAY Spanner watches me when I eat. It's fucking unnatural. It's not like he's looking at me. It's like he follows the food from the moment it leaves the plastic bag, and keeps his eyes on it as it travels the last few inches into my mouth. And all the time, he's holding his own sandwich like it isn't really food at all, but some synthetic approximation of the real thing, the thing that I have and he doesn't. It bugs the fucking tits right off me.

Especially today.

"What the fuck are you lookin' at you retard?"

Spanner moves his eyes from the motion of the concealed food in my cheeks to my eyes, and affects the look of a scolded child.

"Aw, hey, there's no call for that now. No call for that at all."

Belcher looks up from behind his tabloid and shoots me a look.

"Mind your language ye wee cunt."

He sees no humor in that, and the idle line of latent violence in his eyes tells me that even if I do, now is not the time to display it. I glare back at Spanner, whose eyes are fixed back on my hand, the one with the remains of the cheese sandwich in it, and I turn in disgust to look out the window of the Portakabin. I have to wipe an arc in the condensation to see out. It drips all day from the bloody Calor gas fire Belcher keeps on, summer or winter, but through the smear I can make out a figure.

It's not like the hawk guy to be late for his lunch break. That fat moron's as lazy as a fucking woman. But here he comes, ten minutes into the break and only just appearing over the last mound of steaming rubbish, his scabby hooded bird swaying on his wrist, trying blindly to adjust its balance to the bobbing and stumbling gait of its master.

"Door" is the only greeting he gets from Belcher as he enters, and he shuts it behind him obediently.

I watch as he fetches out the stupid wee folding perch he keeps in the pocket of his donkey jacket, erects it on the table, and transfers the bird from his leather glove onto the four-inch piece of doweling. It obliges him by dropping a viscous brown and white marbled shit on the table.

"Aw Jesus Wept, man. We're eatin' here."

Spanner has taken his eyes off my moving jaw long enough to regard the slug-shaped dropping only inches from his Tupperware box of sandwiches.

"It's nature. What d'ye want him do? Go to the fuckin' bog an' wash his hands?"

Belcher looks up again. The motion promotes an instant and respectful silence.

"See anyone?"

The hawk guy looks at each of us turn.

"Naw."

I look out the steamy window again, this time aware that my heart is increasing its pace.

"Naebody," qualifies the hawk guy, as though we misunderstood him the first time.

The Portakabin is right in the middle of the vast toxic plain of the landfill, and today, as most days, the grey Scottish sky can barely distinguish a horizon against the near-colorless piles of waste. I suppose in reality, if you look closely, there's plenty of color in the piles. Mostly primary colors. But it's funny how when you put them altogether like that it just becomes the hue of mud. Sickly, diseased, reeking mud. Only the hooked dinosaur arm of Spanner's J.C.B. breaks the monotony of these man-made rolling hills, abandoned as it is in a frozen predatory pose to the call of lunch. I stare at it for the visual relief it provides, and when Belcher speaks I can barely force myself to turn back towards the room. Of course I do. It wouldn't be smart not to.

"Kids?"

The hawk guy shakes his head.

"They sealed up the gap in the fence. Wee cunts cannae get through any mair."

Belcher looks to Spanner. Tension beats in the air like a pulse.

For a minute we all think Belcher is going to let it pass. He sits back and folds the paper in front of him, examining the walls of the cabin like he's just noticed it. Instinctively I do the same. I let my eyes wander over his gallery. A ceramic plate with transfer pictures of Corfu around the circumference embraces clock hands that have longed since ceased to turn. Next to it a life-size plastic vacuum-moulded head of a Vegas Elvis grins down at all four of us like we were stage-side table guests, and beneath, the Sellotape holding up a silk pennant from Oban is losing the battle to gravity as the red tassels droop and fold back, obscuring the *n*.

But of course he's not looking at all that stuff. He's looking at that fucking doll, Blu-Tacked to the wall, its feet resting on a little souvenir Swiss wooden shelf specially mounted there for the purpose. I glance at Spanner, who's also looking at it, and lower my eyes.

"I telt ye to open it up, Spanner."

Belcher lazily looked back at the transfixed man.

"I believe I telt ye last week."

Spanner opens his mouth, then closes it again. One long wisp of oily grey hair that he combs across and adheres to his bald pate shifts from its base and falls across his shiny face. He pushes it back with familiar attention.

"Ah did."

He's lying so nakedly, even the hawk guy looks away.

"Someone from the estate must've fixed it again since."

We all know it's a lie. Especially me. I look steadily at Spanner to try and hide that.

There hasn't been a stranger on the landfill for over three weeks. Not a kid looking for interesting discarded treasure, not a junkie or wino, not even the illegal dumpers who case the joint after the gates close. No one. Mind, there's nothing strange about that. There's no seagulls either. And that's no thanks to the fucking hawk guy, who's getting paid a fortune to keep these non-existent gulls off the site with his scabby budgie. I sneaked a look at his invoice on Belcher's desk one day. "East Glasgow Hawks" it said at the top of the paper.

And then E.G.H. claimed to be owed nearly two hundred fucking pounds a week, just to keep that lazy bastard's mangy pet flying around all day pretending to keep off imaginary flying vermin. Spanner says the guy's got a contract at the airport too. Must be coining it in, the fat shite. And the worst of it is, the gulls wouldn't come here anymore even if you were pumping fish out your arse. They wouldn't be so daft.

The rats went months ago. That leaves us. Only us.

I force myself to look back up at the doll again. Belcher's had it up there now for three days. That means The Rising is almost here. Like, really really almost here. He wouldn't dare have it out so long in case one of the Council suits dropped by and happened to ask what the fuck it was. So it must be almost now. Shit. Almost time, and no strangers. I can't help wondering what the mad cunt's plan is. You can't tell by looking at Belcher. You can't tell anything very much. So I look at the doll.

This is only the third time I've seen it, since I'm last in. Only been on the site sixteen months. Been to college, blew out, landed here, and it took me at least three months to murder my bloody vocabulary so they'd even talk to me, the undereducated thick bastards. So now I can talk in words of one syllable, or if it's Spanner I'm talking to, less. But I fit in now. I fit in fine. Only seen two Risings, and I can't get the last one out my head when I stare at that thing.

At least the doll can't stare back, on account of having no eyes. The head is a bleached rat's skull, delicate, nearly beautiful. It sits on top of a leather body, attached to it by a separate strip of leather that goes over the top of the skull almost like a World War II flying helmet.

And then that obscene fucking body dangles below it. I can't even bring myself to think about who might have made the thing, what pair of hands held it and stitched it into that shape, but the thought of the maker is worse than the finished work. I used to wonder if Belcher had done it, but one look at his massive chapped hands would reassure you that those fingers would never be capable of any kind of craftsmanship. He can barely make a rollup, and his fingers are so fat it's all he can do to force his forefinger up a nostril to pick the snotter out that ugly nose. Somehow that brings me comfort. No matter how repulsive it is, the doll is a work of art, but the thought that its maker could be in this room would give me the dry boke. Its upper body has two thin arms dangling from it, the hands, or claws, I can't work out which, represented by tiny razor-sharp shards of tin cut meticulously from old cans. On the torso are two half-filled pendulous breasts, the nipples made from the ends of condoms, filled with God knows what that give them a pink fleshy appearance. Hanging below is its distended belly. Maybe it's supposed to be pregnant, maybe not. But there's a slit up it leaving an empty oval chamber about an inch in diameter that's blackened and hardened inside like the interior of a bad walnut shell.

Just below is a two-inch-long, thick wrinkled cock.

The legs that try and straddle the massive swollen organ are stick thin again, and end with the same metal claws, and because they bandy out like an old guy with rickets, those tin claws make its bottom half look reptilian.

Belcher is looking at me now. I felt his gaze shift to my face as tangibly as if he'd stroked me. I look at the doll for a few beats more, resume chewing my sandwich, then try to look away casually.

He'll have a plan. We all trust that he knows what he's doing. The hawk guy makes a wee kind of chucking noise to his bird and strokes its tiny head with a finger, in a kind of affirmation that everything's going to be okay.

But I don't know. It feels different this time. I know I've done wrong but Belcher can't possibly know that. I'm just going to sit it out. The cheese in my mouth tastes like wax. I swallow.

"What about you?"

I blink, then swallow again.

"What?"

He waits. Not honoring my reply with one of his own. Spanner has moved his eyes to my face. The hawk guy is still fingering his fucking bird. I take the back of my hand over my mouth.

"Same, Mr. Belcher. Not a soul."

This time, Belcher gives a slight nod. He picks up his paper again, turns two pages, then folds it in half, in half again, and starts to read the fat origamied rectangle of newsprint as though he had never spoken.

No one breaks the silence. Not even the hawk, and that wee bastard can suddenly give an ear-piercing shriek when you least expect it. Even it senses Belcher's displeasure. We know him too well to think it's finished.

"Sun sets at six-fourteen. Meet at the beds at six."

He smooths the paper, still squinting at the type.

"An' when ah say six, ah mean six, you dozy cunts."

I've been driving the dumper all week. I like it fine. Although it's Spanner who fills me up with his digger, I don't have to see or talk to the stupid bastard. We're safe in our respective cabs, the only communication a wave of a hand from a window or a flash of headlights. And this afternoon all I have to do is think about The Rising.

I'm not thinking about what Belcher has in mind. I'm thinking what we all might get this time. I never thought it would work the first go. And I still don't know if it did, but it felt like it did. And I suppose I need to believe that it did.

Yes, I really do.

I wanted that trail bike and I got that trail bike. Maybe it wasn't quite the way I thought, but I still got it. It was in the auction, the one I saw, sitting up high on its pink shocks the way an Arab race-horse stands on tiptoe before a gallop. I wanted it so badly, and even more badly when it didn't reach the reserve price and it got wheeled away. And then the one I got, just exactly like the one in the auction, was on the site, a few days after The Rising. Just left there, paint as good as new, even sporting two Day-Glo mud guards I hadn't bar-gained for. Well, okay, maybe it wasn't the exact same one. And so the fuck what that it had no back tire and the carburetor was shot. It only took me sixty quid to fix, and that was several hundred notes short of what I'd have needed to buy the thing proper.

See, we all want things. Spanner wanted that woman from his estate. Christ knows why. What a dog. Dyed hair, three kids by three different guys, and her tits nearly down at her ankles. And even though she made Mother Teresa look like a supermodel, she wouldn't spit on Spanner if he was on fire. But he wanted her. And one week after The Rising, he told me as we shovelled that he was getting pissed with her and shagging her from behind in that pit of a flat she has above the shops. You see, that can't be coincidence, can it? I don't know what the hawk guy wants and I don't care. He gets enough for fucking nothing just by chucking that bird around.

But we all know what Belcher wants, and it worries me that it's too big. He's not going to get it. The worst of it is, the thing that really eats me up if I'm being honest, is that I think he'll keep on going, pulling any stunt he can, because he believes that one day his undoable thing will be done.

I saw his face one afternoon and that told me a lot. A lot I didn't want to know. He brought her in the car to the Portakabin on one of his days off, because he was on his way somewhere else. He must have forgotten something important, otherwise he'd never have done it normally.

The engine was still running and he was inside the cabin, but I stopped and looked in the back of the car as I passed. I knew better than to come in because then he'd have known I'd seen her and I know he hates that. It's an old Ford Mondeo, and it's shite. There's rust bleeding all along the underside of the driver's door that you just know creeps right into the chassis where you can't see it, and you can hear that the engine's fucked even when it's idling. You see, that's what he should be asking for. A new car. I just think he'd get it. That The Rising could get him it. But like I said, it's not enough.

She's about fourteen, his daughter. She was strapped into what looked like a giant child seat in the back, except it had kind of head-rest things on either side of her temples with metal arms to position them like an angle-poised lamp. Her face was turned looking out the window, although it was obvious she couldn't look at anything the way her eyes were pointing in different directions and darting around like she was following two different shoals of fast fish. A long thread of foamy spittle hung from her bottom lip and stuck to her chest like a suspension bridge, and on that barrelled chest two thin arms rested, terminating in the clawed spastic hands that seemed frozen in a desire to tear at her own scrawny throat.

Then I glanced up at the Portakabin window and I saw him look-ing at me. His face was a mixture of shame and anger, and much worse, a longing that was almost primeval in intensity. I backed away and he never mentioned I'd even been there. But I couldn't get his face out of my head.

What does he think? Does he think that after fourteen years she'll just get up out of that padded contraption and walk? That she'll open her slack twisted mouth and suddenly say "Daddy?" That she'll untangle her misshapen wasted body and join the other teenagers on the street in choosing clothes, in laughing and drinking and living and shagging boys, and one day even make him a grandfather? It's too much. Way too much.

It's why I closed up that fence. His face. That empty longing. The knowledge that he'd do anything.

I didn't see the first guy. At the first Rising I mean. Knew who he was, though. A good choice. They're all scum, that family of builders that always try and dump when we're on night shift. They used to drop him off by car at the gate. Didn't park, you see, so the night watchman, or the cops who pass regularly couldn't get a licence plate. And then he'd come in and scout about, choose the site, then scarper with the details for the truck to follow in the days after. You see we change the main pit every few days. Move it around. You have to know where we're burying. Fly bastards. Don't know where they picked him up again, but no car meant we could never spot him.

So they never knew where he went, you see. And when the cops came round, we'd never seen him. Like I say, that was the truth for me anyhow. I genuinely never saw him. Just where he was taken, and of course the bit of him that Belcher has to put in the doll's slit belly. Looked like the tip of a finger. Maybe not. I could be wrong. It was the tip of something, though.

But I saw the second guy. And all I can say is that fucking junkie was better off wherever he is now than walking the earth with decent people. Junkies make me boke. I can barely look at their sallow sunken faces in the pub where I drink without wanting to walk up and punch their fucking lights out.

So I watched, and I nearly saw it Rise before I had to look away, but I wasn't shamed that it took the bastard and that I'd helped this time. Those scumbags rob old ladies just to feed their veins. True. I was more shamed I didn't see what came for him. Because I was afraid. Anyway, that was when I got my bike.

But kids. I don't know. I just don't think so. I've watched them, the dirty underfed neglected little shits, pissing around on the heaps of rubbish by the fence in their shiny chain-store sportswear, and could see what Belcher meant. But then you'd chase them, and behind those pinched wee masks of adult defiance that called you things you didn't know were in the English language, there was still glimpses of something like children. So I closed up the fence.

I took care of course to climb over and do it from the other side, so it'd look like one of those hacket hard-faced "mothers" from the estate had done it, the ones with necks so fat their thin gold-chained crucifixes look as though they're choking them to death, instead of protecting their immortal souls.

Belcher'll never know it was me.

Course that's left us without a stranger for this time, but he knows what he's doing. He's the one that really wants something. He'll find a way.

I let myself think about what I want this time and there's no contest. In fact I don't want it, I need it.

Spanner interrupts my dreaming by missing the back of the truck by ten miles, and piles of shit spill over the edge and spew around my cab.

"You blind, you fucking maniac?"

He can't hear me. But I shout anyway, and drive off half full just to bug him. On my way to where this pile of crap needs to be I pass the beds, the mechanically smoothed runways on top of the deepest piles of rubbish that Belcher named, where we'll be meeting in half an hour, and think about it again.

It's a Cosworth. Sex and power. Four doors, black, with a spoiler and alloy wheels. Gerry Kelly, the smooth fucker who works at the bookie's is selling it for near on seven grand, and never in a million years can I get my hands on that kind of cash. But I want it. And you see, a thing like that can't just turn up on the site. Cars don't get dumped on the site. So it'll be interesting to see how I manage to get it. That is, if The Rising really does work. Maybe I want to know for sure that it works more than I actually want the car. Maybe.

I think about it some more as I dump the quarter load that the shit-for-brains Spanner has tossed into the back and then drive back slowly, imagining who I could shag in the backseat of that car and where we could go and how fast.

And before I know what time it is I see the hawk guy and Belcher making their way to the beds, and I pull up the dumper beside Spanner's digger, parked at an angle that'll force him to do a difficult reverse, and go and get ready to join them. Of course there's no sunset. This is Glasgow. The grey sky just turns a darker grey, then the street lights of the city come on and stain it a sickly orange. That's how it works. But if Belcher says it's six-fourteen when the invisible sun pegs out and heads west, then it must be right. The air is thick with methane, so much tonight you can hardly breathe. That happens when the air is still, and even after sixteen months I sometimes think I won't be able to take it. But you do. You get used to anything.

Belcher is holding the doll casually, letting its legs hang from his square fist the way a toddler would take a teddy to bed, and he stops walking at some unspecified spot and waits. Spanner and the hawk guy stand on either side of him but a step behind, and so when I reach them, I choose the hawk guy's side and do the same. It's nearly dark now, but the halogens that ring the perimeter fence are picking us out and lighting up the beds like a football pitch. The shadows are so harsh that the ragged skin of the rubbish almost looks comforting in comparison.

Although it's been compacted, inexpertly by Spanner obviously, you can still make out the variety of human debris that make up this unnatural surface. Cartons and plastic containers, broken bread crates, bits of abandoned machines, handles, telephone handsets, rotting vegetables, dried coffee grounds, ripped mattresses. It doesn't ever do to look too closely. It's best to treat it all like it was one thing. The one big thing that humanity has decided it doesn't want any more. The thing that's been eaten and shat on and torn up and soiled, and needs buried and covered by people like us, kept well out of sight.

I think I can feel something already under my feet, although to tell the truth it might just be my excitement. I never could wait for things.

The hawk guy hasn't got his hawk. I notice this and it's strange. But I don't make the rules, and I don't even know the rules. Maybe it's not always necessary. I don't know if I'm relieved or disappointed. I just know that whatever happens I'm going to watch all the way this time. Not chicken out. Keep looking until it comes and goes.

We wait in silence, hands held in front like we were at church, and then Belcher rubs his face with the hand not holding the doll.

"Ah fuckin' hate it when you wee cunts mess me about."

He says this so quietly and wearily I wonder if he's talking to himself, or even to the doll. But he stops mashing his face and turns to look directly at me. My head feels hot, and I can start to hear my pulse beating in my ears, the way you can sometimes when you're pissed and your pillow's too hard. I stay silent. There might be a mistake. I might be misreading him. The other two are looking at their feet. I wonder if I should also lower my eyes, but Belcher's gaze is too intense.

"Ah mean, whit the fuck was a that aboot? Ye think anybody would miss wan o' the wee bastards? Eh?"

I know, and he knows I know, that he's referring to the fence. I try and hold his gaze.

"Well, do ye?"

He's nearly shouting. That's not like him. I have to answer. I start with a shrug.

"Just thought there'd be a fuss, Mr. Belcher. You know, kids an' that. The cops. You know. The mothers."

He steps right up to me and I can feel his breath on my face. His voice drops again.

"Those fat whores dinnae even know how many fuckin' kids they've got. Even if ye could drag them oot the pub long enough tae line them up and show them, there's no tellin' they'd recognise them."

He closes his mouth and his back teeth grind together and make his jaw move. He speaks next in a near whisper.

"Don't know the meanin' o' the fuckin' word, parent."

When he says this his voice breaks on the word "parent" and I use my embarrassment as a decent excuse to lower my eyes. This disgusting personal display somewhere between sentimentality and rage is making me more nervous than when he's just plain mad. I'm praying he'll stop it and go back to being a one-word fucker. Maybe the prayer works. He's calming down, the hardness back in his voice when he speaks again. All trace of the break healed.

"Ah watched ye close up the fence. You stupid wee arse-wipe."

I think about lying and then he's saying something chilling.

"Ye were last in."

As I look quickly back up again three things happen.

Belcher closes his eyes and nods, like he's fallen asleep. Spanner and the hawk guy grab me by each arm, Spanner surprisingly strong for such a crap wee guy.

Then Belcher takes out his knife and slices the top of my left ear off.

I don't even cry out with the pain. I just open my mouth as wide as my jaw will allow and nothing comes out. Just a kind of gasp. Because I can feel it coming. The ground is moving.

I can't watch as Belcher puts the bit of ear in that oval slit and tosses the doll in front him. I can't watch because I'm looking at the undulating hump in the beds that's growing and changing and coming nearer.

The smell of methane is so strong now that a spark would ignite the whole site, and I gag and cough trying to get my breath and my voice back.

I know stuff now. Here's what I know.

It makes itself. It just fucking makes itself out of whatever it can find. There's two dead dogs' heads melted together to make a thing with three eyes and what looks like all jaws and rotted teeth. The body's a mess of butcher's bones, bottle glass, bits of cat newspaper and broken tiles. But the arms. Oh God, the arms. So much metal. And all ending in blades of tin and steel and rusted pointed broken industrial shrapnel, so that when the first pain comes it's mixed with a sharp, almost fruity tang of oxidising metal. It works fast but clumsily, like a newborn animal, and I know that we're helping make it even as it gets bigger.

And all I can think of as I sink to my knees and drool on the ground in the pool of my own hot piss is his daughter drooling the same way in her bed, and how this isn't going to make it better.

If I could ever talk again, if the ragged hole in my throat would close and stop pumping blood on the milk cartons and broken paperbacks, I would tell the stupid cunt again and again.

Shout it. Scream it.

It isn't going to make it better.

JACK THE RIPPER

SHIRLEY JACKSON

How to reimagine such an infamous, shape-shifting fiend is part of what Shirley Jackson attempts here. Furthermore, she understands that every Jack is now simply part of an aggregate Ripper; each fresh invention only adds energy to the whole.

No, her challenge is to shock us, as economically as possible and taking into account, as her handicap, what we already believe we know.

Does anyone doubt she can do it?

✺

THE MAN HESITATED on the corner under the traffic light, then started off down the side street, walking slowly and watching the few people who passed him. It was long past midnight, and the streets were as nearly deserted as they ever get; as the man went down the dark street he stopped for a minute, thinking he saw a dead girl on the sidewalk. She was nearly against the wall of a building; a few feet beyond her was the small sign of a bar, and seeing that, the man started to walk on, and then turned back to the girl.

She was so drunk that when he shook her and tried to sit her up she sagged backward, her eyes half closed and her hands rolling on the sidewalk. The man stood and looked at her for a minute, and then turned again and went down to the bar. When he opened the door and went in he saw that the place was nearly empty, with only a group of three or four sailors at the farther end of the bar, and the bartender with them, talking and laughing. There was one man standing at the bar near the doorway, and after looking around for a minute, the man who had come in walked over and stood at the end of the bar.

"Listen," he said, "there's a girl lying out on the street outside."

The man farther down the bar looked at him quietly.

"I just happened to be passing down this way," the man who had just come in went on more urgently, "and I saw her, and I think something had better be done. She can't stay out there." The man farther down the bar went on looking. "She isn't but about seventeen."

"There's a phone out back," the man standing down the bar said. "Call the mayor."

The bartender came easily down to the end of the bar, the smile leaving his face as he came. When he got to the end of the bar, beside the man who had just come in, he stood unsmiling, waiting.

"Listen," the man said again, "there's a girl sixteen, seventeen lying outside in the street. We better get her inside."

"Call the mayor," the man down the bar said, "his number's in the book."

"I was just walking by," the man said, "and she was lying there."

"I know," the bartender said.

"Mention my name," the man down the bar said. "Tell him I told you to call."

"I saw that she was nice and comfortable," the bartender said, "and I put her pocketbook beside her, all nice and convenient." He smiled tenderly. "I hope you didn't disturb her," he said.

The man raised his voice slightly. "She can't keep on lying there," he said. "You're not going to say you intend to leave her there?"

"He'll remember me all right," the man down the bar said, nodding. "He won't forget me in a hurry."

"She likes it there," the bartender said. "Sleeps there nearly every night."

"But a girl fifteen, sixteen!" the man cried.

The bartender's voice became harder; he put both hands on the edge of the bar and leaned over toward the man. "Anytime she likes," he said, "she can get up and go home. She doesn't have to stay there. Let her get up and walk home."

"Not in any sort of a hurry he won't," the man down the bar said.

"Comes in here every night and gets drunk," the bartender went on. "I let her have a beer now and then without money, do you want I should rent her a room, too?" He leaned back again and his voice softened. "Sleeps like a baby, don't she?" He turned around abruptly and walked back down the bar to the sailors. "Another drunk," he said to them.

The man turned to the door and opened it, still hesitating. Then he went out. "Don't forget to tell him what I told you," the man down the bar called after him.

When he got back to the girl he saw that she still lay in the same position, face against the sidewalk, with her knees against the wall. Her pocketbook lay on the sidewalk beside her, and the man picked it and opened it. There was no money; there was a lipstick from the five-and-ten, and a key, a comb, and a little notebook. The man put everything back except the notebook; he opened it and found, on the first page, the girl's name and address. When he turned the first page he found a list of about twenty bars, with addresses and, in some cases, names of the bartenders. A few pages later he found another list, this time of sailors, each name followed by the name of a ship, and a date, apparently the date of the last time the ship was in New York. The entries were written in a big, childish writing, with uncrossed T's and an occasional misspelling. Toward the end of the notebook, a picture had been put between the pages. It showed the girl with two sailors, one on each side, their heads together, and all three smiling. The girl in the picture looked pleased and unattractive; lying on the ground, she seemed thin and almost lovely. The man put the picture back into the notebook and the notebook back into the pocketbook, and then, carrying the pocketbook, walked down to the corner and waved down a taxi. With the taxi waiting, he went back to the girl, lifted her, and put her in, and then got in after her. The girl was sprawled out on the seat, and the man had to sit on a corner to give her room. He gave the driver the address he had seen in the notebook, and the driver, after raising his eyes once to the mirror to look at the man, shrugged and drove off.

The house was in a bad neighborhood, old and dirty, and the driver, stopping the taxi, said: "This is it, mister." He turned and looked at the girl, and added doubtfully, "Do I help you?"

The man pulled the girl out of the taxi by taking hold of her legs and dragging her until he could put her feet on the ground, and then taking her by the waist and swinging her over his shoulder. He held her over his shoulder while he took change from his pocket to pay the driver, and then, still holding her by the legs, he went into the house.

The hall was lighted by gaslights, and the stairway was incredibly narrow and steep. The man knocked on the first door, first with his knuckles, and then, grimly, with the girl's shoes, swinging her legs back and forth.

From somewhere on the other side of the door, a woman's voice asked, "What is it?" and finally the door opened a crack and the woman put her face out. It was too dark for the man to see what she looked like, but she said: "Who is it? Rose? She lives on the sixth floor. Last door on the right." The door closed again. The man surveyed the stairway and thought. There was no room in the hallway to put the girl down, so he tightened his grip on her legs and started up the stairs. He stopped for breath on every landing, but by the time he reached the sixth floor he was breathing heavily and moving slowly, putting both feet on each step. He leaned against the wall at the top for a minute, trying to shift the girl's weight, and then went down to the last door on the right. Putting the girl down on the floor, he opened her pocketbook and took out the key and opened the door. It was too dark in the hall to see what was in the room, so he lighted a match and went in, trying to find some light. After lighting three matches he found a candle, which he lit and set on the dresser in its own wax. The room was large enough for a cot and the dresser; on the back of the door were three hooks, on which were hanging a torn silk kimono and a pair of dirty stockings. The bed had a blanket on it, over the mattress, and a dirty, uncovered pillow. On the dresser were a few bobby pins and a package of matches. The man opened the four dresser drawers; all of them were empty except for the top one, which contained a bottle opener and a couple of beer bottle caps. When he had examined the room, the man went outside, where he had left the girl, and picked her up under the arms and dragged her into the room. He dumped her onto the bed and threw the blanket over her. He opened her pocketbook and took out the notebook, glancing through it until he found the picture, which he put in his pocket. He put the key on the dresser and the pocketbook beside it, and then, just before blowing out the candle, took out his knife. It had a polished bone handle, and a long and incredibly sharp blade.

He took a taxi on the corner near the tenement, giving the driver an address in the East Seventies, and was home in a few minutes. When he got out of the elevator in his apartment house he stopped for a minute, looked at his hands and down at his shoes, and carefully took a piece of lint off his sleeve. He let himself into his apartment with his key, and walked softly into the bedroom. When he turned on the light his wife stirred in her bed, and then opened her eyes. "What time is it?" she murmured.

"Late," he said. He went over and kissed her.

"What kept you so long?" she asked.

"I stopped and had a few drinks after the meeting," he said. He went over to the dresser to put down his keys, and looked at his wife's picture in the tall plastic frame. Reaching in his pocket, he found the picture of the girl with the two sailors and thought for a minute; then he went to his wife's dressing table, and with her plastic-handled nail scissors cut the two sailors out of the picture, leaving the girl alone. This fragment of picture he put into the lower corner of the frame holding his wife's picture. He lighted a cigarette and stood looking at it.

"Aren't you coming to bed?" his wife asked sleepily.

"No," he said. "Believe I'll take a bath."

BUTTON, BUTTON

RICHARD MATHESON

For a perfect example of malice served up deadpan, look no further than Richard Matheson's portrait of a marriage undone by expediency. Arthur and Norma Lewis, from the moment we first meet them, are already marked for disaster; the only uncertainty is the path they will take to get there, and how quickly.

And though, like any great conjuror's trick, this tale won't stand up under close scrutiny, the cleverness of its illusions is wholly distracting. Besides, how could I resist the way it stood my theme on its ear?

၆

THE PACKAGE WAS lying by the front door—a cube-shaped carton sealed with tape, the name and address printed by hand: Mr. and Mrs. Arthur Lewis, 217 E. 37th Street, New York, New York 10016. Norma picked it up, unlocked the door, and went into the apartment. It was just getting dark.

After she put the lamb chops in the broiler, she made herself a drink and sat down to open the package.

Inside the carton was a push-button unit fastened to a small wooden box. A glass dome covered the button. Norma tried to lift it off, but it was locked in place. She turned the unit over and saw a folded piece of paper Scotch-taped to the bottom of the box. She pulled it off: "Mr. Steward will call on you at 8 P.M."

Norma put the button unit beside her on the couch. She sipped the drink and reread the typed note, smiling.

A few moments later, she went back into the kitchen to make the salad.

The doorbell rang at eight o'clock. "I'll get it," Norma called from the kitchen. Arthur was in the living room, reading.

There was a small man in the hallway. He removed his hat as Norma opened the door. "Mrs. Lewis?" he inquired politely.

"Yes?"

"I'm Mr. Steward."

"Oh, yes." Norma repressed a smile. She was sure now it was a sales pitch.

"May I come in?" asked Mr. Steward.

"I'm rather busy," Norma said. "I'll get you your watchamacallit, though." She started to turn.

"Don't you want to know what it is?"

Norma turned back. Mr. Steward's tone had been offensive. "No, I don't think so," she said.

"It could prove very valuable," he told her.

"Monetarily?" she challenged.

Mr. Steward nodded. "Monetarily," he said.

Norma frowned. She didn't like his attitude. "What are you trying to sell?" she asked.

"I'm not selling anything," he answered.

Arthur came out of the living room. "Something wrong?"

Mr. Steward introduced himself.

"Oh, the . . ." Arthur pointed toward the living room and smiled. "What is that gadget, anyway?"

"It won't take long to explain," replied Mr. Steward. "May I come in?"

"If you're selling something . . ." Arthur said.

Mr. Steward shook his head. "I'm not."

Arthur looked at Norma. "Up to you," he said.

He hesitated. "Well, why not?" he said.

They went into the living room and Mr. Steward sat in Norma's chair. He reached into an inside coat pocket and withdrew a small sealed envelope. "Inside here is a key to the bell-unit dome," he said. He set the envelope on the chairside table. "The bell is connected to our office."

"What's it for?" asked Arthur.

"If you push the button," Mr. Steward told him, "somewhere in the world, someone you don't know will die. In return for which you will receive a payment of fifty thousand dollars."

Norma stared at the small man. He was smiling.

"What are you talking about?" Arthur asked him.

Mr. Steward looked surprised. "But I've just explained," he said.

"Is this a practical joke?" asked Arthur.

"Not at all. The offer is completely genuine."

"You aren't making sense," Arthur said. "You expect us to believe . . ."

"Whom do you represent?" demanded Norma.

Mr. Steward looked embarrassed. "I'm afraid I'm not at liberty to tell you that," he said. "However, I assure you the organization is of international scope."

"I think you'd better leave," Arthur said, standing.

Mr. Steward rose. "Of course."

"And take your button unit with you."

"Are you sure you wouldn't care to think about it for a day or so?"

Arthur picked up the button unit and the envelope and thrust them into Mr. Steward's hands. He walked into the hall and pulled open the door.

"I'll leave my card," said Mr. Steward. He placed it on the table by the door.

When he was gone, Arthur tore it in half and tossed the pieces onto the table. "God!" he said.

Norma was still sitting on the sofa, "What do you think it was?" she asked.

"I don't care to know," he answered.

She tried to smile but couldn't. "Aren't you curious at all?"

"No," he shook his head.

After Arthur returned to his book, Norma went back to the kitchen and finished washing the dishes.

"Why won't you talk about it?" Norma asked later.

Arthur's eyes shifted as he brushed his teeth. He looked at her reflection in the bathroom mirror.

"Doesn't it intrigue you?"

"It offends me," Arthur said.

"I know, but—" Norma rolled another curler in her hair "—doesn't it intrigue you, too?"

"You think it's a practical joke?" she asked as they went into the bedroom.

"If it is, it's a sick one."

Norma sat on the bed and took off her slippers.

"Maybe it's some kind of psychological research."

Arthur shrugged. "Could be."

"Maybe some eccentric millionaire is doing it."

"Maybe."

"Wouldn't you like to know?"

Arthur shook his head.

"Why?"

"Because it's immoral," he told her.

Norma slid beneath the covers. "Well, I think it's intriguing," she said.

Arthur turned off the lamp and leaned over to kiss her. "Good night," he said.

"Good night." She patted his back.

Norma closed her eyes. Fifty thousand dollars, she thought.

In the morning, as she left the apartment, Norma saw the card halves on the table. Impulsively, she dropped them into her purse.

She locked the front door and joined Arthur in the elevator.

While she was on her coffee break, she took the card halves from her purse and held the torn edges together. Only Mr. Steward's name and telephone number were printed on the card.

After lunch, she took the card halves from her purse again and Scotch-taped the edges together. Why am I doing this? she thought.

Just before five, she dialed the number.

"Good afternoon," said Mr. Steward's voice.

Norma almost hung up but restrained herself. She cleared her throat. "This is Mrs. Lewis," she said.

"Yes, Mrs. Lewis." Mr. Steward sounded pleased.

"I'm curious."

"That's natural," Mr. Steward said.

"Not that I believe a word of what you told us."

"Oh, it's quite authentic," Mr. Steward answered.

"Well, whatever . . ." Norma swallowed. "When you said someone in the world would die, what did you mean?"

"Exactly that," he answered. "It could be anyone. All we guarantee is that you don't know them. And, of course, that you wouldn't have to watch them die."

"For fifty thousand dollars," Norma said.

"That is correct."

She made a scoffing sound. "That's crazy."

"Nonetheless, that is the proposition," Mr. Steward said. "Would you like me to return the button unit?"

Norma stiffened. "Certainly not." She hung up angrily.

The package was lying by the front door; Norma saw it as she left the elevator. Well, of all the nerve, she thought. She glared at the carton as she unlocked the door. I just won't take it in, she thought. She went inside and started dinner.

Later, she carried her drink to the front hall. Opening the door, she picked up the package and carried it into the kitchen, leaving it on the table.

She sat in the living room, sipping her drink and looking out the window. After a while, she went back into the kitchen to turn the cutlets in the broiler. She put the package in a bottom cabinet. She'd throw it out in the morning.

"Maybe some eccentric millionaire is playing games with people," she said.

Arthur looked up from his dinner. "I don't understand you."

"What does that mean?"

"Let it go," he told her.

Norma ate in silence. Suddenly, she put her fork down. "Suppose it's a genuine offer," she said.

Arthur stared at her.

"Suppose it's a genuine offer."

"All right, suppose it is!" He looked incredulous. "What would you like to do? Get the button back and push it? Murder someone?"

Norma looked disgusted. "Murder."

"How would *you* define it?"

"If you don't even know the person?" Norma asked.

Arthur looked astounded. "Are you saying what I think you are?"

"If it's some old Chinese peasant ten thousand miles away? Some diseased native in the Congo?"

"How about some baby boy in Pennsylvania?" Arthur countered. "Some beautiful little girl on the next block?"

"Now you're loading things."

"The point is, Norma," he continued, "that who you kill makes no difference. It's still murder."

"The point is," Norma broke in, "if it's someone you've never seen in your life and never will see, someone whose death you don't even have to know about, you still wouldn't push the button?"

Arthur stared at her, appalled. "You mean you would?"

"Fifty thousand dollars, Arthur."

"What has the amount . . ."

"Fifty thousand dollars, Arthur," Norma interrupted. "A chance to take that trip to Europe we've always talked about."

"Norma, no."

"A chance to buy that cottage on the Island."

"Norma, no." His face was white. "For God's sake, no!"

She shuddered. "All right, take it easy," she said. "Why are you getting so upset? It's only talk."

After dinner, Arthur went into the living room. Before he left the table, he said, "I'd rather not discuss it anymore, if you don't mind."

Norma shrugged. "Fine with me."

She got up earlier than usual to make pancakes, eggs, and bacon for Arthur's breakfast.

"What's the occasion?" he asked with a smile.

"No occasion." Norma looked offended. "I wanted to do it, that's all."

"Good," he said. "I'm glad you did."

She refilled his cup. "Wanted to show you I'm not . . ." she shrugged.

"Not what?"

"Selfish."

"Did I say you were?"

"'Well—" She gestured vaguely. "—last night . . ."

Arthur didn't speak.

"All that talk about the button," Norma said, "I think you—well, misunderstood me."

"In what way?" His voice was guarded.

"I think you felt—" She gestured again. "—that I was only thinking of myself."

"Oh."

"I wasn't."

"Norma."

"Well, I wasn't. When I talked about Europe, a cottage on the Island . . ."

"Norma, why are we getting so involved in this?"

"I'm not involved at all." She drew in a shaking breath. "I'm simply trying to indicate that . . ."

"What?"

"That I'd like for us to go to Europe. Like for us to have a nicer apartment, nicer furniture, nicer clothes. Like for us to finally have a baby, for that matter."

"Norma, we will," he said.

"When?"

He stared at her in dismay. "Norma . . ."

"When?"

"Are you—" He seemed to draw back slightly. "Are you really saying—?"

"I'm saying that they're probably doing it for some research project!" she cut him off. "That they want to know what average people would do under such a circumstance! That they're just saying someone would die, in order to study reactions, see if there'd be guilt, anxiety, whatever! You don't really think they'd kill somebody, do you?"

Arthur didn't answer. She saw his hands trembling. After a while, he got up and left.

When he'd gone to work, Norma remained at the table, staring into her coffee. I'm going to be late, she thought. She shrugged. What difference did it make? She should be home anyway, not working in an office.

While she was stacking the dishes, she turned abruptly, dried her hands, and took the package from the bottom cabinet. Opening it, she set the button unit on the table. She stared at it for a long time before taking the key from its envelope and removing the glass dome. She stared at the button. How ridiculous, she thought. All this over a meaningless button.

Reaching out, she pressed it down. For us, she thought angrily.

She shuddered. Was it happening? A chill of horror swept across her.

In a moment, it had passed. She made a contemptuous noise. Ridiculous, she thought. To get so worked up over nothing.

★　★　★

She had just turned the supper steaks and was making herself another drink when the telephone rang. She picked it up. "Hello?"

"Mrs. Lewis?"

"Yes?"

"This is Lenox Hill Hospital."

She felt unreal as the voice informed her of the subway accident, the shoving crowd. Arthur pushed from the platform in front of the train. She was conscious of shaking her head but couldn't stop.

As she hung up, she remembered Arthur's life insurance policy for twenty-five thousand dollars, with double indemnity for—

"No." She couldn't seem to breathe. She struggled to her feet and walked in to the kitchen numbly. Something cold pressed at her skull as she removed the button unit from the wastebasket. There were no nails or screws visible. She couldn't see how it was put together.

Abruptly, she began to smash it on the sink edge, pounding it harder and harder, until the wood split. She pulled the sides apart, cutting her fingers without noticing. There were no transistors in the box, no wires or tubes. The box was empty.

She whirled with a gasp as the telephone rang. Stumbling into the living room, she picked up the receiver.

"Mrs. Lewis?" Mr. Steward asked.

It wasn't her voice shrieking so; it couldn't be. "You said I wouldn't know the one that died!"

"My dear lady," Mr. Steward said, "do you really think you knew your husband?"

THE ASIAN SHORE

THOMAS M. DISCH

Tourists are strangers who admit the fact, expatriates can remain for years in denial, while "going native" is a well-examined phenomenon. However, to a relatively recent arrival like the American John Benedict Harris, whose residence in Turkey might best be termed a self-inflicted limbo, there is only an increasingly tortuous path to whatever acceptance lies ahead.

And his confusions and hesitations, his stops and starts along the way, have about them not just the mere inevitability of a natural resistance but also the oddness of those alchemic passes employed in urging base ingredients to a higher state.

I

THERE WERE VOICES on the cobbled street, and the sounds of motors. Footsteps, slamming doors, whistles, footsteps. He lived on the ground floor, so there was no way to avoid these evidences of the city's too abundant life. They accumulated in the room like so much dust, like the heaps of unanswered correspondence on the mottled tablecloth.

Every night he would drag a chair into the unfurnished back room—the guest room, as he liked to think of it—and look out over the tiled roofs and across the black waters of the Bosphorus at the lights of Usküdar. But the sounds penetrated this room too. He would sit there, in the darkness, drinking wine, waiting for her knock on the back door.

Or he might try to read: histories, books of travel, the long dull biography of Atatürk. A kind of sedation. Sometimes he would even begin a letter to his wife:

> *Dear Janice,*
>   *No doubt you've been wondering what's become of me these last few months . . .*

But the trouble was that once that part had been written, the frail courtesies, the perfunctory reportage, he could not bring himself to say what *had* become of him.

Voices . . .

It was just as well that he couldn't speak the language. For a while he had studied it, taxiing three times a week to Robert College in Bebek, but the grammar, based on assumptions wholly alien to any other language he knew, with its wavering boundaries between verbs and nouns, nouns and adjectives, withstood every assault of his incorrigibly Aristotelian mind. He sat at the back of the classroom, behind the rows of American teenagers, as sullen as convicts, as comically out of context as the machineries melting in a Dalí landscape—sat there and parroted innocuous dialogues after the teacher, taking both roles in turn, first the trustful, inquisitive John, forever wandering alone and lost in the streets of Istanbul and Ankara, then the helpful, knowing Ahmet Bey. Neither of these interlocutors would admit what had become increasingly evident with each faltering word that John spoke—that he would wander these same streets for years, inarticulate, cheated, and despised.

But these lessons, while they lasted, had one great advantage. They provided an illusion of activity, an obelisk upon which the eye might focus amid the desert of each new day, something to move toward and then something to leave behind.

After the first month it had rained a great deal, and this provided him with a good excuse for staying in. He had mopped up the major attractions of the city in one week, and he persisted at sightseeing long afterward, even in doubtful weather, until at last he had checked off every mosque and ruin, every museum and cistern cited in boldface in the pages of his Hachette. He visited the cemetery of Eyüp, and he devoted an entire Sunday to the land wall, carefully searching for, though he could not read Greek, the inscriptions of the various Byzantine emperors. But more and more often on these excursions he would see the woman or the child or the woman and the child together, until he came almost to dread the sight of any woman or any child in the city. It was not an unreasonable dread.

And always, at nine o'clock, or ten at the very latest, she would come knocking at the door of the apartment. Or, if the outer door of the building had not been left ajar by the people upstairs, at the window of the front room. She knocked patiently, in little clusters of three or four raps spaced several seconds apart, never very loud. Sometimes, but only if she were in the hall, she would accompany her knocking with a few words in Turkish, usually *Yavuz! Yavuz!* He had asked the clerk at the mail desk of the consulate what this meant, for he couldn't find it in his dictionary. It was a common Turkish name, a man's name.

His name was John. John Benedict Harris. He was an American.

She seldom stayed out there for more than half an hour any one night, knocking and calling to him, or to this imaginary Yavuz, and he would remain all that while in the chair in the unfurnished room, drinking Kavak and watching the ferries move back and forth on the dark water between Kabatas and Usküdar, the European and the Asian shore.

He had seen her first outside the fortress of Rumeli Hisar. It was the day, shortly after he'd arrived in the city, that he had come out to register at Robert College. After paying his fees and inspecting the library, he had come down the hill by the wrong path, and there it had stood, mammoth and majestically improbable, a gift. He did not know its name, and his Hachette was at the hotel. There was just the raw fact of the fortress, a mass of gray stone, its towers and crenelations, the gray Bosphorus below. He angled for a photograph, but even that far away it was too big—one could not frame the whole of it in a single shot.

He left the road, taking a path through dry bush that promised to circle the fortress. As he approached, the walls reared higher and higher. Before such walls there could be no question of an assault.

He saw her when she was about fifty feet away. She came toward him on the footpath, carrying a large bundle wrapped in newspaper and bound with twine. Her clothes were the usual motley of washed-out cotton prints that all the poorer women of the city went about in, but she did not, like most other women of her kind, attempt to pull her shawl across her face when she noticed him.

But perhaps it was only that her bundle would have made this conventional gesture of modesty awkward, for after that first glance she did at least lower her eyes to the path. No, it was hard to discover any clear portent in this first encounter.

As they passed each other he stepped off the path, and she did mumble some word in Turkish. Thank you, he supposed. He watched her until she reached the road, wondering whether she would look back, and she didn't.

He followed the walls of the fortress down the steep crumbling hillside to the shore road without finding an entrance. It amused him to think that there might not be one. Between the water and the barbicans there was only a narrow strip of highway.

An absolute daunting structure.

The entrance, which did exist, was just to the side of the central tower. He paid five liras admission and another two and a half liras to bring in his camera.

Of the three principal towers, visitors were allowed to climb only the one at the center of the eastern wall that ran along the Bospho-

rus. He was out of condition and mounted the enclosed spiral staircase slowly. The stone steps had evidently been pirated from other
buildings. Every so often he recognized a fragment of a classic entab-
lature of a wholly inappropriate, intaglio design—a Greek cross or
some crude Byzantine eagle. Each footfall became a symbolic con-
quest: one could not ascend these stairs without becoming impli-
cated in the fall of Constantinople.

This staircase opened out into a kind of wooden catwalk clinging
to the inner wall of the tower at a height of about sixty feet. The
silo-like space was resonant with the coo and flutter of invisible
pigeons, and somewhere the wind was playing with a metal door,
creaking it open, banging it shut. Here, if he so wished, he might discover portents.

He crept along the wooden platform, both hands grasping the
iron rail stapled to the stone wall, feeling just an agreeable amount
of terror, sweating nicely. It occurred to him how much this would
have pleased Janice, whose enthusiasm for heights had equaled his.
He wondered when, if ever, he would see her again, and what she
would be like. By now undoubtedly she had begun divorce proceed-
ings. Perhaps she was already no longer his wife.

The platform led to another stone staircase, shorter than the
first, which ascended to the creaking metal door. He pushed it open
and stepped out amid a flurry of pigeons into the full dazzle of the
noon, the wide splendor of the elevation, sunlight above and the
bright bow of water beneath—and, beyond the water, the surreal
green of the Asian hills, hundred-breasted Cybele. It seemed, all of
this, to demand some kind of affirmation, a yell. But he didn't feel
up to yelling, or large gestures. He could only admire, at this distance, the illusion of tactility, hills as flesh, an illusion that could be
heightened if he laid his hands, still sweaty from his passage along
the catwalk, on the rough warm stone of the balustrade.

Looking down the side of the tower at the empty road, he saw
her again, standing at the very edge of the water. She was looking up
at him. When he noticed her she lifted both hands above her head, as
though signaling, and shouted something that, even if he could have

heard it properly, he would surely not have understood. He supposed that she was asking to have her picture taken, so he turned the
setting ring to the fastest speed to compensate for the glare from the
water. She stood directly below the tower, and there seemed no way
to frame an interesting composition. He released the shutter.
Woman, water, asphalt road: it would be a snapshot, not a photograph, and he didn't believe in taking snapshots.

The woman continued to call up to him, arms raised in that same
hieratic gesture. It made no sense. He waved to her and smiled
uncertainly. It was something of a nuisance, really. He would have
preferred to have this scene to himself. One climbed towers, after all,
in order to be alone.

Altin, the man who had found his apartment for him, worked as a
commission agent for carpet and jewelry shops in the Grand Bazaar.
He would strike up conversations with English and American
tourists and advise them what to buy, and where, and how much to
pay. They spent one day looking and settled on an apartment building near Taksim, the commemorative traffic circle that served the
European quarter of the city as a kind of Broadway. The several
banks of Istanbul demonstrated their modern character here with
neon signs, and in the center of the traffic circle, life-size, Atatürk led
a small but representative group of his countrymen toward their
bright, Western destiny.

The apartment was thought (by Altin) to partake of this same
advanced spirit: it had central heating, a sit-down toilet, a bathtub,
and a defunct but prestigious refrigerator. The rent was six hundred
liras a month, which came to sixty-six dollars at the official rate but
only fifty dollars, at the rate Altin gave. He was anxious to move out
of the hotel, so he agreed to a six-month lease.

He hated it from the day he moved in. Except for the shreds of a
lousy sofa in the guest room, which he obliged the landlord to
remove, he left everything as he found it. Even the blurry pinups
from a Turkish girlie magazine remained where they were to cover

the cracks in the new plaster. He was determined to make no accommodations: he might have to live in this city; it was not required that he *enjoy* it.

Every day he picked up his mail at the consulate. He sampled a variety of restaurants. He saw the sights and made notes for his book.

On Thursdays he visited a *hamam* to sweat out the accumulated poisons of the week and to be kneaded and stomped by a masseur.

He supervised the growth of his young mustache.

He rotted, like a jar of preserves left open and forgotten on the top shelf of a cupboard.

He learned that there was a special Turkish word for the rolls of dirt that are scraped off the skin after a steambath, and another that imitated the sound of boiling water: *fuker, fuker, fuker.* Boiling water signified, to the Turkish mind, the first stages of sexual arousal. It was roughly equivalent to the stateside notion of "electricity."

Occasionally, as he began to construct his own internal map of the unpromising alleyways and ruinous staircase streets of his neighborhood, he fancied that he saw her, that same woman. It was hard to be certain. She would always be some distance away, or he might catch just a glimpse out of the corner of his eye. If it were the same woman, nothing at this stage suggested that she was pursuing him. It was, at most, a coincidence.

In any case, he could not be certain. Her face had not been unusual, and he did not have the photograph to consult, for he had spoiled the entire roll of film removing it from the camera.

Sometimes after one of these failed encounters he would feel a slight uneasiness. It amounted to no more than that.

He met the boy in Üsküdar. It was during the first severe cold spell, in mid-November. His first trip across the Bosphorus, and when he stepped off the ferry onto the very soil (or, anyhow, the very asphalt) of this new continent, the largest of all, he could feel the great mass of it beckoning him toward its vast eastward vortex, tugging at him, sucking at his soul.

It had been his first intention, back in New York, to stop two months at most in Istanbul, learn the language; then into Asia. How often he had mesmerized himself with the litany of its marvels: the grand mosques of Kayseri and Sivas, of Beysehir and Afyon Karahisar; the isolate grandeur of Ararat and then, stiff moving east, the shores of the Caspian; Meshed, Kabul, the Himalayas. It was all these that reached out to him now, singing, stretching forth their siren arms, inviting him to their whirlpool.

And he? He refused. Though he could feel the charm of the invitation, he refused. Though he might have wished very much to unite with them, he still refused. For he had tied himself to the mast, where he was proof against their call. He had his apartment in that city which stood just outside their reach, and he would stay there until it was time to return. In the spring he was going back to the States.

But he did allow the sirens this much—that he would abandon the rational mosque-to-mosque itinerary laid down by his Hachette and entrust the rest of the day to serendipity. While the sun still shone that afternoon they might lead him where they would.

Asphalt gave way to cobbles, and cobbles to packed dirt. The squalor here was on a much less majestic scale than in Stambul, where even the most decrepit hovels had been squeezed by the pressure of population to heights of three and four stories. In Usküdar the same wretched buildings sprawled across the hills like beggars whose crutches had been kicked out from under them, supine; through their rags of unpainted wood one could see the scabbed flesh of mud-and-wattle. As he threaded his way from one dirt street to the next and found each of them sustaining this one unvarying tone, without color, without counterpoint, he began to conceive a new Asia, not of mountains and vast plains, but this same slum rolling on perpetually across grassless hills, a continuum of drabness, of sheer dumb extent.

Because he was short and because he would not dress the part of an American, he could go through these streets without calling attention to himself. The mustache too, probably, helped. Only his conscious, observing eyes (the camera had spoiled a second roll of film and was being repaired) would have betrayed him as a tourist today. Indeed, Altin had assured him (intending, no doubt, a compliment) that as soon as he learned to speak the language he would pass for a Turk.

It grew steadily colder throughout the afternoon. The wind moved a thick veil of mist over the sun and left it there. As the mists thinned and thickened, as the flat disc of sun, sinking westward, would fade and brighten, the vagaries of light whispered conflicting rumors about these houses and their dwellers. But he did not wish to stop and listen. He already knew more concerning these things than he wanted to. He set off at a quicker pace in the supposed direction of the landing stage.

The boy stood crying beside a public fountain, a water faucet projecting from a crude block of concrete, at the intersection of two narrow streets. Five years old, perhaps six. He was carrying a large plastic bucket of water in each hand, one bright red, the other turquoise. The water had splashed over his thin trousers and bare feet.

At first he supposed the boy cried only because of the cold. The damp ground must be near to freezing. To walk on it in bare wet feet . . .

Then he saw the slippers. They were what he would have called shower slippers, small die-stamped ovals of blue plastic with single thongs that had to be grasped between the first and second toes.

The boy would stoop over and force the thongs between his stiff, cold-reddened toes, but after only a step or two the slippers would again fall off his numb feet. With each frustrated progress more water would slop over the sides of the buckets. He could not keep the slippers on his feet, and he would not walk off without them.

With this understanding came a kind of horror, a horror of his own helplessness. He could not go up to the boy and ask him where he lived, lift and carry him—he was so small—to his home. Nor could he scold the child's parents for having sent him out on this errand without proper shoes or winter clothes. He could not even take up the buckets and have the child lead him to his home. For each of these possibilities demanded that he be able to *speak* to the boy, and this he could not do.

What *could* he do? Offer money? As well offer him, at such a moment, a pamphlet, from the U.S. Information Agency!

There was, in fact, nothing, *nothing* he could do.

The boy had become aware of him. Now that he had a sympathetic audience he let himself cry in earnest. Lowering the two buckets to the ground and pointing at these and at the slippers, he spoke pleadingly to this grown-up stranger, to this rescuer, words in Turkish.

He took a step backward, a second step, and the boy shouted at him, what message of pain or uncomprehending indignation he would never know. He turned away and ran back along the street that had brought him to this crossway. It was another hour before he found the landing stage. It had begun to snow.

As he took his seat inside the ferry he found himself glancing at the other passengers, as though expecting to find her there among them.

The next day he came down with a cold. The fever rose through the night. He woke several times, and it was always their two faces that he carried with him from the dreams, like souvenirs whose origin and purpose have been forgotten; the woman at Rumeli Hisar, the child in Usküdar: some part of his mind had already begun to draw the equation between them.

II

It was the thesis of his first book that the quiddity of architecture, its chief claim to an esthetic interest, was its arbitrariness. Once the lintels were lying on the posts, once some kind of roof had been spread across the hollow space, then anything else that might be done was gratuitous. Even the lintel and the post, the roof, the space below, these were gratuitous as well. Stated thus, it was a mild enough notion; the difficulty was in training the eye to see the whole world of usual forms—patterns of brick, painted plaster, carved and car-pentered wood—not as "buildings" and "streets" but as an infinite series of free and arbitrary choices. There was no place in such a scheme for orders, styles, sophistication, taste. Every artifact of the city was anomalous, unique, but living there in the midst of it all you could not allow yourself too fine a sense of this fact. If you did . . .

It had been his task, these last three or four years, to re-educate his eye and mind to just this condition, of innocence. His was the very reverse of the Romantics' aims, for he did not expect to find himself, when this ideal state of "raw" perception was reached (it never would be, of course, for innocence, like justice, is an absolute; it may be approached but never attained), any closer to nature. Nature, as such, did not concern him. What he sought, on the con-trary, was a sense of the great artifice of things, of structures, of the immense interminable wall that has been built just to exclude nature.

The attention that his first book had received showed that he had been at least partially successful, but he knew (and who better?) how far short his aim had fallen, how many clauses of the perceptual social contract he had never even thought to question.

So, since it was now a matter of ridding himself of the sense of the familiar, he had had to find some better laboratory for this pur-pose than New York, somewhere that he could be, more naturally, an alien. This much seemed obvious to him.

It had not seemed so obvious to his wife.

He did not insist. He was willing to be reasonable. He would talk about it. He talked about it whenever they were together—at dinner, at her friends' parties (his friends didn't seem to give parties), in bed—and it came down to this, that Janice objected not so much to the projected trip as to his entire program, the thesis itself.

No doubt her reasons were sound. The sense of the arbitrary did not stop at architecture; it embraced—or it would, if he let it—all phenomena. If there were no fixed laws that governed the furbelows and arabesques out of which a city is composed, there were equally no laws (or only arbitrary laws, which is the same as none at all) to define the relationships woven into the lattice of that city, relationships between man and man, man and woman, John and Janice.

And indeed this had already occurred to him, though he had not spoken of it to her before. He had often had to stop, in the midst of some quotidian ritual like dining out, and take his bearings. As the thesis developed, as he continued to sift away layer after layer of preconception, he found himself more and more astonished at the size of the demesne that recognized the sovereignty of convention. At times he even thought he could trace in his wife's slightest gesture or in her aptest phrase or in a kiss some hint of the Palladian rule book from which it had been derived. Perhaps with practice one would be able to document the entire history of her styles—here an echo of the Gothic Revival, there an imitation of Mies.

When his application for a Guggenheim was rejected, he decided he would make the trip by himself, using the bit of money that was still left from the book. Though he saw no necessity for it, he had agreed to Janice's request for a divorce. They parted on the best of terms. She had even seen him to the boat.

The wet snow would fall for a day, two days, forming knee-deep drifts in the open spaces of the city, in paved courtyards, on vacant lots. Cold winds polished the slush of streets and sidewalks to dull-gleaming lumpy ice. The steeper hills became impassable. The snow and the ice would linger a few days and then a sudden thaw would send it all pouring down the cobbled hillside in a single afternoon, brief alpine cataracts of refuse and brown water. A patch of tolerable weather might follow this flood, and then another blizzard. Altin assured him that this was an unusually fierce winter, unprecedented.

A spiral diminishing.

A tightness.

And each day the light fell more obliquely across the white hills and was more quickly spent.

★   ★   ★

One night, returning from a movie, he slipped on the iced cobbles just outside the door of his building, tearing both knees of his trousers beyond any possibility of repair. It was the only winter suit he had brought. Altin gave him the name of a tailor who could make another suit quickly and for less money than he would have had to pay for a ready-made. Altin did all the bargaining with the tailor and even selected the fabric, a heavy wool-rayon blend of a sickly and slightly iridescent blue, the muted, imprecise color of the more unhappy breeds of pigeons. He understood nothing of the fine points of tailoring, and so he could not decide what it was about this suit—whether the shape of the lapels, the length of the back vent, the width of the pant legs—that made it seem so different from other suits he had worn, so much . . . smaller. And yet it fitted his figure with the exactness one expects of a tailored suit. If he looked smaller now, and thicker, perhaps that was how he *ought* to look and his previous suits had been telling lies about him all these years. The color too performed some nuance of metamorphosis: his skin, balanced against this blue-gray sheen, seemed less "tan" than sallow. When he wore it he became, to all appearances, a Turk.

Not that he wanted to look like a Turk. Turks were, by and large, a homely lot. He only wished to avoid the other Americans who abounded here even at this nadir of the off-season. As their numbers decreased, their gregariousness grew more implacable. The smallest sign—a copy of *Newsweek* or the *Herald-Tribune*, a word of English, an airmail letter with its telltale canceled stamp— could bring them down at once in the full fury of their good-fellowship. It was convenient to have some kind of camouflage, just as it was necessary to learn their haunts in order to avoid them: Divan Yolu and Cumhuriyet Cadessi, the American Library and the consulate, as well as some eight or ten of the principal well-touristed restaurants.

Once the winter had firmly established itself he also put a stop to his sightseeing. Two months of Ottoman mosques and Byzantine rubble had brought his sense of the arbitrary to so fine a pitch that he no longer required the stimulus of the monumental. His own rooms—a rickety table, the flowered drapes, the blurry lurid pinups, the intersecting planes of walls and ceilings—could present as great a plenitude of "problems" as the grand mosques of Suleiman or Sultan Ahmet with all their mihrabs and minbars, their stalactite niches and faienced walls.

Too great a plenitude actually. Day and night the rooms nagged at him. They diverted his attention from anything else he might try to do. He knew them with the enforced intimacy with which a prisoner knows his cell—every defect of construction, every failed grace, the precise incidence of the light at each hour of the day. Had he taken the trouble to rearrange the furniture, to put up his own prints and maps, to clean the windows and scrub the floors, to fashion some kind of bookcase (all his books remained in their two shipping cases), he might have been able to blot these alien presences by the sheer strength of self-assertion, as one can mask bad odors with incense or the smell of flowers. But this would have been admitting defeat. It would have shown how unequal he was to his own thesis.

As a compromise he began to spend his afternoons in a café a short distance down the street on which he lived. There he would sit, at the table nearest the front window, contemplating the spirals of steam that rose from the small corolla of his tea glass. At the back of the long room, beneath the tarnished brass tea urn, there were always two old men playing backgammon. The other patrons sat by themselves and gave no indication that their thoughts were in any way different from his. Even when no one was smoking, the air was pungent with the charcoal fires of nargilehs. Conversation of any kind was rare. The nargilehs bubbled, the tiny die rattled in its leather cup, a newspaper rustled, a glass chinked against its saucer.

His red notebook always lay ready at hand on the table, and on the notebook his ballpoint pen. Once he had placed them there, he never touched them again till it was time to leave.

Though less and less in the habit of analyzing sensation and motive, he was aware that the special virtue of this café was as a bastion, the securest he possessed, against the now omnipresent influence of the arbitrary. If he sat here peacefully, observing the requirements of the ritual, a decorum as simple as the rules of backgammon, gradually the elements in the space about him would cohere. Things settled, unproblematically, into their own contours. Taking the flower-shaped glass as its center, this glass that was now only and exactly a glass of tea, his perceptions slowly spread out through the room, like the concentric ripples passing across the surface of an ornamental pond, embracing all its objects at last in a firm, noumenal grasp. Just so. The room was just what a room should be. It contained him.

He did not take notice of the first rapping on the café window, though he was aware, by some small cold contraction of his thoughts, of an infringement of the rules. The second time he looked up.

They were together. The woman and the child.

He had seen them each on several occasions since his trip to Usküdar three weeks before. The boy once on the torn-up sidewalk outside the consulate, and another time sitting on the railing of the Karaköy bridge. Once, riding in a *dolmus* to Taksim, he had passed within a scant few feet of the woman and they had exchanged a glance of unambiguous recognition. But he had never seen them together before.

But could he be certain, now, that it *was* those two? He saw a woman and a child, and the woman was rapping with one bony knuckle on the window for someone's attention. For his? If he could have seen her face . . .

He looked at the other occupants of the café. The backgammon players. A fat unshaven man reading a newspaper. A dark-skinned man with spectacles and a flaring mustache. The two old men, on opposite sides of the room, puffing on nargilehs. None of them paid any attention to the woman's rapping.

He stared resolutely at his glass of tea, no longer a paradigm of its own necessity. It had become a foreign object, an artifact picked up out of the rubble of a buried city, a shard.

The woman continued to rap at the window. At last the owner of the café went outside and spoke a few sharp words to her. She left without making a reply.

He sat with his cold tea another fifteen minutes. Then he went out into the street. There was no sign of them. He returned the hundred yards to his apartment as calmly as he could. Once inside he fastened the chain lock. He never went back to the café.

When the woman came that night, knocking at his door, it was not a surprise.

And every night at nine or, at the very latest, ten o'clock.

Yavuz! Yavuz! Calling to him.

He stared at the black water, the lights of the other shore. He wondered, often, when he would give in, when he would open the door.

But it was surely a mistake. Some accidental *resemblance*. He was not Yavuz.

John Benedict Harris. An American.

If there had ever been one, if there had ever been a Yavuz.

The man who had tacked the pinups on the walls?

Two women, they might have been twins, in heavy eye make-up, garter belts, mounted on the same white horse. Lewdly smiling.

A bouffant hairdo, puffy lips. Drooping breasts with large brown nipples. A couch.

A beachball. Her skin dark. Bikini. Laughing. Sand. The water unnaturally blue.

Snapshots.

Had these ever been *his* fantasies? If not, why could he not bring himself to take them off the walls? He had prints by Piranesi. A blowup of Sagrada Familia in Barcelona. The Tchernikov sketch. He could have covered the walls.

He found himself trying to imagine this Yavuz . . . what he must be like.

III

Three days after Christmas he received a card from his wife, postmarked Nevada. Janice, he knew, did not believe in Christmas cards. It showed an immense stretch of white desert—a salt-flat, he supposed—with purple mountains in the distance, and above the purple mountains, a heavily retouched sunset. Pink. There were no figures in this landscape, or any sign of vegetation. Inside she had written:

"Merry Christmas! Janice."

The same day he received a manila envelope with a copy of *ARTnews*. A noncommittal note from his friend Raymond was paper-clipped to the cover: "Thought you might like to see this. R."

In the back pages of the magazine there was a long and unsympathetic review of his book by F. R. Robertson. Robertson was known as an authority on Hegel's esthetics. He maintained that *Homo Arbitrans* was nothing but a compendium of truisms and—without seeming to recognize any contradiction in this—a hopelessly muddled reworking of Hegel.

Years ago he had dropped out of a course taught by Robertson after attending the first two lectures. He wondered if Robertson could have remembered this.

The review contained several errors of fact, one misquotation, and failed to mention his central argument, which was not, admittedly, dialectical. He decided he should write a reply and laid the magazine beside his typewriter to remind himself. The same evening he spilled the better part of a bottle of wine on it, so he tore out the review and threw the magazine into the garbage with his wife's card.

The necessity for a movie had compelled him into the streets and kept him in the streets, wandering from marquee to marquee, long after the drizzle of the afternoon had thickened to rain. In New York when this mood came over him he would take in a double bill of science-fiction films or Westerns on Forty-second Street, but here, though cinemas abounded in the absence of television, only the glossiest Hollywood kitsch was presented with the original soundtrack. B-movies were invariably dubbed in Turkish.

So obsessive was this need that he almost passed the man in the skeleton suit without noticing him. He trudged back and forth on the sidewalk, a sodden refugee from Halloween, followed by a small Hamelin of excited children. The rain had curled the corners of his poster (it served him now as an umbrella) and caused the inks to run. He could make out:

After Atatürk, the skeleton-suited Kiling was the principal figure of the new Turkish folklore. Every newsstand was heaped with magazines and comics celebrating his adventures, and here he was himself, or his avatar at least, advertising his latest movie. Yes, and there, down the side street, was the theater where it was playing: *Kiling Istanbulda*. Or: *Kiling in Istanbul*. Beneath the colossal letters a skull-masked Kiling threatened to kiss a lovely and obviously reluctant blonde, while on the larger poster across the street he gunned down two well-dressed men. One could not decide, on the evidence of such tableaus as these, whether Kiling was fundamentally good, like Batman, or bad, like Fantomas. So . . .

He bought a ticket. He would find out. It was the name that intrigued him. It was, distinctly, an English name.

He took a seat four rows from the front just as the feature began, immersing himself gratefully in the familiar urban imagery. Reduced to black and white and framed by darkness, the customary vistas of Istanbul possessed a heightened reality. New American cars drove through the narrow streets at perilous speeds. An old doctor was strangled by an unseen assailant. Then for a long while nothing of interest happened. A tepid romance developed between the blond singer and the young architect, while a number of gangsters, or diplomats, tried to obtain possession of the doctor's black valise. After a confusing sequence in which four of these men were killed in an explosion, the valise fell into the hands of Kiling. But it proved to be empty.

The police chased Kiling over tiled rooftops. But this was a proof only of his agility, not of his guilt: the police can often make mistakes in these matters. Kiling entered, through a window, the bedroom of the blond singer, waking her. Contrary to the advertising posters outside, he made no attempt to kiss her. He addressed her in a hollow bass voice. The editing seemed to suggest that Kiling was actually the young architect whom the singer loved, but as his mask was never removed this too remained in doubt.

He felt a hand on his shoulder.

He was certain it was she and he would not turn around. Had she followed him to the theater? If he rose to leave, would she make a scene? He tried to ignore the pressure of the hand, staring at the screen where the young architect had just received a mysterious telegram. His hands gripped tightly into his thighs. His hands: the hands of John Benedict Harris.

"Mr. Harris, hello!"

A man's voice. He turned around. It was Altin.

"Altin."

Altin smiled. His face flickered. "Yes. Do you think it is anyone?"

"Anyone else?"

"Yes."

"No."

"You are seeing this movie?"

"Yes."

"It is not in English. It is in Turkish."

"I know."

Several people in nearby rows were hissing for them to be quiet. The blond singer had gone down into one of the city's large cisterns. Binbirdirek. He himself had been there. The editing created an illusion that it was larger than it actually was.

"We will come up there," Altin whispered.

He nodded.

Altin sat on his right, and Altin's friend took the seat remaining empty on his left. Altin introduced his friend in a whisper. His name was Yavuz. He did not speak English.

Reluctantly he shook hands with Yavuz.

It was difficult, thereafter, to give his full attention to the film. He kept glancing sideways at Yavuz. He was about his own height and age, but then this seemed to be true of half the men in Istanbul. An unexceptional face, eyes that glistened moistly in the half-light reflected from the screen.

Kiling was climbing up the girders of the building being constructed on a high hillside. In the distance the Bosphorous snaked past misted hills.

There was something so unappealing in almost every Turkish face. He had never been able to pin it down: some weakness of bone structure, the narrow cheekbones; the strong vertical lines that ran down from the hollows of the eyes to the corner of the mouth; the mouth itself, narrow, flat, inflexible. Or some subtler disharmony among all these elements.

Yavuz. A common name, the mail clerk had said.

In the last minutes of the movie there was a fight between two figures dressed in skeleton suits, a true and a false Kiling. One of them was thrown to his death from the steel beams of the unfinished building. The villain, surely—but had it been the true or the false Kiling who died? And come to think of it, which of them had frightened the singer in her bedroom, strangled the old doctor, stolen the valise?

"Did you like it?" Altin asked as they crowded toward the exit.

"Yes, I did."

"And did you understand what the people said?"

"Some of it. Enough."

Altin spoke for a while to Yavuz, who then turned to address his new friend from America in rapid Turkish.

He shook his head apologetically. Altin and Yavuz laughed.

"He says to you that you have the same suit."

"Yes, I noticed that as soon as the lights came on."

"Where do you go now, Mr. Harris?"

"What time is it?"

They were outside the theater. The rain had moderated to a drizzle. Altin looked at his watch. "Seven o'clock. And a half."

"I must go home now."

"We will come with you and buy a bottle of wine. Yes?"

He looked uncertainly at Yavuz. Yavuz smiled.

And when she came tonight, knocking at his door and calling for Yavuz?

"Not tonight, Altin."

"No?"

"I am a little sick."

"Yes?"

"Sick. I have a fever. My head aches." He put his hand, mimetically, to his forehead, and as he did he *could* feel both the fever and the headache. "Some other time perhaps. I'm sorry."

Altin shrugged skeptically.

He shook hands with Altin and then with Yavuz. Clearly, they both felt they had been snubbed.

Returning to his apartment, he took an indirect route that avoided the dark side streets. The tone of the movie lingered, like the taste of a liqueur, to enliven the rhythm of cars and crowds, deepen the chiaroscuro of headlights and shop windows. Once, leaving the Eighth Street Cinema, after *Jules et Jim*, he had discovered all the street signs of the Village translated into French; now the same law of magic allowed him to think that he could understand the fragmented conversation of passers-by. The meaning of an isolated phrase registered with the self-evident uninterpreted immediacy of "fact," the nature of the words mingling with the nature of things. Just so. Each knot in the net of language slipped, without any need of explication, into place. Every nuance of glance and inflection fitted, like a tailored suit, the contours of that moment, this street, the light, his conscious mind.

Inebriated by this fictive empathy, he turned into his own darker street at last and almost walked past the woman—who fitted, like every other element of the scene, so well the corner where she'd taken up her watch—without noticing her.

"You!" he said and stopped.

They stood four feet apart, regarding each other carefully. Perhaps she had been as little prepared for this confrontation as he.

Her thick hair was combed back in stiff waves from a low forehead, falling in massive parentheses to either side of her thin face. Pitted skin, flesh wrinkled in concentration around small pale lips. And tears—yes, tears—just forming in the corners of her staring eyes. With one hand she held a small parcel wrapped in newspaper and string, with the other she clutched the bulky confusion of her skirts. She wore several layers of clothing, rather than a coat, against the cold.

A slight erection stirred and tangled in the flap of his cotton underpants. He blushed. Once, reading a paperback edition of *Krafft-Ebing*, the same embarrassing thing had happened. That time it had been a description of necrophilia.

God, he thought, *if she notices!*

She whispered to him, lowering her gaze. To him, to Yavuz.

To come home with her. Why did he? . . . Yavuz, Yavuz, Yavuz . . . she needed . . . and his son . . .

"I don't *understand* you," he insisted. "Your words make no sense to me. I am an American. My name is John Benedict Harris, not Yavuz. You're making a mistake—can't you see that?"

She nodded her head. "Yavuz."

"*Not* Yavuz! *Yok! Yok, yok!*"

And a word that meant "love" but not exactly that. Her hand tightened in the folds of her several skirts, raising them to show the thin, black-stockinged ankles.

"No!"

She moaned.

. . . wife . . . his home . . . Yalova . . . his life.

"Damn you, go away!"

Her hand let go her skirts and darted quickly to his shoulder, digging into the cheap cloth. Her other hand shoved the wrapped parcel at him. He pushed her back but she clung fiercely, shrieking his name: *Yavuz!* He struck her face.

She fell on the wet cobble. He backed away. The greasy parcel was in his left hand. She pushed herself up to her feet. Tears flowed along the vertical channels from eyes to mouth. A Turkish face. Blood dripped slowly out of one nostril. She began to walk away in the direction of Taksim.

"And don't return, do you understand? Stay away from me!" His voice cracked.

When she was out of sight he looked at the parcel in his hands. He knew he ought not to open it, that the wisest course was to throw it into the nearest garbage can. But even as he warned himself, his fingers had snapped the string.

A large lukewarm doughy mass of *borek*. And an orange. The saliva sprouted in his mouth at the acrid smell of the cheese.

No!

He had not had dinner that night. He was hungry. He ate it. Even the orange.

During the month of January he made only two entries in his notebook. The first, undated, was a long extract copied from A. H. Lybyer's book on the Janissaries, the great slave-corps of the sultans, *The Government of the Ottoman Empire in the Time of Suleiman the Magnificent*. The passage read:

> *Perhaps no more daring experiment has been tried on a large scale upon the face of the earth than that embodied in the Ottoman Ruling Institution. Its nearest ideal analogue is found in the Republic of Plato, its nearest actual parallel in the Mamluk system of Egypt, but it was not restrained within the aristocratic Hellenic limitations of the first, and it subdued and outlived the second. In the United States of America men have risen from the rude work of the backwoods to the presidential chair, but they have done so by their own effort and not through the gradations of a system carefully organized to push them forward. The Roman Catholic Church can still train a peasant to become a pope, but it has never begun by choosing its candidates almost exclusively from families which profess a hostile religion. The Ottoman system deliber-*

ately took slaves and made them ministers of state. It took boys from the sheep-run and the plough-tail and made them courtiers and the husbands of princesses, it took young men whose ancestors had borne the Christian name for centuries and made them rulers in the greatest of Muhammadan states, and soldiers and generals in invincible armies whose chief joy it was to beat down the Cross and elevate the Crescent. It never asked its novices "Who was your father?" or "What do you know?" or even "Can you speak our tongue?" but it studied their faces and their frames and said: "You shall be a soldier and, if you show yourself worthy, a general," or "You shall be a scholar and a gentleman and, if the ability lies in you, a governor and a prime minister." Grandly disregarding the fabric of fundamental customs which is called "human nature," and those religious and social prejudices which are thought to be almost as deep as life itself, the Ottoman system took children forever from parents, discouraged family cares among its members through their most active years, allowed them no certain hold on property, gave them no definite promise that their sons and daughters would profit by their success and sacrifice, raised and lowered them with no regard for ancestry or previous distinction, taught them a strange law, ethics, and religion, and ever kept them conscious of a sword raised above their heads which might put an end at any moment to a brilliant career along a matchless path of human glory.

The second and briefer entry was dated the twenty-third of January and read as follows:

*Heavy rains yesterday. I stayed in drinking. She came around at her usual hour. This morning when I put on my brown shoes to go out shopping they were wet through. Two hours to dry them out over the heater. Yesterday I wore only my sheepskin slippers—*I did not leave the building once.

IV

A human face is a construction, an artifact. The mouth is a little door, and the eyes are windows that look at the street, and all the rest of it, the flesh, the bone beneath, is a wall to which any manner of ornament may be affixed, gewgaws of whatever style or period one takes a fancy to—swags hung below the cheeks and chin, lines chiseled or smoothed away, a recession emphasized, a bit of vegetation here and there. Each addition or subtraction, however minor in itself, will affect the entire composition. Thus, the hair that he had trimmed a bit closer to the temples restores hegemony to the vertical elements of a face that is now noticeably *narrower*. Or is this exclusively a matter of proportion and emphasis? For he has lost weight too (one cannot stop eating regularly without some shrinkage), and the loss has been appreciable. A new darkness has given definition to the always incipient pouches below his eyes, a darkness echoed by the new hollowness of his cheeks.

But the chief agent of metamorphosis is the mustache, which has grown full enough now to obscure the modeling of his upper lip. The ends, which had first shown a tendency to droop, have developed, by his nervous habit of twisting them about his fingers, the flaring upward curve of a scimitar (or *pala*, after which in Turkey this style of mustache is named: *pala biyik*). It is this, the baroque mustache, not a face, that he sees when he looks in a mirror.

Then there is the whole question of "expression," its quickness, constancy, the play of intelligence, the characteristic "tone" and the hundreds upon hundreds of possible gradations within the range of that tone, the eyes' habits of irony and candor, the betraying tension or slackness of a lip. Yet it is scarcely necessary to go into this at all, for his face, when he sees it, or when anyone sees it, could not be said to *have* an expression. What was there, after all, for him to express?

The blurring of edges, whole days lost, long hours awake in bed, books scattered about the room like little animal corpses to be nibbled at when he grew hungry, the endless cups of tea, the tasteless cigarettes. Wine, at least, did what it was supposed to do—it took away the sting. Not that he felt the sting these days with any poignance. But perhaps without the wine he would have.

He piled the nonreturnable bottles in the bathtub, exercising in this act (if in no other) the old discrimination, the "compulsive tact" he had made so much of in his book. The drapes were always drawn. The lights were left burning at all hours, even when he slept, even when he was out, three sixty-watt bulbs in a metal chandelier hanging just out of plumb.

Voices from the street impinged. Vendors in the morning, and the metallic screak of children. At night the radio in the apartment below, drunken arguments. Scatterings of words, like illuminated signs glimpsed driving on a thruway, at high speeds, at night.

Two bottles of wine were not enough if he started early in the afternoon, but three could make him sick.

And though the hours crawled, like wounded insects, so slowly across the floor, the days rushed by in a torrent. The sunlight slipped across the Bosphorus so quickly that there was scarcely time to rise and see it.

One morning when he woke there was a balloon on a stick propped in the dusty flower vase atop his dresser. A crude Mickey Mouse was stenciled on the bright red rubber. He left it there, bobbing in the vase, and watched it shrivel day by day, the face turning small and black and wrinkled.

The next time it was ticket stubs, two of them, from the Kabatas–Uskïdar ferry.

Till that moment he had told himself it was a matter only of holding out until the spring. He had prepared himself for a siege, believing that an assault was not possible. Now he realized that he would actually have to go out there and fight.

Though it was mid-February the weather accommodated his belated resolution with a series of bright blue days, a wholly unseasonable warmth that even tricked early blossoms from a few unsuspecting trees. He went through Topkapi once again, giving a respectful, indiscriminate and puzzled attention to the celadon ware, to golden snuffboxes, to pearly-embroidered pillows, to the portrait miniatures of the sultans, to the fossil footprint of the Prophet, to Iznik tiles, to the lot. There it was, all spread out before him, heaps and masses of it: beauty. Like a salesclerk tying price tags to items of merchandise, he would attach this favorite word of his, provisionally, to these sundry bibelots, then step back a pace or two to see how well or poorly it "matched." Was *this* beautiful? Was *that*?

Amazingly, none of it was beautiful. The priceless baubles all just sat there on their shelves, behind the thick glass, as unresplendent as the drab furniture back in his own room.

He tried the mosques: Sultan Ahmet, Beyazit, Sehazade, Yeni Camii, Laleli Camii. The old magic, the Vitruvian trinity of "commodity, firmness, and delight," had never failed him so enormously before. Even the shock of scale, the gape-mouthed peasant reverence before thick pillars and high domes, even this deserted him. Go where he would through the city, he could not get out of his room.

Then the land walls, where months before he had felt himself rubbing up against the very garment of the past. He stood at the same spot where he had stood then, at the point where Mehmet the Conqueror had breached the walls. Quincunxes of granite cannonballs decorated the grass; they reminded him of the red balloon.

As a last resort he returned to Eyüp. The false spring had reached a tenuous apogee, and the February light flared with deceiving brilliance from the thousand facets of white stone blanketing the steep hillside. Small flocks of three or four sheep browsed between the graves. The turbaned shafts of marble jutted in every direction but the vertical (which it was given to the cypresses to define) or lay, higgledy-piggledy, one atop another. No walls, no ceilings, scarcely a path through the litter: this was an architecture supremely abstract. It seemed to him to have been piled up here, over the centuries, just to vindicate the thesis of his book.

And it worked. It worked splendidly. His mind and his eye came alive. Ideas and images coalesced. The sharp slanting light of the late afternoon caressed the jumbled marble with a cold careful hand, like a beautician adding the last touches to an elaborate coiffure. Beauty? Here it was. Here it was abundantly!

He returned the next day with his camera, redeemed from the repair shop where it had languished for two months. To be on the safe side he had asked the repairman to load it for him. He composed each picture with mathematical punctilio, fussing over the depth of field, crouching or climbing atop sepulchers for a better angle, checking each shot against the reading on the light meter, deliberately avoiding picturesque solutions and easy effects. Even taking these pains, he found that he'd gone through the twenty exposures in under two hours.

He went up to the small café on the top of the hill. Here, his Hachette had noted respectfully, the great Pierre Loti had been wont to come of a summer evening, to drink a glass of tea and look down the sculptured hills and through the pillars of cypress at the Fresh Waters of Europe and the Golden Horn. The café perpetuated the memory of this vanished glory with pictures and mementos. Loti, in a red fez and savage mustachios, glowered at the contemporary patrons from every wall. During the First World War, Loti had remained in Istanbul, taking the part of his friend, the Turkish sultan, against his native France.

He ordered a glass of tea from a waitress who had been got up as a harem girl. Apart from the waitress he had the café to himself. He sat on Pierre Loti's favorite stool. It was delicious. He felt right at home.

He opened his notebook and began to write.

Like an invalid taking his first walk out of doors after a long convalescence, his renascent energies caused him not only the predictable and welcome euphoria of resurrection but also a pronounced intellectual giddiness, as though by the simple act of rising to his feet he had thrust himself up to some really dangerous height. This dizziness became most acute when, in trying to draft a reply to Robertson's review, he was obliged to return to passages in his own book.

Often as not what he found there struck him as incomprehensible. There were entire chapters that might as well have been written in ideograms or futhorc, for all the sense they made to him now. But occasionally, cued by some remark so irrelevant to any issue at hand as to be squeezed into an embarrassed parenthesis, he would sprint off toward the most unforeseen—and undesirable—conclusions. Or rather, each of these tangents led, asymptotically, to a single conclusion: to wit, that his book, or any book he might conceive, was worthless, and worthless not because his thesis was wrong but precisely because it might be right.

There was a realm of judgment and a realm of fact. His book, if only because it was a book, existed within the bounds of the first. There was the trivial fact of its corporeality, but, in this case as in most others, he discounted that. It was a work of criticism, a systematization of judgment, and to the extent that his system was complete, its critical apparatus must be able to measure its own scales of mensuration and judge the justice of its own decrees. But could it? Was not his "system" as arbitrary a construction as any silly pyramid? What was it, after all? A string of words, of more or less agreeable noises, politely assumed to correspond to certain objects and classes of objects, actions and groups of actions, in the realm of fact. And by what subtle magic was this correspondence to be verified? Why, by just the assertion that it was so!

This, admittedly, lacked clarity. It had come to him thick and fast, and it was colored not a little by cheap red wine. To fix its outlines a bit more firmly in his own mind he tried to "get it down" in his letter to *ARTnews*:

> Sirs:
>
> *I write to you concerning F. R. Robertson's review of my book, though the few words I have to say bear but slightly upon Mr. Robertson's oracles, as slightly perhaps as these bore upon* Homo Arbitrans.
>
> *Only this—that, as Gödel has demonstrated in mathematics, Wittgenstein in philosophy, and Duchamp, Cage, and Ashbery in*

their respective fields, the final statement of any system is a self-denunciation, a demonstration of how its particular little tricks are done—not by magic (as magicians have always known) but by the readiness of the magician's audience to be deceived, which readiness is the very glue of the social contract.

Every system, including my own and Mr. Robertson's, is a system of more or less interesting lies, and if one begins to call these lies into question, then one ought really to begin with the first. That is to say, with the very questionable proposition on the title page: Homo Arbitrans by John Benedict Harris.

Now I ask you, Mr. Robertson, what could be more improbable than that? More tentative? More arbitrary?

He sent the letter off, unsigned.

V

He had been promised his photos by Monday, so Monday morning, before the frost had thawed on the plate glass window, he was at the shop. The same immodest anxious interest to see his pictures of Eyüp possessed him as once he had felt to see an essay or a review in print. It was as though these items, the pictures, the printed words, had the power to rescind, for a little while, his banishment to the realm of judgment, as though they said to him: "Yes, look, here we are, right in your hand. We're real, and so you must be too."

The old man behind the counter, a German, looked up mournfully to gargle a mournful *ach*. "Ach, Mr. Harris! Your pictures are not ready yet. Come back soon at twelve o'clock."

He walked through the melting streets that were, this side of the Golden Horn, jokebooks of eclecticism. No mail at the consulate, which was only to be expected. Half past ten.

A pudding at a pudding shop. Two liras. A cigarette. A few more jokes: a bedraggled caryatid, an Egyptian tomb, a Greek temple that had been changed by some Circean wand into a butcher shop. Eleven.

He looked, in the bookshop, at the same shopworn selection of books that he had looked at so often before. Eleven-thirty. Surely, they would be ready by now.

"You are here, Mr. Harris. Very good."

Smiling in anticipation, he opened the envelope, removed the slim warped stack of prints.

No.

"I'm afraid these aren't mine." He handed them back. He didn't want to feel them in his hand.

"What?"

"Those are the wrong pictures. You've made a mistake."

The old man put on a pair of dirty spectacles and shuffled through the prints. He squinted at the name on the envelope. "You are Mr. Harris."

"Yes, that is the name on the envelope. The envelope's all right, the pictures aren't."

"It is not a mistake."

"These are *somebody else's* snapshots. Some family picnic. You can see that."

"I myself took out the roll of film from your camera. Do you remember, Mr. Harris?"

He laughed uneasily. He hated scenes. He considered just walking out of the shop, forgetting all about the pictures. "Yes, I do remember. But I'm afraid you must have gotten that roll of film confused with another. I *didn't* take these pictures. I took pictures at the cemetery in Eyüp. Does that ring a bell?"

Perhaps, he thought, "ring a bell" was not an expression a German would understand.

As a waiter whose honesty has been called into question will go over the bill again with exaggerated attention, the old man frowned and examined each of the pictures in turn. With a triumphant clearing of his throat he laid one of the snapshots face up on the counter. "Who is that, Mr. Harris?"

It was the boy.

"Who! I . . . I don't know his name."

The old German laughed theatrically, lifting his eyes to a witnessing heaven. "It is you, Mr. Harris! It is you!"

He bent over the counter. His fingers still refused to touch the print. The boy was held up in the arms of a man whose head was bent forward as though he were examining the close-cropped scalp for lice. Details were fuzzy, the lens having been mistakenly set at infinity.

Was it his face? The mustache resembled his mustache, the crescents under the eyes, the hair falling forward . . .

But the angle of the head, the lack of focus—there was room for doubt.

"Twenty-four liras please, Mr. Harris."

"Yes. Of course." He took a fifty-lira note from his billfold. The old man dug into a lady's plastic coin purse for change.

"Thank you, Mr. Harris."

"Yes. I'm . . . sorry."

The old man replaced the prints in the envelope, handed them across the counter.

He put the envelope in the pocket of his suit. "It was my mistake."

"Good-bye."

"Yes, good-bye."

He stood on the street, in the sunlight, exposed. Any moment either of them might come up to him, lay a hand on his shoulder, tug at his pant leg. He could not examine the prints here. He returned to the sweetshop and spread them out in four rows on a marble-topped table.

Twenty photographs. A day's outing, as commonplace as it had been impossible.

Of these twenty, three were so overexposed as to be meaningless and should not have been printed at all. Three others showed what appeared to be islands or different sections of a very irregular coastline. They were unimaginatively composed, with great expanses of bleached-out sky and glaring water. Squeezed between these, the land registered merely as long dark blotches flecked with tiny gray rectangles of buildings. There was also a view up a steep street of wooden houses and naked wintry gardens.

The remaining thirteen pictures showed various people, and groups of people, looking at the camera. A heavyset woman in black, with black teeth, squinting into the sun—standing next to a pine tree in one picture, sitting uncomfortably on a natural stone formation in the second. An old man, dark-skinned, bald, with a flaring mustache and several days' stubble of beard. Then these two together—a very blurred print. Three little girls standing in front of a middle-aged woman, who regarded them with a pleased, proprietorial air. The same three girls grouped around the old man, who seemed to take no notice of them whatever. And a group of five men: the spread-legged shadow of the man taking this picture was roughly stenciled across the pebbled foreground.

And the woman. Alone. The wrinkled sallow flesh abraded to a smooth white mask by the harsh midday light.

Then the boy snuggling beside her on a blanket. Nearby small waves lapped at a narrow shingle.

Then these two still together with the old woman and the three little girls. The contiguity of the two women's faces suggested a family resemblance.

The figure that could be identified as himself appeared in only three of the pictures: once holding the boy in his arms; once with his arm around the woman's shoulders, while the boy stood before them scowling; once in a group of thirteen people, all of whom had appeared in one or another of the previous shots. Only the last of these three was in focus. He was one of the least noticeable figures in this group, but the mustached face smiling so rigidly into the camera was undeniably his own.

He had never seen these people, except, of course, for the woman and the boy. Though he had, hundreds of times, seen people just like them in the streets of Istanbul. Nor did he recognize the plots of grass, the stands of pine, the boulders, the shingle beach, though once again they were of such a generic type that he might well have passed such places a dozen times without taking any notice of them. Was the world of fact really as characterless as *this*? That it *was* the world of fact he never for a moment doubted.

And what had *he* to place in the balance against these evidences? A name? A face?

He scanned the walls of the sweetshop for a mirror. There was none. He lifted the spoon, dripping, from his glass of tea to regard the reflection of his face, blurred and inverted, in the concave surface. As he brought the spoon closer, the image grew less distinct, then rotated through one hundred eighty degrees to present, upright, the mirror image of his staring, dilated eye.

He stood on the open upper deck as the ferry churned, hooting, from the deck. Like a man stepping out of doors on a blustery day, the ferry rounded the peninsular tip of the old city, leaving the quiet of the Horn for the rough wind-whitened waters of the Sea of Marmara. A cold south wind stiffened the scarlet star and cresent on the stern mast.

From this vantage the city showed its noblest silhouette: first the great gray horizontal mass of the Topkapi walls, then the delicate swell of the dome of St. Irena, which had been built (like a friend carefully chosen to demonstrate, by contrast, one's own virtues) just to point up the swaggering impossibility of the neighboring Holy Wisdom, that graceless and abstract issue of the union commemorated on every capital within by the twined monograms of the demon-emperor Justinian and his whore and consort Theodora; then, bringing both the topographic and historic sequence to an end, the proud finality of the Blue Mosque.

The ferry began to roll in the rougher water of the open sea. Clouds moved across the sun at quicker intervals to mass in the north above the dwindling city. It was four-thirty. By five o'clock he would reach Heybeli, the island identified by both Altin and the mail clerk at the consulate as the setting of the photographs.

The airline ticket to New York was in his pocket. His bags, all but the one he would take on the plane, had been packed and shipped off in a single afternoon and morning of headlong drunken fear. Now he was safe. The certain knowledge that tomorrow he would be thousands of miles away had shored up the crumbling walls of confidence like the promise of a prophet who cannot err, Tiresias in balmy weather. Admittedly this was the shameful safety of a rout so complete that the enemy had almost captured his baggage train—but it was safety for all that, as definite as tomorrow. Indeed, this "tomorrow" was more definite, more present to his mind and senses, than the actual limbo of its preparation, just as, when a boy, he had endured the dreadful tedium of Christmas Eve by projecting himself into the morning that would have to follow and which, when it did finally arrive, was never so real, by half, as his anticipations.

Because he was this safe, he dared today confront the enemy (if the enemy would confront *him*) head on. It risked nothing, and there was no telling what it might yield. Though if it were the *frisson* that he was after, then he should have stayed and seen the thing through to its end. No, this last excursion was more a gesture than an act, bravado rather than bravery. The very self-consciousness with which he had set out seemed to ensure that nothing really disastrous could happen. Had it not always been their strategy before to catch him unaware?

Finally, of course, he could not explain to himself why he had gone to the ferry, bought his ticket, embarked, except that each successive act seemed to heighten the delectable sense of his own inexorable advance, a sensation at once of almost insupportable tension and of dream-like lassitude. He could no more have turned back along this path once he had entered on it than at the coda of a symphony he could have refused to listen. Beauty? Oh yes, intolerably! He had *never* known anything so beautiful as this.

The ferry pulled into the quay of Kinali Ada, the first of the islands. People got on and off. Now the ferry turned directly into the wind, toward Burgaz. Behind them the European coast vanished into the haze.

The ferry had left the Burgaz dock and was rounding the tiny islet of Kasik. He watched with fascination as the dark hills of Kasik,

Burgaz, and Kinali slipped slowly into perfect alignment with their positions in the photograph. He could almost hear the click of the shutter.

And the other relationships between these simple sliding planes of sea and land—was there not something nearly as *familiar* in each infinitesimal shift of perspective? When he looked at these islands with his eyes, half closed, attention unfocused, he could almost . . .

But whenever he tried to take this up, however gently, between the needle-tipped compasses of analysis, it crumbled into dust.

It began to snow just as the ferry approached Heybeli. He stood at the end of the pier. The ferry was moving eastward, into the white air, toward BÜYÜK ADA.

He looked up a steep street of wooden houses and naked wintry gardens. Clusters of snowflakes fell on the wet cobbles and melted. At irregular intervals street lamps glowed yellow in the dusk, but the houses remained dark. Heybeli was a summer resort. Few people lived here in the winter months. He walked halfway up the hill, then turned to the right. Certain details of woodwork, the proportion of a window, a sagging roof caught his attention momentarily, like the flicker of wings in the foliage of a tree, twenty, fifty, a hundred yards ahead.

The houses were fewer, spaced farther apart. In the gardens snow covered the leaves of cabbages. The road wound up the hill toward a stone building. It was just possible to make out the flag waving against the gray sky. He turned onto a footpath that skirted the base of the hill. It led into the pines. The thick carpet of fallen needles was more slippery than ice. He rested his cheek against the bark of a tree and heard, again, the camera's click, systole and diastole of his heart.

He heard the water, before he saw it, lapping on the beach. He stopped. He focused. He recognized the rock. He walked toward it. So encompassing was his sense of this scene, so inclusive, that he could feel the footsteps he left behind in the snow, feel the snow slowly covering them again. He stopped.

It was here he had stood with the boy in his arms. The woman had held the camera to her eye with reverent awkwardness. He had bent his head forward to avoid looking directly into the glare of the setting sun. The boy's scalp was covered with the scabs of insect bites.

He was ready to admit that all this had happened, the whole impossible event. He did admit it. He lifted his head proudly and smiled, as though to say: *All right—and then? No matter what you do, I'm safe! Because, really, I'm not here at all. I'm already in New York.*

He laid his hands in a gesture of defiance on the outcropping of rock before him. His fingers brushed the resilient thong of the slipper. Covered with snow, the small oval of blue plastic had completely escaped his attention.

He spun around to face the forest, then round again to stare at the slipper lying there. He reached for it, thinking to throw it into the water, then drew his hand back.

He turned back to the forest. A man was standing just outside the line of the trees, on the path. It was too dark to discern any more of his features than that he had a mustache.

On his left the snowy beach ended in a wall of sandstone. To his right the path swung back into the forest, and behind him the sea dragged the shingle back and forth.

"Yes?"

The man bent his head attentively, but said nothing.

"Well, yes? Say it."

The man walked back into the forest.

The ferry was just pulling in as he stumbled up to the quay. He ran onto it without stopping at the booth to buy a ticket. Inside under the electric light he could see the tear in his trousers and a cut on the palm of his right hand. He had fallen many times, on the pine needles, over rocks in furrowed fields, on cobbles.

He took a seat by the coal stove. When his breath returned to him, he found that he was shivering violently. A boy came round with a tray of tea. He bought a glass for one lira. He asked the boy, in Turkish, what time it was. It was ten o'clock.

The ferry pulled up to the dock. The sign over the ticket booth said BÜYÜK ADA. The ferry pulled away from the dock.

The ticket taker came for his ticket. He held out a ten-lira note and said, "Istanbul."

The ticket taker nodded his head, which meant no.

"*Yok.*"

"No? How much then? *Kaç para?*"

"*Yok Istanbul—Yalova.*" He took the money offered him and gave him back in exchange eight liras and a ticket to Yalova on the Asian coast.

He had got onto a ferry going in the wrong direction. He was not returning to Istanbul, but to Yalova.

He explained, first in slow precise English, then in a desperate fragmentary Turkish, that he could not go to Yalova, that it was impossible. He produced his airline ticket, pointed at the eight o'clock departure time, but he could not remember the Turkish word for "tomorrow." Even in his desperation he could see the futility of all this: between Büyük Ada and Yalova there were no more stops, and there would be no ferries returning to Istanbul that night. When he got to Yalova he would have to get off the boat.

A woman and a boy stood at the end of the wooden dock, at the base of a cone of snowy light. The lights were turned off on the middle deck of the ferry. The man who had been standing so long at the railing stepped, stiffly, down to the dock. He walked directly toward the woman and the boy. Scraps of paper eddied about his feet then, caught up in a strong gust, sailed out at a great height over the dark water.

The man nodded sullenly at the woman, who mumbled a few rapid words of Turkish. Then they set off, as they had so many times before, toward their home, the man leading the way, his wife and son following a few paces behind, taking the road along the shore.

THE HOBBY

ERIC MCCORMACK

It's not that literature lacks for extraordinary stories, it's that Eric McCormack has created this tour de force—a world beyond a door beyond an obsession—so economically.

Each time I read it, I discover something new; always when I finish it, I gasp.

᪪

THE WRINKLES ON his face were as complex as a railroad junction, a chain of mandalas converging on his eyes and mouth. Somewhere within them lay a secret not disclosed by the facts: sixty years working for the LMS (London-Midland-Scottish), a terminal "thank-you-very-much," a silver pocket-watch in remembrance. Began his travels then, always by train, and came to be in southern Ontario for a time, took a room with a Kitchener man and his wife who'd only ever boarded a cat before, never had a human being winter over with them.

Like a cat, too, he nuzzled around their house on the first day, unselfconscious, sniffing into all the corners, a lithe old man looking for a particular place. And settled on the basement. The man and his wife agreed to install a bed there. The basement was his. He brought down his suitcase, later his wooden box of equipment. He told them that between journeys he liked to build his own railroad, an old man's hobby, an old man with railroads on the brain. Who hoarded words like nuts, occasionally squandering them in reminiscences. As on a morning of snow in January:

"There was a lot of snow that day. Still the plough should have been able to clear the lines. They nearly had to cancel the parade. That was a good fire in the waiting-room, but the station-master wouldn't let us enjoy it. 'Do this, do that.' Keeping the platforms clear for the spectators. We were just as glad when the trains arrived. They came right out of the snow. The Flying Scotsman, the Royal Scot, the Caerphilly Castle, the Lord Nelson, the Princess Elizabeth. You could see the names right on their sides. Those engineers ignored us as though we weren't even there waving and shouting at them. The noise made us forget the cold. The ground was trembling and people were laughing, even the station-master, and he never used to laugh. After they were all past he said, 'You'll not see anything like that again.' I said, 'Maybe not.'"

Always remembering the old days on the railroads. But talking was not his hobby, he had to get on with his work behind the locked basement door. Then he would emerge late in the day, grimy, nod over a snack, and off to bed. He always locked the basement door after him and made it plain they must on no account go down until he had finished his work, whenever that might be. For he had so much to do, laying the tracks, wiring the dynamos, installing complicated parallels, cycles, assembling the platforms, the station itself.

Yet by the end of January they suspected he was nearly finished, for one night as they sat in the living-room overhead, they heard what sounded like a train pecking its way along the tracks. They smiled and went to the basement door. But the noise stopped and he did not answer their knock.

Next day he told them they must be patient, he would not abide prying into his work. Right now he was organizing a full timetable and was too busy to amuse sightseers. He had crews to dispatch, mail-loading to supervise, tracks to inspect, all the burdens of assembling an intricate operation.

They co-operated. Instead of setting a place for him at table, they would leave his dinner on a tray at the door of the basement. Often when they went to pick up the tray they would find the meal untouched and so they worried about his health too. When he did consent to come to table, it was usually by way of celebration, some difficult piece of machinery successfully installed. He would wash the grease from his face and hands, and sit cheerfully, quietly, his mind elsewhere planning the next move. Only on Sundays would he luxuriate in bed late, storing up strength for the Monday morning onslaught. On one of those Sundays, he rose late and had lunch with them. Over coffee he looked at them directly and spoke:

"That boy wore me out. I tried to get him to help me build a railroad after I retired. I showed him how to put it together and how to fix it when it broke down. But the tunnel frightened him the way it gobbled things down like a snake. I told him you couldn't do without a tunnel. He said he was scared it would swallow him, and me too, if I didn't look out. He just wanted to sit upstairs in his room, all alone, like he always did. She was the one that found him in the bath, and she never recovered from that. I always feel bad when I think about it, for I loved them both, and I think they loved me."

They wondered what he meant by it all, but he looked desolated and they could think of nothing to say.

Mostly at table he listened absently to their small talk now, every so often checking his LMS silver pocket-watch with furrowed brow. They sensed that he grudged the time away from his hobby. When they would gently try to interest him in a stroll along the neat, tree-lined Kitchener streets, or coax him to come with them in the car to inspect the lush Mennonite farmlands of Waterloo County or see Niagara Falls, he would excuse himself, pointing out, as to irresponsible children, that there were schedules that had to be met. For their part, they accepted all his rebukes with remorse, perhaps pride. They were thankful for him, their lives were curiously purposeful as they had seldom been before.

And now a manic period began. He would start work in the basement at first light and they would hear him hammering urgently all day long and into the night. Whenever they saw him he was covered in grease, eyes red-rimmed, clothes dirty. His face had become so wrinkled it might have been a mask under which a stranger hid. They fretted over his neglect of himself, they did not want him to die on them from exhaustion. Yet their concern seemed to menace him, and he would mutter cagily that they should not worry, he was used to this, his railroad must be finished on time.

They did not have long to wait.

The next Sunday morning. Two A.M. They had gone to bed at midnight. He had stayed up late working in the basement. A tremendous howl awakened them abruptly, the whole house vibrated with it. Oh my God, they thought as they rushed downstairs into a cloud of foul smoke that made them wheeze and cough, he's set the place on fire.

The basement door was locked from the inside. A terrifying grinding and screaming came from behind it. They stood helpless, then put their bodies resolutely to the door and splintered it open. They stumbled inside onto the landing at the top of the little staircase, and through the smoke they saw his work.

Under the dim ceiling lights, the basement was transformed. It was now a grimy old British railway station bustling with activity. On the platform beneath them a swarm of people they had never seen before, one of them carrying a baby in her arms, jostled onto a single passenger carriage attached to a huge, old-fashioned glistening black locomotive, a monster of hissing steam. A golden LMS was emblazoned on its side. Paralyzed, they watched as officious-looking porters in dowdy uniforms with tin buttons began slamming the carriage doors behind the last passengers, and an amplified voice whined something about a departure. Other travellers on the congested platform seemed to have recently disembarked and uncertainly escorted trolley-loads of luggage pulled by brisk porters towards various murky apertures. A guard waved a red flag.

That was when they saw him. He was in the engineer's cabin, leaning his left elbow on the window ledge, peering ahead of the train up into a vast tunnel. The brakes exhaled numbingly. The wheels began slowly to lumber towards the tunnel. With his right arm they saw him reach expertly in front of him and pull back and forth, back and forth. A shattering double wail permeated the air. He glanced back in their direction for a moment. He was all concentration, he was all contentment.

They did not know what moved them. Hand in hand they rushed down the stairs in desperation, yanked open the last door of the moving carriage and scrambled aboard. One of the porters slammed the door shut behind them as the train entered the tunnel.

A sudden silence. The smell of stale cigarette smoke. Before them stretched an aisle giving access to half a dozen compartments. As they swayed along the aisle, the passengers behind the glass paid no attention to them: some were reading newspapers, some conversing with their neighbors, some staring idly out of the windows into the darkness, the train advancing further into the tunnel picking up speed. All the compartments were filled except for the very last, marked FIRST CLASS. The only occupant was a bushy-haired man who loured up at them as they gazed in. Distantly they heard the engine screech a muffled defiance of the darkness. They entered the compartment, slid the door shut and sat down opposite me. They told me how they came to be on that train. Then they asked me who I was, and we looked at each other with growing anxiety.

THE TWO-HEADED MAN

NANCY A. COLLINS

Out there, where the dark night road is its own world, the rules are as short as the miles are long. And Nancy Collins, never shy about twisting them, dares us to flinch at her audacity.

Though set in a truck stop, its air perfumed by diesel fumes and bacon grease, the story she offers is nonetheless a fairy tale. Cinderella may be a weary waitress, a bit shopworn, and her suitor as perverse a Prince Charming as ever was imagined—still, the dream is dreamed and the dance begun, and who's to say otherwise?

❧

IT WAS GOING on midnight when the two-headed man walked into Kelly's Stop.

The short-order cook glanced up when the burst of cold air rifled the newspaper spread across the Formica serving counter. The man stood in the diner's doorway, the fur-fringed hood of the parka casting his face in deep shadow. He tugged off his mittens and stuffed them into one pocket, flexing his fingers like a pianist before a recital.

"You're in luck, buddy," said the cook, refolding the newspaper. "We was just about ready to call it an early night."

The waitress stabbed out a cigarette and pivoted on her stool to get a better look at the stranger. She tugged at her blouse waist, causing her name, LOUISE, to twitch over her heart.

"Car had a flat . . . up the road . . ." came a voice from inside the shadow of the parka's hood. "We don't . . . have a spare . . ."

The cook shrugged, his back to the stranger. "Can't help you there, bub. Mike Keekhaver runs the Shell station down the road a piece, but he don't open up till tomorrow morning."

"Then we'll . . . have to wait."

"We?" Louise moved to the front window and peered out between the neon Miller High Life and Schlitz signs. The gravel parking lot fronting the diner was empty. "You got somebody with you, mister?"

"Yes . . . you could say that," answered the stranger as he unzipped the parka and tossed back the hood.

Louise gasped and clamped a hand over her mouth, smearing lipstick against her palm. The cook spun around to see what was going on, butcher knife in hand: late-night truck-stop robberies were not uncommon along Highway 65.

The stranger had two heads. One was where heads are supposed to be. And a damn fine one at that. It was the handsomest head Louise had seen this side of a TV screen. The stranger's hair was longish and curly and the color of winter wheat. It framed a face designed for a movie star: straight nose, strong and beardless chin, high cheekbones, and eyes bluer than Paul Newman's.

The second head looked over the stranger's left shoulder, perched on his collarbone like a parrot. It wasn't a deformed or even unsightly head—just average. But its extreme proximity to such masculine perfection made it seem . . . repulsive. The second head was dark where the other was fair, brown-eyed where the first was blue. It regarded Louise with a distant, oddly disturbing intelligence, then turned so its lips moved against its fellow's left ear. The stranger laughed without much humor.

"Yeah, guess I *did* scare 'em some . . ." The stranger shrugged off his coat. "Sorry, didn't mean to startle you like that."

Now that the parka was all the way off they could see that the stranger really didn't have two heads. A padded leather harness, like those worn by professional hitchhikers, was strapped to his shoulders and midsection. But instead of a bedroll and an army surplus duffel bag, he carried a little man on his back.

The stranger seated himself on one of the stools, leaning slightly forward under the weight of his burden.

"What is he? A dwarf or somethin'?" The cook ignored the look Louise shot him.

The man did not seem at all insulted. "Nope. Human Worm."

"Huh?"

"Carl's got no arms . . . or legs."

"That so? Was he in Viet Nam?"

"No. Just born that way."

"How about that. Don't see that every day."

"No, you don't, " he agreed amiably. The Human Worm leaned closer and whispered into his ear again. The stranger nodded. "Okay. Why not, long as we're here. We'll have two orders of bacon and eggs . . . one scrambled . . . one sunny-side up . . . two orders of toast . . . and two coffees. Got that?" The stranger pulled a cloth hankie out of his pants pocket and draped it over his left shoulder.

"Uh, yeah. Sure. Comin' right up."

"Name's Gary. This here's Carl." The stranger jerked a thumb to indicate his piggyback passenger.

"Pleased t'meetcha," the cook grunted.

Carl bobbed his head in silent acknowledgment.

Louise stood near the end of the serving counter, debating on whether she should try to talk to the handsome stranger with the freak tied to his back.

Talking to the various strangers that found their way into Kelly's Stop was one of the few perks the job had to offer. The trouble with the locals was that she knew what they were going to say before they even opened their mouths. She hated living in a pissant little town like Seven Devils.

She envied the strangers she met; travelers from somewhere on their way to someplace. She liked to pretend that maybe one of them would be her long-awaited Dream Prince and take her away from Kelly's Stop—just like Leslie Howard rescued Bette Davis in *The Petrified Forest*. But if her Prince was going to put in an appearance, it was going to have to be pretty damn soon. Her tits were starting to sag and the laugh-lines at the corners of her eyes were threatening to become crow's-feet.

She studied the two men as they waited to be served. It was sure as hell a *weird* setup. But that face . . . Gary's face . . . was the one she'd pictured in her fantasies. It was the face of the Prince who would deliver her from a lifetime of bunions, corn plasters, varicose veins and cheap beer.

The more she thought about it, he wasn't really *that* strange. It was kind of sweet, really, the way he carried the crippled guy on his back. It wasn't that much different than pushing a wheelchair.

The cook plopped the eggs and bacon onto the grill, slammed twin slices of bread into the toaster and returned his attention to the spitting bacon.

"Louise! Get th' man his coffee, willya?" The command made her jump and she scurried over to the Mr. Coffee machine.

"How you like it?" she asked, hoping she didn't sound shrill. Her hands were shaking. She took a deep breath before she poured.

"Black. Cream and sugar."

She slid the cups across the counter and located a sugar dispenser. She felt his gaze on her as she moved to get the cream from the cooler, but she wasn't sure which one was doing the looking.

Gary picked up the cup of black coffee with his left, blew on it a couple times, then lifted it over his shoulder. Carl lowered his head and noisily sipped from the lip of the cup while Gary stirred his coffee with his right hand.

"Wow. Neat trick." She kicked herself the minute she said it. What a *hick* thing to say.

Gary shrugged, causing Carl to bounce slightly. "Helps if you're ambidextrous."

"Ambiwhat?"

"Carl says that's being good with both hands," he explained, ges-

turing with a piece of bacon. Carl leaned forward, grasping the proffered strip with surprisingly white, even teeth before bolting it down
like a lizard.

Louise watched as Gary fed himself and his rider, both hands
moving with unthinking grace. He acted as if it was as natural for
him as breathing. Carl wiped his mouth and chin, shiny with grease
and butter, on the napkin draped over his companion's shoulder. His
eyes met Louise's and she hastily looked away.

There was something hot and alive in those eyes; something hungry and all too familiar. Her cheeks burned and she dropped a bou-
quet of clean flatware onto the floor.

"Look, mister, I'm gonna be closin' shop real soon. Like I said,
the Shell station don't open till seven or eight. There's a motel up the
road a bit, the Driftwood Inn. You shouldn't have no trouble findin' a
place there. They're right off th' highway, so they're open all night.
I'd give you a lift but, uh, my car's in the shop an' I live in town, so . . ."
The cook fell silent and returned to cleaning the grill.

The two-headed man sat and drank coffee while Louise and her
boss busied themselves with the ritual of closing. Louise mopped
the floor faster than usual, trying not to look at the stranger and his
freakish papoose.

"Well, lights-out, folks," the cook announced with a forced smile.
The two-headed man stood up and began shouldering themselves
back into the parka. "Uh, look, Louise . . . Why don't you lock up for
me, huh? Laurie's waitin' up on me and you know how she gets."

Louise certainly did. Laurie had had enough of waiting up for
her husband three years back and joined the others who'd abandoned Seven Devils, Arkansas. She nodded and watched him flee the
diner for the safety of a nonexistent wife.

Gary pulled the parka's hood over his head and zipped up. All she
could see was his face—that achingly handsome face—with its baby-
smooth jaw and electric blue eyes.

It was bitterly cold outside, their breath wreathing their heads.
The hard frost had turned the highway into a strip of polished onyx.
Gary stuffed his hands into his mittens, gave Louise a nod and a half-

wave and began to walk away, the parking lot's gravel crunching under his boot heels. The lump under his parka stirred.

Do something, girl! Say something! Don't just let him walk off!

"Hey, mister . . . er, misters!"

He turned to smile at her. She felt her bravado slip. *Dear God, what am I getting myself into?* But it was two in the morning and everyone in Choctaw County was asleep except for her and the blue-eyed stranger . . . and his traveling companion.

"I've got a place 'round back. It's not much, but it's warm. You're welcome to stay . . . I hate to think of you walking all the way to the motel and then it turn out to be full-up."

Gary stood there for a moment, his hands in his pockets and his head cocked to one side as if he was listening to something. Then he smiled.

"We'd be delighted."

The frozen grass crunched gently under their feet. The dark bulk of Louise's trailer loomed ahead of them, resting on its bed of cinder blocks.

"Where are we . . . exactly? We've no real idea . . ."

"You're in Choctaw County."

"That's the name of this place?"

"No. Not really. This here's Seven Devils. Or its outskirts, at least. Not much to it, except that it's th' county seat. This used to be a railroad town, back before the war. But now that everything's shipped by trucks, there ain't a whole lot left. What makes you want to drive around in this part of Arkansas in the first place? There's nothing down here but rice fields, bayous and broke farmers."

"We like the old highways . . . we meet much nicer people that way . . ."

Louise stopped to glance over her shoulder as she dug the house-key from her coat pocket. Had it been Gary's voice she'd heard that time? All she could see was shadow inside the parka's hood. She stood on the cinder block that served as her front stoop and fussed with her key chain. She could hear him breathing at her elbow.

"Welcome to my humble abode! It ain't much, but it's home. It used to belong to the boss. I keep an eye on the place for him."

Why was she so anxious? He certainly wasn't the first man she'd invited back to her trailer. She'd known her share of truckers, salesmen, and hitchhikers tricked out in their elaborate backpacks. Some of them she'd even deluded herself into thinking might be her Prince in disguise.

Each time there had been the meeting of tongues, the grunts in the dark as loins slapped together, and the cool evaporation of sweat on naked flesh. Each time she woke up alone. Sometimes there'd be money on the dresser.

She flicked on the lights and she entered the trailer. The tiny kitchen and shoebox-sized den emerged from the darkness.

"Like I said; it ain't much."

He stood on the threshold, one hand on the doorknob. "It's nice, Louise."

She shivered at the sound of her name in his mouth. She moved into the living room, hoping for a chance to compose herself. She needed to think.

"Close the door! You're lettin' the cold air in!" Her voice was unnaturally chirpy.

Gary closed the door behind him. She felt a bit more secure, but she couldn't help but notice how worn and tacky everything looked: the sofa, the dinette set, the easy chair . . . For a fleeting second she was overwhelmed by a desire to cry.

Gary removed his parka, carefully draping it over the back of the easy chair. He was wearing faded denims and a flannel shirt and he was so beautiful it scared her to look at him. He was so perfect she could almost ignore the Human Worm strapped to his back.

"Get you a drink?"

"That would be . . . nice."

She hurried past him and back into the kitchen. She retrieved her bottle of Evan Williams and a couple of highball glasses. She poured herself two fingers, knocked it back, then poured another two before preparing a drink for her guest. She returned to the living room—he was standing in the exact same spot—and handed Gary the glass.

"Skoal."

"Cheers," he replied, lifting the glass to Carl's lips.

While his partner drank, Gary's eyes met and held hers. "We know why you invited us here, Louise . . ."

Her heart began to beat funny, as if she'd been given a powerful but dangerous drug. She wanted this man, this gorgeous stranger. She wanted to feel his weight on her, pressing her into the mattress of her bed.

". . . but there's one thing you ought to know before we get started . . . and that's Carl's got to go first."

She stood perfectly still for a second before the words her Dream Prince had spoken sank in. She was keenly aware of Carl's eyes watching her. Her face burned and her stomach balled itself into a fist. She felt as if she'd awakened from a dream to find herself trapped in the punch line of a dirty joke.

"What kind of *pervert* do you think I am?" The tightness in her throat pitched her voice even higher.

"I don't think you're a pervert, Louise. I think you're a very sweet, very special lady. I didn't mean to hurt you." There was no cynicism in his voice. His tone was that of a child confused by the irrationality of adults.

She felt her anger fade. She gulped down the rest of her drink, hoping it would fan the fires of her indignation. "I expected *something* kinky out of you—like maybe letting th' little guy *watch* . . . but not, y'know . . ."

"I see."

Gary moved to retrieve his parka. Before she realized what she was doing, she grabbed his arm. She was astonished by the intensity of her reaction.

"No! Don't leave! Please . . . it's so lonely here . . ."

"Yes, it *is* lonely," he whispered. His eyes would not meet hers. "Go stand over there. By the sofa. Where we can see you."

Louise did as she was told. Everything seemed so far away, as if she were watching a movie through the wrong end of a pair of binoculars. Her arms and legs felt so fragile they might have been made of light and glass.

Carl whispered into Gary's ear. His eyes had grown sharp and alive while Gary's seemed to lose their focus.

"Take off your blouse. Please." The words came from someplace far away.

She hesitated, then her hands moved to the throat of her blouse. The buttons seemed cold and alien, designed to frustrate her fingers. One by one they surrendered until her shirtfront fell open, revealing pale flesh. She shrugged her shoulders and the blouse fell to the floor.

Carl once more whispered something to Gary, never taking his eyes off Louise. "The skirt. Take it off."

Her hands found the fastener at her waist. Plastic teeth purred on plastic zipper and her skirt dropped to the floor, a dark puddle at her ankles. She took a step forward, abandoning her clothes.

Carl murmured into Gary's ear. She unhooked her bra, revealing her breasts. Her skin was milky white and decorated by dark aureoles. Her nipples were as hard as corn kernels.

On Carl's relayed command she skinned herself free of her pantyhose. When the cool air struck her damp pubic patch, her clitoris stirred.

Gary moved toward her, bringing Carl with him.

She gasped aloud when Gary's hands touched her breasts. His thumbs flicked expertly over her nipples, sending shudders of pleasure through her. Then one hand was between her legs, teasing and gently massaging her.

Louise felt her knees buckle and she grabbed hold of Gary's shoulders to keep from falling backwards. Her eyes opened and she found herself staring into Carl's dark, intense eyes. She felt a brief surge of shame that her orgasm had become a spectator event, then Gary worked a finger past her labia and sank it to the second joint. Louise groaned aloud and all thoughts of shame disappeared.

He moved swiftly and quietly, wrapping her in his powerful arms and lifting her bodily. She felt a different form of pleasure now, as if she were once more within her father's safe embrace. He moved down the narrow hall, past the cramped bathroom alcove and into the tiny bedroom at the back of the trailer. He lowered her trembling body onto the bed, draping her legs over the edge of the mattress.

His left hand continued to trace delicate patterns along her exposed flesh while his right loosened the harness that held Carl in place. He only halted his exploration of her body when he moved to free his burden.

Louise saw that Carl was dressed in a flannel shirt identical to Gary's, except that the empty sleeves had been pinned up and the shirttail folded back on itself and fastened shut, just like a diaper. Gary removed the shirt and Louise swore out loud.

Even on a normal man's body Carl's penis would have been unusually large. It stood red and erect against the thick dark hair of his belly. Louise was so taken aback she scarcely noticed the smooth lumps of flesh that should have been Carl's arms and legs.

Gary positioned Carl's naked torso between her spread thighs. His gaze met and held her own so intently Louise almost forgot the absurd perversity of what they were doing.

"We love you," said Gary, and shoved Carl on top of her.

Louise cried out as Carl penetrated her. It had been a long time since she'd been with a man, and she had never known one of such proportions. She involuntarily contracted her hips, taking him in deeper. Gary's right hand kneaded the flesh of her breasts. His left hand helped Carl move. She could also feel something warm and damp just below her breasts. She suddenly realized it was Carl's face.

Gary's face was closer to hers now, his eyes mirroring her heat. She snared a handful of his hair, drawing him closer. His mouth was warm and wet as he clumsily returned the kiss. She felt the quivering that signaled the approach of orgasm and her moans became cries, giving voice to an exquisite wounding. Her hips bucked wildly with each spasm, but Carl refused to be unseated. As she lay dazed and gasping in her own sweat, she was dimly aware of him still working between her legs. Then there was a deep groan, muffled by her own flesh, and she felt him stiffen and then relax.

Louise rarely experienced orgasms during intercourse. She had been unprepared for such intensity; it was if Gary had stuck his finger in her brain and swirled everything around so she was no longer sure what she thought or knew.

No. Not Gary. Carl.

The thought made her catch her breath and she raised herself onto her elbows, staring down at the thing cradled between her thighs. Carl's face was still buried in her breast. She touched his hair and felt him start from the unexpected contact. It was the first time since their strange rut had begun that she'd acknowledged his presence.

She felt Gary watching her as she moved back farther onto the bed. Carl remained curled at the foot of the mattress, his eyes fixed on her. Gary stood in the narrow space between the bed and the dresser, his hands at his sides.

"What about you? Aren't you interested?" Her voice was hoarse.

Gary did not meet her gaze as he shifted his weight from foot to foot.

"What's the matter? Is it me?"

His head jerked up. "No! It's not you. You're fine. It's just . . ." He fell silent and looked to Carl, who nodded slightly.

Gary took a deep breath and loosened his belt buckle. His manner had changed completely. His movements had lost their previous grace. Biting his lower lip and tensing as if in anticipation of a blow, he dropped his pants.

Gary's sex organs were the size of a two-year-old child's. They lay exposed like fragile spring blossoms, his pubic area as smooth and hairless as his face. His eyes remained cast down.

Louise's lips twisted into a wry smile. She had willingly serviced a freak in order to please her long-awaited Prince, only to find him gelded. Yet all she could feel for the handsome near-man was sorrow.

"You poor thing. You poor, poor thing." She reached out and touched his hand, drawing him into the warmth of her arms. Surprised, Gary eagerly returned her embrace. To her own surprise, she reached down to pull Carl toward her. The three of them lay together on the bed like a nest of snakes, Louise gently caressing her lovers. After a while Gary began to talk.

"I've known Carl since we were kids. My mama used to cook and clean for his folks and I kept Carl company. His mama and daddy were real rich, that's how they could afford to keep him home. At least his mama wanted him home. Carl's daddy drank a lot and used to say how it wasn't *his* fault in front of Carl. I knew how he felt. About having your daddy hate you because of the way you was born. Maybe that's why me and Carl made such good friends. You see, I can't read so good. And I'm really bad with math and things like that. My daddy got mad at my mama when they found out what was wrong with me and he ran away. I never really went to school. When Carl was five, his daddy got real mad and started kickin' him. And Carl hadn't even done anything bad! He kicked Carl in the throat and they took him to the hospital. That's why Carl can't talk too good. But he's real smart! Smarter than most people with arms and legs! He knows a lot about history and math and important stuff like that. Carl tells me what to say and how to act and what to do so people don't know I've got something wrong with me. If people ever knew I wasn't smart they'd be even meaner to us." He exchanged a warm, brotherly smile with the silent man and squeezed him where his shoulder should have been. "Carl looks after me. I'm his arms and legs and voice and he's my brain and, you know." He blushed.

"You're lucky. Both of you. Not everyone is as . . . whole."

"But we're not!" He folded her hands inside his own. "Not really. That's why we've been traveling. We've been trying to find the last part of us. The part that *will* make us whole."

Louise did not know what to say to this, so she simply kissed him. Sometime later they fell asleep, Carl's torso curled between them like a dozing pet.

The alarm went off at eight-thirty, jarring Louise from a dream-less sleep. She lay there for a moment, staring at Gary, then Carl. She should have felt soiled, but there was no indignation inside her. She gently shook Gary's beautiful naked shoulder.

"It's morning already. The filling station must be open by now. You can get your tire fixed."

"Yes." His voice sounded strangely hollow.

She got out of the rumpled bed, careful to keep from kicking Carl, and put on a house coat. Now that it was daylight she felt embarrassed to be naked. She hurried into the kitchen and made coffee.

Gary emerged from the bedroom, dressed, with Carl once more harnessed to his back. She handed him two mugs, one black and one with cream and sugar, and watched, a faint smile on her lips, as they repeated their one-as-two act.

After they finished, Gary picked his parka up and laid it across one arm. He glanced first at her, then angled his head so that he was as close to face-to-face with his passenger as possible. After a moment's silent communion, he once more turned to look at her, and his eyes lost their focus. Carl's lips moved at his ear and Louise could hear the faint rasping of his ruined voice.

Gary spoke, like a man reading back dictation.

"Louise . . . you're a wonderful woman . . . I know you're not attracted to me, that's understandable . . . but I see something in you that might, someday . . . respond to *me* too . . ."

As Gary continued his halting recitation, Louise's gaze moved from his face to Carl's. For the first time since she'd met them, she really looked at *him*.

She studied his plain, everyday face and his brown eyes. As she listened, the voice she heard was Carl's and she felt something inside her change.

"We'll stop back after we get the tire repaired . . . It's up to you . . . We shouldn't be more than an hour at the most. Please think about it."

Gary began to put his parka on, but before the jacket hid Carl completely she darted forward and kissed both of them. First Gary, and then, with great care, Carl. They paused for a second and then smiled.

Louise stood in the middle of the trailer, hugging herself against the morning cold, as she watched her lovers leave. Funny. She'd always imagined her Prince having blue eyes . . .

HIDES

JAY RUSSELL

A man already fighting his own destruction on one front is often less well prepared to defend himself on another. Inspired by classic traveler's tales, Jay Russell imagines one very specific and afflicted hero, a celebrated writer, determined to cross an entire continent in pursuit of his heart's desire. Yet when the territory he enters—a landscape forbidding enough on its own—turns out to be very, very deadly, we can only put our trust in the immutability of biography, in the facts we already know.

But, meanwhile, we hold our breath.

✺

"You ain't from here."

Stevenson did his best to smile. The smell wafting off the man was atrocious, like something that should have been buried weeks before. Stevenson hadn't noticed it so much while the man slept through the first several hours of the journey, but now that he was up and moving, waving his arms about, the smell was impossible to avoid. The others in the stage didn't seem to mind, but Stevenson couldn't stop coughing; had to will himself not to retch with every fresh wrack of his aching lungs. He spat a wad of phlegm out into his dirty handkerchief. The blonde man who smelled like a dead thing hawked up a brown lugie of his own and spat it out the window, largely missing.

"Lunger?" the man asked.

Stevenson nodded, started coughing again and lost all control. He turned, leaned over the sleeping, red-haired woman to his right and vomited out the window. Bloody wads of mucus came up along with the too-big breakfast of hotcakes, bacon and coffee he'd forced down in the dining car of the train. The train that was supposed to take him all the way to Sacramento, but which had been forced to discharge its passengers at Carson City where the track had flooded out. Stevenson had been reluctant to board the uncomfortable stage-coach, but hadn't seen any choice. Not if he wanted to get to Fanny.

And seeing her again was the only thing in the world that truly mattered. His desire had driven him across an ocean and this massive, mad continent.

Stevenson held his head outside as the stage rattled along the choppy dirt trail. The dry air did his lungs some good—just not enough. And nothing could change the smell of the man sitting across from him. Stevenson would never have gotten on board if he'd known, but the blonde man had jumped on just as the stage pulled out of Carson City. So there was nothing to do but ride it out. Reluctantly, gulping a last tubercular lungful of fresh air, Stevenson withdrew back into the coach. He started to apologize to the young woman he'd leaned across, but saw that she hadn't so much as stirred. The acid taste of bile coated his tongue and palate, but Stevenson found that it cut into his sense of smell, and he accepted the small mercy. The blonde man watched him with an unpleasant smile plastered across his unshaved face. The other passengers—a stiff-backed, elderly man in a black suit and stovepipe hat, and his horse-faced, pursed-lipped wife, also in black—simply looked bored.

"Nasty," the blonde man said.

"Aye," Stevenson agreed.

"You what?"

"Sorry?" Stevenson was confused.

"You said 'I,' but you didn't say what. Then you said 'Sorry,' but you didn't say what you's apologizing for."

"Aye," Stevenson repeated, catching on. "I meant to say yes. Aye means yes, ye see. Ken?"

"Not in these parts it don't. And my name ain't Ken. It's Jackworth." He looked at the elderly man. "You Ken?"

The old man offered the slightest, unfriendliest-possible shake of his head. His wife screwed her face up into an even uglier expression.

"No Kens here," the blonde man said.

"My mistake," Stevenson said. He sighed.

"You talk funny, mister." Jackworth hawked another wad of phlegm toward the window. Given his own condition, it didn't bother Stevenson—not like the smell—though Stevenson had now seen enough of the American West to realize that there was nothing likely wrong with the man's lungs; it was the egg-sized wad of tobacco stuffed in his cheek that was to blame.

"So where's you from then?"

The smell was starting to get to Stevenson again. He put his hand up to his mouth and nose to stem the effects. It didn't help much.

"Edinburgh," he said, and coughed.

"Enburr?" the man puzzled.

Stevenson lowered his hand, tried not to roll his *r*'s so much. "Ed-in-burgh."

Jackworth scratched his head, pulling out a louse which he briefly inspected before squashing it between thumb and forefinger. "Ed-and-burg," he repeated. "That up Nebraska way?"

Stevenson coughed again, but this time to disguise a laugh. The blonde man might be stupid—might be?—but he looked like the type who wouldn't take kindly to being mocked. And he was watching Stevenson very closely.

"Edinburgh's a city in Scotland."

Jackworth just frowned.

"Scotland. It's a country."

Nothing. A blank stare.

"It's a part of Great Britain. England?"

The man shook his head.

"Across the Atlantic Ocean."

Jackworth's eyes lit up. "I heard of that," he yelled, slapping his hat against his thigh. "Never seed it, though. Seed Wichita once. Big old town." He leaned forward—bringing his smell with him—and held a hand up to his cheek to confer on Stevenson a conspiratorial whisper. "Got me some fine cunny there, tight as a baby sheep. Ain't never forgot it."

Appalled, Stevenson nonetheless smiled and nodded, then turned toward the window for a taste of clean air and the hope of an end to the conversation.

"Where's abouts—"

The question was interrupted by a monstrous lurch of the stage-coach. The sleeping woman rolled on top of Stevenson and both fell to the far side of the compartment. Jackworth was quick—very quick—and grabbed hold of the door handle, but the old man and his wife tumbled to the floor, like a pair of coupling crows in flight. The man's stovepipe hat zipped right out the window. The wheels on the right side of the coach lifted off the ground, and for a very long second Stevenson felt certain that the vehicle was going to flip over. But with a gut and lung–shuddering thud, followed by a loud crunch from the undercarriage, the coach righted itself. The driver shouted a stream of curses as he tried to bring the horses to rein. Stevenson couldn't see much with the no-longer-sleeping woman sprawled on top of him, but he could hear the horses shriek and whinny as they went down and the rear axle of the coach was ripped out from underneath. The carriage hit the dirt trail hard, and Stevenson smacked his jaw against the wooden bench, biting into his upper lip as he did so. His mouth filled with the too-familiar taste of blood.

There was another jerk, and then everything came to a blessed stop.

Jackworth was out of the coach before Stevenson could even right himself. The woman had rolled back off of him with the coach's final lurch and spilled into the old man and woman. Stevenson pressed the back of his hand to his mouth and, examining the volume of blood, decided that the cut wasn't too bad. He got to his feet as best he could—at better than six feet tall, he couldn't stand up straight—and offered a hand to help untangle his fellow passengers. The young woman appeared dazed, but had no visible injuries. Stevenson lifted her up and sat her down on the bench, where she rubbed her stomach. The old man had gotten to his knees and now fussed over his wife, who sat whimpering on the floor. The man had a long gash across his forehead, and had torn his undertaker's suit, but the woman was hurt much worse. Her black skirt had ridden up and Stevenson saw that her leg was badly broken. An ivory cane of bone poked out through a bloody tear in her left thigh. The woman touched the bone with her finger, unable, it seemed, to recognize it for what it was. She'd gone very pale indeed, and started to cry out with the pain, but her husband, studying Stevenson's gaze, seemed more concerned with drawing the hem of her skirt back over the exposed expanse of her ghost-white thigh. The man's lips drew back in a snarl, but before Stevenson could say anything, two shots sounded from outside. Another pair swiftly followed.

Stevenson leaped out the open door, misjudged the distance and took a face-first fall into the dirt. More embarrassed than hurt, he scrambled to his feet. He came around to the front of the coach just in time to see the driver put a final bullet into the head of a dying horse. A second dead animal lay beside it.

"There's my job," the driver said, and spat onto the corpse. The pair of horses that had survived the accident whinnied nervously a dozen yards up the road.

"The old woman is hurt quite badly," Stevenson announced. "She's broken her leg clear through the skin."

The driver turned to Jackworth, who was dancing excitedly between the dead animals. "What in hell'd he say?"

"He ain't from here," Jackworth reported. "Come from 'cross the ocean. Atlantic, you know it?"

"The old woman inside the carriage is badly injured," Stevenson repeated, slowly. "Her leg is broken."

"Shee-it," the driver said, and spat again. "Ain't that just the fly on the turd."

"You a doc there, Ed-and-burg?" Jackworth asked. He practically leaped from leg to leg, like a man desperate to urinate. What was he so bloody excited about, Stevenson wondered.

"Nae . . . no. But ye can see bone through the flesh. There's not a lot of doubt as to what's wrong."

"Hot damn! Got to get me a lookee-loo at that." And Jackworth jumped back into the coach.

A moment later the younger woman leaned out, still rubbing at her belly, but looking less dazed. Stevenson went to help her out, and together they studied the wreck of the stagecoach. The rear axle had snapped in two and lay a dozen yards up the road, near the two-foot-deep gully in the trail that had caused the crash. The front axle was still attached, but it too was as broken as the old woman's leg. It was clear that they wouldn't be going any farther in this coach, though, looking at the damage, Stevenson felt lucky to be alive and essentially uninjured.

"What do we do now?" Stevenson asked the driver.

The man picked his nose and spat. He looked aggrieved to have to answer the question. Or perhaps just scared about the consequences of the crash, Stevenson considered.

"We's caught what you'd call 'twixt and 'tween and halfway to neither. Too far to the company post, especially with the womenfolk and such. There is a old way station not too far from here. Five, maybe seven miles, best I reckon. Don't generally like to stop there, though."

"Why not?"

"Company don't like it. Had some trouble there a while back. S'all I know."

"Will there be a doctor there?" Stevenson asked.

The driver chuckled. "Barely a *there* there, friend. But I reckon she'll have to do us. Feller runs things there knows some doctoring. Claims to, anyway, what I hear. Queer feller, I thought; makes your blood run like the wrong way."

Stevenson didn't much care for the sound of that. "Is there nae a better destination for us?"

"Not to make before nightfall. We put the old lady on the one horse, and the ma'am here on t'other, should make it right enough. Not too bad a hike, these things go. Bit uphill. Not that I sees much choice in the matter."

And thus did Robert Louis Stevenson, late of Edinburgh, Scotland (across the Atlantic Ocean, of which many people have heard), set out on the road to Hides.

The old woman screamed something fierce as they dragged her out of the remains of the coach, but mercifully she passed out as they settled her onto the horse, making the task that much easier. Jackworth continued to marvel at the length of bone protruding through her thigh, though to his credit he did the lion's share of carrying her without complaint. Her husband, who'd reluctantly introduced himself as Mr. Anderson Balfour—he stressed the *Mister*—looked on disapprovingly, constantly tugging her dress down over her exposed leg, and proving himself to be of little help. The driver—Grey, he called himself, though if that was his first name or last, or merely an encapsulation of his life, Stevenson never learned—was only slightly more helpful, utterly preoccupied, it seemed, with the wreckage of his stagecoach and his livelihood. Little Jackworth was a ball of energy, though, and while Stevenson felt that there was something odd about the fellow (not just his smell), he decided Jackworth's primary offense was that of being somewhat juvenile. Indeed, as he studied the blonde man, Stevenson guessed that Jackworth couldn't be much more than nineteen or twenty years old. Though he did wear a pair of guns on his belt.

The other woman, who eventually introduced herself as Mrs. Timothy Reilly, continued to clutch at her belly, while denying any specific discomfort or injury. She showed some initial reluctance at mounting the remaining horse, and in the end would only ride sidesaddle. Stevenson might have assumed she was fearful of the steed, but she seemed confident enough once in place.

Grey led the way, taking the reins of the horse bearing the unconscious old woman, along with the lockbox from the stagecoach; the other bags would have to be left behind with the wreckage, though the driver secreted the passengers' belongings in the woods off the trail to be safe, then covered his tracks. Balfour followed directly behind Grey, eyes glued to his wife's leg, then came Mrs. Reilly on her horse. Stevenson, already feeling the effects of the strain on his lungs, brought up the rear. Much to his chagrin, Jackworth fell into place beside him, swinging his arms back and forth as he walked, like a kid in a holiday parade. A light breeze from the north brought with it just a hint of storm; Stevenson took advantage of it to position himself upwind of the man.

"So, Ed, what's yer business?" Jackworth asked.

Stevenson didn't much want to talk—he was finding it difficult enough just walking and breathing—but neither did he like to be rude.

"I've trained and toiled as both a lawyer and an engineer, though neither vocation proved much to my liking. I do a wee bit of writing now, and am told I've a flair for it. And most people call me Louis." *Except for one who calls me Robbie*, he thought.

"No fooling. Sorry 'bout that, Lou. Well, gee. I always did want to learn to read, you know. Got a cousin who knows his ABCs right through, mostly. Smart as a whip and hung like a bear. Beat that if you can! What ya write?"

"Stories about my travels, mostly. People and things I've seen, and places I've visited. France and Germany most recently. And about my home in Scotland, of course."

"Hooo-weee! You been all them places? I heard of France, you know. That 'cross the Atlantic, too?"

Stevenson merely nodded. "My health compels me to travel. The climate back home is particularly unsuitable to my condition. More's the pity, because I do love it so."

"So what brings yer hell and gone out here? You fixing to write another story?"

Stevenson hesitated. He didn't much care to discuss his life and plans with this stranger. And he couldn't talk about Fanny to anyone. She was . . . hard to explain.

"In fact, I'm just now thinking about something entirely different: a work of pure fiction. A pirate story, I ken. I find that my imagination grows keener than my powers of observation with each passing year." Stevenson offered himself a slight chuckle.

"Don't know no pirates, so I can't help you there, Lou. Plenty good tales 'round these parts, though."

"Is that right?"

"You must know 'bout the Donners," Jackworth whispered.

"Not to my recollection."

Jackworth took off his hat and slapped it against his thigh. He grinned so wide, Stevenson could see all his missing back teeth. "You ain't heard of the Donner party?" he practically yelled.

The others all turned around and the driver, Grey, offered a particularly disgusted look. Jackworth slapped his hand over his mouth.

"What was the Donner party?" Stevenson asked.

When it was clear that the others were again facing front, Jackworth continued, determinedly sotto voce: "Cannibals."

Stevenson assumed he misunderstood. "I beg your pardon?"

Jackworth feverishly nodded his head. "They was cannibals. I mean, not to start, but that's how it come out in the end."

"I don't think I follow ye."

"Thirty years or so back. Donners and Reeds was travelling west. Two big families. Got trapped up in the Sierra, just a piece aways from here, by the winter snows. Damn fools, but ain't no shortage of them. Supplies run out, animals run out, luck run out, mostly. Nothing left for it but to chomp each other. Told folks after that they only et the ones what was already dead, but there's them what say elsewise. Some claim they drew lots and slaughtered the losers like sows. Others that the families set up camps and went at each other like in a war and et their enemies what they captured. Eighty-odd went into that pass in winter, forty-odd come out the other end in spring. Others all got et."

"Good Lord!"

"Yessir. There's folks 'round who still remember, can tell you the gruesome details if you can stand to hear 'em. It's a wonder, ain't it? Imagine how'd it be like to end your days getting et."

"And you're certain that this is true?"

A darkness crossed Jackworth's face. "You calling me a liar?"

"Nae, certainly not." Stevenson had learned that, in this part of the world, short of stealing a man's horse there was no offense worse than questioning his word. "I just wondered if this is not, perhaps, some wee tall tale which is told in the region. I have heard a few others. Some nonsense about a giant lumberjack for one. And it reminds me of the stories told of old Sawney Bean in and around Ballantrae."

Jackworth nodded, seemingly appeased. "Well, this ain't no tall tale, that's for sure. It's a damn historical fact. They even started to call the old canyon trail where it happened Donner Pass."

"Remarkable," Stevenson mused. "How could anyone do that?"

"How's you mean?"

Stevenson found himself intrigued and repelled by the story in equal measure. "Imagine eating human flesh. Not just eating it, but slaughtering it yourself. A friend, a cousin, a brother. Even if they were already dead, the things ye'd have to do. Draining the blood. Cutting the muscle from the bone. Carving the organs from their cavities. Cooking the meat, putting the morsels in your mouth. Chewing. Swallowing." He shuddered. "Doesn't seem possible."

"I could do it."

Stevenson studied the young man. Jackworth stared ahead with an intense, very serious expression, nodding to himself. "Ye couldn't."

Jackworth looked up at the writer. "Oh, yeah. I been hungry. I done things. I seen things."

"Not like that, surely."

"Naw, not exactly. But then I ain't never been stuck in no mountain pass in no blizzard with nothing to eat but a third cousin twice removed. I seen men kilt, though, and it were for less than not starving to death. People is funny animals, Lou. My daddy used to say never turn your back on a animal 'cause you never can tell what it's likely to do. Well, I turned my back on lots of critters and I ain't never suffered no harm. Okay, mebbe a bite on the ankle. But turn your back on a man, and you're likely as not to take a bullet in the ass. Or worser. People is just animals when day turns to night, you gotta know that. And you can't never be surprised by the things they's prone to do. Aw, hell, I got to take a piss something fierce. Burns like hell when I do it, too. Don't know what that's about."

As Jackworth dashed off into the trees, unbuttoning his fly, Stevenson increased his stride. He thought he could do with some different company for a while.

They stopped after an hour of mostly uphill walking. It was Mrs. Reilly who asked if they could rest, and though Grey glanced up at the darkening skies with a frown, he nodded his assent. Stevenson went over to help the woman down from the horse, but a fresh coughing fit overcame him, and ultimately she had to help him to sit on an outcropping of rock above a gurgling stream. He waved her away, nodding his thanks, and hawked up a bloody wad of phlegm against the white stone. He lay flat on the rocks and reached down to scoop up handfuls of clear water. It was so cold that it sent a spike of pain up through his head, but after a few swallows, the coughing once again subsided. He rolled over, breathing slowly, enjoying the dim rays of late afternoon sun that penetrated the mounting overcast.

Balfour stood guard beside his wife, still out cold. With Grey's help, they'd lowered her off the horse, to give the animal a chance to rest and drink from the stream. Jackworth kept an excited eye on the enterprise, eager, it seemed, to catch another glance at the woman's protruding leg bone. Mrs. Reilly had wandered off behind the trees, to answer nature's call no doubt. She returned a few minutes later, still rubbing her stomach, a dyspeptic expression distorting her otherwise pleasant features. She went over to see if she could be of help with Mrs. Balfour. The four of them stood in a circle around the old woman, none of them quite knowing what to do. Jackworth saw Stevenson studying the tableau and grinned at the writer. Stevenson groaned to himself as the blonde man came over to his spot on the rock. Jackworth leaned over and whispered into Stevenson's ear: "You're trying to figure which of us you'd eat, ain't ya?"

Stevenson had been thinking no such thing. Before he could say so, Jackworth added: "Well, I got dibs on the Irish cunny, hear?" and he licked his lips lasciviously. To Stevenson's relief, Jackworth stood up and wandered back toward the trail.

Mrs. Reilly was gesticulating forcefully at the old woman. Mr. Balfour crossed his arms over his chest and firmly shook his head from side to side. She then pointed at the driver, but he raised his hands in a "no sir, not me" gesture and walked away, back to the horses. Mrs. Reilly again made a pleading gesture at the old man, but he just turned his back on her. Exasperated, she walked away and sat down beside Stevenson.

"She's going to lose that leg," Mrs. Reilly informed him. "He's tied a sash around the top to stem the bleeding, but it's fastened too tight and the leg's gone all blue. The blasted man won't listen to a word I say."

"He looks a stubborn old mule."

"Impossible. I told him she'll lose the leg and he just insists that 'the Lord will provide.' And beggars will ride, I say."

Stevenson raised an eyebrow. "Not one for Providence then?"

"I didn't mean to shock you. I understood you to be a writer of tales. I always heard writers were open-minded, liberal types."

Jackworth liked to talk, Stevenson realized. "Aye, but I'm also a lay preacher's son."

"No offense meant, I'm sure."

"None taken, missus. I'm just surprised to hear a good Irish lass like yourself express such a sentiment."

"Who said I was Irish?"

Stevenson felt slightly flustered. "Well, it's just . . . your look and your hair and . . . Mrs. *Reilly* and all that."

Mrs. Reilly dragged her rear end across the rock, closer to Stevenson. "May I confess something to you?" Stevenson nodded. "My name isn't really Mrs. Reilly."

"Nae?"

She shook her head. "There is no Mr. Reilly."

"Is there not?"

She shook her head. Suddenly, a picture took shape in Stevenson's head. He didn't know how he knew, but he knew. He said it out loud. "Then who's the father of the bairn?"

The woman's eyes went wide, and the hand that had been rubbing her stomach froze.

"I didn't mean to shock ye," Stevenson said, touching a hand lightly to the woman's arm.

"How did you know?" she whispered.

"I didn't for certain. Until this second. But the way ye touch your belly, and the way ye ride the horse and, well, ye've probably heard it said before, but as I look at ye there's a kind of a glow about ye. I just put a series of observations together and invented the story that tied them up in a neat package. That's what I do, after all. It's true then?"

She nodded. "You won't say—"

"It's none of their concern," he said, patting her hand. "Nor mine. As an open-minded writer."

The woman looked relieved. "I'm travelling to find the father. Let him know the situation. I hope to *become* Mrs. Reilly. Well, a missus at least, whatever the name." She studied Stevenson carefully. "I bet you're a good writer."

Before he could reply, or recover from his blush, their attention was distracted by a piercing scream from the old woman. She'd come to, and didn't much like the feeling. As she continued to shriek, Grey had to rush over and try to settle the horses. Jackworth came running back from wherever he'd been, and made straight toward the Balfours. He stood directly over the old woman, breathing hard from his exertions, but seemingly excited by her agony. Mr. Balfour was struggling with his wife, holding her from behind, trying to calm her down. Stevenson and Mrs. Reilly both stood up, but before they could make a move to help, Jackworth hauled off and punched the old woman in the jaw with all his might. Her head rocked back and she tipped over, smacking the ground hard.

She was out cold again.

Mr. Balfour studied his wife, then glanced up at the still-grinning Jackworth. The old man nodded his thanks and Jackworth winked at him.

They loaded the women back on the horses and set off up the road.

The trail levelled out, but the early evening air took on a chill. Stevenson had left his coat in his travelling bag and had to make do with cinching tight his waistcoat. Jackworth was up in front with Grey—every so often the two men broke out in fits of ugly laughter—and Mrs. Reilly seemed to be half dozing in the saddle as they made slow progress. Stevenson had been lagging behind and increased his pace, as much to keep warm as anything else, and without really meaning to, found himself beside Mr. Balfour. He thought about walking on past, but another burst of vile hilarity from Grey and Jackworth restrained him. He matched strides with Balfour, offering a glance back at the old man's wife, still enjoying Jackworth's ministrations on the back of the horse. They walked like that for some ways.

"Has she stirred?" Stevenson asked, unable to endure any more of the uncomfortable silence.

"No."

"With fortune this gentleman at the way station will be able to help."

"Can't say."

"Do you know anything about this place? The driver doesn't seem to care for it."

"Nnnn."

Stevenson tried a different tack: "So where are ye and your wife headed?"

"West."

Stevenson coughed. "Getting a tad cold now," he said.

"You say so."

Balfour walked a little quicker. Stevenson slowed his pace again, allowing Balfour and the horse bearing his wife to advance past him once more.

Coughing, shaking his head, crossing his arms over his chilled body, Stevenson walked on alone.

There was just enough light to make out the sign. It had been crudely burned into a strip of old wood that might once have been part of a door. It dangled on frayed hemp rope from the dead branches of a lightning-struck willow tree. Just the one word:

HIDES

"There she is," Grey announced.

The building was roughly oblong, but none of the angles were quite straight. Several crude windows had been carved out of the mismatched wooden walls, but there was no glass in the frames, only flimsy shutters to keep out the wet and the cold. One whole side of the structure was black and charred, though some makeshift effort to patch up the worst of the fire damage was in evidence. Bright light glinted out through holes in the door and gaps in the frame, suggesting that someone waited inside. Though who could regard such a wreck as *home*, Stevenson couldn't imagine. His heart sank at the prospect of finding proper attention for the injured old woman from anyone residing here.

"Hides," Stevenson whispered. He shuddered.

"They say it used to be a big trading post," Grey explained. "Been here since Hector was a pup. The Yana and the Atsugewi'd come swap their pelts and beads and such for heap big firewater. Heh-heh. Don't think I even seen a Atsugewi for going on ten years now. Kilt 'em all, I reckon. Or drank 'emselves to death, filthy red buggers."

And he spat. "Don't know what keeps the place going these days. Not much from the look of her."

Mrs. Balfour began to stir again on the back of the horse. She wasn't quite awake, but she was moaning slightly and her teeth chattered like cicadas at sunrise. Stevenson saw Jackworth ball his fingers into a preparatory fist, but Mrs. Reilly slid down from her mount and stood between the blonde man and the old woman.

"We'd best get her inside," she said to Mr. Balfour. The old man glanced at Jackworth, as if considering the fist option, then nodded at Mrs. Reilly. Jackworth looked briefly disappointed, but he was all smiles as he helped Grey carry the woman into the old trading post.

Mrs. Reilly opened the door for them as Grey and Jackworth hauled Mrs. Balfour across the threshold. Mr. Balfour scurried right behind. Mrs. Reilly held the door for Stevenson, who entered last.

The trading post consisted of a single large room, broken up only by a counter that ran the length of the far wall. The room was lit every which way by gas lamps and fat tallow candles that stank to high hell but provided an unexpectedly warm glow. All manner of furry hides had been draped across the walls and over the rough wooden floor. Stevenson didn't know his American fauna too well, but he recognized bits of beaver, raccoon, deer and an immense bearskin that covered the whole center of the room. A grizzly, possibly. The hides smelt musky and mildewed, but their softness and heat sucked the worst of the chill right out of his lungs.

Sitting in a rocking chair by a roaring fire in the comer was a rotund ball of a man with a misshapen, bald head. He wore wire-rim spectacles and was reading from a tattered yellowed copy of Beadle's Dime Novels. His dark brown eyes opened wide at the sight of the group that had intruded on his quiet evening.

"Howdy," Grey said. He hawked into a spittoon by the door. "Paul, ain't it?"

"Poole," the round man said. He had a soft, almost girlish voice. He pulled a pocket watch from his vest, frowned. "You should have passed hours ago. Why are you here?"

"Accident. Busted both axles, believe that? Been hoofing it for miles. Coach is a wreck and I had to put down two the horses. I'm through, that's for your certain."

"My," Poole replied.

Everyone stood and stared at each other then, Jackworth and Grey still supporting Mrs. Balfour between them. Her groaning had gotten louder.

"This woman needs some attention," Stevenson finally said. "She's broken her leg in the accident."

"He's from Ed-and-burg," Jackworth helpfully pointed out.

Poole continued to sit there.

"Can ye help her?" Stevenson urged. "Or is there someone else?"

"No one else. Just me now." The fat man blinked. He put down his book, pointed at the opposite corner of the room. "Bring her this way."

Jackworth and Grey carried Mrs. Balfour over to a bench and put her down—a bit roughly, Stevenson thought—then stepped away. Mr. Balfour walked around behind the bench, hovering protectively over his wife. The old woman's eyes fluttered open and she immediately began to shriek in pain. Poole waddled over and lifted the hem of her black dress without so much as a by-your-leave. Mr. Balfour gasped, but offered no more substantive objection. Poole knelt down and ran his fingers up the woman's leg, gently prodding at the exposed shank of bone. Mrs. Balfour screamed.

"Well," Poole said.

"Won't you do something?" Mrs. Reilly asked.

"This tourniquet has been fastened much too tightly," Poole announced. Mrs. Reilly issued a harrumph. Poole loosened the sash and kneaded the flesh of the woman's upper thigh. Mr. Balfour took a white-knuckle grip on the back of the bench, but held his tongue. His wife wailed in such agony that, had there been any glass in the windows, Stevenson felt sure that the sound would have shattered it. Blood oozed out of the open wound, but in lesser volume than before.

"First things first," Poole said. He got up and slowly walked behind the counter, not at all bothered by the old woman's cries. A series of ill-balanced shelves and cubbyholes along the back wall held a plethora of mismatched jars and beakers, filled to varying levels with multicolored liquids. As the old woman continued to shriek —Stevenson wanted to cover his ears—Poole calmly went about pouring drops and drains out of different bottles into a chipped whiskey glass. He glanced up and down the counter for something, shrugged to himself, then stuck his finger in the glass to stir the potion. He sniffed his finger as he withdrew it and nodded in approval. He handed the glass to Mr. Balfour.

"Make her drink that," he said.

The old man tried to put the glass in his wife's hand, but she was beyond reasoning. She flailed at him, nearly emptying the glass of its contents. Balfour didn't seem to know what to do. Poole shook his head and sighed.

"A bit of help, if you would."

Grey and Jackworth had retreated near the fire with a bottle of rye. The two men exchanged a glance and got up. Grey took the old woman's arms, Jackworth, grinning, her feet. When she opened her mouth to let out a wail, Poole snatched the glass back from her husband and poured the contents down her gullet.

Mrs. Balfour choked on the stuff at first and spat some of it out, but enough of it must have gone down, because in less than a minute she was asleep again.

"What was in that?" Stevenson asked.

"Oh, just a little elixir I know," Poole said. "She'll be out till morning if we're lucky. We could saw that leg right off, and she wouldn't feel a thing." He looked up then at Mr. Balfour. "I'm not planning on sawing it off. At least not yet. But you shouldn't have tied that knot so tight. I'll try and fix her up, but I don't know that it will take. Time, as is its wont, will be the final arbiter. And circumstance."

Mr. Balfour nodded.

Stevenson was impressed as he and Mrs. Reilly assisted Poole with setting the leg. Poole decided that Grey and Jackworth were too indelicate for the task, and though the process had its difficult moments—Stevenson had to look away as Poole forced the exposed length of bone back inside Mrs. Balfour's torn flesh, then twisted and pulled at the leg until he felt the broken ends grind together and mesh—Poole worked quickly and with a minimum of spilled blood. They used two lengths of worm-eaten board for a splint, and secured it with strips of muskrat hide. Poole couldn't decide what to do about the open wound, then opted for stitching it closed with some catgut and a needle made from bone that must have been meant for sewing hides. Stevenson again found it difficult to watch as Poole darned together the torn flaps of skin but suspected that, all in all, Mrs. Balfour could have had worse luck than to have alighted at Hides. Poole finished up by dousing the wound with rotgut whiskey. As the amber liquid washed over the stitched opening, Mrs. Balfour shuddered in her induced slumber. Poole lay a blanket on top of her, and gave another to her husband, who settled in for the night on the floor beside her.

By the time they were done with the old woman and had cleaned themselves up, Jackworth and Grey had finished off their bottle of hootch and had both passed out on the floor in front of the dying fire. "Leave them be," Poole said, and hauled out a couple of louse-ridden horse blankets which he gently laid over the sleeping men. He searched around in a trunk until he found a length of calico. He hung it up across a corner of the room, making a private sleeping space for Mrs. Reilly. He found a somewhat softer and cleaner blanket for her and piled some furs on the floor into a little mattress.

"I'm not really equipped for ladies," he said, "but you should be able to make do with that. I receive so few guests."

Mrs. Reilly gratefully retreated behind the curtain, still rubbing her belly and saying her good-nights. Poole gathered another set of furs together and flung them on the floor beside his own bed. "That should do you," he said.

"That'll be dandy," Stevenson replied.

Poole went about damping out the candles and lamps until the only light came from the embers of the fire in the corner. Stevenson removed his boots and waistcoat, unfastened the top buttons of his trousers and chemise and lay down.

The sound of snoring soon filled Hides.

The rain woke Stevenson up. The rain and the coughing.

The storm that had threatened to break all during their long hike finally arrived, and with a fury. Water sloshed into the corners of the room, from the spots where the walls and roof were poorly joined, and through gaps in the wall and windows and door. The sudden concentration of humidity and moisture in the air sat heavily in Stevenson's lungs and provoked a diabolical coughing fit.

At first, Stevenson could barely stop hacking long enough to take a breath. He crawled off his pallet of furs toward the door, made it to the spittoon to hawk up a wad of dark mucus. He was able to take several deep breaths after that, until a fresh spell of coughing possessed him. Not wanting to wake the others, he dragged himself out the door and into the wet night. His stockinged feet plunged ankle-deep into the mud, but a slight overhang in the roof kept the worst of the rain off of his head.

The coughing, however, simply wouldn't stop.

Stevenson sank back to his knees as the pain exploded through his chest. This was as bad as it had ever felt. His lungs were on fire and something wet and thick got caught in his throat; he couldn't draw sufficient breath to expel it. He opened his mouth as wide as it would go, began clawing at the air with his muddy hands as if he could physically wrench some of it into his lungs.

He was choking to death.

As veins of darkness seeped in at the edges of his vision, Stevenson saw, in his mind's eye, Fanny's sweet face. As he made one, last effort to draw a saving breath, his only regret was that he'd never kiss that face again, feel her lips on his.

Something struck him hard across the back, knocking him face-first into the mud. A hand grabbed at the hair on the back of his neck, yanked him up sharply, then another blow to the back. And another.

With the fourth hammer strike, a fist-sized chunk of phlegm exploded from his throat, passed his lips and disappeared into the black swamp around him. With a gasp like rattling bones, he drew in a wet lungful of air, and nothing had ever tasted so sweet. He exhaled, coughed, took another slap on the back—but didn't need it. Just like that he was breathing normally, though tears continued to stream from his eyes.

"Better?"

Stevenson turned around in the slick mud and saw Poole, mud-spattered as well, staring down at him. Poole put out a hand, helped Stevenson back to his feet.

"I thank ye, sir."

"I heard the ruckus. You was looking a little peaked there, friend."

"I believe, Mr. Poole," Stevenson said, through another small cough, "that ye just saved my life."

Poole shrugged, but smiled. He looked embarrassed. "Just a little pat on the back's all it was. Could have gone either way. How long you suffered the consumption?"

"Always. It's afflicted me in one way or the other since I was a boy."

The rain had slowed, but Stevenson stepped out into it, allowing the cool drops to wash the sweat and blood from his face. He breathed deep, found he wasn't coughing at all.

"That's rough," Poole said. "But you beat the odds still being alive this long. I'm impressed by that. We live with long odds and brief lives. Tried anything for the consumption?"

"Medicines are largely useless. I travel. I find some climes more amenable than others, at least for a time. I hadn't expected this one to be so . . . ungracious."

"This can be rough country."

Stevenson stepped back under the protection of the overhang, stared out into the night with Poole, who'd lit up a cheroot. "So I've been told. Though I thought only in winter."

"Heard about that, huh? Well, I guess everyone knows about the Donners by now."

"I hadn't until Mr. Jackworth in there told me the tale during our sojourn here. Quite gruesome."

"You have no idea, friend."

Stevenson raised an eyebrow. "Ye weren't . . ."

"Seen and done a lot," Poole said, not meeting Stevenson's gaze. "It's rough country and it's a rougher life. You can't really understand if you ain't a part of it. Some see things out here and call them cruelties, but everything is relative. Ever seen how a cat plays with a rat? What a fox'll do to a chicken or a bear to a sheep? Eaten alive is nature's rule and it's just our civilized—so-called—selves who've got nancy-prance ideas about such things. Ideas that we deserve better than being eaten alive. Better than nature."

"And don't we?"

Poole shrugged. "Maybe some. Not most."

"But surely the whole purpose of civilization, its primary virtue, is to escape those very cruelties of nature. To celebrate our unique ability to rise above such cruelty, to transcend nature. Even if it's our own nature."

"Think so? Think anyone rises above their nature? That that's possible to do?" Poole turned his gaze back on Stevenson, who wanted to respond in the affirmative, but who didn't fancy arguing with a man who'd just saved his life, who suddenly looked very intense. Poole answered his own questions anyway: "Just ask the Donners," he said.

As the storm swelled again Stevenson felt a fresh cough coming on, so Poole led him back inside and out of the rain. Mr. Balfour raised his head, scowled, and went back to sleep beside his still-slumbering wife. Jackworth and Grey continued to snore on the floor, Mrs. Reilly hadn't so much as stirred from behind her curtain.

"I got something here that might help you out a bit," Poole whispered, and led Stevenson back to his collection of jars and beakers. He had to stand on a chair to get a bottle of clear liquid down from a high shelf. "Try this."

"What is it?"

"Laudanum. Mostly. Ever try it?"

Stevenson nodded. "The effects are salubrious, but short-lived. The afterward is like drinking a barrel of cheap gin."

"Get you through the night," Poole suggested.

Stevenson considered, then nodded. Poole poured him a measured glassful, which Stevenson raised to his host in a toast. "You don't regard this as too intrusive of civilization on nature?" Stevenson asked. He meant it as a joke.

"Some interventions are necessary. And it'll get you through the night," Poole repeated, mirthlessly.

Stevenson downed the drink, which was extremely potent. Poole had to help him back to his makeshift bed.

Breathing comfortably, Stevenson was asleep within seconds.

And awoke to the familiar smell of blood.

Stevenson was so used to spitting up blood in the night that he didn't think much of it. He had trouble, thanks to the laudanum, thinking straight at all. The storm had passed and the morning sunlight pierced his eyes like knitting needles. Stevenson tried to lift his head, but couldn't do it. He lay there for a while, breathing deeply but without difficulty. Bits of dried mud spotted the furs and floor beneath him, flaked off his hands and arms as he raised them to rub at his bleary eyes.

The smell of blood was very strong.

Stevenson forced himself to a half-sitting position and glanced down at the front of his shirt. He saw more mud there, but no sign of having bled from his mouth in the night. He touched his fingers to his lips, came away with no trace of red there, either. The scent, however, was overpowering.

Stevenson looked behind him, saw the arc of Poole's sleeping back, the slight rise and fall of his round shoulders. Glancing across the room, he could make out Grey's and Jackworth's legs poking out from the far end of the counter. They didn't appear to have moved at all in the night. The Balfours were silent, as well. As he groggily got to his feet he stole a guilty glance at Mrs. Reilly's curtained corner.

The calico lay on the floor, revealing the exposed flesh of the young woman sprawled across the bed of furs. Embarrassed, Stevenson looked away, but even as he did so, he knew that something was very wrong.

That bloody smell had to be coming from somewhere.

Stevenson turned back toward Mrs. Reilly. He took a tentative step, saw that the pile of hides on which she slept were dark and wet. She was entirely naked, and though his gaze fell at first on the swell of her exposed breast, he saw that something dark sat upon her abdomen. As he drew nearer, his head began to swim with the sanguine odor that wafted off of and out of her. There was nothing atop her stomach, he saw as he neared her bed, but rather her abdomen had been cut open; peeled apart and turned inside out. She'd been slit from between the legs up to her navel. Most of what had been contained within was untidily piled without.

"Jackworth," Stevenson whispered.

He spun around, but there was no movement from the pairs of legs on the floor. Stevenson grabbed at an empty whiskey bottle, holding it by the neck like a club. He advanced along the counter, raising the bottle high above his head as he turned the corner.

The legs were unattached to any bodies. The bloody stumps had been neatly arranged on the floor, but the bulk of neither Grey nor Jackworth was anywhere to be seen. Stevenson dropped the bottle, opened and closed his eyes several times, convinced that he must be trapped in some laudanum-inspired nightmare.

The sight—and smell—of the Balfours' bodies, husband's head on wife's shoulders and vice versa, eventually convinced him otherwise. The old woman's carefully splinted leg was untouched.

Stevenson stared at the carnage around him, his head still fuzzy from the drug and the shock.

What had happened? Who could have done this? What kind of animal . . .

Poole.

Stevenson grabbed the bottle again and smashed it against the counter. Holding the jagged edge in front of him, he advanced on his host—his savior of only hours previous who still lay in his bed.

Stevenson could hear the fat man's heavy breathing, saw now that his blanket and straw mattress were drenched in drying blood.

Poole slowly rolled over as Stevenson approached. His eyes were glazed, his features dotted with splotches of red.

Stevenson moved closer, saw that the man's hands were cupped over his chest, something wet and dark clutched within.

Stevenson raised up the broken bottle.

Poole stared dully at him; made no move to attack or get up. He just lay there in his blood-soaked bedclothes.

"Why?" Stevenson asked.

Poole didn't respond, didn't so much as blink.

"Why?" Stevenson demanded, voice breaking. "Why did you do this?"

"Eaten alive," Poole whispered. "Eaten alive."

Stevenson waited for more. He had to blink away the fuzziness that continued to dance at the edge of his consciousness.

". . . alive," Poole croaked.

Stevenson lowered his weapon. He looked into Poole's eyes and saw only a reflection of the morning sunlight.

"Why not me?" Stevenson begged.

Poole swallowed hard, and his eyes flicked down to his chest. Stevenson followed his gaze.

Poole opened his hands to show Stevenson what he held. So tiny but so unmistakable in form.

He shovelled it into his fat mouth.

Stevenson screamed.

He lifted the sharp-edged glass high above his head.

Fanny's skin glowed in the lamplight with the sweat of their exertions. A snail's trail of semen dried on her thigh, matted the softness between her legs. Her head rested on his shoulder and he stroked her long hair. She held his spent organ delicately in her hand; his arm beneath her, his hand cupping the outer curve of her breast.

"He must have been alone out there for a very long time," she said.

"The stagecoaches passed by, stopped in when they had to. The driver, Grey, knew the place, knew the man's name. He wasn't a hermit."

"I'm trying to think how he could have . . ."

"Do ye think I'm not? Don't ye know I can't think of anything else now?"

She didn't reply.

"Other than ye," he added. And kissed her hair.

"He could have taken you, too," she said, and shuddered. "So easily. Why didn't he, Robbie? Why did he spare you?"

"I haven't a clue. Perhaps because he saved my life in the night."

"He saved the old woman, too. It didn't help her."

"Aye. I don't know. That's why I say. There was nothing but madness in his act, so where do ye look for the logic, for the reason in such a thing?"

"And there was no clue? No sense of, I don't know, danger or menace from him?"

"Not a bit. Like I say, the conversation we had in the night, about human nature and the quality of civilization, was a bit peculiar, but it was just words in the night. Or so I thought. And if ye'd seen him treating that old woman the night before—he seemed so clear-headed, so knowledgeable. But it's like there was some other man hiding inside the one I could see, ken? Imprisoned within the first, waiting to come out. But damned if I know what the key was that opened the door and set the monster free. Was it something I said to him? Is that why he spared me? Damned if I know anything at all about people."

"Eaten alive," Fanny whispered.

"What's that?"

"Isn't that what he kept repeating to you? Eaten alive?"

"Aye. That's all I could understand. Not that I do understand."

"Perhaps he was describing himself. Perhaps he was talking about something that happened to him?"

"I don't know, love, I feel like I don't know anything anymore. I just feel lost. Like a stranger even within myself. "

"Eaten alive," Fanny repeated.

Stevenson turned his head, but, in spite of the topic of conversation, had grown hard again in her hand. She slipped out of his grasp and climbed astride him, slipping him back inside herself. She rocked slowly back and forth on top of him.

"Robbie?"

"Aye," he groaned.

"You didn't tell me what you did."

"Eh?" he said, understandably distracted.

"You didn't finish the story. You said you had the broken bottle, and that you raised it up. But you didn't tell me what you did. What happened to Poole."

"Oh, Fanny. Oh my, Fanny."

She grasped his head and looked hard into his eyes.

"Tell me what you did, Robbie. You know that you can tell me anything. You can tell your Fanny."

"Eaten alive," Stevenson gasped, and exploded inside her.

"Robbie?"

CONTRIBUTORS

TABITHA KING'S first novel was the fantasy *Small World*. For her series which includes *The Caretakers*, *The Trap*, and *Pearl*, she invented a fictional Maine town, Nodds Ridge. *One on One*, both a gritty love story and a loving ode to high school basketball, is also set in Maine, where she lives with her husband, Stephen.

THOMAS TESSIER is the author of several novels of terror and suspense, including *The Nightwalker*, *Phantom*, *Finishing Touches*, *Rapture*, and, most recently, *Fog Heart*. He has also published a collection of short fiction, *Ghost Music and Other Tales*.

ALEX HAMILTON, a longtime feature writer for *The Guardian* and radio critic for *The Listener*, has also written extensively for the BBC.

Among his short story-collections are *Beam of Malice, Flies on the Wall*, and *Wild Track*, and his novels include *As If She Were Mine* and *The Needle*. He has edited numerous anthologies, *The Cold Embrace* and *Splinters* being two of them.

JOHN PEYTON COOKE'S novels are *The Lake, Out for Blood, Torsos, The Chimney Sweeper*, and *Haven*. He sold his first short story, "The Cat's Meow," to *Eldritch Tales* when he was sixteen.

H. P. LOVECRAFT is one of the most famous names in fantasy and horror literature: his readership has increased steadily since his death more than six decades ago. Among his influential works are the collections *The Outsider, Beyond the Wall of Sleep, At the Mountains of Madness*, and *The Dunwich Horror*.

PATRICIA HIGHSMITH gained fame with her debut novel, *Strangers on a Train*. Her other books include *The Talented Mr. Ripley, This Sweet Sickness, The Tremor of Forgery, A Dog's Ransom*, and *Edith's Diary*. Her short stories have been collected in such volumes as *The Snail-Watcher* and *Mermaids on the Golf Course*.

G. K. WUORI has published a collection of short stories, *Nude in Tub: Stories of Quillifarkeag, Maine*, and a novel, *An American Outrage*.

LISA TUTTLE is the author of the novel *The Pillow Friend* and editor of the anthology *Crossing the Border: Tales of Erotic Ambiguity*. Her handbook, *Writing Science Fiction and Fantasy*, has recently been published. Her other works include the novels *Familiar Spirit, Gabriel*, and *Lost Futures*, and the collections *A Nest of Nightmares, A Spaceship Built of Stone*, and *Memories of the Body*.

MARK HELPRIN'S novels include *A Soldier of the Great War* and *Winter's Tale*. His short stories have been collected in *A Dove of the East* and *Ellis Island and Other Stories*, and he has collaborated with artist Chris Van Allsburg on two books for children, *Swan Lake* and *A City in Winter*.

JACK KETCHUM'S first novel was *Off Season* (recently republished as *The Unexpurgated Off Season*). Other full-length works include *Hide and Seek*,

Cover, The Lost, Offspring, Ladies' Night, and *Red.* His short-story collections are *The Exit at Toledo Blade Boulevard* and *Broken on the Wheel of Sex.*

EDITH WHARTON, one of the twentieth century's most celebrated writers, actually published her first collection of short stories, *The Greater Inclination,* in the final year of the nineteenth. Her best-known works include *The House of Mirth, Ethan Frome, The Custom of the Country,* and *The Age of Innocence,* for which she won the Pulitzer Prize in 1921.

RAY BRADBURY has had few equals as a writer of fantasy and an American original. Among his many unforgettable works are the short-story collections *The Martian Chronicles, The October Country, The Illustrated Man,* and *Something Wicked This Way Comes.* He wrote the screenplay for John Huston's film adaptation of *Moby-Dick* and has seen sixty-five of his stories adapted for television's *Ray Bradbury Theater.* His most recent novel was *From the Dust Returned;* his newest collections, *Driving Blind* and *One More for the Road.*

CHRISTOPHER FOWLER'S latest collection of short fiction is *Uncut.* Earlier volumes include *Personal Demons, Sharper Knives,* and *Flesh Wounds.* Among his novels are *Roofworld, Rune, Darkest Day, Psychoville, Disturbia, Soho Black,* and *Calabash.*

VICTORIA ROTHSCHILD is a great-niece of the actress and novelist F. M. Mayor, whose own stories of mystery and imagination were published posthumously as *The Room Opposite.* An associate fellow of medieval literature at London University, she has published both poetry and short stories and is currently researching the life of George Anne Bellamy, an eighteenth-century woman of the theater.

JOHN WYNDHAM'S last novel was *Chocky.* Earlier ones include *The Day of the Triffids, The Midwich Cuckoos* (filmed as *Village of the Damned*), *The Chrysalids,* and *The Kraken Wakes.* Among his acclaimed short-story collections are *The Seeds of Time* and *Consider Her Ways.*

MURIEL GRAY is a former designer and illustrator who bypassed punk-rock stardom to become one of Britain's leading television interviewers and presenters. Now head of the largest independent television company in Scotland, she is also the author of two novels, *The Trickster* and *Furnace*, the latter an homage to M. R. James's "Casting the Runes."

SHIRLEY JACKSON'S best-known works are the short story "The Lottery" and the novels *The Haunting of Hill House* and *We Have Always Lived in the Castle*. Posthumous collections are *Come Along with Me* and *Just an Ordinary Day*.

RICHARD MATHESON has written seventeen novels and more than one hundred short stories and adapted many works for the screen, including tales by Edgar Allan Poe, Jules Verne, and Bram Stoker. His best-known books include *I Am Legend, The Shrinking Man, Hell House,* and *What Dreams May Come*.

THOMAS M. DISCH is a versatile writer with science fiction, suspense, horror, poetry, plays, and theater and film criticism among his many credits. His more recent works are *The Dreams Our Stuff Is Made Of: How Science Fiction Conquered the World, The Castle of Indolence: On Poetry, Poets, and Poetasters,* and *The Sub: A Study in Witchcraft*. His novels include *Black Alice* and *The Businessman: A Tale of Terror,* while among his volumes of short fiction are *Getting into Death* and *Fun with Your New Head*.

ERIC McCORMACK is the author of the novels *The Paradise Motel, The Mysterium,* and *First Blast of the Trumpet Against the Monstrous Regiment of Women*. His story collection, *Inspecting the Vaults,* was short-listed for the Commonwealth Writers Prize.

NANCY A. COLLINS has written novels, graphic novels, and short stories. Among her full-length works are *Angels on Fire, A Dozen Black Roses, Sunglasses After Dark, Tempter,* and *In the Blood*. She has had stories published in more than fifty anthologies and edited the collection *Dark Love*.

JAY RUSSELL is the author of the novels *Greed & Stuff, Brown Harvest, Celestial Dogs, Burning Bright,* and *Blood,* as well as the short-story collection, *Waltzes and Whispers*.

PERMISSIONS

TALL MEN,
SHORT SHORTS